Next Year

in

Avaria

Jennifer Paller Girard

Ballast Books, LLC
www.ballastbooks.com

ISBN: 978-1-966786-55-9

Printed in the United States of America

Published by Ballast Books
www.ballastbooks.com

For more information, bulk orders, appearances, or speaking requests, please email: info@ballastbooks.com

Sea of Orion
Xhartana
Pax
Channel of Arcturus
Terebet
Ma'adim Desert
Latros Mountains
Forest of Rian
Kokhav Valley
Bai Llai Glade
Imiris Tundra

Realm of Avaria
Isle of Ori
Sands of Sivan
Mesios Rainforest
River of Pyxis
Zokhara Savanna
Sea of Tehom

PROLOGUE

"One hundred years ago, on this very eve, the darkest of the dark time cloaked our homeland of Avaria under its suffocating veil. The Jesimi people inhabited Avaria for thousands of years before the dark time—we were its first inhabitants, in fact. A malevolent sect of Marre people wove their wicked spell and destroyed the last of our defenses. They took up the mantle of power over all the realms, outlawing magic except their own, unleashing their reign of fury, and forcing the Jesimi people out of Avaria and into exile across the continent. Our ancestors were too late to leave. They recalled that the ground beneath their very feet began to tremble and quake as the realm of Avaria mysteriously fragmented into three parts, snapping off the continent. Each island was magically propelled out into the dark Sea of Orion, becoming our own Isle of Ori, Pax, and Xhartana, where the worst of the Marre people rule from. Some say it was that very moment that the Leviathan slithered to the surface from the abyss to haunt our waters once more.

"The tale goes that El selected twelve representatives from the Jesimi people to guard twelve enchanted keys before they fled. It is fated that someday, a hero will be born, and they will traverse the continent to assemble the twelve keys and gather our people once more. Together, our people will rise up, they will fight for freedom, and they will be reunited in our homeland, thereby banishing the Leviathan back to the depths from whence it came."

"Do you mean Elia the Light Bringer, Mother?" Adam wondered with wide eyes as he tugged the cozy, light-blue blanket, adorned with little stitched-on moons, closer to his chin.

"No, my son. While we pray for the return of Elia the Light Bringer, I speak of a person, just a person. They will be incredibly brave and courageous, kind and true. They will bring our people home," Rachel said in a near whisper as Adam's eyelids began to droop.

"Please, Mother, tell it again. It's my favorite story," Adam begged, as he did every night before bed.

Like every other night, his mother gently responded, "Tomorrow, my love. Now, you must sleep and dream big, wild dreams."

She placed a gentle kiss on his forehead as he gave in to the sleep he so valiantly fought. She blew out the candle on the windowsill beside Adam's small, wooden bed plumped full of straw. Rachel looked back at her sleeping child and smiled, hopeful for the adventures his future was sure to bring and, in equal measure, fearful of the pain he would face simply because he had been born Jesimi.

CHAPTER 1

15 years later

Adam's hands crashed over his ears, and he ducked his head intuitively as the deafening sounds of destruction surrounded Zera, his village. Homes and buildings had been set on fire, walls and beams crashing to the ground beneath them. He raced through the devastation as cries from women, men, and children pierced his soul. Zev, his soul-sealed great white wolf, bounded in his footsteps, his penetrating melted-caramel eyes menacing, as if he might dismantle anyone who stood in their way. Others threaded through the village with a similarly furrowed brow, wandering in sheer panic as they searched for their families and friends.

Adam forced himself to carry on until he turned down the familiar path his feet had carried him down countless times before. He slowed, and Zev nearly toppled over him, sliding to slow behind him. On the left corner was the olive tree that had once towered over Adam but now didn't look quite so tall, the village well on the right, reddish-brown dirt beneath them. The sky was fraught with falling cinders and glowing with the fury of the flames. Time ceased to exist as he beheld his home, alight. Adam's limbs fought his every step, seeming to sink in quicksand, knowing what might await him. The door to his home was ajar, and though it was sure to fall at any moment, he dashed through it, pulling up the tail of his handmade white shirt to cover his mouth.

"Stay back, Zev. I don't want you getting hurt!" Adam shouted behind him in vain, as Zev warily followed, never having allowed Adam to face any potential danger alone.

Their home was so small, his eyes fell on his mother immediately, her body still, blanketed in ash, aglow in the embers. He jumped into action, seizing her under the arms and quickly dragging her outside.

"Mother! Please, Mother, I can't lose you. Don't leave me alone." Adam choked back sobs as he surveyed her; she hadn't even twitched. He prayed to El it was not too late, even if he felt that praying to El hadn't gotten him anywhere before. Rachel's eyes fluttered briefly, and somehow, her face was still full of warmth.

"Mother, I'm right here. Please come back to me. Keep fighting!" Adam cried as a well of tears sprang from his eyes and splashed across her face, leaving streaks in the ash and on what he knew was her favorite dress. Zev sat back on his haunches and let out a deep whine, nuzzling Adam's shoulder.

"Adam, listen carefully, my son." Rachel peeled one eye open and whispered with gravel in her voice, wincing; the smoke had clearly done its damage. She strained to grasp Adam's hand that lay on her shoulder and squeezed with the little that was left of her surprisingly vast might for her small frame. Adam snapped to attention, brimming with hope, with fear, and he listened raptly, pushing her salt-and-pepper hair out of her face.

"When it is safe again, you must enter what is left of our home and retrieve a wooden box I buried under the head of your bed when you were small. I have written you a letter that explains everything you need for your future. I hoped it would not come to this and I would be able to tell you everything myself; alas, that is not our fate, my love. Know that I will always be with you . . ." Rachel's final words faded out as she lost consciousness once again, for good, dropping Adam's hand as hers fell limp by her side.

"Mother, no. Please . . . What does that mean? I can't do this without you. Please, I love you," Adam pleaded as he placed his head on her chest, where he had found so much comfort and love from his mother's kind heart. No more, as her heartbeat fell further behind until it beat no more. The vessel that held Adam's mother, his world, felt suddenly hollow and empty as her soul ascended. He shuddered as body-wracking sobs took him over; he felt every agonizing moment of the process.

"Nooooo!" Adam released a guttural scream, which was echoed by an unearthly howl from deep in the hollow of Zev, where their souls connected.

Pleas and sobs and mourning sounded throughout the village as more lives reached their untimely end. He continued to lie his head there on her chest, incapacitated by his grief. Zev lay beside him with one enormous paw over Rachel's leg. Adam didn't know how much time had passed, but the moon rose over the burning ruins, and the sky bled from thick, gray smoke to black.

Adam lifted his head slowly from his mother's body, finding himself momentarily out of tears. He noticed that while he had lain there with his mother, the roof of their home had caved in and the walls had burned to the ground, leaving nothing but soot in the aftermath.

The only thing that could have drawn him away from his mother was her final words to him. His curiosity grew as he dragged himself up, feeling much older than he had a day ago, and wiped some of the ash off his tear-streaked face onto the once-white shirt his mother had made him. He cautiously entered the ruins of his life, pushing aside debris and piles of soot and ash to get to where his too-small-for-him bed had once stood. Adam collapsed onto his knees, pushed up his sleeves, and shoved the mess aside until he reached the dirt floor that had grounded him since his birth. He began to claw into the dirt where the head of the bed would have been, as if digging for his life. Dirt flew everywhere, into his eyes, covering his already-ash-smeared clothing until he felt something solid beneath the dirt. Brushing the earth from the top, he beheld the lid of an ornately carved wooden box with his name in the center, surrounded by intricately intertwined flowers and vines. He dug around the sides to free the box and tugged it into his lap with a groan. He paused for a moment before opening it, uneasy, clinging to the words that would resound in his head forever.

Finally, he flung the lid to the side and pulled out a single roll of parchment. He carefully unfurled it, and sprawled across the page was his mother's elegant penmanship, honed after years of tireless work as a preserver. Adam felt a tug of pride; he had followed in her footsteps to train in the same profession. The pride swiftly fell to a new bottomless pit of despair and emptiness as the events of the last hours folded in on him. He forced his attention to return to the letter, and he read.

My Dearest Adam,

If you are reading this, I fear the worst. I am likely no longer with you. Do not fret; my spirit is bound to yours, and you will never be alone, my son. Do you remember the story I used to tell you when you were a boy? I told you the tale of the person who is destined to bring our people, the Jesimi people, together again from exile, gather the twelve keys, and free our homeland from the wrath and the tyranny of the radical Marre people of Xhartana. I have always suspected that person to be you.

When you were born, at your naming ceremony, your left palm glowed a rare, bright white with a symbol of a lone man. That is how I chose your name, Adam, "the first man." Your gift may not have manifested the way others have, but it will. You're special. While I know you would likely prefer to spend your time among the scrolls, it is time for your great adventure. You will journey through the realms to meet with our people living in exile across the continent and convince them to join together to fight for Avaria. You will gain their trust using your gift and collect the twelve enchanted keys. With our people and the keys reunited, the Jesimi people will be unstoppable, free, and reunited in Avaria.

To undertake this immense task, you will need to learn to wield your gift, and you will require assistance, as none of us can do this alone. My brother, Benjamin, whom you have not met—we have had much strife between us, which I have begun to regret as I write this letter—will guide you. Benjamin lives alone on the other side of the Isle; you can find him where the edge of salt flats meets the river and the trees. His gift is that he is able to help others hone their abilities and wield them for good. He does not use his gift often, preferring to be alone, not vastly different than you. He knows all about you, and he will be the one to help you learn about your gift and how to use it to aid you before your great adventure. Please go see him at once so you can begin preparations; time is of the essence. You will bring our people together once again. Remember that fear itself is not to be afraid of, but refusing to live because of fear is the worst of fates. You are loved.

Yours Eternally, Mother

Adam read and reread the letter a dozen times, and each time sent his jaw falling to the floor. He could not wrap his mind around any of it. His mother was gone. He had an uncle he had never met who was supposed to help him. He was somehow also supposed to travel the entire continent to gather his people together to fight against the very monsters who were responsible for his mother's death. His mind raced as he tried to make sense of the nonsensical.

Only hours before, Adam, his mother, and a number of other friends and neighbors from the village had secretly gathered together to celebrate the Day of the Great Scroll. They danced and sang, ate and drank, merrily rejoicing together, celebrating the finishing of this year's reading of the Great Scroll. After a much-too-brief celebration, the people decided to part ways to avoid unwanted attention from the tyrannical leaders stationed on their island. Adam had gone back to work with Zev in tow, while his mother returned home to rest, as she had tired after baking so much bread.

These sorts of gatherings, especially Jesimi traditions, were banned by Xhartana, who controlled the Isle of Ori and much of the continent. There were a few villagers posted as lookouts while they had their quick celebration. Somehow, their wardens must have found out, as their troops had descended like a swarm of bloodthirsty locusts, marching through the streets with torches and destroying everything in their wake, stabbing those who got in their way with daggers and swords.

Adam returned to his mother's side, letter in hand, and crumpled down next to her body. Zev had not budged from his position; he whimpered as he acknowledged Adam's pain and confusion. Adam scanned the neighborhood, taking in similar scenes in every direction, wondering who had survived Xhartana's wrath this time, who was spared. He couldn't help but feel a sense of guilt begin to build deep in his gut that he had not been home. Maybe he could have saved her. He shrugged the thought off, as he knew once those evil, cruel-hearted men set their sights on you, there was no way to survive. There never had been. Many had been lost to their hatred and violence before. Avaria had been lost.

Time passed painfully, slower and faster at the same time, and Adam sat in the dirt and the ash, holding the letter and his mother's hand, waiting—though he wasn't entirely sure for what. He mindlessly ran his other hand over Zev's silky coat, over the beige angelwing markings that spread their way down each side of his body behind his broad shoulders, feeling ever so slightly less than alone.

Adam could barely bring himself to look up as a wagon, pulled by two stout, gray donkeys, rounded the corner by the olive tree and slowed to a stop in front of his home. He knew why it was there. Lemuel, Isle of Ori's Keeper of the Great Scroll, leaped down from the wagon with his hedgehog on his shoulder. He treaded over and knelt down beside Adam, placing his weathered hand firmly on his shoulder. Lemuel met his eyes with great warmth and sadness and held his gaze for a moment, bringing a tinge of comfort that could only come from someone you have known your entire life.

"Dearest Adam . . ." He trailed off regretfully. "I am so devastated for you. Rachel is so meaningful to all of us, but there are no words to describe the kind of mother she has been to you. May her memory be for a blessing." Lemuel's head appeared heavy on his shoulders, his chin almost resting on his chest, his hedgehog clawing to hold on. The worn lines that usually framed his smile now highlighted the depths of his lamentation. He tugged uncomfortably on his blue prayer shawl with its white, woven details and silently prayed, facing east and bowing, before returning his attention to Adam and Zev.

"I want to help dig the graves. I know there aren't enough builders or makers to get them dug quickly enough. We must bury them as soon as possible," Adam insisted breathlessly.

"Of course. That would be greatly appreciated. We have sustained great loss this night; we will honor the lives of our loved ones in the week to come, and always. Take heart; El is with us. You are not alone," Lemuel encouraged kindly, echoing the words Adam's mother had spoken before her death.

"I appreciate it, but I think if El were here, my mother would be as well," Adam replied gruffly and strode over to his mother's limp body, where he gathered her into his arms and carried her to the back of the wagon. He gently placed her body down on the bed of straw and covered her with the blanket that Lemuel had draped across the side. Adam set a tender kiss on his mother's cheek before pulling the blanket over her head and convincing himself to stumble a few steps back, out of the way, just as the subtle orange glow of dawn began.

"I shall keep her safe until it is time," Lemuel said. "You are welcome to head to the cemetery to help with preparations. We are working to determine plans for housing those who have lost their homes, so when you are ready, head to the Temple, and we will make sure you are cared for." Lemuel hopped back into the seat of the wagon, took the reins, and went on his way, taking Adam's world with him. Adam watched with a blank stare until the dust and soot the wagon stirred up fell back to the ground.

Come, look. Through their soul-sealed inner communication, Zev beckoned Adam over to where the front door of their home had stood just one day before. Zev pawed at something metal buried under the debris. Adam reached down and plucked out a small, decorative metal box that he knew held a tiny parchment scroll.

"Our mizzur," Adam said in wonder. His fingers brushed the lettering on the metal box as they had each time he had entered the home. The mizzur serves as a reminder of who the Jesimi people are and who El is, and it protects the home and the space they share together. This was all that was left of the first twenty years of his life, and the irony was not lost on him. As he held this last symbol in his hands, tears escaped his eyes once more, blurring out the world and inviting a lifetime of memories they had shared in this home to flow through him as naturally as breath through his lungs. His legs grew weary, his soul was weary, but he knew he must do something, or the darkness hovering around him, waiting for him to drop his shield, would consume him.

Adam looked down at Zev. "We have to help. We have to do something."

Anything. You know I will stand with you through any challenge that may arise. I made that oath when you turned thirteen and completed your task with honor, and we were soul-sealed. I am with you, always, Zev promised.

Adam innately knew that to be true—Zev had proven it since that very day—and he had a feeling he would desperately need that promise in the coming days and months with this grand adventure his mother spoke of in her letter.

CHAPTER 2

Adam pocketed the mizzur and the letter and willed himself to look away from where his home had once stood. He began to walk toward the cemetery, Zev following. As they threaded their way through the narrow roads of the village, it was difficult for Adam not to gasp repeatedly as the breadth of the destruction sank in. They passed neighbors, and they would have normally stopped to say a quick hello, but not today. Solemn faces and tears took precedence over niceties, and Adam and Zev pushed on.

Some odd homes and buildings had been spared, and it appeared the Temple was one of them, which was surprising, as the Xhartanians despised anything and everything Jesimi. The culture, beliefs, the way of life. It seemed that their only goal for tens of years was Jesimi suffering and destruction. They relied on the Isle of Ori and Jesimi people across the continent for money through taxation. They also had nearly no resources on Xhartana and made no effort to build or grow anything, preferring to simply steal it from the Jesimi and any other people they could overpower, which was pretty much everyone. Adam was certain he would be hearing about the survival of the Temple being a miracle from El at some point in the near future.

He swept around the Temple to the back, where the Jesimi cemetery lay. Rows of headstones lined the grassy knoll, and red anemone blossoms burst forth from the earth in between. Small stones and pebbles adorned the tops of the headstones, as was Jesimi custom to leave as protection from evil spirits or demons.

Adam approached David, Lemuel's right hand, who seemed to be managing the sudden and tragic need for expanding the cemetery far more than it should have been this quickly. The deeply pained look on his face painted the story that he had not been spared loss.

The two men briefly embraced in the place of the words they could not yet find. A striking red deer with white markings along its back exited David's shadow and took an awkward step closer to Zev, causing Zev to take a much larger step backward. Many soul-sealed animals took an interest in Zev on the Isle because he was so unheard of. Wolves were not native to Avaria, including on the Isle. It was always safe to say that Zev never took any interest back. Much like Adam, he preferred solitude, the two of them often sitting in silence in each other's company, content.

"How can I help?" Adam asked hesitantly, feeling deeply out of sorts, as if he might burst into tears at any moment. Everyone knew he would never do so publicly—he was known for his stoicism, his intelligence, his quiet wit. He had to keep busy.

"Sela is on her way to help, so we will be able to make use of her gift of strength. You are welcome to begin if you would like. I have begun marking where each grave will be." David pointed toward a new row of chalk outlines on the grass beyond the existing rows. Adam took the shovel David offered and nodded, heading in that direction with Zev on his heels.

Adam was not much of a hard laborer with his tall and lanky figure, but he thought now was as good a time as any to begin, if only as a distraction from the pain that constantly threatened to disassemble his very existence. He once again rolled up the sleeves of the same white shirt he had been wearing since yesterday, revealing his warm olive skin with a smattering of thick, black hair. Zev brushed up against his legs, then wound himself up in a ball to lie at the foot of the first grave.

Adam gripped the shovel tightly and used his foot to press it deeper into the soil, then heaved a chunk of it behind him. The sun was climbing higher, causing sweat to bead on Adam's upper lip, which he could only take as a poor sign of what was to come with this level of exertion. He continued to dig, slowly finding his rhythm as Zev looked on. Others began digging next to him, and he wondered whether they had lost family or friends as well, or whether they were just helpful neighbors. On the Isle of Ori, they were often one and the same. Adam mopped his brow with the back of his hand as the hours passed and it grew hotter with the early-autumn heat.

"Hey, Adam, I heard about your mother. I am so very sorry; she was so wonderful. My uncle and aunt were taken as well," a petite woman with bright-blonde hair and equally bright-blue eyes stammered in Adam's direction.

"Thanks, Sela. I am so sorry to hear that too. I just can't believe it happened. Again," Adam replied, finding it hard to continue to form words that oozed with grief. This was certainly not the first Xhartanian attack since the dark time, and there was no reason to believe it would be the last. As Adam pondered this reality, something unfamiliar bloomed deep within him, something uncomfortable, something he knew he would not be able to ignore for long.

"Here, let me help you finish this," Sela offered, moving to Adam's side. She took the shovel with her right hand and drove it into the soil of the grave he'd been digging, which was no more than a couple feet deep at this point.

"Thank you," Adam said, grateful to not be alone.

"Of course," Sela replied, gently running her hand over Adam's arm comfortingly.

When they'd finished the job, Adam sighed and headed back toward the Temple. He walked up the three steps and pulled open the large oak doors into a bright and open space—a sanctuary. He stopped for a second, closing his eyes as the sun beamed through the large picture windows set into the walls of wood and reddish-brown mud.

Although Adam struggled with belief in El, with belief that Elia the Light Bringer would come, this place always brought him a sense of peace. The villagers could no longer gather here together for services on the Day of Rest, but they often found themselves here for whatever it was they might need.

Lemuel had returned from what Adam imagined was a very long and painful night, and the old man walked down the side of the sanctuary toward him.

"Adam, my son, the rest of the villagers are working together to find places for those of you who lost your homes. Some will stay here, and some with other families, and some in the day school. They are making enough food for everyone, and they have clothes and other things you might need at the school. I am making arrangements for sitting the zayin; some of you will sit here, some elsewhere," Lemuel said, referring to another Jesimi custom of sitting for seven days after the loss of a loved one and receiving people, generally to your home, to mourn. The visitors bring food and share stories of the person who has died while the family receives these stories and offerings.

"Thank you, Keeper," Adam replied, bowing his head.

"Why don't you head to the school to try to eat something and maybe find a change of clothing?" Lemuel offered.

"I suppose I could," Adam responded, shoving his hands in his pockets. The last thing he wanted right now was to be surrounded by even well-meaning people. He did not like to be around groups of people on his best days, let alone his worst. Surveying his tattered shirt and no-longer-tan linen trousers, he realized he would need to find something more suitable to bury his mother in. She would be furious if she saw how filthy he was right now and would order him to remove the clothes immediately so she could wash them, and so help her if the stains did not come out. He nearly laughed at the thought only to be slammed by the flood of agony that he would never anger her again. He wouldn't hear her laugh, hear her sing . . .

"Adam?" Lemuel broached the silence.

"Oh, yes, sorry. Lost in my head. We'll head there now," Adam said, nodding to Zev beside him.

Adam and Zev headed over to the day school that Adam had attended at Lemuel's behest. He was greeted by fleeting memories of his time there, out by the edge of the ominous forest, where his passion for knowledge had flourished. With the reminiscent whiff of endless papyrus scrolls came memories of his childhood bully and nemesis, Samuel, who had made it his purpose to torment Adam.

In the present, the school had been made to suit the needs of Zera villagers who had lost everything. Adam was tended to by a kind maker, who fitted Adam with new clothing: a beautifully made, dark-blue cotton shirt with buttons crafted from shells and beige, lightweight trousers that actually fit his lengthy legs.

He and Zev were then shuffled over to the Jesimi mothers bustling around with endless homemade food: chicken soup like his mother had made, bread, brisket, potatoes. A generous spread, yet no amount of delicious food and motherly encouragement could convince Adam's stomach, sickened with grief, to comply. Zev's, however, was happy to do so, and he was quickly sated from all the scraps and the attention of the hovering women.

They expressed their gratitude and made their exit, heading back to the Temple. Adam assumed they would be done digging the graves and Lemuel would know when they planned to begin the burials. He thought to himself that it might be odd to be in a rush to bury your loved ones, but he heard his mother's words once again that they must return the body, the vessel, to the earth as soon as possible to ease the journey of the soul. He wouldn't know a moment of peace until her wishes had been fulfilled.

Back at the Temple, a larger group of people had gathered, some weeping, some stone-faced, but all clearly suffering. Adam entered the sanctuary and saw that Lemuel was deep in conversation with another family, so he took a seat over to the side to wait. Zev slid to the floor and took the opportunity to take a quick nap.

After a short time, Lemuel made his way over to them and shared the plans for the rest of the evening. "The builders have been working frantically to make enough plain pine coffins, the makers have made white linen wrappings, and we are about to get started. Do you have anyone you would like here with you?" Lemuel asked hopefully, his hedgehog nuzzling into his neck.

"It's just us. Although, apparently . . ." Adam trailed off.

Lemuel squeezed his arm and told him to wait there while he started with a couple of other families. He would come when it was Adam's turn.

Adam felt like he was sinking into the floor, or maybe he simply wanted to, as the realization continued to barrel into him over and over again that he was here to bury his beloved mother. Alone. She was gone. Zev's giant head landed on his lap as he sensed the depth of Adam's pain, and Adam mindlessly patted Zev behind the ears. He watched mourners come and go as if he were a ghost observing from beyond the veil, like he was stuck in some time bubble while life lurched on all around him.

Lemuel popped the bubble as he approached and said, in a somber tone, "It's time."

Adam and Zev followed him out the back doors of the Temple to the same scene they had left earlier, but it felt wholly different under the eerie shroud of dusk. Beside the grave that Adam had partially dug sat a plain pine coffin, and he knew that within its walls, his mother was carefully wrapped in white linen so she could be returned the earth as El intended. Zev let out a small howl—Adam was unsure whether it was in response to Adam's pain or Zev's own, as Rachel had been a mother to him as well.

"Do you want to see her again, son?" Lemuel asked kindly, now flanked by David, Sela, and a few others whom Adam had seen around the Temple often.

"I've said my goodbyes. Let's bring her peace," Adam said, choking on his words, grasping his throat as his voice escaped him.

Sela wove around the others to make her way next to Adam and placed her hand on his. A few of the men lifted the coffin to lower it into the grave, and Adam stopped them for a brief moment, kissed his fingers, and pressed them to the top of the coffin before gesturing for the men to continue. Lemuel began to speak, pray, and chant, but Adam was miles away, numb, utterly broken inside. Sela handed him the shovel, and he filled it with the dirt they had removed earlier. With only slight hesitation, he tossed it over the coffin at the bottom of the grave. He then handed the shovel to Sela, who added a shovelful of dirt, followed by Lemuel and the few others present. The men then made quick work of filling the grave to the top, then stomped down the soil and added a patch of grass on top to make it flat. Almost as if the hole in the ground that held Adam's mother had never been there. There would be no grave marker until one year after her death, per Jesimi custom.

Adam had expected to cry, to be inconsolable, but there was only emptiness. He held a blank stare on his face as the people around him said, "May her memory be for a blessing," and left him there, alone again. His mother, his light, his world, was gone. Adam turned on his heels and sped out of there, Zev on his heels, wondering where he thought he was going. Adam didn't know; he just knew he couldn't be there for one more second. He had no aim; his thoughts were all consuming and blank at the same time, no direction, no plan for the first time in his life. The thick aroma of smoke and death hung in the air. He was untethered.

He raced through the roads of the village, gasping for air, everything a blur. Once he reached the edge of the village, he did something he never did and kept running across the rolling hills filled with roving cattle and goats. The moon had begun its rise as its opposite sank below the horizon. He noticed he was almost to the salt flats bordering the Sea of Orion, where he and the other children had been taken once in school to learn about how salt was gleaned and made usable. Adam intuitively banked left and continued around the edge of the blue-green salt flats, toward the forest. He was nearly bowled over by the smell of sulfur, but it quickly gave way to a brisk, salty breeze that flowed through his jet-black hair, freeing his trapped breath.

He heard the swiftly growing sound of roaring water and eventually ran into the edge of the forest, which coincided with this side of the raging Copper River before it fell into the inky-black sea. Adam whipped his head around and realized he had found himself where the edge of the salt flats met the river and the trees. His head spun, wondering why on earth he would run from his mother's burial to his unknown uncle's house. He squinted his eyes in the descending darkness to make out a small hut at the edge of the wood.

CHAPTER 3

Zev gave Adam's leg a nudge. *Come on, let's go. Is this not what your mother wanted in her letter? Are you not curious as to why she sent you here?* Zev gave him a familiar look that let Adam know he saw all the way into the depth of each corner of his very soul.

"Of course I'm curious; that's how I ended up here." Adam was still reeling from his sudden flight past the bounds of the village, which was wildly out of character for him. Not only were they not supposed to leave the confines of the village unless doing so for vocational purposes that served Xhartana, but he had also never had any interest in it before. Adam preferred to spend his days poring over ancient scrolls and creating new scrolls of his own, etching the lives and adventures of other Jesimi onto the pages of history. As a preserver, he was better suited to scribing and studying than wasting his time pressing boundaries.

That life suddenly seemed a world away. He had to figure out what his mother meant about his gift, about this great adventure across the continent; he owed her that much. With a scowl on his face, he began to move cautiously toward the hut at the edge of the wood, signaling to Zev to keep quiet. He wasn't quite sure why, but it seemed appropriate, as he didn't often approach unknown huts at night. Adam stepped onto the stone path that led to a slightly warped front door and lifted his hand to knock.

"Who's out there?" A deep voice boomed through the large crack in the door.

"Erm, um, it's Adam, your nephew . . . I think. Are you Benjamin?" Adam swallowed the lump in his throat and took a couple large steps back. Zev snaked his way in front of him, uttering a low growl.

The door flung open and an unkempt, grizzly, middle-aged man loomed in the doorway. He wasn't much taller than Adam, but he was intimidating. He had a skeptical look and gazed up and down at Adam and Zev, taking in his uninvited callers.

Benjamin paused much too long for comfort before groaning, "All right, then, come in." He stepped aside with a sweeping gesture of his arm, waving toward the inside of his home.

Though the hut was tiny from the outside, it was surprisingly warm and cozy on the inside. The hearth was blazing with a fire that immediately cured the bite of cold Adam hadn't noticed before. Benjamin strode over to the fire, took a couple of logs from the stack next to the stone hearth, and tossed them in, causing the fire to pop and crack. He didn't bother to step aside, telling Adam that Benjamin's gruff exterior and his blistered, filthy hands paralleled what was inside. There were beeswax candles giving off a toasty glow to match the brilliance of the fire around the single-room home.

Adam and Zev hovered near the door, unsure of what to do next, Adam anxiously tapping his toes. A very large lizard lumbered out from under the wooden bed frame in the corner of the room, and Adam gasped. Zev crouched down on his front paws, growling out a warning to the other animal.

"Relax; he won't hurt you," Benjamin said casually. "That's just old George. He's a water monitor." He fell back into one of two shoddily constructed wooden chairs that flanked a small, similarly shoddy wooden table, lacing his large hands together behind his head. He gestured for Adam to take the other seat. "I guess I should offer you something to drink or eat. I don't have guests very often, as you could probably tell."

"I'm fine, thank you," Adam politely answered, knowing full well that "fine" was the last thing he was.

Sitting face-to-face with his uncle, he was struck by how much his image mirrored his mother. They shared the same warm olive skin and dark-brown hair, now with streaks of gray. Her dark-brown eyes peered back at Adam, but the skin surrounding them appeared more weathered, worn. He noted that these dark-brown eyes were a little emptier and momentarily wondered why. Zev sat back on his haunches at his side, but he was clearly on guard, watching the large lizard waddle back under the bed after taking a drink from a tin bowl of water.

"So, what brings you?" Benjamin inquired in his gritty, low voice.

Adam squeezed his eyes closed, preventing the tears that had dried up from re-forming. He brushed his hair out of his eyes to look at his uncle, trying to figure out how to tell him why he had suddenly made an appearance. He had not even known he had an uncle before last night, and now he sat before him, his blood, a stranger.

Adam rubbed his hand over his forehead and choked out, "It's Mother. Xhartana, they came . . ." He continued to try to expel the words looming in his head. "They burned our home down." He paused for a long moment, then took a deep breath. "She's gone."

The words echoed through the small room, and Benjamin's head fell into his hands. When he finally looked back up, despair was painted across his wizened face and in the way his limbs fell limp. A pitter-patter of clawed feet came scampering across the floor as George came to his side, recognizing that his soul-seal was in pain. The four of them sat silently for what seemed like a very long time, individually reexamining the events that had led them to this moment.

Benjamin was the first to break the silence. "I loved your mother. We were close as children . . ." He trailed off, clearing his throat, staving off the emotions that had probably lain dormant for years. Adam nodded in acknowledgment.

"She left me a letter," Adam announced as he carefully withdrew it from the pocket of his new trousers, noticing the hems were already muddy from his excursion. "She told me to come here, that you knew about me. She said that you were going to help me." Adam slid the scroll across the table as if it were his most prized possession and realized that it very well may be.

Benjamin raised an eyebrow and opened the scroll to read his sister's letter to her son. He took his time, nodding occasionally, while Adam waited impatiently. Benjamin nodded again, closing his eyes for a moment and sighing deeply.

"Yes, I was there at your naming ceremony after your birth. We were still close then. That was before . . . I kept track of you, though, and agreed that if anything happened to Rachel, I would help you prepare."

"Prepare for what? She wrote about some great journey across the continent, twelve keys. I have barely left Zera. And I don't even have a gift!" Adam cried in frustration at the sharp left turn life had taken.

"We have a lot to talk about. I'll answer your questions eventually, but not tonight. I can see how tired you are," Benjamin insisted brusquely, looking rather conflicted about it all himself. "Where are you gonna sleep? Do you have a friend who'll take you in?"

Adam, defeated, confused, shook his head. "Lemuel said that there are people offering to share their homes, and people are staying at the day school and the Temple. I can go back and ask him."

"No, you'll stay here. You're family. I'll honor my sister's wishes and look after you," Benjamin declared.

As he seemed like the wrong type of man to argue with, Adam nodded and muttered his thanks. Benjamin led him around the hut and told him to take whatever he needed, showing him his food stores, the water he had fetched from the river that morning to drink or clean his feet of the mud that clung to them, and the outhouse. He disappeared outside for a moment and brought back an armful of hay to create a makeshift bed for Adam and Zev. He spread it out in the corner of the hut and covered it with a pilled woolen blanket he'd pulled off a shelf above the stack of firewood.

Adam eyed the bed warily, more due to sharing the space with the shockingly large lizard than the condition of the bed itself. He allowed himself to reel for a few moments—his home was destroyed, his mother was gone, in the blink of an eye—then snapped himself out of it and again thanked Benjamin for his hospitality, grateful he did not have to stay with strangers. The strange familiarity he already had with his uncle struck him as a new feeling. He was rather friendly and got along fine with others, aside from that bully, Samuel, a thorn in his side throughout his life. But Adam wasn't someone who thrived in the company of others and did not experience the type of kinship he had seen others partake in, outside of his soul-seal with Zev and his mother. He figured that if his uncle lived all the way out here, they might have that in common.

Adam clumsily, as usual, lowered himself onto the hay bed, letting out a grunt as he landed on his tailbone. He removed his sandals and scooted around until he got comfortable, then pulled a second blanket over his long legs, leaving his clothing in place. He watched as his uncle puttered around the hut, snuffing out candles and doing what Adam imagined was his nighttime routine.

"So, what should I call you? Uncle? Benjamin?"

"Not Benjamin; that was our father. Just Ben is fine." He made his way to his bed in the other corner, George scurrying after him and taking his place underneath. "We'll figure this out tomorrow. Try to get some rest."

Adam interpreted that to be about as close as Ben got to warmth. "Thank you. I'm glad to meet you. I wish I would have known about you." Adam felt the sentiment floating in the room between them, a million unspoken words, most of which would never be heard.

With that, Ben snuffed out the last candle, leaving the menacing shadows to dance along the walls to the glow of the embers crackling in the hearth. Zev butted up against Adam's side to provide warmth, comfort, and safety from anyone and anything that might hurt him, though he knew he could not heal the aching pain that had split Adam's heart in two.

He's right, Adam; you should try to sleep. I'll never leave your side, Zev whispered. Adam closed his eyes and stroked Zev's fur as he tried to push it all away, heavy with loss and fear. A thick fog rolled over him, freeing him from consciousness for now.

CHAPTER 4

Adam slowly opened one eye and let out a shriek as he was met with a beady black eyeball and a lengthy, darting tongue, altogether too close for comfort. Zev loped over from where he had been standing on the other side of the hut with Adam's uncle.

Right, he had an uncle. He was in his uncle's house. He let out a gasp as it all flooded back in, and he scanned his surroundings. The pale dawn light burst through the few small windows scattered across the mud walls of the hut, drawing geometric shapes that continually moved. It looked much the same in the daylight, but he realized how tidy and well kept it was, in opposition to the way Ben appeared to keep himself.

Ben was busy in the kitchen area, stirring some unknown liquid in a metal cup, which he brought over to Adam. Adam looked up inquisitively, as if to ask what it was.

"Drink; it'll help. This is gonna be a long week." He ignored the unspoken question, so Adam took his chances and sipped the hot, comforting liquid. It seemed to be some kind of herbal tea. He shrugged and kept drinking.

"I have to go back to Zera. For the zayin," Adam said, as unsure about it as he sounded. Sitting the zayin usually occurred at one's home, and he no longer had a home. Though Lemuel had said he was making plans to address this problem, he dreaded the seven days of pitying gazes, seven days of being offered food he likely couldn't stomach.

Still, the tradition was important, and he wouldn't think of letting his mother down. He would mourn for seven days, he would sit in an uncomfortable chair because grief should be painful, he would be grateful for the support. That didn't make him dread it any less. "Will you . . . Are you going to come?"

"Hmm, I dunno. I haven't been back in years. There is no love lost between me and that place. Especially now, without Rachel there," Ben pondered aloud.

"I understand. I just hoped I wouldn't have to face it alone." Adam looked at the floor again, making a circle with his toe.

Ben cracked a handful of eggs into an iron pan and walked over to the fire that was roaring once again in the hearth. He slid the eggs over the fire to let them cook. Adam wondered where he got fresh eggs all the way out here. The smell elicited a loud gurgle from his stomach, to his surprise, reminding him that it continued to be very empty, save the herbal tea.

Ben removed the pan from the fire and set it down on a stone ledge. He scooped the eggs from the pan, dropped them onto two plates, and strode over to hand one to Adam. He moved to refuse, and Ben just shoved them closer, handing over a fork to go with them. It wasn't a question, so Adam accepted with a nod of thanks and reminded himself he needed to eat to get through what was to come. After the first couple of forced bites, he realized it wasn't so bad and finished them.

"Thank you for everything. Should I plan to return after the zayin so you can tell me more about what my mother wanted?" Adam asked with furrowed brow.

"That would be fine. Sure, you could do that," Ben sputtered, clearly as uncomfortable as Adam was with the very odd situation they found themselves in.

"I guess I should be on my way, then. It took me nearly half an hour to get here last night, and I was mostly running. The Keeper will be wondering where I've gone," Adam nervously rattled.

Ben met him with a curious stare in response to the running confession, but his curiosity went unanswered. Adam made his way toward the warped wooden door, with Zev a step behind him, and looked back briefly. "I guess I will see you in a week." He gave a half smile, and they made their exit.

Adam slowed as he took in his surroundings. He had never seen anything so beautiful, and his breath was stolen for a moment. Just beyond the hut was the swirling, dark-blue Copper River effortlessly tumbling into the endless well that was the Sea of Orion, which wound its way around the grassy area the hut lay on, surging to meet the turquoise-and-rust salt flats ahead. To the right was the vast emerald wood that from this angle looked endless, though nothing was on this tiny slice of Avaria, amid the blackest sea.

Adam turned and noticed a small chicken coop he hadn't seen in the dark beside the hut, explaining their breakfast. Behind the coop was a large pen, where a single chocolate-brown cow and a pair of small black goats roamed freely. Adam wondered how he hadn't heard them from inside the hut and guessed perhaps the sound of the river had drowned them out.

Adam liked it here. He took a deep breath, and the air felt clearer, cleaner . . . free. A foreign sensation. Just as quickly as it came, the shackles of grief encroached upon him again, and he tapped Zev's head, letting him know it was time to go. He began walking, begrudgingly shuffling his feet in the direction of Zera, his home, though it didn't feel like home without her there.

As he made it clear of the edge of the wood toward the salt flats, he heard shouting.

"Wait! Wait for me!"

Adam whipped his head around to look back toward the voice and saw his disheveled uncle, running his fingers through his hair as if trying to tame it. Ben jogged to catch up as he finished buttoning a loose, black long-sleeved shirt to match his black trousers, not bothering to tuck it in, which seemed to suit him well.

"You changed your mind?" Adam asked in bewilderment. He had steeled himself to do this alone, as he imagined he would from now forward. Well, not alone; he had Zev. He certainly couldn't say that company was unwelcome, especially from someone who had loved his mother too.

"I should be there. I need to swallow my pride for Rachel; she would want me there, with you." Ben said, but something about his demeanor read that swallowing his pride didn't come naturally to him and that he would pay a substantial price to do so. He fell into stride beside Adam and Zev, George tagging along behind.

Adam asked what he knew Zev was thinking. "Can he keep up? His legs are so short."

"He's actually very fast when he wants to be. He goes with me to walk beside the river and through the woods every day," Ben informed them, making eye contact with George. Adam couldn't imagine being sealed with a giant lizard, but he wasn't one to judge. Most of the time.

They all followed the rounded edge of the impressive salt flats and walked inland, the ground now mostly flat beneath their feet and alternating between dirt and clumpy, fading grass. They journeyed in near silence, listening to the birds chirping, which dwindled the farther they moved from the wood. They did not yet know how to make small talk and were not the types to force it.

It was cooler than it had been yesterday; nevertheless, the sun shone, ignoring that it should have been hanging its head as well.

They took in the outskirts of the village, and Adam noticed Ben visibly tighten his jaw, yet again making Adam wonder how his uncle had come to be the way he was—what had happened to him, to his relationship with his sister. The wondering shrank as it made way for the mix of emotions he'd always imagined sitting zayin would bring.

The four of them silently walked the quiet streets toward the Temple, and Ben's face scrunched with pain as he was privy to the horror of what the villagers had experienced in the latest attack.

Entire streets of only ash and scraps. He seemed to understand there was nothing he could say, so he simply bore witness; he did not look away. Adam admired that in him, though he didn't say so. They made their way up the steps of the Temple and through the large oak doors in the front of the sanctuary.

"Adam, there you are!" Lemuel exclaimed, looking him up and down. "I was wondering if you had found a place to sleep comfortably last night."

Adam nodded, curious if the man made this much space for all those who were grieving, showed this much compassion. He imagined so.

"Oh, heavens to El, Benjamin, is that you? I have not seen you for so many years!"

"Hello, Keeper," Ben responded, folding his arms over his chest, distant.

"Well, it's pleasant to see you again, though I wish it were under different circumstances. I am deeply sorry about Rachel. I remember you two as children," Lemuel said. "Many of those who lost loved ones have family or friends who are hosting them in their homes for sitting the zayin. The few who do not shall sit it here, in the sanctuary. Rachel loved it here; she would sit in her seat, and I would catch her closing her eyes to feel the glow of the sunlight on her face. She truly loved life." He looked as if he might burst into tears at his own sweet memory. "If you'll help me move some of the chairs around to create some space for each of the families." He gestured to the rows of wooden chairs.

Adam and Ben both followed Lemuel's lead, separating the chairs into different groups and dragging a handful of large wooden tables from the back doors after David hoisted them through, his red deer peeking over his shoulder. Adam and David gave each other grim smiles in greeting. Once everything looked to be in place, Lemuel gestured to a table near the front of the sanctuary, perpendicular to two wooden chairs for Adam and Ben and facing a group of chairs for visitors.

Adam and Ben looked at each other apprehensively as they sat down, side by side, the wood creaking under their larger-than-average frames. Ben appeared to be packed with muscle in contrast to Adam's lanky build, though both towered over the usually short people on the Isle. Adam tapped his foot while Ben folded his idle hands over his crossed arms. Adam fanned himself a bit—it could get warm in the sanctuary when the sun was at its peak—but stopped himself, not wanting to look as if he was not honoring this sacred tradition. He had to be uncomfortable; grief was supposed to be painful.

Small groups of people began to trickle into the Temple, pausing to wash their hands in the buckets outside, fresh from the well, and pray. People that Adam had known his whole life—neighbors, those he attended school with—and acquaintances alike sat in the chairs before him and Ben and prayed. They prayed for them, for Rachel; they brought food, so much food, and piled it onto the table next to them. They placed their hands warmly on Adam's and Ben's shoulders in support. It became a blur; people cycled through for hours as Adam and Ben shifted in their chairs, prayed with the visitors, and thanked them for their blessings and for sharing their memories of Rachel. Though Adam and Ben barely spoke a word to each other the entire day, Adam took comfort in having another person there. Even though Adam and Ben had known these people for a very long time, they didn't *really* know them, not deeply. He supposed Shai, his preserver mentor, knew him as well as anyone there did. Shai had come to offer his sympathy, embracing Adam warmly, which was welcomed, maybe even needed, and delivering a delicious-looking bread that appeared to be infused with cinnamon. Adam hoped his appetite would return in time to savor a bite or two.

As the day began to withdraw and the sanctuary emptied, Adam and Ben looked at the tableful of food that people had brought for them, though they hadn't eaten any of it. They imagined just how much food these people had prepared and shared with so many mourners, and Adam found himself once again glad to have grown up here.

They finally stood and stretched their legs, and George and Zev mirrored their actions. Lemuel noticed and came over.

"Are you planning to head all the way to your home each night, or shall I find you a place to rest your heads?"

Ben piped up immediately. "I'm heading home. It's not too far, and I just like being at home." He turned to look at Adam. "You can come with, or stay."

"If you're sure, I suppose I'll come with you. I don't want to impose," Adam replied, understanding that his uncle had gained a nephew and his very large wolf instantaneously while learning of the death of his estranged, yet beloved, sister. He knew it had to be a lot to handle.

"Like I said, you can come. You're all that's left of my sister, and I've gotta live with the fact that we won't get our moment. I'll keep my promise to her to help you." Ben made keen eye contact as he spoke, impressing upon Adam how much he meant it.

Lemuel looked between the two with hope and clapped each of them on the shoulder. "I shall see you both tomorrow morning." He handed them a couple of large woven baskets with handles to fill with the food from their table. Ben and Adam each took one and filled it to the brim.

Noting their pained expressions, Lemuel continued, "Xhartana can't break us. We will always have each other, and their hearts will always be black and empty. We are deeply connected to our homeland of Avaria. Though they wreak untold horrors on us, they can never take that away from us."

Adam and Ben shared their thanks and made their exit, retracing the steps they had made that morning, soul-seals beside them. Once again, they journeyed in silence, gazing up at the stars as they appeared. They were far brighter than usual, and Adam tripped over his sandal a couple times trying to look up.

Adam took pieces of food from the basket and handed them to Zev as they walked. He noticed Ben doing the same thing with George.

Thanks. I wasn't going to say anything, but I am starved, Zev rumbled to him. They usually spoke far more to each other, but Adam guessed there wasn't much to say these days. True friendship, partnership, was not in spoken words; it was in shared moments.

They rounded the salt flats again, that sulfur stench hanging in the air, and wandered closer to the river and the edge of the wood beyond. Ben let out a sigh of relief as the hut fell within view. Clearly this was heavy for Adam, but he knew leaving home was a challenge for Ben too.

Once inside, Ben quickly made a fire by stuffing some of the kindling at the base, setting it alight, and adding a couple logs to lend them warmth through the night. They sat at the table as they picked through some of the food from their baskets, chatting a bit about some of the people who had stopped by to see them, sharing the odd memory like old, reunited friends would. They headed to bed to try to shut the darkness out for a brief moment before starting anew.

CHAPTER 5

Adam, Ben, Zev, and George fell into a pattern for the next six days: Wake up, face reality, try to eat, walk for miles through remarkable places, sit in their grief, try not to wallow in it, wallow anyway, return the few miles to the hut, eat again, sleep, repeat. By the end of the seven days, Adam and Ben had gotten into a fairly comfortable rhythm with each other, able to communicate with few words, as they both seemed to prefer. However, the time for talking was abruptly upon them as their shared purpose of sitting the zayin ended, and that knowledge hung in the air between them. Adam had not forgotten the letter from his mother for a moment, often drifting off during the sitting to imagine what might have caused her to spill those words on the page—her final words. While Adam and Ben both would have likely preferred to not dip below the surface, they had shared a profoundly emotional experience over the past week, and simply choosing not to express it through words did not mean it had not begun to knit a bond.

They found themselves in the chairs at the wobbly table, facing each other as they had each of the seven days before, listening to the crackle of the fire after having eaten the last of the food from the zayin. Adam shifted back and forth as he considered how best to broach the topic that had been on the tip of his tongue since his life had collapsed. Ben pushed a few lyar, or copper coins, back and forth across the table, nervously twiddling them between his fingers.

The silence that had grown peaceful and comfortable between them became unmanageable with the threat of what was to come.

Adam broke it first. "So, I suppose it's time to talk about my mother's letter." He sat back uncomfortably.

"I guess so," Ben said with a deep, resigned sigh, placing the coins in his pocket and running a finger along his shredded, sun-worn knuckles.

"I have so many questions."

"I'm sure you do, and I'll answer them. I'll explain what I know, and we'll figure out the rest together." Ben took a swig of his tea and cleared his throat. "As you know, I was at your naming ceremony. Your chubby palm glowed blinding white, which is a rare color, with an image of a lone man. That's why Rachel named you Adam, 'the first man.'"

"Wait just one moment!" Adam interjected, with heat flaring through his nostrils in a way that made Zev rise to his feet. Adam patted him lovingly on his side, letting him know to stand down. "I don't have a gift. I've never shown a single sign of a gift. In fact, there is nothing special about me at all!"

"I haven't known you for long, but I doubt there is nothing special about you at all," Ben retorted. "You're Adam, son of Rachel, and you were born with a powerful gift. It's no surprise to me it's been hiding, because it's so different from the others. If you're not careful, it could do a lot of harm."

"My schoolmates' gifts emerged many, many years ago, when we were children. I am fairly certain I would know by now if I could heal, if I had the vision, if I could wield light or water, fire or emotions," Adam said indignantly, with just a tinge of jealousy.

There was very little separation between those with gifts and those without on the Isle, very little judgment, as the Jesimi people felt everyone had something to offer. The fact that the use of any type of magic was banned by Xhartana probably helped soothe any possible tension. Since the dark time, once a gift emerged, instead of training in school to manage it, the child was trained to subdue it. It seemed that about half of people were born with gifts. Adam had always wished he could be happy with his place, not pining for more. And now this.

"Your gift wouldn't be as obvious and wouldn't have naturally shown itself. Especially as you tend to keep to yourself."

"Well, what in the name of Avaria is it?" Adam shouted. Ben let out the slightest chuckle. "You think this is funny, do you? My mother *and* my home are gone, and I have some kind of secret magical power that you are tiptoeing around!" Adam sank back into his chair, folding his arms across his chest like a young child not getting his way. Zev groaned at his side.

"You're a leader. You were born pure of heart, and as far as I can see, you've stayed that way. With your gift, you can see the collective past of a people, allowing you to understand them in a distinctive way. You'll innately have the words that will connect your heart to theirs and speak to their souls." Ben spun the words like thread on a spindle as they unwound everything Adam had known about himself prior to this moment. They fell into silence that was fraught with questions and teeming with worry.

"I am no leader. I can't be. I'm like you; I like to be alone," Adam stuttered. "I don't want to manipulate people. I don't want to see their pain."

"First, you don't know if you are a true leader until you've been in a spot to lead. Second, and listen close, I have scraped the bottoms of every scroll, digging for information on this gift once I saw that symbol. This isn't a gift that's manipulative; it's the opposite, if wielded by a decent person. If someone wanted to use it for evil, to prey on people's memories, their joy, their pain, they could. Of course, they would pay the price. As you know, if gifts are used for dark purposes—not just on our people, but on any people—the glow fades each time and eventually disappears altogether, bye-bye magic. And yeah, you'll see pain. That's the thing about life—it's painful. That's not an excuse to hide, though I'm not one to talk, living out here on the edge of civilization. You'll see it all and speak truth and honesty. People will believe in you, and you'll bring our people, scattered in exile across the continent, together again. That's why people will give you their most sacred possessions: the twelve keys. Xhartana and their sidekicks on Pax have tortured our people, controlled us; it's time to fight back. We can't do it alone. There have been whispers about a person who would come to lead us to peace like we had before the dark time. Once your mother and I saw that symbol on your hand, we knew it was you." Ben drew in a deep breath, and Adam could tell these were important words he had been waiting forever to speak. He wrung his brawny hands, waiting for a response.

A glimpse of flames burned in Adam's eyes, and he allowed last week's attack to simmer in his veins while he built up to a response. "I don't quite know what to say. Why me?" he murmured, looking his uncle in the eyes.

"Why not you?" Ben asked, staring back. "It's fated, written. Who knows why anyone receives the gifts they do, or don't. That's for El alone to know. We've gotta decide what to do with it. Are you gonna train with me or return to Zera and hide from the future your mother saw for you?" That last little dig stoked the flames further.

"I don't hide! I was fine before this latest attack. We were fine. I enjoy my work; I like to read and to write and to observe," Adam contended.

"So, you wanna sit on the sidelines? Haven't you ever wondered what it would be like to make history, to become part of our history instead of just recording it?" Ben asked intentionally, poking into a neglected corner of Adam's soul that he had never shared, let alone acknowledged, where his imagination bloomed and he could be any-thing, do anything. Adam's heart fluttered at the sheer possibility that any of this could be true, that he even had a gift, that he could be part of something bigger than himself. It terrified him and thrilled him in equal measure.

"Maybe I don't," Adam let slip through his lips and clapped his hand over his mouth, not believing he admitted it out loud. Ben snickered again, and Zev tilted his thick neck to look up at Adam, wondering what this all meant for them. "Even if I wanted to consider this crazy idea, and it is crazy, considering I've only left Zera a handful of times and have certainly never stepped foot off this little moon-shaped Isle, I wouldn't know where to begin."

"That's why your mother sent you to me. She told you that I have a gift fit for this exact situation. My gift helps lure out developing magic. I help to nudge the magic into the person's control, to help them safely wield it and master it. Hell of a gift for a loner who can barely stand his own shadow, huh?" Ben slapped his knee, laughing at his own joke. "Many people with gifts don't need assistance, depending on their gift and the strength of it." Shadows began to leap through the irises of his eyes. Adam wondered what caused the sudden shift in his uncle's demeanor and looked at him speculatively.

"You can tell me; why are you all the way out here?" Adam asked gently, intuiting that his gift may be part of the reason.

Ben hesitated, then said, "A long time ago, when I was about your age, I still lived at home with your grandparents and your mother. I was helping a young girl, Adala, with her new gift. She was a talented seer, and it took all my power to help her control it. One day, I got distracted for a second, and she fell deep into a vision. By the time I noticed how far she'd fallen and tried to pull her back, I'd reached my power limit and couldn't get to her. Her mind was lost. She's been lost ever since; she just sits with glassy eyes, muttering warnings under her breath about great peril and some special weapon. Nonsense, really, and no healer has been able to bring her back." Ben slumped in resignation. "Of course, I was blamed, and they were right. I should've been paying closer attention while she was practicing. Zera turned against me. Mother and Father were disappointed. Rachel, she wanted to help me, but she couldn't go against them. So I left. And I never came back, until last week, with you.

Adala's glazed-over eyes creep me out to this day, and I haven't used my gift since." Ben gritted his teeth.

"I am so very sorry that happened to you. You were young yourself; everyone makes mistakes. It shouldn't have cost you your whole life," Adam offered his uncle, shocked at his openness about his past but grateful to be trusted with it. "Thank you for telling me that. It couldn't have been easy to say out loud, even after all this time."

"It was a long time ago, and my life here, on this little slice of land, is enough for me. I stick just outside the attention of the Xhartanians occupying the Isle out here, and I've made it work. I knew one day you'd come knocking. I can't say I didn't hope you'd be with my sister when you did."

"Wait, hold on. Here we are talking about wielding magic. Using our gifts is outlawed. I've read the commands from Xhartana; they can read magical signatures. Wouldn't power like that have been discovered?" Adam tried to put the pieces of a messy puzzle together in his head.

"Ah, I forgot; you haven't known me long enough to know that I can be very crafty. Back in my schoolboy days, I was known for getting mixed up into some trouble for my tinkering with any magical plants or substances I could get my hands on. Me and a couple of friends ended up creating a concoction that accidentally subdues large magical signatures from being discoverable. It's a combination of crushed-up clear quartz, a pinch of salt from the salt flats, ground-up leaves, and the essence of a very rare herb found only in the Rian Forest. Luckily for us, I still have a decent amount saved up, if you're man enough to try using your gift." Ben winked arrogantly, in a flashback to his youth.

Adam let out a laugh, his first in some time. "Do I even want to know how you figured that out? Or how you got your hands on those ingredients?"

Ben simply shook his head, lifting his hands up and shrugging with a charming smile. Adam was once again warmed by the likeness to his mother.

"You look so much like her, you know?"

"People thought we were twins growing up. That is, until I sprouted up about a foot taller than her." Ben gestured toward his height, and he looked like he wanted to say more but was emotionally spent. "So, nephew, what do you think? Are you gonna help save our people?"

"Ha, no pressure at all there," Adam said, smiling in response to being called a nephew. "I can't promise that, but I would like to learn about my gift, maybe learn to use it. Then we can begin to discuss the bigger things." Adam thought he had lost his mind; all that had happened in the past week, all he had lost, and what he stood to gain was baffling. He sat there, head spinning.

"We start tomorrow. Let's get to bed," Ben said, a look of hope and promise on his face that made Adam a little uneasy and a little excited. Adam was way too tired and way too perplexed to do anything but rest, so they tucked in for the night.

CHAPTER 6

Adam peeled one eye open, prepared for a lizard surprise that didn't come. He pulled himself up to see Ben scrambling around the hut in some kind of preparation. Adam stretched his arms over his head and let out a lengthy yawn. Today was the day his uncle would try to lure his gift out. At Adam's age, it was unheard of. He revisited the conversation they'd had yesterday, still full of disbelief. Adam was supposed to believe he had a gift that had been lurking under the surface, a gift of leadership, of always being able to find the right words that people need to hear, a gift from his pure heart. He had never thought of himself as impure, though his mother would likely disagree after finding him in the barn after the Day of Triumph celebrations a couple of years ago with a girl he had been courting at the time. He laughed to himself at the memory, though it most certainly had not been funny and had resulted in many unpleasant consequences and lengthy talks with the Keeper.

Adam mostly couldn't come to terms with having a gift that allowed him to connect with other people on such a meaningful level. That was certainly not a talent he naturally possessed, often tripping over his words and keeping people at arm's length. He wasn't comfortable around many people, though as he looked over at his uncle handing some bread to Zev and George, who seemed to be tolerating each other a bit more, he felt that may be shifting.

He accepted the plate of eggs and bread he was handed and finished them off, then headed over to the bucket to wash his dish.

"All right, no more dillydallying. It's time," Ben pronounced.

"Dillydallying?" Adam smirked.

"Oh, quit. Are you ready to start?" A serious expression fell over Ben's stubbled face.

"As ready as I'll ever be. Though I will say, the world does seem to be upside down," Adam responded honestly. He was ready, though, ready for something new, something that was just his.

Ben gestured for Adam and company to follow him out the warped wooden front door, and they did. He skirted the chicken coop and the goat and cow corral toward the wood and the mighty Copper River as the other three trailed behind. They walked in silence for a short time, Adam enjoying the crisp freshness of the fall air tickling his skin. They approached the bank of the fierce river that wasn't all that wide, but it was forbidding where it met the edge of the vast wood. Ben scouted for a good place to sit, his eyes landing on a tuft of grass in the shade of a billowing willow tree that stood out of place among a legion of spruces and pines that blurred together as far as the eye could see. Ben and Adam sat opposite each other and Zev and George took their places at the sides of their soul-seals, notably selecting the same side. Ben scraped through the pocket of his brown trousers and pulled forth a jar of what appeared to be dirt and maybe some sticks. He placed it between them, unscrewing the lid that tightly held its contents in place.

"This is the concoction I told you about. It's not really an elixir or a potion, because it's not liquid, but it works. Anything to keep those monsters away." He got to work coating his left palm in the dirt from the jar and reached to do the same to Adam's.

Adam scrunched his nose at the scent: dirt mixed with some kind of potent herb. He lifted his head to the sky to take a deep breath away from the protective substance on his hand and inhaled the captivating forest fragrance, centering himself in the process.

"Try to clear your mind, much as you can. It won't always be like this, but for now, I just need to call to your power, to wake it up. Close your eyes and put your left palm on mine." Ben held his dirt-coated left palm up for Adam to meet.

He did, though he couldn't imagine anything more awkward than sort of holding hands with your new uncle. Adam took a deep breath again and tried to clear his mind. Considering the whole world was on his mind—the plight of his people and his own dire losses—this was no easy task. He tried to picture a blank space, he tried counting, he tried many things, and Ben opened one eye in an accusatory fashion. Adam doubled down. If there was one thing he was sure of, it was that when he put his mind to something, he willed his way to accomplishing it. The hum of the energy that flowed within him quieted, thoughts and memories in his mind came and went. As he acknowledged and then sent away a poignant memory he'd shared with his mother, an entirely foreign sensation careened its way into his body, burning as it lit a path, weaving through every fiber of his being. It was so all-consuming, he felt as if it might burst through every pore in his skin all at once. He was overtaken by this novel feeling and was wildly uncomfortable at the unknown he had willingly invited in. He opened his eyes timidly and immediately had to squint; the glow from his left hand was blinding, streaks of bright white and green. His eyes met Ben's, which were wide with amazement at the power that surged between them.

"I'm gonna let go, and we'll see what happens. I'm right here with you," Ben reassured Adam and tentatively pulled back his hand, revealing a vivid-green, glowing symbol of two people shaking hands on his palm.

Adam simultaneously realized most of the blinding quality of the light was emanating from him. As Ben withdrew, Adam felt that strange, consuming feeling begin to subside, and his hand dimmed in time. His mouth hung open as the realization clung to him that he did, in fact, have a gift, and it wasn't all some kind of sick joke.

"You did it your first try! I knew you'd be powerful, but I didn't expect you to be *that* powerful. I've never seen anybody with this much." Ben looked genuinely surprised and equally delighted.

"Technically, you did it. As soon as you let go, it stopped." Self-doubt rang through Adam's tone, as it often did.

"You'll be wielding on your own soon enough. This was a hell of a start. Wanna go again?" Ben challenged, raising his left hand.

As uncomfortable as the experience had been the first time, it dawned on Adam that he now felt like something was missing that had never existed before. He stepped up to the challenge, and they repeated the same routine a handful of times. Each time Ben let go, Adam was able to hold on to the magic a bit longer. After their last attempt, Ben lay back in the grass and Adam followed suit, absent-mindedly stroking Zev's fur. Both men were exhausted by the effort it had taken to come so far in a day. No words passed between them as they watched the willow tree dance with the clouds above their heads. Eventually the hunger that had thankfully returned to Adam required that they venture back to the hut. The hut that held the straw bed and the new uncle with his giant lizard. Adam had a strange feeling it held a piece of him and Zev now too. It felt oddly like a new version of home.

They said hello to the goats, the cow, and the chickens as they passed by and went inside to make a hearty stew with potatoes, beans, meat, and lots of spices.

After a fitful night of sleep, tossing and turning under the spell of what his body had done—accepting his gift—Adam shook his head in disbelief. He missed his mother. He was growing rather fond of his uncle, and tolerating George, and maybe part of him was even a little excited and proud. Foreign feelings or not, he craved routine and the familiar. He liked to eat the same things, walk to his place of business the same way, dress the same; it was comfortable, easy. It kept that tiny piece of him that begged for excitement at bay. If you would have told him this was where he'd be a little over a week ago, he would have laughed, because deep down in his bones, he felt average. What was now being asked of him was anything but; it was a calling for someone extraordinary. Adam made his way out to the chicken coop to snag some eggs in preparation for what he assumed would be another thoroughly wild day.

The four of them made a habit of heading to that perfect spot under the willow tree, near the banks of the gushing river at the edge of the wood, until the days began to blend together. Adam was comforted by this regularity, being able to rely on something remaining the same, even as absolutely nothing they did there was ordinary. They basked in the autumn sun, calling on Adam's gift, pushing it further into his bones, into every cell. That strange, unnerving feeling Adam had felt when his magic had first surfaced began to slowly give way to a sort of ease, a flow that felt as easy as breathing. The days were seemingly endless as they rose and fell with the freedom of his and Ben's magic, almost strong enough to push down the shadows that constantly crept up from every beautiful corner. They began to share stories about their separate lives with Rachel between attempts, blending their blood deeper into true family. Adam worked tirelessly to sustain the magic on his own each time his uncle removed his hand. Ben's eyes shone with pride as the intensity of the white symbol on Adam's hand blazed longer and brighter with each attempt, wrapping Adam's entire body in tendrils of glowing power of his own making.

One morning, as the chill bit at their exposed ears and noses, Adam was able to summon his gift alone, mustering all his concentration, and rather than emptying his mind, he held on to the feeling that had become so familiar. The power snaked through him, filling him with light and a sense of deep pride. He raised his head to the sky and basked in the feeling as it made its home within his very skin. Zev no longer flinched each time Adam attempted to make the connection, simply lying next to him and watching appreciatively out of the corner of his eye. Adam slumped over his own lap as he let the power flow back to whence it came, releasing its grip. He found that even when he was not actively wielding it, his very makeup had changed—he was changed. He feared what that might mean for his future; it didn't bode well for the cozy, comfortable life he had planned. That life had included his mother and her plentiful recent attempts to marry him off, much to his dismay. Back to the future it was.

"You're ready for the next step," Ben announced, beaming at him with pride, light shining through his dark-brown eyes like Adam hadn't yet witnessed. Light he suspected had lain dormant for many years. The thought pinched at Adam's heart; the man he had grown to know was good, and he didn't deserve to have been banished for making a mistake he'd spent his life regretting.

"Okay . . . What might that be?" Adam eyed him suspiciously.

"Right now, your magic is adjusting to you, and you're adjusting to it. Like I said, it is a very different gift than the others. If you had speed, you'd already be a blur. Because this magic is so different, you'll have to learn to use it on other people, to receive their collective memory. Then, you'll be able to find the right words to connect with them. This magic will work on individuals, but you should really ask before digging into people's personal memories; it can really fire them up. That's not how you'll wield it on your journey. When you get to each of the twelve Jesimi villages or cities, you'll be able to tap into each people's life experiences and histories as a whole—less personal, and necessary to understand how different we all are, but in some ways, kind of the same. Seeing their truth will allow your magic to find the right words straight from your heart to theirs, convincing them to have faith in you, agree to hand over their key, and be a part of the fight for freedom," Ben explained, as if that made all the sense in the world.

Adam balked. "Yes, simple as that. I'll go around the continent, and people will somehow listen to me and agree to hand over their most prized possessions and join in a fight that could get them killed. That makes sense. Me, the preserver, who spends his days among the scrolls, trips over his own way-too-large feet, I am going to bring people together." He anxiously wiped the dirt off his left hand in the grass.

Zev let out a low growl. *Come on, Adam. How could you think so lowly of yourself? I wish you could see yourself how I see you. And I see you best, considering our soul-seal. Why don't you try to have some faith? I rather like the idea of a grand expedition.* His enormous mouth pulled up at one corner in a half smile, revealing frightening incisors.

"What'd he say?" Ben asked curiously, watching the exchange.

"He thinks I'm too hard on myself; he always has. He believes in me like my mother did, more than I've ever believed in myself," Adam relayed, with a hint of frustration, but mostly with fondness for his beloved white wolf.

"I've gotta agree with him there." Ben reached out to graze Zev's great shoulder, pausing to request permission. Zev stood to push himself into Ben's hand, the ultimate compliment. To touch another person's soul-sealed animal was only granted when the animal knew their person trusted them unequivocally. Adam looked on in awe, as his mother had been the only other human Zev had ever allowed to lay a hand on his milky fur. Of course, the two men didn't verbally acknowledge it, but it certainly felt like a big deal, and it was.

The next day, they plopped down in their idyllic spot that they seemed to have permanently claimed. Adam knew by the grave look on Ben's face that their lesson today would be different. He also guessed that his past with Adala was clashing with his present, and he took his gift very seriously.

"Today, we've gotta move forward. Time is running out, and you have to start the journey soon, before it's too late," Ben warned. Adam wondered what Ben knew that he didn't but knew better than to question it at this point. "You have to learn to shape your gift rather than just letting it take hold of you. I told you yesterday that your magic would allow you to see a glimpse of the past of a person or a group; it works the same either way. We'll start with me; I'll guide you to see my past to practice. Once you have that down, then we'll have to figure out what's next."

Ben began the process of smudging the mixture on their left hands. He was using the same jar that he'd used on the first day, though they had made quite a dent in its contents. Adam swallowed down the many fears that broke through the surface as he considered what it might be like to see his uncle's memories. He quickly shoved it back down, knowing he had to do this, knowing he *wanted* to do this. He squeezed his eyes shut in concentration as Ben began to whisper instructions.

"Palm up to mine again. Physically touching the subject makes this part easier but usually won't be possible. We'll start here. I am not gonna call your magic; you are. Pull it up and into your veins, letting it flow free." Ben paused for a moment as Adam's magic pushed against his. "Good. Okay, now concentrate on the connection between our palms; feel my energy shift against yours. This'll let you open a window into my memory. Let the white light flow through my body, up to my mind, and stay open—accept me as I am with all you are. Sit with the feeling of our connection and allow it to take root within you."

"Ugh, I can't get through the barriers." Adam gritted his teeth in frustration. Using this gift seemed like one step forward, two steps back. Determined, he pushed harder against the brick walls he seemed to be up against. He felt the sensation of stumbling forward, though he remained rooted in the seated position. "Whoa, what was that? It feels different now."

"You forced your way through; good. Now, open your heart to me. For you to see other people's memories, you've got to earn it, like you had to earn Zev's trust during your task when he picked you as his soul-seal. You must have pure intentions. Open your heart and listen, pulling on that connection between us." Ben's tone was breathier than usual, obviously impacted by having Adam in his head.

Adam did as he was told, trying to lower his own barriers and hush his worries to a whisper, listening for whatever his uncle might have to share. Quieting his own thoughts was hard enough; trying to tune in to someone else's was another challenge entirely. He drew another deep breath, feeling the dewy blades of grass push up through the fingers of his right hand, and he listened. Suddenly, the image of a little girl flowed through his vision, laughing as she ran from someone, her dark-brown hair flowing in ribbons behind her. He continued to watch as he realized the person chasing her was himself—or, he guessed, his uncle—in a hazy memory. The little girl disappeared into the edge of a forest for a moment, popping out from behind a tree a second later, earning a laugh that he felt echo from his own throat. Just as quickly as the girl had appeared, the wispy memory faded from view. Adam felt himself being shoved backward, though he was still firmly planted on the ground and his body hadn't actually moved. He felt his magic withdraw from his uncle as if he was pulling it back himself, and it coiled up in its normal resting place in his chest. He opened his eyes as his uncle covered his own face, and Adam wondered for a moment if he might be crying. He wasn't, but whatever that memory had been, it was powerful.

The awkwardness and not knowing what to say that Adam usually felt in these situations was inexplicably gone. The words wove together from the depths of his soul and began to pour from his lips. "Ben, thank you for sharing such a beautiful memory with me. I can only imagine how painful it must have been to dig deeply into a time in your life right before things became complicated and difficult. That was my mother, wasn't it?" he asked, with more nerve than he had ever held.

Ben plucked a tiny yellow flower from the grass beside him and twirled it between his fingers without looking up. "Yes, it was her," he admitted, pausing to gather his thoughts. "Although Xhartana has always been a threat, controlling our magic, our gatherings, even trying to control our beliefs. Our childhood here on the Isle was full of warm, sunny days, just like the one you saw. We played hide-and-seek, we searched for wood nymphs in the trees, we laughed. So much laughter. That was the happiest time of my life, so it's no surprise they are the first memories you found. Some people are easier to reach than others; that's just how people are. I've spent my life building walls to keep people out, and look how far you've come in such a short time, already knocking them down. And you knew exactly what to say to make me feel better." Ben looked distant, lost to the past.

"Erm, I suppose. It was only one memory, though. Aren't I supposed to see an entire people's collective history? If I can only receive one singular memory from you, how will I gather them from an entire people?" Adam threw his hands up in frustration.

"This is the first time you've ever tried. Just weeks ago, you didn't even believe you had a gift. You have so much more power than you know. Beyond your gift. I guess I'll just have to help Zev remind you till you figure it out for yourself," Ben ribbed, jabbing Adam in the arm. "Do you wanna try again?" He gave Adam his signature mischievous smile that didn't quite meet his haunted eyes.

"I don't want to hurt you. This has to be very difficult for you," Adam said gently.

"I'm a big boy; I can take it," Ben replied, gesturing to his rather swollen bicep in jest. "If you really wanna master this, you'll have to believe that you can. I can't do that part for you."

"I guess that's something I will have to work on as well," Adam agreed. "Let's go again."

They pushed their dirty palms together and tried again, both facing their respective fears by choosing to connect with each other and open themselves up. Neither really understood—at least, not yet—that all their grief and pain and fear had just a little less power over them when they joined together.

They practiced over and over, Adam cracking more and more of Ben's walls in his mind, illuminating moments from Ben's life that had made him who he was. Each revealed Ben as he had grown up, and the memories became marked by darkness, the color dripping from them bit by bit. Adam pushed further, trying to understand how Ben had come to be in that little hut where the edge of the salt flats meets the river and the trees, alone.

Finally, a full, luminous moon rose over the wood as the sun slipped into the blackest sea just beyond, and darkness embraced them like welcome old friends. Adam and Ben could barely stand under the weight of the magic they had expelled mixed with the heaviness of the memories they now shared. Ben placed his hand on Adam's shoulder for a moment and looked at him with an expression that he had only ever received from his mother—a look that was a mixture of pride and affection. Adam had never known a father, and other than Lemuel and Shai, he had never really had a man in his life to look after him and teach him. He wished deeply that he had not lost his mother and his home, but he found himself reassured by this growing bond. Ben's look and grasp on his shoulder told him the feeling was reciprocal, and Adam smiled broadly in response. They returned to the hut in silence, ate in silence, and then went to bed in silence. Too many words and memories had been spilled to address when they were as bone tired as they were.

Over the next few days, they ate like fiends and slept like babies as they poured their all into practicing connecting and receiving Ben's past. The cracks and small doorways Adam had created in Ben's mind were shattered open as the two of them moved forward, deepening both Adam's ability and their friendship in time. Adam grew familiar with the burden of carrying the pain of two people as he witnessed some of the ugliest moments of Ben's life. He watched as Ben was shunned from the community and turned away by his own parents, which was a memory that gnawed at Adam deeply. He figured he would have to learn to manage that feeling somehow if he was going to carry even more painful memories with him eventually. Once Adam had smashed the last piece of the last wall between them, energy flowed between them in a new way, without tethers, connecting them on a new level that washed over them both with glowing light.

"You did it!" Ben exclaimed. A second layer of meaning lurked beneath the surface—maybe Ben would find a second chance at his life. A new purpose. Using his own magic, connecting with his blood, maybe even starting over somehow. Maybe he didn't need to remain alone.

"I guess I did. I could never have done it without you. I couldn't have done what you did, letting me in like that. You don't even know me that well." Adam said in his usual self-effacing manner, giving Ben a gentle punch on the shoulder. El forbid these two actually hug. Refreshed hope shone in the spark that never seemed to leave the whites of Adam's eyes, the perfect opposition to his nearly black irises.

"We're almost there. Your mother'd be so proud. I know she wanted to be here to see all this herself, but I have a strange feeling she may be watching over us somehow," Ben said, desperately wanting that to be true. "She knew time was running out and the only thing standing between you and your great adventure was a plan. And maybe practicing on a group of people to make sure you feel strong before you go."

"You know, calling it my 'great adventure' doesn't instill any confidence in me about the nature of this trip you are sending me on," Adam said, with more than a hint of sass.

Ben bellowed out a laugh. "I guess not, but it sounds way more exciting. It'll be the adventure of a lifetime, if you can pull it off. And I know you can."

"Why aren't you joining me on this exciting, great adventure if it's going to be *so* good?"

"It's not my journey to take. It's yours, alone. Your mother and I knew that the minute that symbol glowed on your hand and fixed itself in our minds. You were given this gift. You. I didn't know you before, which is too bad, but you're a different man than the one who knocked on my door, scared out of your mind, weeks ago." With that, Ben strode over to the shelves above the stacks of firewood and pulled out a long scroll, which he unfurled and smacked down on the wooden table.

Adam gasped as he beheld an ancient map that depicted Avaria as one with the continent, before the dark times. That meant the map had to be over one hundred years old. The preserver in him buzzed with excitement as he reached out to run his fingers over the slightly bumpy papyrus with deep-black ink gracing the lines and words, pale blue depicting the Sea of Orion and the Sea of Tehom on the south side of the continent. Rust and bronze and taupe and every shade of green dripped across the map of the continent with its many realms: the Mesios Rainforest, the Imiris Tundra, the Zokhara Plains, the Forest of Rian, and Terebet flecked with vast, gray mountains. The top of the map held Avaria, which had been hugged at the bottom by the Ma'adim Desert before it was split into Xhartana, Pax, and the Isle of Ori. Seeing it whole, when it was the Jesimi homeland, as El had made it, was something to behold. Though Adam's work as a preserver granted him access to countless historical scrolls and records, a map of the old continent was incredibly rare, and probably illegal. Xhartana didn't acknowledge that there was a time before they laid claim and waste to not only Avaria but the continent as well. As Adam marveled at the map, he froze; the reality that Ben and his mother intended for him to traverse this immense land full of unimaginable obstacles fully set in, and his eyes widened in horror.

Ben took notice of Adam's growing fear. "Whoa, slow down. Let's not get worked up yet. We are gonna plan your journey; it's important to take it one step at a time. One Jesimi village at a time." He gestured for Adam to calm down by lowering his hands. "I have marked the twelve Jesimi villages, towns, and cities on the map so we can plot a path. But during an adventure like this, you've gotta be prepared to change course for any number of reasons. You might encounter severe weather, danger from magical creatures, danger from Xhartana—you'll need to be flexible. I know, not your strong suit."

"You have to be joking about all of this. I like routine, structure, plans, and you're telling me not only am I going to cross the continent, but I also have to be *flexible*?" Adam's heart beat faster just thinking of the possibilities this seemingly impossible task might bring. He felt like he was sinking in quicksand, and no one was going to be there to pull him back out. And he might actually end up in quicksand! Something he did not have to worry about in his day-to-day, in the little village on the Isle. Being burned or stabbed by Xhartanian combatants? Yes. Quicksand? No.

"We've been over this. What else are you gonna do? Go back to Zera, back to preserving, alone? Knowing what you know now? Knowing who you are now? What you're capable of? I think it's too late to turn back." The flicker of the fire reflected in Ben's eyes, and Adam sunk into his seat, trying to quiet the warring in his head between this new, potentially powerful man and the man he had always been, just getting by. The latter was safer, but maybe even scarier than the unknown. He lay his head on the table, and Zev shoved his under Adam's hand. Ben started to roll the map up and suggested they might revisit the plan soon.

"G'night, kid."

"Good night, Ben," Adam responded with a faint smile. He was glad he had an uncle, no matter how overwhelmed he was about absolutely everything else.

CHAPTER 7

The first thing Adam saw when he opened his eyes was all three of the others looking at him as if they were annoyed by waiting for him to awaken. He rolled his eyes and laughed, throwing off the blanket, and tugged on the too-large pants and shirt he was borrowing from Ben. The shirt was made for much broader shoulders, and the clothes hung off him as if he were a strawman as he lifted his arms to the side disapprovingly. Ben snuck a laugh under his breath. At least they were both tall, so the length suited him. He folded the sleeves up and considered he was lucky to not be stark naked, as all of his clothing had been burned in the fire, and the one outfit he had been given the day after was not quite enough.

"We are gonna have to get you some appropriate clothing for your journey and shoes that your toes don't dangle off the front, of" Ben said, pointing toward the worn black leather sandals that had graced Adam's sizeable feet for far too long.

"I don't know how to weave or sew, and I don't have a single lyar to my name. Shai has been so kind to give me this time to grieve Mother, but eventually I need to return so I can forge a living." Adam folded his arms across his chest.

Ben strode over to the corner of the hut and reached underneath the table that sat beside his bed. He lugged out a decent-sized, dark-wooden chest with black iron forming a cage around the exterior, culminating in a padlock adorning the front. Ben shot Adam a sly grin as he pulled a black iron key from some unknown pocket and inserted it into the lock, popping it open with a half turn to the right. He removed the padlock and, in a far too leisurely manner, cracked open the lid to unveil a rather large pile of copper lyat. Interspersed among the coins lay an assortment of semiprecious crystals: amethyst, rose quartz, malachite, lapis lazuli, and more gleamed in the chest, catching the sun. Adam gaped at Ben, his emotions beginning with shock and ending with suspicious curiosity.

"Care to explain how you have amassed more wealth than my mother or I have ever seen in our lives while we have barely gotten by just down the road?" Adam asked in an accusatory tone.

"Well, your mother and I knew this day would come. We've been planning. Putting away any extra lyat we were able to make to prepare for your journey," Ben confessed. "The crystals I got in various ways over the years, won them in games, traded for them. Most gemstones are mined in the Mesios Rainforest and somehow make their way here. They each hold power of their own and are useful for a variety of things somebody might need to keep in their back pocket."

Adam stepped back as he realized that Ben had never done anything to earn his distrust. He had told him everything he had wanted to know even when it had caused him pain. He felt a tinge of frustration at his mother for keeping this from him, though he suspected she must have had good reason.

"It's all just so much. It's hard to believe my mother would have hidden this all from me." Adam breathed out a pained sigh.

"Don't blame her; she wanted to wait until you were ready, until it got closer to the time the stars would align for you to begin your journey," Ben replied.

"I don't blame her; I'm just still so confused. And more than a little dumbfounded by that mountain of coins." Adam remained wide-eyed, his knuckles nearly raw from grinding them together.

"You'll need it if you're gonna succeed. Before we buy the things you'll need for your journey, you still have some practicing to do to prove you're ready. I wanna know you're able to use your gift on a group of people, accurately and safely. We won't start in Zera . . ." Ben trailed off, and Adam knew deep in his heart that he was being protected from seeing his very own painful history. All the times Xhartana abused his people, stole from them, forced them to work, tortured them, killed them. He knew it all too well.

Ben continued, "If we are going to win our righteous battle against evil, we'll need all the Jesimi on this Isle to fight with us, along with the rest scattered around the continent. We'll need all twelve keys and all twelve groups. There aren't many of us, but we sure are mighty when we stand together. We're weak because we've been separated and spread throughout the land, and they're able to control us. We'll start by visiting a couple of the other Jesimi villages on the Isle, and you'll use your gift to earn their trust and, hopefully, their keys."

Ben seemed to love giving an empowering speech, but Adam didn't mind; he needed all the inspiration he could get.

"Once you feel more confident in your abilities, we'll plot your course as best we can, outfit you, and then find a way to smuggle you across the sea to the continent."

Adam smirked at the certainty his uncle spoke with. "So, no big deal?" He casually shrugged as if he believed the words he spoke.

They launched into such an intense bout of laughter that Adam's stomach began to ache. Adam looked down at George and Zev, and it seemed that their lizard and wolf shoulders were bouncing in silent amusement too. His heart warmed as he sat among this group that had grown to feel like his, and he vowed not to take this second chance at family for granted.

"No time like the present. Let's go. This Isle is very small; there are only two other villages besides the city: one near the south end of the Isle, close to where Xhartana has their post, and another out on the peninsula on the far north side, across the Copper River and through the vast wood. Where should we start?" Ben ground his knuckles together, rearing to go.

"You know they don't like when we leave our own villages. How will we explain what we are doing if we get caught?" Adam asked, truly afraid of the answer. In the short time he'd come to know his uncle, he seemed rather fearless, and Adam most certainly was not.

"We won't get caught." As if that was a sufficient answer to someone who was known for being practical. "I've been sneaking around this Isle my entire life. Also been preparing for this moment with you for many years. Have faith in me, as you'll ask others to have faith in you." A sly look crossed Ben's face, exactly as Adam imagined him as a young boy when he inevitably got into trouble.

"I will likely live to regret this, but I do trust you. You've given me no reason not to. Against my better judgment, I will follow your lead," Adam said resignedly, that same combination of fear and exhilaration filling his every fiber.

Ben nonchalantly tossed a small loaf of bread and a couple of small red apples into a woven bag and hauled the strap across his chest. He went to a shelf above the hearth, reached into a basket, and pulled out a blade, maybe seven or eight inches long, made of the shiniest steel—Adam caught a glimpse of Ben's reflection in it. Ben carefully put the blade back in its black leather sheath and fastened it to his side. Adam gave him a quizzical look, which Ben haughtily ignored, and without a word, he marched out the warped wooden door, letting it swing closed behind him before the other three could pass through. *Rude*, Adam thought, *but in character*.

"We'll start by going north. I'd rather face the woods and any creatures we might find there before those monster soldiers." Ben shivered.

Adam wondered what Ben had been through to make his seemingly infallible uncle shiver. He rushed to catch up, barely avoiding the same root that he had tripped over for days.

Klutz, Zev muttered under his breath.

"I heard that, and I don't appreciate it," Adam retorted, giving his wolf a look.

"You say something?" Ben called over his shoulder.

"Nothing," Adam grunted.

Zev and George slinked along behind them, walking in stride with each other somehow, though their legs were feet apart in length. They passed their spot, and Adam beamed as his gift rose, licking at the surface of his skin, pressing him to release it as it seemed to recognize where it was.

They pushed on into the edge of the endless wood, dipping under the dark-green canopy that quickly stamped out the light of day. A chill flirted with Adam, dancing along his skin. The scent of pine overtook him, soothing him from within the endless sea of trees. Adam had to stare at the ground as he followed Ben, Zev at his side now managing to help keep him on track as the uneven forest floor threatened to upend him at any moment. The deafening drone of rushing water filled the air as they approached the bank of the Copper River. They all stopped to take it in as its natural beauty wrestled with its formidable existence. Ben surveyed the river, presumably seeking a way to cross. He told them to wait while he took off jogging farther into the forest, George scuttling along in his wake.

Adam sat on a stump a few feet away from the edge of the water, watching it lap against the pine-needle-coated forest floor. The sun peeked through the open slice of air above the water, giving temporary respite from the darkness. Adam found himself deeply grateful that his uncle seemed to be skilled at navigation; without him, Adam would have been lost from the moment he entered the wood.

He scanned his surroundings, listening, drawing in the soothing fragrance through his nostrils and letting the breath seep back out of his mouth. He let his mind wander to the tales the other children told in day school about the Mazzikin, the invisible demons. He would be embarrassed to admit the very real dread that took hold of him for a time as he sat alone on his stump, wondering if fairy tales could be real. He talked to his soul-sealed wolf and had magical powers, so it wasn't that far-fetched to think there were meddlesome demons who gallivanted through the wood, looking for a soul to harass.

Adam heard sticks snap as someone or something moved toward him in the shadows, and he stood suspiciously, Zev on high alert at his side. Ben glided into view as easy as a Sunday and gave him a very amused look when he saw the panic imprinted on Adam's and Zev's faces.

"Did you think I was a Mazzik or something?" Ben let out a laugh that came straight from his belly.

"No!" Adam snapped. "Maybe. I dunno. Do you know for sure they aren't real?"

"They're real. I just didn't know how much of a fearful fanny you were." Ben slapped his knees as he resorted to childhood name-calling.

"Fearful fanny, really?" Adam squeezed his fists, and his mostly dormant muscles tensed.

"Come on, I found a way across. You're probably not gonna like it, though," Ben taunted, and he ambled back through the thicket.

Adam and Zev followed, Adam still seething, trying to come up with a witty retort. Just up ahead, he noticed a colossal pine tree had fallen across the river's wide path, with the unforgiving fresh water far below.

Adam stopped in his tracks, taking in Ben's plan. "You want us to cross that tree without plunging to our deaths? Great idea. Have you met me?"

That elicited a snort. "Yeah, I do. The river runs through the entire width of the Isle; we have to cross—no other choice. You can do this. But not with those El-forsaken sandals. Hand them over." Ben beckoned toward Adam's feet as Adam looked on with increasing disbelief.

"So, not only do you want me to cross a tree trunk when I can barely walk on flat ground, but you want me to do it barefoot?" Adam raised his voice incredulously.

"How long are we gonna keep doing this back-and-forth thing where you pretend you can't do new things, I tell you that you can, and then you do it and end up liking it?" Ben said, looking over a blister on his hand as if he could not be less interested in the conversation.

Adam thought for a moment, and though it irritated him to no end, Ben was right. This was all totally new for him, and he had been forced to adjust to it, but he would be lying if he said that he wasn't sort of enjoying it. That thought dipped into the seeping well of guilt that he was having fun without his mother.

A new sense of resolve bloomed within him, mostly born out of a desire to prove to his uncle that he wasn't afraid. He tore off his sandals and tossed them to Ben, who threw them in his bag and started toward the end of the mammoth tree. Its roots had been ripped from the earth and now flew in every direction, making it difficult for Adam to fathom how he would even get up onto the trunk. Zev brushed him aside as he took a graceful flying leap onto the log as if it was nothing, then began to pad gently across the log, looking straight ahead the whole time. Adam reminded himself to thank Zev for going first, though his performance was a little arrogant for his taste.

Adam began to scale the peeling log, digging his hands and toes between the cracks to drag his tall body up onto it. He swung a leg across and cursed to himself as he sliced his leg on the sharp bark, dribbling blood across it, then straddled the log and steadied himself to stand.

The thunder of the water threatened to toss him in as he took his first steps, arms straight out from his sides for balance—not his forte. He continued one step at a time, gripping the log with his bare feet, starting to build confidence just as a gust of wind came and toppled him off his lengthy legs. Adam nearly fell down the side of the log but managed to find a handhold at the very last second. As he dangled there, he made the grave mistake of looking down at the churning water and the sharp, protruding rocks.

He swung a leg up once again and seriously considered crawling across, but meeting his uncle's eyes, shining with pride, he stood again, bolstered. Adam turned, fixing his eyes on Zev's great white form beckoning him to safety, and he trembled as he took his last step and was above solid ground again. He hopped down, finding it hard to believe that he was still in one piece and that he felt . . . exhilarated. He wiped some of the blood on his borrowed pants and watched as Ben hoisted George up, then effortlessly followed. George's long claws assisted him, piercing the bark as he waddled across.

"Told you you could do it." Ben threw Adam's sandals over his shoulder to him as he cut a path through the woods once again.

Adam puffed his chest a little and followed, deliberating whether he had made a mistake blocking out the world for so long.

They continued in comfortable silence, navigating their way somehow through the very dim wood to the other side, where beams of light trickled through the trees. As they reached the tree line, they fell in next to each other, Ben smiling at some unknown memory and Adam's mouth once again falling open. They stood atop a fairly large, grassy hill blanketed by a brilliant array of wildflowers swaying in the breeze. At the bottom of the hill, a quaint village unfolded, hugging the curves of a slim peninsula suspended above the gloomy Sea of Orion.

Adam could hardly keep himself from running to the welcoming place before them, kicking himself for never exploring the tiny moon-shaped Isle he had lived on his whole life. He could not believe that this picturesque place was less than a couple hours' walk from his home.

Zev rolled down part of the hill, giddy as he shoved his muzzle through the endless blossoms, unfazed by a sneeze or two. Even George's lizard mouth seemed to turn up at the edges as he scurried surprisingly quickly down the hill in his soul-seal's wake. Adam took his time meandering down after them, plucking flowers and inhaling their unique and captivating scents, making sure to take in every detail so as never to forget this feeling. Freedom, adventure, hope.

As they reached the bottom of the hill, they strolled through the arched stone village entrance, which was draped with the greenest of vines, onto the main cobblestone road. Adam couldn't believe how vastly different this was to his home, down to every detail. Each of the buildings and homes they passed were built of matching stone and mortar, with wooden roofs. It was bustling as villagers passed them with babies in their arms and buckets of water they had fetched from the well, nodding in greeting to the visitors as they passed. The main street trailed off, ending with a steep slope into the mysterious and murky sea. Adam and Ben approached a beautifully carved wooden bench adorned with many names. They ran their fingers along, taking in the names and wondering why they had been etched there. A jolly, large-bellied man with a long gray beard stopped as he noticed their curiosity.

He hung his head and said, "Those are the folks that we lost in the last attack by Xhartana when we didn't pay our taxes on time here in Mezarim. Though we like to make a very big celebration around here of Katziyr, the Day of the Harvest, the harvest was unkind to us that year. We simply couldn't feed ourselves and supply their stores on top of paying into their coffers." The man pinched his lips together, taking his hat into his hands and uttering a silent prayer to El. It was hard to imagine the evil force that was Xhartana tainting this serene place, but they tainted everything. It was who they were.

"We are so terribly sorry to hear that, kind sir. Xhartana just struck us; they burned many of our homes and killed so many of our people. My mother," Adam just barely edged out, realizing it was the first time he had to tell someone about her since his uncle.

He hoped someday it might get easier, but he knew that it likely never would. The man reached out, grasped Adam's shoulder, and gave him a knowing look. They had all suffered at the hands of Xhartana for over a hundred years. The resolve that had been lit in Adam's gut burned brighter and stronger. The man continued on as he and Ben sank onto the bench.

"I know this is hard, but should we try to tap into your gift? These are our people; they're Jesimi. Their pain is your pain already. It lives in you." Ben bumped his shoulder into Adam's gently.

"Now is as good a time as any. Again, not sure how I earned the right to see their history," Adam said, looking at the ground.

"That's why. Because you get that it's a privilege—a heavy one. You're pure goodness, and *you* were given the gift," Ben replied earnestly.

Yes, that message was beginning to sink in. It didn't make any more sense than it had the day he'd first read it in his mother's letter, but it had become more real each time he'd wielded his gift, each time he'd succeeded at something new. He didn't know about pure of heart, but he did know that if he had been given such an important gift, he couldn't let his people down.

Ben took the special mixture from his bag and handed it to Adam. Adam smeared it across his left palm and handed it back to Ben, assuming he would do the same.

"You're ready to do this on your own, and since you aren't connecting with me, you don't need my gift to help. I'll be here the whole time, walking you through it, but it's the same thing you've been working on while connecting with me. You'll let your magic flow freely under your skin, and instead of focusing on reading and meeting my energy, you'll concentrate on what's right in front of you: the beating heart of this village. Where the people here come together when they can safely. Right here along this street, it looks like there is a food shop, a maker's shop, their Temple, some sort of village hall, their day school, their water well." Ben gestured to the places as he mentioned them.

They sat in silence, smiling, watching the children run after squirrels in the center of the large cobblestone circle that decorated the beating heart Ben described. Adam pondered how resilient the Jesimi people were, though they shouldn't have to be. Never losing their sense of wonder, their love of life, of each other.

With that inspiration, Adam beckoned his gift, welcoming its strange grasp, asking it to wander freely through him. Then he focused on the center of this sweet little village by the sea. He looked at the faces of the people, the passersby, and wondered what more they had faced, what they had celebrated, and what they had lost. A foreign sensation like a deep pressure fell over him, and he squeezed his eyes shut.

He gasped as a memory filled the void that he had created for this moment, wrapping its way along the far corners of his vision, tinged with sepia as if it was from long, long ago. People danced outside in large circles, holding hands and kicking their legs, the circles moving opposite ways. They laughed and smiled so hard it looked like it might have even hurt. The memory gave way to another that appeared to be a wedding: A woman, covered from head to toe in white, her face veiled, circled a man, wearing a black suit and hat, seven times. The man looked like he was so happy, he could burst. Dozens of people stood around them, burgeoning with love.

The next vision crashed into that beautiful scene, this one splashed with darkness, and Adam quickly realized he was witnessing the time before Avaria split off the continent. The village wasn't too different from the one that stood before him today, but it felt distant, out of reach. He hoped he'd get better at differentiating between them.

The memories continued to sweep over him, flickering back and forth between pure joy—soul-seal ceremonies, naming ceremonies, holidays—and the evil that had swept the land—Xhartanians attacking mercilessly and without notice, time and time again. Tears slipped from his eyes as he scrunched them tight, weathering the impact of the collective pain this village held. The details were different, but the similarities between this village and his own were astounding.

The magic began to lighten its grip, and he felt lightheaded as his mind was once again his; his body wobbled a bit as he slowly opened his eyes. He jumped back as he realized he was surrounded by quite the crowd of curious onlookers. The white light of his left palm was fading but remained rather bright as his gift folded itself nicely in his chest where it lived. The people, a variety of ages and appearances, were flanked by animals he assumed were soul-seals. All of them were clearly wondering what this strange magic was.

"Hello, I am Adam, son of Rachel. This is my uncle Ben, son of Idit, and that's George and Zev." He nodded to each individual as he introduced them, not recognizing the seriousness in his tone. The ease of his words did not match his usual speech, which tended to sound deflated. "Your village is truly breathtaking. I come from Zera, a village much like yours up the hill, across the vast wood and the mighty Copper River, and past the salt flats. We were recently attacked by Xhartana. They burned many homes and buildings, killing many of our own, including my beloved mother." He sucked in a breath and paused as his audience leaned in, listening to his every word. He got a feeling they did not have many visitors.

While the words that fell from his lips were genuine, he wasn't working hard to form them as he usually did. He tugged on his magic and felt it flow from its nest within him. "My mother left me a letter that said that I was born with a gift: I would be able to see the collective past of a people, allowing me to truly see them, to connect with them on a soul level. The gift then helps me form the words to speak to your hearts from mine." A little girl with light-brown pigtails was so close to Adam, she was nearly falling into his lap. "Your home is so very like mine. As Jesimi, we share so many of the same customs and beliefs, the same values, and unfortunately, the same enemies and pain. My mother wrote in her letter that the time was near to gather the Jesimi people from all over the continent, reuniting the twelve keys, to rise up against Xhartana, to take back Avaria and free our people from their reign of tyranny. She believed it was my fate to travel the realms and use my gift to join our people once again. I begin with you." Adam slipped back to himself, surprised that his gift could make him suddenly less terrified of speaking to more than one person— heck, even just one person. He folded his hands in his lap and tapped his foot as he awaited any kind of response to his words.

The crowd parted, and a stern-looking woman waded through. She was bordering on frail with her petite frame, her dark hair speckled with streaks of gray that matched her weary, almond-shaped eyes.

Her skin was a faded sienna. She was shadowed by a small but equally formidable sand cat who bore holes into the visitors with unblinking eyes in an undeniably adorable face. The woman looked as if she carried the weight of the world on her shoulders, and Adam wondered if maybe she did. She gave them a guarded look.

"I am Irena, daughter of Naomi. Welcome to Mezarim," she said through her teeth. "My name means harmony, and my gift matches, though we don't use our gifts. Nevertheless, I have been called to guide my people, and it is my honor to protect them. Xhartana is a great enemy to all who seek peace; you will find no argument on that here. However, we are but a simple people. We are not fighters; we do not wield weapons except to hunt. I fear we would be of little aid to any kind of battle." Irena stamped her lips into a thin line.

"There are many ways to fight the upcoming battle," Adam said in a tone that could have convinced a mouse to jump into a cat's mouth. "We will need skills of all kinds, gifts of all kinds. There are so few of us; we must all decide we will not stand for this a moment longer if we want to succeed. We will succeed, because we must—we are the side of good. It certainly won't be easy, but nothing is easy, and we are Jesimi."

"I hear you; I hear you. I must speak with our people about this. We must pray about it. Please, be our guests this eve. You must be starved from your journey; you must eat. You shall stay with us in our home," Irena insisted rather forcefully, and Adam had to admit, he was hungry.

They warmly accepted the invitation of the indomitable leader and followed her down the pockmarked cobblestone road to her home. It was quite a bit larger than Adam and Rachel's had been, or Ben's, offering a few separate spaces for Irena, her husband, and their two children, aged eight and eleven, who were introduced as the group walked over.

Adam and Ben were rushed into chairs at the round wooden table, which was cloaked with a deep-blue linen tablecloth adorned with small white stars and tucked into a corner of the cozy stone abode. The children swiftly brought them cups brimming with hot herbal tea, smiled widely, and then ran off to their room, making all kinds of ruckus playing. George and Zev made their place at Ben's and Adam's feet, giving a wide berth to the suspicious-looking sand cat, who was aggressively purring and guarding his soul-seal. Adam looked over at Ben, who had been watching him like a proud father. Adam slumped under the heft of that unfamiliar feeling and loved it at the same time.

Irena was spinning around, preparing food, as her husband stoked the fire. They were strikingly different; his warmth met her chill head-on, and their love for each other clung to every surface in their inviting home. Adam couldn't help but be comforted by a mother fussing over him, as it reminded him of his own.

At a dizzying pace, Irena set down dishes of food: a platter of fish surrounded by slices of bright-yellow lemons, diced potatoes coated with some kind of herb that smelled delightful. She handed them empty plates and called to the children to come eat. She filled metal goblets with sweet wine, and the adults lifted their glasses high, slamming them together and all but yelling in unison, "Next year reunited in Avaria!"

They all filled their plates, and as they consumed the delicious food, they shared stories with each other about their homes and their lives. Adam and Ben looked at each other, observing how much lighter Irena's demeanor appeared—the best conversations always happened around food.

Irena rushed over to where she had prepped the food and brought back a beautifully browned, rectangular cake that set all their mouths to watering. They enjoyed every last morsel of the honey cake as laughter flowed easily through the ranks of new friends. The children were eventually sent off to bed begrudgingly as the adults continued to visit.

"Thank you for this delicious meal and for inviting us to join your family this eve. It has been an honor to visit your village and to have you consider helping us," Adam said, Ben nodding along with him and trying to get food out of his teeth without anyone noticing.

"The pleasure is ours. We do not get visitors often, and it makes it seem like we are alone. It is nice to be reminded we are not."

With those words, Irena showed them the beds she had made up at the foot of the fire, having managed to juggle that with making a full meal, and they all retired for the night. And not a moment too soon, as Adam realized he had never felt so tired. The first use of his gift on a larger scale had taken its toll, but truth be told, his soul felt alight with purpose, fatigue be damned. The blanket snagged the cut Adam had earned crossing the river earlier, and the twinge of pain made him feel alive, maybe more alive than he had ever been. He had seen and held great pain, not unlike his own, but maybe he could be part of doing something about it. Once and for all.

Adam, Ben, Zev, and George awoke to the sounds of children snickering as little faces peered at them from around the corner. The rare scent of coffee, which had to be imported in, and that of eggs filled their nostrils, causing them to bolt upright. They stood to fold the hand-knitted blankets they had been generously lent.

Irena pointed to the table once again, and they made their way over to sit. She set down cups of steaming coffee, sending a few drops toppling over the edges, and a small container of fresh milk. She slid full plates of bread and eggs across the table, and Adam and Ben both caught them just before they flew off, eliciting some snickers from the children. The two sat together and ate, sipping at their coffee, waiting for their host to join them or inform them what their next steps might be. Stripes of daylight shone through the windows, and Adam traced them with his finger as he wondered how his first real attempt at using his gift the way his mother had intended was received. He had known it would be the challenge of his life; he believed that sentiment every moment he moved closer to accepting fate and embracing this wild future.

"I was up early, meeting with the unofficial council here to discuss your message," Irena said casually.

It was as if the painfully serious woman they had met just yesterday had morphed into this much gentler creature. The weight still sat firmly upon her shoulders, even when smiling and laughing, but her demeanor had softened.

"We stand by what I said: We are not trained fighters, and we do not wield weapons." She paused, and Adam's heart skipped a beat. "However, we have many other abilities among us; some of us have powerful magic gifts we have had to subdue that could be beneficial. We also have other skills that may prove useful. Ultimately, though we would not make a suitable front line in your battle, we are Jesimi, and that means we have warrior blood. If we allowed this battle to take place and simply sat back, we would not deserve to reap the benefits of the freedom that will be ever sweeter when we earn it. We hope you find some tough, well-trained Jesimi on your journey, but you are not alone. Adam, Ben, we are with you."

Adam's eyes clouded with tears, and this time, it wasn't his grief trying to escape its prison—it was hope. There was always going to be hope. He felt a strange inkling that his mother's words—that she would never truly leave him—might, in fact, be true. She would be proud. They all stood to shake hands and pat each other on the back warmly.

"That's quite a gift you hold, Adam," Irena continued. "I, for one, am rather glad you decided to face this monstrous challenge head-on. You are a brave young man; I will be glad to stand beside you when the time comes." She pulled him into a brief, firm hug, then released him, and he could swear her pallor brightened ever so slightly. Hope seemed to have that effect.

She strode over to the stone hearth, calling to her husband. They both anchored themselves and slid aside a slab of sandstone that sat atop the mantel. Irena wicked away the beads of sweat that had formed on her gently lined forehead, and from the hollow space, she withdrew a key from a brass hook. Irena returned to Adam, reached for his hand, and pressed the key into his palm, curling his fingers over it with a knowing smile.

Adam unfurled his fist and beheld the most unique key he had ever laid eyes upon. It had been etched from a brilliant turquoise stone native to the Isle, formerly Avaria. The first key—one down, eleven to go. It wasn't until now that Adam realized he did not know what the keys unlocked. He simply knew that gathering them all was paramount to their triumph.

"Thank you for trusting me with this most precious resource. I promise to keep it safe and use it only for good." Adam closed his fingers around the cold stone key once again, holding it his chest.

Adam and Ben said thank you a dozen times, assuring Irena that they would send word with any updates and agreeing to return when they could. They would have been happy to stay for quite a while longer in Mezarim, hovering above the darkest sea with the kindest of people.

They looked back, out of breath, as they crested the wildflower-covered hill and smiled before they plunged into the dark, cold wood to make their way home. Adam's mood couldn't even be tempered by twigs snapping and pine needles crunching nearby, though they did set his spine a bit straighter. He was surprised at the comfort he felt returning to the little hut; it felt like home. Through the thickness of his grief, he was grateful for his uncle and a sort of home. And, most of all, he was hopeful.

CHAPTER 8

Adam, Ben, and their soul-seals stepped outside after another good night's sleep, full from breakfast and giddy from their collaboration with Mezarim. With buoyed spirits, they set out again, hoping for a similar result with the other Jesimi village on the southern part of the Isle. They looked up as the clouds became tinged with darkness and quickly knitted together over their heads. An ostentatious crack of thunder, seemingly close by, had them jumping in surprise. In contrast to the fierceness of the thunder and accompanying blinding flashes of lightning, the gentlest of rain fell from the sky, landing on them with such grace, they didn't run. Zev cried out with joy as he began to dance his wolf dance, frolicking beneath the stormy sky. George made a run for it back toward the hut, but Ben dragged him back. The men laughed and considered whether this was a foreboding sign or simply autumn's way of invoking her changes on their world. The Jesimi people were known to be rather superstitious. Adam had always laughed at his mother's "warning signs" that never seemed to amount to anything and special routines she performed to be sure not to provoke El or tempt fate.

The group pushed through the rain, unaffected, except Zev, who couldn't help but dive like a cub into every new mud puddle they passed. He may have been a majestic white wolf, but he was still full of youth. Adam envied that in him, as he did not remember a time when he'd felt playful, unencumbered; he had always been quite serious.

They rounded the salt flats, the usually vivid greens and blues muddied from the falling rain, and the overwhelming sulfur smell was allayed. They followed the path they would take to go to Zera but eventually passed the turnoff, continuing their voyage south. This southern half of the Isle was all fairly open to the elements, though dotted with the occasional olive tree and rolling hill. After yesterday's challenges crossing the river and traversing the dark wood, this seemed like an easy task. Adam began to whistle to himself as they walked along, absentmindedly twisting the turquoise key that now hung from a piece of twine around his neck. Ben burned a hole in the side of his head with his eyes, making it very clear he was not planning to listen to that much longer, and Adam snickered and stopped.

Ben stopped walking and turned to face him. "The village we're going to now is on the far side of the Isle from the Xhartanian base, but they do patrol the area closely. They use this as a training ground for their boys when they graduate from their religious military school at age fourteen. You would think younger and less experienced would be a good thing for us, but these children are trained in the most brutal forms of combat from the time they can walk. Their extreme form of Marre beliefs is vicious. They're raised with one purpose: defending the reign of the Xhartanian empire and crushing the Jesimi people," Ben explained as Adam frowned deeply, nodding in understanding. "We'll have to be really careful from this point on and be prepared to hide quickly and quietly. We don't wanna get caught." Ben's eyebrows knitted together with a seriousness that made Adam shudder at what capture might bring. Xhartana had taken people from his village before, and the conversation brought back teeth-chattering memories.

"Follow me closely, no talking, and definitely no whistling from here. Once we get to the village walls, we'll be much safer since they have better defenders than Zera," Ben said as he started off again, scanning his surroundings carefully as he moved.

Adam also surveyed the landscape, and he began to wonder where they would hide, should the need arise, as he could see nothing but patches of tall grass and the same hard-packed, reddish-brown dirt that lined the streets of his village, now clumped and muddy. He made a valiant attempt at stealth as he followed in Ben's and George's steps, one foot after the other, about as gracefully as an ox. They moved like this in a straight line for a time, which he imagined would appear strange to an outside eye, until Ben halted abruptly, pushing a single finger to his lips to silence them, the other hand signaling to stop. The clopping of hooves crescendoed as it drew closer.

Ben looked around furiously, hunting for a place to hide, in case the oncoming were the enemy. He grabbed Adam's arm, ripping him from the spot where he stood, and they flew away from the muddy road. Ben was all but holding Adam up, as his sandals were not built for fleeing from danger. They spotted a rocky outcropping that spread out over a barren field, which stretched far into the distance. Ben continued to drag Adam, hopping down to the bottom of the stack of rocks and tucking them both underneath the narrow overhang. Ben swore under his breath and whispered, "I hope it's enough."

Adam became panic stricken as reality set in—this wasn't simply a river he needed to brave crossing; this was a real-life nightmare. The horses—a number of them, from the sound of it—drew closer to where the group had just stood. All four held their breath as they waited to see whether the riders would notice anything was amiss, if they were even Xhartanian. Voices boomed across the expanse, thick with a Marre accent, echoing across their hiding place. Ben and Adam didn't have to strain much to hear their lively conversation, their faces turning a horrid shade of greenish-yellow as they recognized what the guards were discussing. Zev let out a throaty growl.

"And then, and then, praise the Deity on high, I slashed their throats. The kids first so the parents had to watch, of course." Rounds of depraved, venomous laughter followed the boast. It sounded like at least three or four men, maybe teenagers, judging by the youthful lilt of their sinister voices.

Another voice penetrated the thick air hanging between villains and their soon-to-be foe. "I liked the part where we lit everything on fire. I like fire."

Adam lunged to attack, nearly giving them away, but Zev latched onto his pant leg and Ben yanked him back under just in time. They both had to physically cover their mouths to prevent sound from escaping their lips as they listened to a play-by-play celebration of the attack on Zera that had cost Adam his mother and home and Ben his sister. The lives and homes of so many others as well.

"Well, it's about to get even better," a nasally voice claimed, his vile words bounding across the rolling hills. "No more of these small-time raids. I've heard the whispers of Jesimi pig rebels across the continent, and Balian, Namtar, and Vardas have big plans to squash them all like the bugs they are. We're going to be patrolling larger areas of the continent; we will be in control, as it should be, praise the Deity."

"Did you hear about the platinum? I never had no magic, but everyone is all excited about it."

"Of course. I'm higher up than you; they trust me more," said the nasally voice. "I hear everything. They finally struck a deposit in the mine. They thought it was empty, but the Deity always provides. As soon as they can get it all out, our soldiers can get back their powers, and we'll finally be able to destroy them. Sweep them from every last corner of our land, the land we took for ourselves because we are stronger, better. Soon, we will extinguish all Jesimi rats from all the realms as if they had never existed." With that, the voices faded, and the descent into murderous cackles fell away.

Adam, Ben, George, and Zev waited, frozen in torment, in revulsion. Ben ordered them to wait while he popped his head just over the top of the overhang, then reported nothing but hoof prints in the mud where the soldiers had stomped all over their hope for a peaceful future. How could they ever share a land with savages like that?

"Sick bastards," Ben muttered, shaking his head with disgust. "I knew time was running thin, but I didn't know they had gotten their filthy hands on more platinum. That changes things. Your great journey may be our last chance before it's too late. You'll have to warn everyone you meet about these advances."

"Gee, thanks. No pressure or anything." Adam had to force himself to breathe, vibrating with fear at having been so close to the men who had taken his mother from him—and been thrilled to do it.

They were all the same cutthroat, ruthless tyrants. The Jesimi people had done everything they could over the past hundred years to make peace, to come to any sort of terms with Xhartana, like Xhartana had with Pax—the third island that had come from Avaria splitting off the continent and whose leaders had helped Xhartana take the helm of power. Xhartana could not be moved from their reign of evil; nothing stopped them or even slowed them down. The one thing they had not faced in over one hundred years was a united Jesimi front. That is what needed to happen—their only chance. With that in mind, Adam stood and followed Ben back to the rutted road.

They made haste this time, nearly jogging, hoping to avoid further run-ins with the rogues. Before they knew it, they approached a gray stone wall that towered above their heads. They wove their way around the curve of the wall until they reached a large wooden gate that looked like it should be guarding a castle. They peered through the lattice work, and two men entered their field of vision. They wore guardian garb, head to toe, and held spears nearly the length of their bodies, with carved wooden handles and sharp steel heads. They did not make eye contact or break their grave expressions as their spears descended to point directly at Adam and Ben.

"Um, hello there. We are from Zera, just north of here. We have come to meet you," Adam said in his usual awkward way, wearing a sheepish smile. He figured nonthreatening was the way to go with spears that large pointed at them.

"No visitors shall go here," the guardians responded in deep, bellowing unison. Ben and Adam made brief eye contact that screamed how creepy this was.

"We made our way down here, and it's very important that we speak to someone today," Ben said, puffing up his muscular chest and taking the opposite tack to Adam.

"No visitors shall go here," they repeated, staunchly unmoved by Adam's and Ben's insistence.

"Helpful, thanks," Adam whispered under his breath. He turned to his uncle. "Well, what are we going to do now?" he asked, throwing his hands up in the air in frustration.

Before Ben could respond, they noticed a young man strolling languidly toward the wooden gate that separated them.

"Well, what do we have here? We weren't expecting any visitors," the man rolled off his tongue, resting a hand on one hip.

Unsure of the nature of his tone, Adam repeated, "We are from Zera. We have come to speak with you about something very important." He hoped that would be enough to let them in.

"We keep things pretty well locked down here in Kesil, for obvious reasons, so you can see why we are hesitant to let in strangers," he said, with an air bordering on arrogance. "What is it you would like to speak with us about?"

Adam glanced at Ben—they had not prepared for this—before responding, "My name is Adam, son of Rachel. This is Ben, son of Idit, and Zev and George. I have a gift that allows me to see a people's collective experience, their joy and their pain. I am able to join together with them and speak to their hearts. My fate is to travel to the continent and gather the Jesimi people together once more, collecting the twelve keys, as it is time we fight against the horrors inflicted upon us for over a hundred years. The only way we can do this is together." Adam felt ablaze with passion for the words he spoke; his gift had mingled with his soul, solidifying his belief in it.

The man looked wholly unfazed and replied, "That's nice, but we have found a way to manage it, for the most part." He gestured to the wall that wrapped around the village. "It is naïve to think anyone could fight against them. Their numbers are only matched by their cruelty. We will have no part in any sort of uprising that is sure to be crushed." His tone made it clear his part in the conversation was over. Adam and Ben looked at each other with the aching feeling of having failed to convince him before they had even started.

"Ethan, come on, it's time!" a distant voice shouted.

"Now, if you'll excuse me, I have important matters to attend to." The cocky man, apparently named Ethan, gave them a faux smile and a dramatic bow at the waist.

"Thanks for your time," said Ben, his tone matter of fact. "I guess we'll be on our way. If you change your mind, you can find me where the salt flats meet the edge of the wood and the Copper River meets its end in the darkest sea." He turned on his heels to begin the journey back, the other three trailing behind silently.

Adam opened his mouth to speak, but Ben pressed his finger to his lips again, warning him to silence. The sky was clear, and the birds had resumed their endless chirping without a care in the world, as if Adam and Ben hadn't just risked their lives to be turned down cold. The silence was helpful as their shared irritation with the situation floated in their heads. Once they were back near the outskirts of Zera, their shoulders fell a little in relief.

"You couldn't have done anything differently," Ben said, speaking the first words in what seemed like forever, knowing exactly what Adam was thinking. "It's actually a good lesson, because you will face untold hurdles on your great journey. Great journeys are never easy, or they wouldn't be great, now, would they?"

Adam didn't respond, thinking to himself that Ben was probably right, but that didn't make it easier. Failure wasn't a familiar concept for Adam; he had never really tried anything new to fail at. He was very dedicated and successful in his studies, which carried over into his work. Though they didn't fully know the purpose of the twelve keys, he imagined coming up one key short might pose a problem. While he continued to be annoyed that he didn't have another group of Jesimi friends, he worked to let that feeling subside as they made their way back home, one lone key hanging from the twine around Adam's neck.

"I have to go take care of a few things today," Ben said as he popped open the chest from under his bedside table. He scooped a handful of lyat into a small linen pouch and dropped it into the pocket of his trousers. "You should rest while you can. Time is running short now; you'll be leaving soon."

"Should I ask what you're going to do?" Adam raised an eyebrow suspiciously.

"You probably don't wanna know. If I'm successful, I'll have to tell you anyway. Tonight, when I come back." Ben stuffed another crust of bread into his mouth and waved a hasty goodbye.

Adam mustered a half wave in return and sunk back down in his chair, sipping his tea. He realized he hadn't been really alone since he had lost his mother and found his uncle, and that thought alone was enough to set him on a path to unraveling completely. He felt such a sharp sting, he grasped his hands together over his heart as if to stop it from bleeding. He'd relied on the distraction of his new gift and crazy adventure, along with the oddly comforting company of his gruff uncle who, as it turned out, was soft inside, and his giant lizard. He intuitively reached for Zev just as the wolf's head plopped into Adam's lap, ever so slightly taking the edge off of his pain. Zev kept his head in position for a few minutes, easing Adam's burden, and then moved to nudge his leg.

Let us go outdoors. If we remain, I'm afraid I will lose you to your pain, Zev said, weaving the beautiful, awful words into Adam.

Adam knew he was right—he was always right, but especially now. He had the whole of the Jesimi people to think of; if he fell apart, how would he possibly achieve anything? He sat there a few moments longer, lingering in the shadows that toyed with him, threatening to squeeze the breath from his lungs. The loneliness of being without his mother was a thousand-pound weight around his neck. He looked down into Zev's eyes, sustained by their strength, and pushed on his knees to stand, despite the weight hanging like a noose.

They wandered outside, instantly in awe of the pinks, oranges, and purples splattered across the sky. They stood in front of the dawn as if it were a painting to be admired, drinking in every glorious inch side by side, allowing each stroke of El's brush to sketch them back to life. After their legs had fallen asleep from standing so still and the sun was well on its daily arc across the sky, Adam went over to feed the animals. Zev wasn't allowed the temptation of getting too close to animals he would naturally hunt, though he had never crossed that line before. Adam drifted through the chicken coop, spreading feed and gathering their morning offerings. He plucked some hay from a nearby bale and gave it to the cow and goats. Though the pain still raged within him, this was medicine to his soul, in this beautiful patch of the world. His uncle had done something right choosing this spot.

Adam and Zev squandered the day away, walking along the Sea of Orion, lying in the grass, avoiding the gloomy wood, even snoozing to the tune of the waves lapping at the rock-strewn shore before it was time to prepare supper. Adam was most definitely not a cook, but he figured he could throw something together. Zev watched him warily as he bustled about, gathering ingredients to make some kind of soup. He tossed them all together in a pot with a little water and left the concoction to boil above the measly fire he had made. He had been the designated firewood chopper in his home, but his mother had loved to make the fire she would cook on, so his skills could use some improvement. He busied himself with other tasks until Ben swung through the warped door, his large frame announcing itself as he made his entrance.

"What's that smell?" Ben's face crinkled as Zev and George turned their noses up.

"Oh no!" Adam rushed over to the fire to check the soup, finding it to be badly singed, smoke billowing from beneath the cast iron lid. "Sorry, I was trying to make something for when you returned. I'm afraid I'm not very skilled at cooking." He looked down at his feet.

Ben burst out laughing, straight from his gut, while Adam awkwardly removed the pot from the hearth and peered in to see if any of it was salvageable. It wasn't. Ben took it from him and assured him that the goats and the cow would love it. He pulled the bag he was carrying off his shoulder and brandished a wedge of cheese and a buttery, braided loaf of bread. Adam shrugged, and they tore apart the bread and cheese, which ended up making a delicious meal.

"So, aren't you gonna ask where I was?" Ben inquired. Adam gesticulated for him to go on. "I was finding you a place stowed away on a ship that will be crossing the Channel of Arcturus to the continent," he said casually.

"Excuse me?" Adam cried. "When is this big crossing that you have planned to take place?" He wasn't entirely sure he desired the answer.

"In one week," Ben replied, with slightly more tenderness, as the seriousness of the situation warranted.

"One week? How in Avaria am I supposed to prepare for a journey to the continent in one week! I thought I had more time!" Adam shouted, feeling as if he might really burst into tears.

"I have an old friend, a builder of ships. I went to see him today about our problem, as we can't travel to the continent freely, and Xhartana guards the docks. Since he built the ships and knows how they're boarded and guarded along with every little compartment, he came up with the perfect plan to get you over there without being caught, hopefully. He is from the city; his wife runs the place, actually. The problem is that the only ship heading to the continent for the next two months leaves in a week. We don't have a choice. We can't wait months; your journey must begin. It was written." Ben sounded more like he was trying to convince himself. Perhaps he had grown fond of having his nephew around, and though Adam showed great promise, mastering his gift quickly, Ben likely worried about his physical strength and safety.

"Well, I suppose that's it, then. I have one week to prepare for my great journey." Adam sank back into the chair he had jumped from. Ben nodded, reassuring him very little.

The following week was packed full of trips into the village to fit Adam for travel clothing. The clothing maker they saw was the same one who had been so kind to Adam before his mother's burial. They also went to see a leather maker for boots and a large rucksack to carry his belongings. They used the chest of lyat to purchase supplies from harvesters, gatherers, and makers across the village. Adam got a haircut, and though his hair no longer fell into his eyes, it still left an incredibly thick nest of black locks atop his head. Adam went to see Shai, his mentor, to update him on all that had happened and what was to come. He apologized profusely for not fulfilling his responsibility as a preserver, but Shai brushed it off, saying that this calling was far more important.

Adam and Ben met with Lemuel to fill him in about the great journey and the conversation they had overheard from the Xhartanian guards. Adam didn't have to use his gift to get him on board for whatever battle was to come; their trust was implicit. Lemuel readily handed over the key that had been safely kept for over a century with the Great Scroll in its wooden ark in the Temple. A beautifully crafted copper key, tinged green from age and inscribed with the number eighteen, now hung beside the turquoise one around Adam's neck. It was made of the same copper as lyat, mined there on the Isle of Ori. The number eighteen holds prodigious significance to the Jesimi people, as it represents life.

By the time their business in Zera was complete, Adam was overcome, realizing that it would always be home, even without his mother. He may have kept his heart guarded, but the people who knew him would always be there, knocking at its door.

Every night that week, they pored over the ancient map of the realms. Ben marked what he knew of each of the twelve Jesimi villages, which was unfortunately very little. When magic ran deep and free throughout the continent, there was a connection, communication between the people, but over the years of being under the rule of Xhartana, they had grown further apart. Adam's pride grew, knowing that he might be part of restoring that unity among his people, as did his curiosity at what he might find.

Ben pointed out geographical features that Adam might encounter and what he knew of the climate of each realm. He shared bartering advice, as Adam would never be able to carry enough on his back to wind his way through the wildly different regions. He would need to be smart and keep his wits about him to ensure he had what he needed to stay safe and complete his journey successfully. They went over the charted path repeatedly until Ben felt satisfied that Adam was as prepared as he could possibly be.

Dusk fell the night before Adam was to stow away on the ship and begin his great journey. The constant fear that flickered within him could barely be restrained from full-blown panic as he considered the many ways this could go sideways. By this point, turning back scared him just as much and seemed to be ever less of an option, so he grew comfortable with debilitating fear as his baseline.

Ben made a special roast chicken with potatoes for supper and had bought little jelly-filled pastries wrapped in delicious buttery dough from a maker in the village for dessert. After they had their fill and had lulled themselves into their usual post-meal haze, Ben ambled over to the shelves above the hearth. He brought something over and delicately placed it on the table in front of Adam. Adam gasped as he took in Ben's steel dagger shrouded in its black leather case.

"I want you to take this with you. Never take this off. Xhartana is not the only danger you'll face; you'd be a fool to think otherwise. I know it's not in your nature to hurt anybody or anything, but we have to protect ourselves or pay the price. I know you have Zev, but I wanna know you can protect yourself as well," Ben said solemnly, pushing the weapon closer. Adam ran his finger over the hilt of the blade, realizing that the dark-wooden handle had an incandescent mother-of-pearl inlay. He marveled at the delicate craftsmanship of something so violent.

"Thank you, but I wouldn't have the first clue how to use it," Adam said.

"When the time comes that you need it, you'll know. Your hand is about the same size as mine; it should work just fine. Try to be careful not to cut yourself," Ben warned as Adam unsheathed the blade and held it up to the candlelight. Adam shuddered, imagining what he might be facing that he would need to use it.

He supposed he was glad he had it, just in case. He placed it back in its home and twiddled his fingers anxiously. Sleep did not take hold that eve for any of them as they all lay in that small, cozy hut, eyes closed, imagining the dizzying twists and turns of the road ahead.

CHAPTER 9

When the time came to gather their things and take their leave to the western docks, they were already stirring, no longer pretending to sleep. Tension fogged the air as Adam donned slightly thicker black trousers, buttoned his ivory shirt, and pulled a black knit sweater over his head to stave off the growing chill. As he pulled on each boot, created just for him out of strong black leather and thick soles, his forehead creased, and he laced each boot just a bit too tightly. He stood and scanned his new attire, nodding his head in general approval but wiggling his toes, which were not used to being bound within enclosed footwear. Ben had made enough jokes about his sandals and the many things that could happen to dangling toes on his journey that Adam had readily agreed to the sturdy and practical boots he now wore. Standing tall, he swung the dagger in its scabbard around his hips and fastened it carefully, patting the weapon, equally uncomfortable and glad it was there, and shooting a tight smile at his uncle.

They had already packed the large leather rucksack the previous night with provisions and now swirled around each other by candlelight as they double-checked and added things that had been missed. A minimal amount of clothing layers for diverse climates, a small canvas tent, food that would hold over for some time, and a larger bag of lyat than he had ever held at one time.

Ben carefully wrapped the jar of his accidental invention in cloth—Adam would need it whenever he accessed his gift to prevent Xhartana from being able to get a read on his magical signature—and tucked it into Adam's bag. "Since you're going to be passing through the Forest of Rian anyway, I need you to stop and find this magical herb to make more of this mixture. You may even have run out by then, but we will most definitely need more leading up to battle to prevent Xhartana from getting wind of anything we might be preparing. You will have to ask a local where to detect it, as I've never actually been there; we simply found it at the market and used it in our experimenting." Adam noticed a rebellious light in Ben's eyes, and though he could not relate, he sort of loved it.

Ben handed him a hand-drawn picture of a leafy-looking plant with what appeared to be upside-down, heart-shaped blossoms. The plant was labeled as a spring green and the blossoms as fuchsia. The plant was aptly called a weeping heart.

Ben passed Adam a couple of clear quartz crystals as well as another small container full to the brim of salt, noting it had come from the salt flats. Ben shared that to make the unnamed mixture, Adam would need to blend crushed clear quartz, a pinch of salt from the salt flats, and ground-up leaves from the weeping heart, then squeeze in the essence from the blossoms last. Adam nodded, hoping that he would remember the recipe.

He went over to the pile of things that had quickly accumulated beside his hay bed and withdrew the small metal box containing the mizzur scroll from his home. He pocketed it, deciding that it would make the journey with him. Seeing as he no longer had a house to protect, maybe it would protect him. He unrolled the letter from his mother, running a finger over the words that were embedded into his memory by now, then rolled it back up and placed it in the box for safekeeping.

Adam looked around. That seemed to be the last of it, so he drew the drawstring at the top of the rucksack tight and pulled the flap over, then fastened the brass buckle with a click. Ben handed him another piece of bread, encouraging him to eat before the long journey ahead, as he had not been able to thus far that morning. Adam tore off a piece of the dark-brown bread topped with oats and forced himself to chew and swallow, his dry throat bobbing as the bite got stuck on the way down. He took a swig of Ben's special herbal tea, cursing as he burnt his tongue—he shoved the tea aside, correctly assuming nothing could calm him at this point. The grimace on his uncle's face told him that he wasn't alone in that feeling.

Adam fastened a smaller replica of the antique map, which he had made as he and Ben had plotted his course, to the outside of his pack, as well as his water jug, tightening the cap after drops of water splashed out. He slung the pack over his shoulders, and its weight humbled him. He had assumed his tall frame would absorb it easily, but he was wrong, and his shoulders hung low from the impact.

Ben looked Adam up and down and broke his scowl. "You look so different from the kid who came running to my door not so long ago. You're a man, and you're ready." He looked as proud as he was worried, his eyes growing glassy. "It's time to go; we've gotta meet Gideon before the sun rises so we can get you settled before the guards and passengers show up."

"It's time," Adam agreed, feeling his knees grow weak beneath him. He looked around the cozy little hut and its inhabitants that had so quickly become his in the wake of the darkest time of his life, and he knew he would miss them, he would miss this place. He drew the strength from El knows where to pull himself away and exited the warped door toward his destiny, whatever it may bring. The cold stole the air from his lungs as he stepped outside, as if he hadn't already been holding his breath. Zev was pinned to Adam's side, maybe a bit closer than usual, knowing he was the only thing keeping Adam together as they stared down the nose of fear itself.

The foursome moved stealthily in the pitch-dark early morning, before dawn performed its kiss. Their usual silence was constantly interrupted by whispered warnings and tips from Ben, as if Adam was actually taking in a word he was saying. If it hadn't been said before, hopefully it wasn't important.

Adam's palms were slick with apprehensive sweat. With each step the pressure grew, and he felt as though his chest might burst; nevertheless, he marched on. Though they had grown to know the path by heart and Ben had no difficulty navigating it in the dark, every pebble threatened to topple Adam. With every rock that met the toe of his boots, he grew more grateful he had them, though they felt the slightest bit suffocating.

When they could barely make out the turn to Zera, Adam hesitated for a moment, feeling as though he could not turn back past this point. Down that path was the life he had spent twenty years building with his mother and for himself. If he kept going, he had little idea of what he was going to face. As he squinted to look down the familiar path lined with the story of his life, he imagined what it would be like to return there without his mother, going back to his work as a preserver while knowing now what he was truly capable of. He was shocked when he found the thought to be drenched in melancholy and marked with the emptiness he had only entertained in the dark of night, when he was alone and let his imagination off its taut leash. His mother was not there anymore—she was everywhere, she was anywhere he was, and his heart was lifted in that moment enough to take the first step past the turnoff, and then the one after that. Ben said nothing, seeming to know he needed the space to be able to move forward, and simply brushed his elbow as they walked on.

They began to hurry as dawn grew nearer, Adam towing the substantial load of his rucksack and his decision to follow his mother's request to gather his people. His nostrils filled with the tang of the salty sea breeze, and all four of their heads lifted in unison, drifting under its spell. They approached the dock, watching their footing as they drew closer. A tall ship loomed in front of them. It was still too dark to make out any details, and the sky and the sea melted together into the dark endlessness. Ben, Adam, Zev, and George all froze as a large figure strode toward them.

"It's just me, Ben," a deep, inviting voice called out.

Ben moved toward the man in the dark and gathered him in a manly embrace, clapping him on the back. "Adam, this is Gideon, son of Hersch, the old friend I was telling you about. He worked out your passage."

"It's nice to meet you, Gideon. This is Zev. You must know George already," Adam said, politely offering his hand to the man who towered over him and his uncle. Gideon grasped it with a warmth that took him by surprise.

The man was as broad as he was tall, a dark-brown wall of muscle, barely discernable from the night. His imposing stature was hardly a match to the kind-heartedness that emanated from him in spades. Adam didn't usually want to be friends with the people he met, but that was different with Gideon. From the shadows beside him emerged a large ibex, his hooves clopping along the creaky wooden docks. It was too dark to make out the color of his massive coat, but two giant horns adorned his head, curling back toward his shoulders. Though the creature who moved to Gideon's side was clearly a force to be reckoned with, they shared the same kind eyes.

"So, this is the kid you were telling me about, huh? He doesn't look much like a kid." Gideon chortled as he sized Adam up. Aside from the nervous smile, Adam supposed he really didn't.

"That's him, all right. My nephew. Gonna use his gift to gather our people so we can drive Xhartana out once and for all," Ben said boastfully. "And not a moment too soon. We overheard some guards when we went south to Kesil; they struck platinum deep in the mine, lots of it. And they have big plans to infiltrate the rest of the continent and wipe out all of us Jesimi for good. With all that platinum and their powers recharged, they just might be able to."

Gideon closed his eyes and sighed deeply. "Well, listen, you don't have to use your gift to convince me to join you; I'm all in. I am a builder of ships, and I have to deal with these Xhartanian brutes most every day. I also have a gift; my name means 'great warrior.' I have to say my gift lives up to my name; though I have been forced to suppress it my whole life, I am a warrior through and through, and I will fight at your side for Avaria, for our people." Somehow, Adam knew he could count on that as truth, and he nodded his thanks firmly. "My beautiful wife is the head of our fair city; she leads as boldly as she is able under the thumb of Xhartanian cruelty. I shared your story with her, and we both trust your uncle enough to trust you."

Adam couldn't believe his luck as this kind giant of a man handed him a dark-wooden box with the emblem of the Isle inlaid in black pearl. Adam held his breath as he popped it open, and on a bed of netting lay his third key. This one had been rendered from lustrous cream shells plucked from the Sea of Orion, as the city lay nestled around the bay, their way of life intricately intertwined with its bounty. Adam carefully looped the third key onto his twine necklace, imagining how much more challenging it would be to assemble the rest.

"Thank you for trusting me. I won't let you down," Adam declared, the fire born of his pain burning hotter, the weight of the keys around his neck serving as a constant reminder of the stakes of his success.

"Let's get you on board before this place fills up. Follow me." Gideon surveyed his surroundings before beckoning them to follow.

They followed Gideon up the wooden gangway, Zev pausing as the swell of the sea began to move beneath them, making the planks creak and groan. They hurried across the deck and descended into the hull, and Gideon pointed out a narrow, well-covered spot in a far corner, deep in the belly of the ship, where Adam and Zev were to hide for the entirety of the crossing to the continent. Gideon said he could not be certain Xhartanian officials or guards would not be on board, though this was generally a merchant route used for trade. They all gathered at the bottom of the stairs leading back to the deck.

Gideon warned in jest, "Watch out for the Leviathan during your crossing; you know they say he rose from the deep when Avaria split in three off the continent over a hundred years ago. Good luck, kid." He chuckled as he made his way back to the dock so the family could say goodbye.

Ben and Adam just looked at each other for a while, unable to find words to meet the gravitas of the moment. Adam bent down and gave George a little pat on the head, and the water monitor closed his eyes, basking in the moment—his goodbye.

"Well, now's not the time for a big speech; it won't help, so I won't make one. I will repeat that you're ready for this; you were made for it. You'll never feel ready, but you are. Try to be flexible and stay safe. Let people in. I know it's hard, especially after losing someone. I'm not one to talk," Ben said with an expression that gave away his real feeling in the moment: worry. But he would never voice that. He simply reached out and pulled Adam in for their first-ever hug.

As Ben pulled him tight to his broad chest, Adam gathered all his strength to not fall apart into the man who had become his family. It meant more to both of them than all the words in the world. They gripped each other for some time, every moment illustrating the trust and love they had grown.

Ben finally stepped back. "The sun is gonna come up; we've gotta get going, or this'll be over before it starts."

Adam nodded, gulping for air that wouldn't come. "Thank you, Uncle. I will do this, for all of us," he whispered, making a very shoddy attempt at confidence.

With that, Ben smiled, and he and George turned and climbed the stairs to the deck. Adam and Zev didn't move as they listened to footsteps cross the deck and descend the gangway. Tears welled in Adam's eyes as he stood frozen in the panic that he could no longer keep at bay. His breathing quickened as reality set in on him like a ton of bricks. His heart had never beat so fast, and he worried his chest might actually explode. In that moment, at the base of the steps in the hull, Adam peered out the single porthole as dawn broke, giving way to the glimmer of the sun as it pushed up out of the sea. He let the light fill his body with breath and slow his heart, assuring him that darkness could always be driven out. Zev nuzzled his hand as he drew a few deep breaths, trying to focus on the moment instead of fearing what would come next.

The Sea of Orion shifted beneath their feet, causing Adam and Zev to stumble back and forth across the slowly rotting wood hull that failed to instill much confidence. The sea was the murkiest black, so black he thought that if he fell in, he might never surface again.

Adam heard voices coming from the docks and hurried over to the tiny cargo space. He carefully laid the net over the entrance to their spot to better disguise their hiding place. While tiny beams of sun streamed in above their heads, it was rather gloomy and damp. The ship gave off a moldy, foul odor, awash with stale beer and rot. Adam and Zev leaned against each other for comfort as their entire lives were upended again, and by choice at that.

They remained very quiet as steps began to trail across the deck above them. They heard mostly male voices that seemed to be talking about business, but some women and even a few children laughed and stomped. Adam and Zev noticed the sway of the ship as the tide changed, and they worried over what it would be like on the open sea.

Adam thought about Gideon's parting jest. He did not know if the Leviathan was simply a folk tale, like the Mazzikin in the wood, or if it was a real threat they might face during the crossing of the Channel of Arcturus. The vast, deadly beast was said to patrol these waters between the three islands and the continent, looking for ships to spill and people to drag to its lair in the fathoms below. Adam's life had not been devoid of peril living under the thumb of Xhartana, but he had never faced what lay ahead.

He gritted his teeth and gripped Zev's snow-white fur tighter as they heard men clomping down the stairs into the hull they were hiding in. The footsteps inched closer to them, and they held their breath. A man was close enough that they could smell the wine he had drunk the eve before and hear him rummaging around the cargo hold as if he was looking for something. From what Adam could see, he did not appear to be a Xhartanian soldier, more likely a crew member on the ship. He apparently found what he was looking for and trudged to the other side of the hull. Zev and Adam simultaneously released their breath, both slightly lightheaded.

"Hoist the sails!" someone bellowed from above, and the ship shuddered to life beneath them.

Adam was glad he had met Gideon, who'd had a hand in building this ship; it gave him just enough confidence that it would not sink to the bottom of the channel the second it left the dock. It lurched sideways in time with their stomachs as the ship floated away and made its bearing. Zev and Adam looked at each other, wondering how in Avaria they'd gotten here, hiding on a ship, on their way to the continent. Beneath the fear, however, lay something much deeper in both of them, nagging and tugging under the surface, trying to punch through. The same feeling that never seemed to leave, as if it was written into the fabric of their very souls, the souls of all Jesimi. Something like hope.

The seconds drowned into minutes and the minutes drowned into hours as Adam and Zev were tossed back and forth like sacks of flour beneath the deck of the ship. The bread and eggs that Ben had forced them to consume prior to their departure sloshed around in their stomachs, leaving them too nauseated to communicate. The groans surrounding them informed them they weren't alone.

Gideon had said the crossing would not take more than three or four hours, depending upon the winds, and they were both hoping with everything they had it was closer to three. The sticky heat was oppressive in this hidden compartment, adding heavily to the discomfort. Adam stripped off his black sweater, quietly stuffed it into the top of his very full rucksack, and wiped the sweat beading on the top of his lip. He supposed he was glad that feeling awful distracted him from thinking too deeply about an ancient, monstrous sea creature slithering through the sea beneath them, threatening to crash through the wooden hull of the ship at that very moment to swallow it whole.

He tried to stay focused, one step at a time. Ben's request that he remain flexible was strongly deterred by Adam's security in the plan they had constructed. They would land at the edge of the realm of the Mesios Rainforest and begin their trek there. Having never left the Isle of Ori, he couldn't begin to imagine what they might find. As a preserver, he had access to many scrolls containing information about the other realms, and some even had renderings of far-off places, but he had never really allowed himself to think too deeply about the rest of the world. It didn't factor into his previous plans, not really. He hoped that he had somehow retained some of what he had learned and what his uncle had taught him in the past few weeks. He had loosened the lid of the well within him where he had shoved these thoughts and dreams away, and they began to flow through him freely. The excitement was nearly tipping fear off the scale, though honestly, the scale was fairly overwhelmed with the unrelenting rocking of the ship. Poor Zev's fur was all but turning green. Adam seriously wondered what was wrong with people who chose to travel by sea, or worse, work the open sea day after day.

More shouting ensued above deck, and they hoped that meant this joyless ride was about to meet its end. The ship lurched from side to side, and Adam figured it was being maneuvered into docking position. Zev toppled over Adam's knees as the ship knocked into something—the dock, most likely. The ship groaned and creaked as it recovered from the hit. Men bustled above them as they lowered the sails, dropped the anchor, and rolled out the gangplank with a crash. It sounded as if passengers were gathering to depart the ship; peeking through a crack, Adam could see the men who had been underneath with them holding their stomachs, queasy, and gripping the handrail to go up the stairs.

Gideon had instructed them to wait for ten full minutes after they heard the last steps before making a swift exit themselves. They remained in their hiding spot for fifteen—Adam was nothing if not thorough—and when they heard nothing but distant voices, they slowly emerged, Zev first. They tiptoed up the stairs and peeked out onto the deck in all directions—no one was in sight. They hastily ran across the deck and down the gangway, both praising El as they touched solid ground again. There was a single guard, not in Xhartana's colors, at the end of the dock, so they casually walked past as quickly as they could, hoping they would not be stopped. They were starting to get comfortable holding their breath and hoping something bad didn't befall them. In this case, it worked; they were not stopped as they made their way off the docks.

As soon as they felt they were out of danger, they took in their surroundings and staggered back, still feeling as if they were bobbing up and down in the water. The black sea butted up to a wall of trees every hue of green they could have imagined. They had thought the wood by Ben's hut on the Isle was endless, but this gave the word *endless* new meaning. The brightness of the foliage wasn't foreboding in the same way, either; it was downright resplendent. It gave off an air of excitement, of possibility. The canopy loomed above them, splashed with endless twisting and looping vines and scattered with brilliant blossoms of radiant reds, yellows, oranges, and pinks, welcoming them as they walked closer.

Adam and Zev looked at each other, wide-eyed, and though neither was steady on his feet yet, they had no time to waste. They grinned and bounded into the sea of green, and unlike the wood on their Isle, they weren't plunged into darkness. Light shone through the thick vegetation, illuminating the path that lay ahead, as if it had been made just for them.

CHAPTER 10

Zev's and Adam's spirits were fortified by the exhilaration of being on steady land and not getting caught during their crossing. They continued at a dizzying pace, laughing and jokingly bumping into each other, causing Adam to spill over into the swollen bushes that lined the pinched trail more than once. Zev visibly snickered as Adam flew out each time, kicking high and wiping any trace of potential spider webs from his body. As it turned out, a healthy fear of arachnids and the rainforest didn't mix.

They began to slow as their legs begged it of them, and they shared their water stores. Ben had taught them how to find clean water, and they knew they would need to do so by this eve to ensure they didn't run out. None of them knew how long it would take to cross this part of the jungle to get to their first stop. Ben had spoken of a city in the trees but had not provided many details, mostly because he simply didn't know much.

Adam kept the compass Ben had provided him easily accessible to check their bearing regularly; it would be all too easy to become lost in this endless parade of vegetation. The aged bronze compass had been imbued with magic so that it did not point true north—it pointed toward their heart's truest course, and they could not be led astray.

Neither Adam nor Zev were the least bit concerned as the sunlight poured over their heads and the warmth molded around their skin, inviting them to stay awhile. Adam marveled at nature herself and how a setting so wild, untouched, and teeming with life could even be real. There were endless layers, and everything seemed to be full of life, from the very soil they tread on to the air, full of the calls of the cockatoos, howls of the monkeys, and chirps of the cicadas. The boldest, most vivid shades of green masterfully painted the magical canvas they had stepped into. Adam didn't think he had ever felt more alive, and judging by Zev's zesty behavior, chasing his tail and bounding around like it was the best day of his life, the feeling seemed mutual.

Can you believe this place? Who could have imagined this was what we were missing? Zev cooed in awe, swiping a butterfly of the truest azure dotted with black as it pirouetted on his snout.

"Unbelievable," Adam said as he took a moment to look up, so far up. "Are you too hot? I didn't really think about how this stuffy heat might affect you."

When we were soul-sealed, the magic that bonded us ensured that nothing would stand in the way of my promise to be by your side, and vice versa. I can feel it flowing beneath my skin, allowing me to be comfortable wherever you are so I am able to protect you and remain near, Zev said, suddenly very serious as he spoke about his duties.

"Thank El for that. I would never have considered making this journey without you, but I would hate it if you felt uncomfortable at all." Adam reached over to stroke Zev's soft, pointed ear.

I am proud to be by your side on this most important of quests. Zev continued to casually stroll down the path, unable to prevent himself from getting smacked in the face by hanging vines and tree branches.

Adam grasped one of the vines that fell into his face after Zev had managed to dart around it. He tested it to see if it was firmly attached to the absolutely monstrous tree beside them, so tall they couldn't even make out the top. Adam took a few steps back, hoisted himself up on the vine, and swung past Zev, laughing maniacally as he clung to the vine for dear life. Losing his grip on the backswing due to sweaty palms, he barreled into Zev at full speed, and they flew top over tail into the massive tree trunk and its sprawling, exposed roots. They landed with a couple of loud thuds, looked at each other in shock, and burst out laughing again. Zev's shoulders bounced up and down, caramel eyes bright with joy.

"So, that's a lot harder than it looks." Adam shrugged, trying to keep a straight face as he fought another bout of hysterics. They wiped off the dirt and mud they'd accumulated in their tumble and started off once again, having to work hard to keep the giggles at bay.

Try to be the slightest bit more careful, why don't you? You aren't exactly the most agile human I know, Zev reminded him with a wink and a nudge.

They snacked on the salty dried meat that Ben had prepared as they continued to blaze their path through the midst of the dense jungle. The sun started to gradually filter out, and weariness tugged at their aching muscles. It was hard to believe that just that morning they had awakened in that cozy little hut. Adam found that he missed it, especially as dusk neared and he knew that meant finding shelter on the rainforest floor. Ben had warned of the creatures that lurked in the night, and Adam didn't want to encounter any of them if he could avoid it, shivering at the thought.

They began to look around for a suitable spot and came across a massive tree that had fallen across the path. The trunk was plenty wide enough for even Zev's large wolf frame, and he leaped onto it and curled up, showing that he had found his bed for the evening. Adam smiled at him and examined his options as he contended with the waning light. He took off his knapsack, and the lack of weight was an immediate relief, which was quickly replaced with a wave of fire that swept up his spine and spread across his shoulders. He winced as he flipped up the top of the bag, opened the drawstring, and spilled the topmost contents as he dug for the small tent. He pulled it out, shoving the things that had fallen out back in, and decided to fashion a hammock by tying the tent with rope to branches on the fallen tree so he could tuck himself against it and off of the ground. It took him quite a few tries and just as many falls to get the knots right, but he succeeded just in the nick of time, right as they were plunged into the purest darkness. Adam swore as he fumbled around for his flint, wishing he would have built the fire before it was pitch black. The cadence of the birds of the jungle, the symphony of cicadas, and distant howls and growls made up the score of their eve.

Not allowing himself to wonder what might be lurking nearby, he cracked some extra branches from the fallen tree and prepared to light a haphazard fire. He felt around in the dark and was glad Zev could see better than he could—he was completely disarmed, struggling to even strike the flint in his own hands. In the moment before he found success, the rainforest around them on all sides, from floor to canopy, came alive again with a warm glow. Relief filled them, and they released their breath.

"Fireflies!" Adam exclaimed with joy at a distant memory that tugged at his heart: running after them and catching them before returning them to the skies, with his mother looking on. He wondered to himself if this was some kind of sign from her, letting them know she was looking out for them. It was, in fact, his mother who had gotten them into this mess to begin with, he thought with a chuckle.

Zev pawed at the air as the wood and the sky alike bloomed with a greenish-yellow glow. Adam felt like a boy again as he quietly waited until one floated close enough to him, then snatched it in his hand, pulling it in close to look at with Zev. He opened his palm and leaped back in disbelief, blinking his eyes furiously, trying to see more clearly as the tiny face attached to the glowing, humanoid body scowled up at him. He shook his head as everything he had ever known and believed crashed all around him in pieces. What was this thing? What did it mean? And perhaps the scariest thought of all—if this was real, then what else was?

The tiny being, still on his palm, tapped her tiny toes and folded her tiny arms in frustration. Adam looked at Zev, who had stumbled back in concern, which was as close to fear as Zev really got.

"What do you think they are?" Adam asked Zev.

"We talk, you idiot. We are pixies." Her face turned red as she spoke, though her voice was lilting. She couldn't have been larger than the length of his palm. She had bright-red hair piled high on her head, large green eyes disproportionate to the rest of her freckled face, a tiny button nose, and a perfect pink pout.

"My apologies, um, ma'am? It's just, I thought you were a firefly. I didn't know pixies existed," Adam stuttered, wondering what the appropriate thing to say might possibly be when meeting a pixie.

"What is a firefly?" she asked, voice tinged with disgust.

"Well, it's a kind of insect, and it glows. Very magical," Adam replied, holding his pixie-laden hand at a distance.

"You thought I was an insect? How dare you! Insects are most certainly not magical. It seems you confused a bug with the pixie evening call to each other after we spent a long day working away in our colony in the treetops. If you look closely now, you will see each of us has a slightly different coloring—our lights are different based on the color of our wings." She spun around to show off her delicate jade wings as she flapped them in and out a couple of times.

Still in shock, Zev and Adam looked closer at the lights around them and realized she was right—these were certainly no fireflies. Some of the pixies hovered closer, scoping out the intruders. While they were all tiny, they each bore unique coloring and markings. They were breathtaking. Ethereal.

"We have been rude. My name is Adam, son of Rachel, and this is Zev. We are just passing through on our way to the great city in the trees," Adam said, hoping it wasn't too late to make amends.

The corners of her lips began to turn up, and she let her toothpick arms fall loosely at her sides. "I am Ivy. Welcome to the Mesios Rainforest," she said with dignity, complete with a small curtsy.

"This is my family." The pixies swooped over their heads and began flying in collective figure eights while humming a very catchy tune, showing off their enviable beauty and grace. "We see so few humans, and even fewer wolves, here. What draws you toward the great city?" She plopped down on his palm, crossed her legs, and folded her hands under her chin, settling in for the answer.

Adam laughed, thinking he may have really lost it this time. "We are on a great adventure across the continent in search of the Jesimi people, who were exiled from Avaria over one hundred years ago when Xhartana took power with the help of the people now living on Pax Island. Our people have been persecuted for too long; we have lost far too many and far too much. My mother used to tell a tale of a person who would be born with a gift to bring the Jesimi people together again, gather the twelve keys, and fight a great battle so we can once again be free in our realm of Avaria. She left me a letter that I read after she was slain by them recently; she said I was that person, and I was fated to take this journey."

Ivy batted her long eyelashes as she listened, captivated by his tale. "Wow, that was most certainly not what I was expecting. What a story that is, and what a journey you shall have. We mostly keep to ourselves, but we hear voices drift up to us on the breeze, from our colony way up high in the trees. We know the rule of the Marre people of Xhartana to be brutal and not righteous. Fairness is of the utmost importance to pixies, and though we will protect ourselves if we are attacked, we are a peaceful group. Your plight is true, and I will gladly aid you in your quest to find the great city among the trees. As great as it is, it is well hidden to outsiders; you will need my help to find it," she said in her wispy voice as she stood once again.

"We would be most grateful for your assistance. Before this journey, I had never left the Isle of Ori. I was a preserver of Jesimi history, of our culture and our beliefs and our lives. Now, I've stepped into it, and it's rather overwhelming, to say the least," Adam admitted honestly, deep into reevaluating all he had ever known as a pixie sat in his hand.

"I'll be off for the eve—my family must feast and celebrate—but I shall return by first light to guide you, Sir Adam and Sir Zev, on your noble quest." Ivy saluted before flapping her wings and rising into the air. All of the pixies ascended, and their glow grew faint. Adam's knees buckled, and he caught himself and sat in the dirt, head in hands.

"Did that really just happen, or did I imagine that? That can't have been real, right?" Adam asked a blank-faced Zev, unsure of which answer he wanted. If pixies were real, then anything could be real, which was terrifying and thrilling.

It happened, my friend. Pixies are real, and they are beautiful, tiny winged creatures who are known for their attitudes but are generally very helpful and honest, Zev said matter-of-factly.

"Wait, did you know they were real?" Adam asked.

I had never laid eyes on them, but I suspected our realms were full of magic we had yet to unveil, Zev said mysteriously.

"Yeah, that clears it up. Thanks, bud," Adam snapped sarcastically. "You suspected that magical creatures existed and never told me?"

It never came up. You would not have believed it had you not seen it with your own eyes, anyway. You only trust the scrolls. Zev heaved back on his haunches, grooming his fur languidly.

Adam knew Zev was right—he liked facts, history, things that could be relied upon. He had always harbored a sneaking suspicion that the folktales back home about the things that went bump in the night were real. A shiver ran down his neck as he considered the possibility that if pixies were real, magic was real, and maybe *everything* was real.

Adam managed to light a small fire, and they ate more of the food stashed away in his bag, being cautious to ration it as planned. Their minds raced and their bodies ached from the incredibly long day, and Zev hopped up on the tree stump, curling up on the numerous circles that signified the immense length of its life. Adam ungracefully tucked himself into the makeshift hammock, and surprisingly, the overbearing heat that remained long after the sun had disappeared lulled them into sound sleep.

Adam rose to consciousness, swatting at a buzzing sound surrounding him. He slowly peeled his eyes open, and they landed on a once-again-angry Ivy.

"You know, one swat could be the end for me!" she shouted, wagging a miniature finger at him.

"Apologies; I didn't know you were there." Adam groaned as he stretched his very sore and tight muscles, raising his arms above his head.

With that, he awkwardly popped out of the thick natural tent material and collapsed to the ground, which was thankfully not far below. Ivy and Zev snickered, not even trying to hide it, as Adam peeled himself off the ground, dancing around, brushing off the ants that had taken hold of his bare feet.

"Good thing you got those trigger ants off quickly. The rainforest is immensely beauteous, but it is full of the deadliest of creatures," Ivy said in her singsong cadence as if it wasn't a chilling warning.

Ivy landed on the thick, dead gray bark of the fallen tree. Zev and Adam looked at each other, as they could have sworn that when she landed, the spot under her feet glowed and looked far more deep brown than dead gray, almost alive. Ivy chattered away, telling them everything they could ever want to know about her home, and much that they didn't.

"I guess we should be off. This is only the very beginning of a very long journey ahead—we need to make headway," Adam said when she had finished, reaching for his boots apprehensively. He winced at the aches and pains that he seemed to be collecting.

"We really aren't too far off. Just follow me; I vow to get you there as swiftly as I can," Ivy said, her giddy grin fading into seriousness at her promise. It reminded Adam of Zev's attitude toward protecting him, which warmed his heart.

Adam quickly swapped his shirt to one better suited to the heat, which was starting to get to him. He left the pants and dagger fastened to his waist. It wasn't so much the temperature as the thickness of the air; it felt suffocating, as if it could trap him. He looked around, making sure he had everything, and yanked the knapsack onto his back once more, nearly folding under its weight. He heard stirring and clicking through the dense verdant foliage, which was more than enough to send him headlong after a waiting Ivy farther into the jungle.

The undergrowth grew thicker and fuller on their path, and as they went, curtains of green would often tumble down in front of them, so they had to squeeze through sideways, shoving the vibrant plant life to the side to make their way. Ivy flitted about, telling them about the various plants and flowers and the animals they heard calling in the distance. She especially seemed to love the flamboyant birds that sought shelter under the canopy as the group passed by. Adam trudged on, not quite as taken by the beauty of his surroundings as he spent an inordinate amount of time wiping away sweat. The lack of breeze and the glaring sunlight that should not have been so harsh through the treetops.

"We are not too far now. Prepare yourselves for the most spectacular sight you will ever see," Ivy announced dramatically.

"You wouldn't be overselling it or anything, would you?" Adam laughed.

"See for yourself when we arrive. Keep up; I had forgotten how slow humans are," Ivy whined. Zev nodded his agreement.

They pressed on, sincerely hoping their new pixie friend was right, because even though they hadn't been walking very long, their exhaustion was evident. Adam wondered to himself how that might affect his gift once he got there. It set in that he had no idea what to expect, and he had only successfully wielded his gift with a group of Jesimi once. He knew that turning back wasn't an option at this point—well, he supposed it never really had been from the moment he'd read his mother's letter. He brushed the mizzur taking up residence in his pocket, a souvenir of a former life and a promise for a different future.

They smacked into a wall of intertwined vines, branches, and other plants, and Adam had to free his dagger to cut some of it loose. He held the opening for Ivy and Zev and stepped out from under the canopy into another world.

They found themselves teetering at the top of a sheer cliff face, and small rocks tumbled down under their feet. Adam's stomach dropped like a ton of lead, and his palms became laced with sweat as he took a large step back. A hint of a breeze swept across his face— he took in a deep breath of the open air. They were looking down on endless clouds of treetops as far as the eye could see. Upon further inspection, Adam was physically taken aback as he made out a sea of wooden roofs that blended in among the tree canopy below. They had made it to the city, and he could hardly wait to explore. Now, how in all the realms would they get down there?

CHAPTER 11

"It would be rather easier if you could simply fly," Ivy teased, her cheeks filling in rosy red. "Since you cannot, there is a secret ladder just down this way."

"If it's so secret, how do you know about it?" Adam asked.

"I am a distinguished pixie. We are an important part of the fabric of the Mesios Rainforest, as are the citizens of the city, and as such, we keep each other apprised of goings-on across our realm," Ivy said indignantly, giving her signature foot stomp for effect.

"Okay, then, we'll follow you," Adam replied, with a light eye roll once she had turned her back and floated along the edge of the cliff. He and Zev walked closely to the thick hedge of vegetation to avoid having to look down. They stopped as Ivy held up her hand and pointed downward.

"You call that a ladder?" Adam cried as he took in the disintegrating ladder formed from timeworn vines twisted around each other, tied to the trunk of a vast tree, and tossed over the edge, plunging into the abyss, the bottom of which they could not see below the canopy. Zev let out a low, throaty growl, reminding them of his presence.

"Seeing as how Zev is a quadruped, that ladder really isn't an option," Adam said. Then, under his breath, he added, "Which is a good thing, considering I hadn't planned on us dying today." Zev stood tall, flashing his broad chest.

"Well, if you are too frightened to take the easy way, there is a cave system right over there that leads down to the great city," Ivy said, pointing back into the thick foliage they had emerged from.

"You think that the ladder is the easy way? We'll take our chances with a nice, indoor stroll to cool off," Adam replied with an air of arrogance, as if they had found an easy solution.

"Sure, but don't say I didn't warn you," Ivy hummed as she disappeared once again behind the forest's curtain of foliage.

Adam and Zev shoved their way after her. It wasn't long before Ivy guided them to the ominous mouth of a cave that formed a semicircle rising from the forest floor. It was set into a rock face covered in billowing vermillion blossoms with garish pops of red spilling from their centers, as if they were sticking out their tongues. It was a strange juxtaposition: the beauty of the flora and the depth of the darkness they were about to enter. For a moment, Adam thought back to the lousy ladder, but looking down at Zev beside him, he knew this was the only choice.

The three of them pushed forward, slipping behind the veil of flowering vines, into the mouth of the cave. Ivy concentrated intensely, and her yellowish-green glow burst forth from her tiny body, gently outlining the narrow tunnel they found themselves in. They began to wind their way down the gradient, the rock walls surrounding them seeming to edge closer and closer with every step. Zev stepped into place behind Adam as the path tapered inward—they both tried not to think about that fact. It was much cooler inside, but just as humid, and the wet air clung to their lungs.

"Watch your head, Adam; it gets a bit tight up ahead," Ivy warned, turning back and throwing a half smile over her shoulder.

Just as she said it, Adam barely ducked in time to avoid a sharp, skinny chunk of rock descending from the cave ceiling. These became more frequent, causing Adam to bend in half, trying to balance the weight of his rucksack on his back as it slid back and forth, pulling him to and fro. He wondered if he might be on his hands and knees soon as his arms easily reached out to brush both sides of the hollow tunnel. He continued running his hand over the surprisingly smooth, damp surface as they walked and listened to the dull ricochet of water dripping endlessly.

Adam felt a slight tingle on his fingers and across his hand, up his forearm, a gentle kiss of sensation. He looked down and saw a line of spiders of the brightest shades marching up his arm, each one the size of his fist. As momentary shock wore off and horror set in, Adam let out an unearthly shriek that caused Ivy and Zev to double over as it echoed off the jagged walls. He jumped so high he cracked his head repeatedly on the rock ceiling as he smacked his left arm and viciously tried to shove the spiders off. The scaly yet also horrifically furry eight-legged monstrosities flew off of him and splattered against the wall like bursts of paint—lemon yellow, scarlet red, deep plum. Even once they were off, he kept scrubbing his skin as if he wouldn't be satisfied until a layer or two had come off, the memory of them on his body seared in forever.

Zev nudged him out of his panic bubble. Adam had apparently awoken some type of hell nest; a kaleidoscope of thousands of super-sized spiders spilled from a crack in the cold, dark cave, a rainbow of doom as they coated the narrow tunnel from the ground to the ceiling, their beady eyes that extended from their monstrous forms waggling every which way in what seemed to be a desperate hunt for blood. Adam's continued shrieks were matched by the high-pitched wails coming from Ivy as she flew deeper into the cavern and the intense howls from Zev, which were only usually heard when he ran under a full moon. Ducking and keeping his arms pressed tightly to his sides, Adam raced to catch up to Ivy—who flew awfully fast for someone with such small wings. He was wildly out of breath, still brushing his arms and shaking his hands as phantom spiders haunted him. Zev was hot on his heels, but the tidal wave of arachnids seemed barely quelled by their speed. Eventually, after running for what felt like hours Zev looked back, and they had finally fully outrun them.

They are gone now, Zev said, signaling for Adam to slow down.

Ivy looked back and slowed to a hover, bobbing up and down in the air as she worked to catch her breath too. "I did warn you," she said with a sly grin.

Adam was already bent in half to protect his head, and he placed his hands on his knees and waited for his heart to drop back into his chest from the place it had lodged itself in his throat, though he wondered if it ever would. He thought for a moment how glad he was that at least they had been running in large downward spirals rather than up. Adam pushed his damp, sweaty jet-black hair off his forehead as he stretched his arms above his head, very careful not to touch the rock walls ever again. Zev looked on with concern as Adam wrapped his arms around himself in an attempt to stop the body-racking shakes stemming from visceral fear.

Ivy had darted forward a bit as they recovered, and she called out, "Hey, you two, come and have a look at this."

They lumbered after her slowly and noticed the tight walls falling away, while the blanket of darkness remained firmly in place. The illumination of Ivy's body was enough to know the cave had opened up into something pretty spectacular. Adam pulled the flint from his pocket and detached the large stick he had fastened to the outside of his rucksack for a situation just like this and thanked his former self for thinking of it. A much-needed win with so much embarrassment coursing through him. He struck the flint a few times, the damp air pressing down on him; eventually, it sparked, and the end of the branch blazed bright. They blinked heavily to adjust to the sudden light and gasped in unison as the fire cast flickering light across an immense chamber deep in the belly of the cave. The ceiling was stories above their heads, the floor was lined with elaborate rock sculptures, and multihued crystals were embedded in the walls, glinting in the firelight, shadows marking their presence. It was plain to see why this realm was legendary for its gems.

At the bottom lay a glistening pool of the purest turquoise, looking as if it had never been disturbed, aside from a steady drip-drop from far above the chasm sending serene ripples across the surface. A strong sense fell over them that this was the way it must remain: untouched, perfect. They marveled at every detail of this creation as if every single piece was crafted by hand with the utmost care. Though they could have stayed for hours, none of them forgot the spiders that had chased them here, and they knew time was of the essence in getting to the city. They tore their gazes away and continued to follow the cave downward, sincerely hoping Ivy was right and it would spit them out at some point. Adam was grateful that their path remained fairly open and he was able to remain upright through the remainder of the damp, dark cavity deep in the rainforest. He wondered if he was seeing things or if he was beginning to see glimpses of light accumulating before them.

Ivy flew a bit farther ahead. "Ooh, this is going to be so good!" She rubbed her hands together quickly.

Adam and Zev looked at each other, trying to prepare for whatever she might mean and hoping their definitions of *good* were similar. Both were suspicious and just a bit disturbed by all that had transpired since they'd entered the Mesios Rainforest. The reality that they had known, even with its own dangers, was long gone; a new day had dawned, and they were fairly certain it would be full of both terror and magic. If they had to have the terror to get the magic, they supposed they were willing to pay that price. The pair nodded to each other in their way, acknowledging that they were on the same page, as they always were.

Ahead of them, a semicircular opening brushed with blinding beams of sunlight beckoned them out of the dark. Though they did not know what lay ahead, they embraced it fully and hurried out. They all blinked rapidly again, Adam shielding his eyes as they tried to adjust, and he watched Zev's pupils return to normal. Adam doused the torch in the dirt beneath them, and their eyes focused forward, blinking again in case their eyes deceived them.

They were once again under the soaring canopy of the rainforest, and the sun beat down on them, warming and drying their bones. Unfolding before them into the distance was a city, very much great, as they had been told. The entire sprawling city had been built into the trees—not a single structure touched the ground. Adam and Zev's jaws fell open once again, Adam thinking that at this point, they might fall off. They stood frozen in their tracks, admiring the ingenuity it must have taken to construct a fully functional treehouse city for what appeared to be thousands of people. Ivy flitted around them, sprinkling them with laughter and joy as she witnessed their reaction.

Adam remembered that he was here for a reason, and since his vital organs had returned to where they were intended to be in the time since the gruesome arachnid incident, now was as good a time as any to use his gift. They made their way over to sit at the base of an expansive tree, Adam checking vigilantly for any creepy-crawlies. They popped some dried fruit into their mouths as Adam pulled the jar of magical signature protectant dirt from his knapsack. He took some deep breaths, trying to center himself and shake off the beginning of their outlandish adventure, focusing on Zev's calming presence as he coated his left palm. He stilled himself and centered all of his energy on the people who lived within this glorious city among the trees. He allowed his curiosity about who they were and his pure desire to get to know them to fill his heart and carry him away. He inhaled as the familiar sensation of his power unfurled in his chest and spread to the farthest reaches of his body, taking him over. It was still slightly foreign, but every time it grew less so as it was entirely his.

Adam opened his eyes for a moment to observe the people he could see living their lives in the trees and tried to connect. He was knocked off-balance as the visions swooped in, almost forcefully this time, beginning with the sepia-glazed memories that he associated with being further back in time. He saw the very place they sat before it was a city. Many lived here in hammocks and tent-like dwellings long ago, but he could tell instinctively they weren't Jesimi. Then he saw Jesimi people being forced from Avaria. The pained looks on their faces seemed universal, though the faces themselves were vastly different.

These people made their way here, and they were welcomed with open arms to build something great together. Adam smiled with his eyes closed as he watched the city sprout up, its people—Jesimi and many others, with many different backgrounds and beliefs—living there in harmony. He witnessed their struggles and felt their joy and the love they shared, and he saw the children they raised.

The visions grew crystal clear, which he took to mean they were more recent. Xhartana troops came in, demanding resources, accusing them of using magic, trying to destroy them. Calling the Jesimi and their neighbors hateful names, beating them, destroying their homes and belongings. Then he observed the people rebuilding. That was unfortunately and fortunately what it meant to be Jesimi.

The present moment returned as the visions faded from his mind, and a single tear fell from his eye. A tear that held their shared pain, the pride he had in his people. As it dropped, it began to burn; the desire to fight back simmered stronger in a way that he knew couldn't be assuaged. He flicked the tear from his chin and gathered his bearings. He felt taller, stronger somehow, claiming his birthright, his gift, and following this wild twist of fate. Ivy hovered over Zev, gently stroking the soft spot behind his ear, watching Adam and waiting.

"Well, I suppose we should head into the city and see if we can find someone in charge," Adam proposed, and the other two nodded, following behind as he lugged his pack off the ground.

Adam couldn't help but look up in awe at the sweeping city above them. They didn't have to go too far, as a few people soon strode toward them with purpose and neutral expressions. Adam and Zev continued moving forward tentatively, Ivy in their shadows, remembering Ben's warning that like Kesil, some places will be less receptive than others. As Adam smiled hopefully, the woman in the center stepped forward, grasping both of Adam's arms in greeting, forearm to forearm, and broke out into a sincere grin. The two men flanking her offered their own greetings.

"We have been expecting you," the woman said, nodding confidently.

A golden curtain of hair tumbled over her shoulders, nearly meeting her slender waist. Her pale, porcelain skin blossomed with pink on her cheeks, and she had used some kind of paint to highlight her honey-colored eyes, which were flecked with the gold of her hair. A giant, mousey-brown otter, who appeared to be soaking wet, wove its way back and forth between her feet. She moved from grasping Adam's forearms to gracefully tugging him to her chest for a hug. She was rather tall for a Jesimi woman, but Adam still had a head's height over her. He let out a nervous laugh and patted her upper back gently. If he was honest, he'd needed a hug from who seemed at first glance to be the nicest person in all the realms.

"You have?" Adam asked with a tone of surprise, suppressing the pull of his gift wanting to assist him in getting his message across more eloquently. How could they have possibly known he was coming?

"Phineas here saw you coming. We already know what you are here for, and we are overjoyed you have come. He has foreseen that the time is upon us when we will stand and fight against evil as one. I am Lian, daughter of Dalia; my name means 'of willow,' so the rare chance I can get away with it, I am able to dance among the treetops, gracefully flowing from branch to branch."

One of the men at her side had deep-brown eyes that were matched by his deep-brown skin. His cheekbones sat high on his face and rounded with a genuine smile. Adam imagined the gift of sight to be heavy, as it held the utmost importance and value among the Jesimi people—really any people. He could merely see the collective past of a people and sometimes felt he might crumble; he couldn't imagine seeing the future. At the man's side, a majestic ocelot stood, statuesque, as it did not flinch or blink from its penetrating stare.

Phineas seemed to catch Adam's line of thinking and reached out his hand to him; he grasped Adam's wrist tightly in greeting and understanding that Adam had not felt before, and it comforted him greatly.

"And this is my husband, Raviv. His name means 'raindrops.' So, when he is able to sneak using his gift, he can make the rain come or stay away." She giggled, grasping his hand and placing her head on his shoulder. The man was about the same height as his wife and looked at her adoringly, brushing his warm, curly brown hair out of his eyes as the red howler monkey perched on his shoulder picked at it.

"This is my beloved Lily," Lian said with stars in her eyes, pointing to the giant otter at her feet. "That is sweet Mayim." She pointed at the monkey now climbing Raviv's limbs as if he were one of the trees they lived among.

"This is Zev and Ivy. Since you saw me coming, you likely are already aware that I was able to utilize my gift to see glimpses of your lives here. It is incredible that you came here after being forced into exile, that you joined together with the others and built this magnificent city. I could see it has been fraught with pain and brimming with success in equal measure. I continue to be moved by how vastly different we are as Jesimi in every way, yet our plight is much the same. We share common enemies and common friends. We want to be free and live in peace." Adam let his gift flow through him again, his hand warm with white light as he spoke.

"You do not have to convince us, Adam. We were with you long before you arrived. Xhartana has crossed us one too many times, and it is past time we rise against them. Welcome to Talus, the great city among the trees. We just have to show you around!" Lian announced excitedly as she held her husband's hand and raised them together. Phineas smirked at them, and Adam let out a chuckle, finding these people really easy to like.

"Our prized key shall be yours; I can see how crucial it will be to collect them all. I shall speak with you later," Phineas said mysteriously, and he swiftly walked away. The ocelot lingered a moment longer, then prowled after him.

Lian beckoned them to follow as she led them to the base of the city, her excitable soul-seal scampering after her. Adam snickered under his breath—the giant otter looked somewhat like a limp noodle when it ran.

Adam couldn't help but wonder how one was to get up there if nothing touched the ground, flashing back to the shoddy ladder. Before them, a large wooden platform descended, engraved with intricate floral designs of Mesios origin. Lian skipped onto the platform, pulling Raviv behind her, and Adam and Zev hesitantly stepped on as well. Ivy was nearly bursting with excitement. The platform lurched under their feet, nearly knocking Adam off-balance, and he caught himself on Zev. It steadily rose rather high into the trees until it seamlessly became part of what Adam imagined was their version of a city street, suspended in the sky.

"It's an intricate pulley system, operated by the very best," Lian answered the unasked question, eyes gleaming. "We don't get visitors often, so forgive me my slight overzealousness." She tittered, and her husband kept making the same moony eyes at her.

Adam wondered if they were newly married; they both looked rather young in comparison to Phineas, who he guessed was maybe in his forties.

"Follow me, and watch your step," Lian continued. "Though the design is seamless, if I say so myself, if you're not used to being suspended high in the trees, you might misstep and fall off." She let another giggle loose, as if that was funny, and walked on.

The city was even more impressive from up here; the construction was incredible. Adam had never seen homes or buildings this beautifully designed. Even the stone homes in the Mezarim didn't compare.

"Everything here is made from locally sourced elements within our rainforest. Everything you see is built from the wood of these very trees and hardened by natural materials we have mined, such as rubber and metals. There are about three thousand four hundred of us living here at present, and we all have a wide variety of skills. Our builders and creators are unparalleled, clearly, but equality takes precedence here. We all consider ourselves to be of the same value, regardless of our gifts, our cultural background, or our abilities. We are an amalgamation of Jesimi people here, varying in the way we look, what part of Avaria we came from, and our beliefs. There are many El nonbelievers who live here, but they participate in our cultural activities as a community just the same. As you know, being Jesimi isn't just about our beliefs; it's who we are, through and through—it's in our blood. This openness allows us to live in harmony with all the non-Jesimi people who make up about thirty percent of our population. They join in on our holidays and celebrations, and we join in on theirs. Of course, it isn't perfect, but due to the distance and how difficult it is for Xhartana to get here, we are able to govern ourselves, for the most part, with a council of twelve. Problems do arise, but we work them out among ourselves." Lian beamed with pride.

They walked on, just beneath the canopy. Firm wooden decking jutted out from each cluster of trees, with homes built into the centers. Large parts of walls were left open for air to flow in and out, some with horizontal wooden siding, some with vertical, some slanted. Different shades of wood and different smells wound around them as they pushed deeper into the city. Between each cluster of trees were well-constructed rope swing bridges; a far cry from the ladder on top of the cliff, these were solidly secured and only swayed lightly as they crossed them. Enough to add a layer of sweat to Adam's palms, however.

Adam hadn't even noticed their return to the oppressive, wet heat after leaving the cave, but now, his clothes were plastered to his skin again. The absolute magic of this place, the resilience of its people, made him not even care.

After another rope bridge—which Adam held on to rather tightly—lay the largest cluster of monumental trees they had seen thus far, their collective trunks taking up more space than Adam's entire village. The structures built into the trees and rambling around them were not dissimilar to what they had seen, just more. Layers and layers of wooden decking spiraled around what appeared to be dozens of pods intermingled with the branches, as if they were meant to be there. People milled about, and some sat on benches carved out of the trees themselves. Kids climbed and wound around between the trunks, whooping and hollering on their natural playground.

"And this, this is the heart of our city," Lian explained with a deep sigh of awe, as if seeing it through fresh eyes.

"It's . . . it's. Well, there aren't words for what it is," Adam said as he followed.

Zev cut in front of him, eyes gleaming. Adam thought Zev had been made for this, and maybe he had. They wove their way in and out of the main part of the city, Lian buzzing around and showing them different stores where makers and creators sold their wares, from lightweight garments dyed every color under the sun to everyday items carved out of wood: plates, cutlery, containers, art, décor. The meeting chamber for the council was carved out of what had been an insignificant hollow relative to the size of the tree. She showed them the schools and the thrumming open-air market, where the harvesters and gatherers sold their commodities on built-in tables, which were piled high with fruits, corn, grains, coffee, and cocoa beans, with people clambering to gather what they needed for the week. Lian introduced them to people as they went by, but Adam found it difficult to keep track.

She led them to a dark hollow filled to the brim with scrolls and introduced him to Talus's preservers, who were busy at work with piles of new papyrus and wells of ink so full, they spilled over, dripping inky blackness onto the honey-stained wood. Seeing the people of Talus live in peace was inspiring and gave Adam hope for the future.

As the streams of light flooding between the trees began to dim, Lian must have realized how exhausted Adam and Zev looked.

Ivy had just been floating along on a cloud all day, happy to be given a special tour, though she had been there before.

"We would love for you to be our guests this evening," Lian said, Raviv nodding along with her.

"We would be honored, if it's not too much of a burden," Adam responded.

"You could never be a burden. You are so brave to take on this adventure, and we would do anything to aid you," Lian pledged.

She led the way across another bridge and around a number of other dwellings, stopping to pick up her towheaded, brown-eyed toddler, whom she introduced as Asher, from a neighbor before arriving at a hexagonal home built around a tree. The wood that had been used to build it had a warm orange tint to it, which suited its owners. The slats of wood that made up the siding were laid horizontally, and the shingles of the roof were made of something much darker and thicker.

They made their way to the door, which was painted bright yellow, and Mayim and Lily pushed through first, followed by Lian, Raviv, and little Asher. Adam, Zev, and Ivy came in last. The yellow didn't stop at the front door; it coated the wooden furniture and graced the cushions, drapery, and, well, pretty much everything.

"Welcome!" Lian and Raviv said in sync, smiling proudly before Lian peppered Asher's round, cherubic face with kisses for the tenth time in the last couple of minutes.

"What can I get you to drink? How about some wine? You must all be starving!" Lian fired in quick succession, hurrying to tuck them, even Zev, into the bench built into the side of the home. A large rectangular table butted up to the bench and was flanked by a couple of chairs that the yellow had skipped over, making them appear out of place.

Mayim and Lily bounded around the circular room, chasing each other and playing, as Asher squealed with excitement. Zev looked on suspiciously, and Adam elbowed him gently for being judgmental.

Lian and Raviv busied themselves, tossing things back and forth between them. Raviv held Asher tight to his hip, doling out endless snacks to the toddler. Adam got the idea that Asher's small feet didn't often grace the floors, as his parents revolved around him like moons around the realms.

Lian placed a carved walnut cup full of wine in front of Adam, water in front of Zev, and a tiny cup full of nectar in front of Ivy. Adam took a sip of the achingly sweet yet strong liquid and looked around at the massive tree trunk in the middle of the room. Raviv took out a knife, sliced up a dark-yellow banana, and brought it over to the table. Adam had never quite tasted a banana like it, and he handed some to Zev to try.

Exhaustion set in; Adam was sitting for the first time in a long time, and the letdown from all the adrenaline he was expelling these days was hitting him like a sack of rocks. He noticed Zev's head falling toward his lap, eyes closed, and then catching himself and snapping back to attention at any sound.

Lian brought over a large platter full of a variety of food Adam had never seen before. She raised her cup, and everyone followed suit. "Next year reunited in Avaria!" they all cried, knocking their cups together before taking a sip. Asher clapped his chubby, dimpled hands and reached out to lace his fingers through Zev's fur, which was surprisingly well received. Brave kid, considering the wolf was three, maybe four times his size, Adam thought.

"Now, eat! You must be starved!" Lian said. She loaded two plates and pushed them closer to Adam and Zev while Ivy kept working on her nectar, her wings fluttering with satisfaction. Adam hesitantly used his wooden utensil and drew a bite to his mouth. It was bursting with unfamiliar flavors and spice. He picked out that there was some kind of grain and corn, with some wild garlic, and then so many unknown spices, it made his head spin. He dug in, not refusing the second plate Lian demanded both he and Zev eat as she wrangled Asher back to his seat, cooing as she encouraged him to eat.

Adam rubbed his belly, sighing deeply. Just as he thought the meal had concluded, Raviv announced dessert.

"You can't come to the rainforest, the home of the most delicious cocoa beans in the world, and not eat chocolate," Lian said frankly, and Adam had to agree, accepting a chunk of chocolate that Lian explained was made by crushing the cocoa beans and melting them down with milk, then letting the mixture reform. Adam groaned as he took a bite and quickly inhaled the rest, thinking it might just be the best thing he'd ever tasted. He looked teasingly at Zev, who growled in return at being denied the sweet treat. He was not alone; Asher began to scream in protest as he was denied the chocolate as well.

"Not until you finish, my love," Raviv insisted, clearly trying to hold to the rules. His attempts were effective, and Asher plugged his nose and shoved the rest of his squash into his mouth, quickly followed by presenting his open hands, chocolate-ready. Lian swooped in to fulfill his wish, all of them laughing together.

Adam's stomach dropped as the lightness of the mood struck a place deep in that well of guilt. It wasn't long ago that he'd lost his mother; he should be suffering more. He quickly reminded himself that the purpose of sitting zayin is to feel the grief up front, feel it fully, cope with it, and then go on living. He knew she would want him to feel joy.

"Well, my dears, now that you have made it to the great city and are settled in nicely, and now that I have been replenished by your generous nectar, I must be getting back to my family for the evening." Ivy sniffed back against the tears welling in her eyes.

Adam was taken aback by how sad the thought made him; she had nestled her way into his heart in such a short time, and he found that he might even miss her. "Do you have to go so soon?"

"You have no further need of me for now. Fear not; I am certain we shall meet again. We pixies may be small, but you know that fairness is our most vital quality, and we may yet find a way to stand with you against your ghastly foe." She pressed her tiny, freckled hand to Adam's face and then Zev's. Glowing once more, she took off out the open window.

"Goodbye! Thank you!" Adam called after her, and another hole punctured his wounded heart—this felt like another loss. He would see her again; he had to stay focused.

"Thank you for welcoming us so warmly. We are so very glad to be here with you all," Adam said graciously to their hosts, more than ready to fall asleep at any moment.

Lian led them up the spiral of stairs that jutted out from the center tree to their guest quarters, decorated generously in canary yellow, and bid them good night. The moment they laid their heads down, they disappeared into dreams and nightmares.

CHAPTER 12

Adam awoke to the strong scent of coffee filling the air, and something else he couldn't put his finger on as he sat up and stretched. Mmm, cinnamon; that was it. The sounds of some kind of stringed instrument being strummed floated up from beneath them.

As it did nearly every day now, the mashup of shock and grief and fear that made up Adam's current circumstances made themselves known as soon as consciousness came. He thought of his mother most when he first woke up, though if he was honest, he thought of her all day, and though the piercing, agonizing pain had shifted, it wasn't necessarily any better. He missed her endlessly; he missed their home, the comfort of their lives together. Though he would do anything to get her back, he was glad to be on this adventure, to have new purpose driving him; otherwise, he feared he might go mad. He thought of his uncle and found he sort of missed him too. The complexity of these warring emotions stirring within him was altogether new and not particularly comfortable, but he accepted them all. There was no other choice.

Are you okay? Zev asked, reading Adam's expression like a book.

"Not really, but also very much okay, you know?" Adam scrunched his face in confusion at his own words.

That does not make a lot of sense, but okay. Did you have nightmares about spiders last night? Zev jested, nudging Adam's shoulder.

"No, jerk. I was not in any way physically prepared for this journey." Adam groaned in pain as he kneaded the muscles in his legs, then brushed a phantom sensation off with a shudder as he viscerally remembered yesterday's arachnid encounter.

Adam tugged on an olive-green T-shirt that brought out his deeply tanned skin, some lightweight trousers, and the black sandals he had snuck in his rucksack when Ben wasn't looking. He chuckled, thinking of how distraught his mother would be at the wrinkled state of him. They looped their way downstairs, following the wafting cinnamon and coffee.

"I hope we didn't wake you with our playing," Lian said when she saw them. "Raviv and I play music together; we are performing at our friend's naming ceremony later and needed to practice. Oh, you must join us. You will be most welcome!" Her voice was inflected with sunshine, matching her home décor of choice.

"Not at all; it sounded lovely. And we wouldn't want to intrude on something so personal," Adam responded respectfully.

"Nonsense. Nearly every Jesimi in the city is invited, and many non-Jesimi residents as well. Naming ceremonies are very sacred, as you must know. We take any chance we can get to celebrate around here." Lian folded her long, toned arms across her chest.

"Well, we would be honored. Since the Isle of Ori, where I came from, has a Xhartanian outpost on it, they monitor us much more closely. I know the same laws apply to you, but we aren't able to have any kind of gatherings or celebrations. Our naming ceremonies are held in secret, with only close family and the Keeper of the Great Scroll," Adam said, his smile fading in anger as he recalled the onslaught of terror following their recent attempt to gather together, resulting in carnage and death.

"That's just terrible. That's what you're here for, though; that's why you're on your great journey. Because it's past time that we are all free to live in peace," Lian asserted, her eyes clouding with an intensity Adam hadn't seen before. Their shared pain clung to the air between them as she crossed the distance and placed her hand gently on his shoulder.

They all sat and chatted while they had breakfast: bananas and some kind of tomato concoction that was, once again, mouthwatering and surprisingly spicy. Raviv regaled them with tales of his work as a gatherer—collecting items and foods that grew naturally in the rainforest. He told Adam and Zev of the harvesters, who grew their food using slash-and-burn farming methods appropriate to their location. Adam and Zev were amused by his passion, and Lian all but dragged them out the door on their way back to the city center among the cluster of trees.

They rose to the top of a large tree right under the canopy, the bushy leaves brushing their shoulders, and Lian beckoned them into a packed Temple. It was built right into the top of the tree, so the light ebbed and flowed with the wind through the thinning branches. Two large men stood guard outside, and Adam wondered why that was necessary here, making a mental note to ask. He assumed they were far enough removed from Xhartana's grasp, but he remembered what he had seen when he used his gift—they were everywhere.

The sanctuary was so packed full of people, there was no room to sit, and all kinds of animals flew above and darted through the crowd, from macaws to capybaras, poison dart frogs to tapirs. Lian tugged Adam to the front, yanking his arm as he apologized to everyone he bumped into on the way. There were three men standing up on the pulpit above the throng of well-wishers; one of the men held a newborn baby wrapped tightly in soft, pink blankets. The infant peacefully dozed in his arms as he showed her around, glowing with pride. The second man gently kissed the infant's forehead and placed his arm lovingly around his partner.

The Keeper of the Great Scroll called for everyone's attention, and the large room bathed in warm sunshine fell silent. The Keeper introduced the couple, then said some prayers in the ancient language. Both of the men spoke briefly of their love for each other and their excitement to be fathers to their bundle of joy, and then they tucked her tightly into the wicker basket between them. The Keeper stood behind it, and Adam heard all breath draw out of the room as the crowd waited to see if the baby had been gifted. She let out a fierce wail and raised her arms in protest at having been put down; judging by the discomfort on her fathers' faces, it wasn't common. Her tiny hands opened, and her left palm began to glow the most vivid shade of orchid, revealing a symbol: a circle around a jeweled crown. It quickly faded as the people gave a resounding cheer. Adam suspected their response would have been the same had she not been given a gift. He knew some Jesimi people placed more weight behind the gifted, but in places like this, where equality was truly valued, everyone had their own abilities that helped, threading them deeply into the tapestry of their community. One of the men scooped the baby up, and they both covered her and each other in kisses as they proudly announced her name: Atara, meaning 'crown.'

Adam couldn't help but be softened by the apparent depth of their love, wondering if he would ever experience it. He'd had a few girlfriends over the years, but he hadn't felt that longing for someone deep in his soul. He hadn't been in love, not like these two, not like Lian and Raviv. What an incredible place this was.

Lian squeezed his arm as she shoved past him and hopped up onto the ledge. Raviv followed with two wooden instruments, having placed Asher in the arms of a friend, and handed her one. They moved to sit on chairs placed over to the side and began to play a happy, upbeat melody, strumming together in perfect harmony as the crowd began to sing and sway, with overwhelming joy emanating from them. Adam swayed right along even though he didn't know the words, letting the contagious joy infect him. Zev seemed less moved as he was continually shoved back and forth at Adam's feet.

After a few songs, the people lined up to congratulate the couple and Atara. Adam and Zev waited for Lian and Raviv, leaning against the railing of the dark-wooden deck overlooking the city. Adam held on tight, as they were stories above the ground, but it was breathtaking—the natural beauty matched the ingenuity of these people. The moist air settled as a cool breeze trickled down from the clouds hanging low above the canopy, and Adam wondered if a storm might be brewing.

They were soon joined by Lian, Raviv, and a boisterous Asher, and Adam commended them on their musical talents and offered thanks for inviting them to attend the ceremony.

The next couple of days were filled with meeting countless people, too many to remember their names, and seeing the rest of the city among the trees. They joined Lian at a council meeting so she could show them off and confirm Talus's support of Adam's efforts. Every last one of the councilors readily agreed to be a part of the upcoming battle to free the Jesimi people and reunite in Avaria, their homeland. Adam took the opportunity to impart the chilling information he and Ben had accidentally overheard on their way to Kesil on the Isle: Xhartana had struck more platinum, making them even more formidable and backing their plan to expand their reach into the farthest corners of the continent, removing all Jesimi from existence.

With this in mind, Phineas strode purposefully over to a knothole in the chamber and delicately extracted a key. It was whittled out of fine wood and had seven glittering emeralds affixed to its bow. He placed the key in Adam's hands, and once again, Adam pledged to treat it with the utmost care as he gently strung it onto the nowweighty twine around his neck and tucked it carefully beneath the collar of his shirt. One key closer to freeing his people.

Adam's spirits were well and truly buoyed by these incredibly warm and vibrant people. They shared so many of the same customs, beliefs, language, but they went about it so differently. He supposed that was what was so special about his people, and his pride for being Jesimi soared. Adam felt they could have stayed forever—he could see them fitting in and even being happy there—but he couldn't allow anything to distract him from his mother's final wish, from his purpose. Though it pained them both, Adam and Zev said goodbye to the people who had become fast friends.

"Our time here has been so wonderful. You have a beautiful family, a beautiful city full of amazing people. Meeting all of you was such an honor. I feel even more motivated and prepared for my great journey after your encouragement," Adam said as they walked him and Zev back to the platform that would deliver them to the forest floor.

"The honor has been in getting to know you. You truly are pure of heart, just as Phineas foresaw. We shall meet again, even nearer to a better future. Because of you," Lian stammered as the dam burst and hot tears slid down her face, Raviv holding Asher between them, nodding along and comforting her. Even Lily and Mayim fell still, which seemed very rare due to the gravity of the moment. Lian gracefully pulled Adam and Zev into a group hug and not-so-gracefully squeezed them extra hard before releasing them. Asher reached out to give Zev one last pat, and Adam felt the pain a little more sharply. Adam and Zev stepped onto the large wooden platform as its operators began to work the pulley system, and they began their descent.

"Goodbye for now. Thank you again!" Adam shouted, waving zealously, feeling the same tug he felt in his heart when they'd left Ben and then again when Ivy left. He wasn't used to missing people, but he supposed this was the price he paid for letting them in. For loving. A price well worth the cost.

He reached down to scratch the top of Zev's head, which was resting on Adam's leg, partially to steady Adam and partially because he didn't much like all these goodbyes either. The platform lurched as it drew level with the ground, creating a cloud of dirt. Adam waved it away as they stepped off, checking his enchanted bronze compass and sighing as they treaded farther into the rainforest. Ben figured after the great city in the trees, they would have to journey maybe three or four days to the border of the next realm, one of the largest.

CHAPTER 13

They trekked across the jungle, fighting their way through oppressive heat and endless insects, finding places off the ground to sleep for a few hours in the night. Their aptitude for adventure had quickly grown, and they worked as a team to navigate their path. The change in scenery wasn't rapid; the thickness of the foliage that had swallowed them for days began to gradually subside, the air slowly becoming thinner and dryer. The forms of the trees and the types of flora and fauna they observed began to change. There was not an obvious barrier between the two realms, so they were unsure whether they had crossed onto the Zokhara Savanna, but as the trees became fewer and farther between and the shades of green traded for shades of browns and reds, they figured it was safe to assume they had made the transition.

Adam pulled out the map and pointed to the spot where they stood, just on this side of the border in the southern part of the savanna. He couldn't help but feel proud to even have made it this far, though his feet and his shoulders continued to cry out from his boots and rucksack. He stroked the keys around his neck, a constant reminder of his purpose. He and Zev were well on their way and had many incredible Jesimi friends who would join them in their impending battle, even some non-Jesimi allies, to his pleasant surprise. He took a long chug of the water that Lian had provided and a little nibble of the chocolate she had insisted he take when she'd restored their supplies for this next leg.

Taking a deep breath in, and inhaling mostly dirt, he wasn't certain whether he preferred this drier heat to the wet heat of the rainforest. The undulating land sprawled out in front of them, stippled with oddly shaped trees and swept with tall, yellowish grasses. Towering termite hills popped up from the sand like art sculptures, making them wary. The barren landscape was breathtaking in its own austere, unending way.

The lack of shade was problematic as they headed toward the next village. Adam's boots and Zev's paws became coated with the grime that they kicked up as they went, both tempted to cover their faces to prevent so much of it ending up in their mouths, but they kept moving.

The scenery began to look almost alien; very little changed over the hours they trudged through the savanna, their eyes red as they continually tried to rub the dirt out. Adam began to grow concerned over how they might find water in a place such as this, in stark contrast to the last realm, where water oozed from everything.

They preserved their precious energy rather than talking, focusing on making it to the village Ben had told them was half a day's journey across the border. Half a day had come and gone, and no sooner had the words primed themselves to spill from his lips when in the distance, the village appeared, as if it had sprung from their very imaginations. They simultaneously drew in breaths of relief that they were nearly there. Adam wrestled with whether he should stop and try to utilize his gift before entering, as he had before, or wait until he was inside. The landscape answered the question for him: All that stood between them and the village was open dirt, some bumbling tumbleweed, and what seemed to be some kind of den. They made a wide berth, leaving space for whatever lived beneath, sure they didn't want to meet it.

As they moved closer, they realized the village was rather small, surrounded by tall wooden posts that were sharpened at the top and driven into the ground side by side, forming a barrier.

Adam wondered what it was they were trying to keep out, ignoring the chill that brushed its finger down his spine.

They slowed their pace, moving around the perimeter to look for an entrance, anxiety building within them as they wondered how they would be received. Adam ran his hand over the blade strapped to his side, hoping with all his might he'd never have to use it.

Around the far side, they discovered an opening in the fence and hesitated before stepping through. Before they could get their bearings, they were swarmed by at least four people who seized Adam's hands and bound them behind his back. Zev morphed into a vicious version of himself, trying to tear through those who held him back to protect Adam; it was his most sacred responsibility. He threw all of his weight against those restraining him, but it was of no use; he thrashed his head around, gnashing his teeth, looking for flesh to sink them into.

"What in all the realms is going on?" Adam cried out as the men and women gained full control over him and Zev.

No one responded as they pushed Adam and Zev forward. Unsure of what was happening, blood whooshing in his ears, he decided he didn't really have much of an alternative at this point and allowed himself to be dragged along. Zev never stopped thrashing to get to Adam.

They walked through the center of the village, which was skirted by mud cottages with grass thatched roofs on either side. They noticed a lack of villagers as they continued on, drenched in dread. Adam knew this was a Jesimi village—it had been marked carefully on the map—and hadn't expected this type of welcome. He looked down at his side and realized the dagger was gone. He hung his head for a moment, and though it looked bad—really bad—maybe he could talk their way out of it.

At the end of the rows of cottages, the village opened up, and they were surrounded by people sparring with each other one-on-one as others cheered them on, booed them, or both. They filed through the middle, trying to make themselves small so as not to get hit with any errant bodies or weapons. What a peculiar place; Adam had never happened upon Jesimi warriors. Guardians protected his village, but not particularly well. This was entirely new and wholly nerve-racking.

At the back edge of the village fence, there were a handful of people draped across blankets on the ground or sitting in wooden chairs, conversing naturally with each other and shaded by massive, billowing fabric the color of the earth beneath them. Adam and Zev were shoved toward them.

"We found these two sneaking around the village, so we brought them to you right away, sir!" one of their captors, a sizeable and intimidating woman, bellowed. Adam was unsure who that was addressed to, as no one made any quick moves while Adam and Zev waited to hear their fate, trembling, knowing it was on the line.

After Adam nearly passed out from holding his breath so long, a broad-shouldered, square-jawed man tossed some kind of nut in his mouth and deigned to face them. "What do you have to say for yourselves? What brings you to our little village on the savanna?" he asked in a menacing tone, letting them know that if they answered incorrectly, it would not bode well for them. An enormous, prehistoric monster lumbered out from behind him—a saltwater crocodile that hissed at his side ominously.

"I am Adam, son of Rachel, and this is Zev. We are from the Isle of Ori. I am on a great journey across the continent to gather the Jesimi people scattered in exile together once more to fight the tyrannical rule of Xhartana." Adam hoped his paralyzing fear and weakness wasn't as obvious on the outside. He considered going on, but the man looked as if he was thinking deeply, so he waited.

The man stood, casting a powerful shadow over all those before him, and strode toward Adam and Zev. Zev's caramel eyes bore into the man as he approached, and Adam flinched, bracing for whatever was coming next.

The man broke out into a wide grin and clapped him on the shoulder, pulling him free of those restraining him and gesturing for them to let Zev go. "Well, why didn't you say so!" his husky voice boomed, echoing across the endless panorama with nothing to stop it from going on forever. Adam and Zev looked around, very confused and equally suspicious as to the sudden change in tune. "We are a village of warriors. We protect ourselves and our homes with everything that we are; it's our most precious value. We never have unannounced visitors, so our guardians thought you meant us harm. Our apologies for that, boys!" He chuckled deep in his belly, and the guardians looked on sheepishly, offering unspoken apologies and handing back Adam's dagger.

"Welcome to Kiritum! I am Arnon, son of Ruth, and I am descended from a long line of warriors of Avaria. My name means 'torrent valley,' and my gift empowers me to unleash a river of fury upon my enemies. We are happy to welcome a guest from a part of the homeland we long for so deeply, though we have never touched its soil. You will have to tell us everything of your journey. As Jesimi warriors, our plight is your plight, and we will fight to end the dastardly grasp of Xhartana over our people." As he spoke, everyone in sight, who seemed to be much of the village, stopped to listen to his words in reverence. It seemed clear that Arnon, swathed in fine, white material, was in charge and well respected. Adam stood back, listening and trying to keep his facial expressions in check as he took it all in, not sure how to feel. He and Zev kept their eyes pinned on the gigantic croc lounging in the sun.

"Don't concern yourselves with him; he's a big baby, really. That's Spike." Arnon then introduced some of the people who were in the tent with him and the vast array of soul-sealed animals, ranging from a kangaroo and a fluffy wombat to a warthog and a wildebeest from further north on the savanna. Adam laughed at the strange scene; one never got used to the concept of assorted animals presenting themselves to children when they turned thirteen in a rite of passage, soul-sealing to them, thereby agreeing to protect them forever.

Adam remained semi-amused, though still fairly distressed from their terrifying entrance, when the crowd that had accumulated in front of them parted. A woman effortlessly stood from her chair, kicking it back, and strolled toward them lackadaisically. Adam stepped back as the air was whisked from his windpipe; he had never in the entirety of his life laid eyes on anyone half as stunning as the woman before him. He tried not to gape as he took in every perfect detail of her face. Her deep-tan skin was kissed by the sunlight that struck her face, brightening it further, reflecting the glint in her eyes. He could not bring himself to look away, noticing as she moved closer that her eyes were a mesmerizing hazel that could hypnotize anyone who peered into them for too long. A large scar traversed her left cheekbone and up across the edge of her eye. She made sure her long mahogany curls didn't cover it, instead keeping them tucked them behind her ears. A glance at the rest of her, quick so as not to be disrespectful, revealed significant womanly curves that were well exposed in a black top that crisscrossed over her chest, winding around her neck and fastening there. She wore matching short pants that could have been painted on, bare feet beneath. There were two spears fastened to her back in the shape of an X. As she came to a halt right in front of Adam, he could have sworn he saw actual flames in her eyes, and he was completely captivated by her. His heart fluttered as if it might take flight, more than when they had run from thousands of arachnids; he wasn't sure he entirely liked it, feeling almost beholden to another person.

Adam tried to shake off the spell she had woven over him as Arnon spoke. "This is my beloved daughter, Serafine, daughter of Rivka. Her name means 'burning one,' and she possesses the gift of fire wielding. She is a fierce warrior, like all of us that came before her, and someday she will take my place as the head of Kiritum."

Serafine lowered her head slightly in greeting, her expression remaining stagnant, unreadable, her presence almost royal. Out from under a blanket of her hair, a small, shiny black fire salamander with large orange-red spots slipped onto the notch above her collarbone. Adam nodded with a dumb smile, not knowing how to properly respond or even form words.

"Serafine will show the two of you around and enlighten you on the ways of our village. We shall have a feast this eve in your honor. Then we can discuss what brought you to us." Arnon didn't leave room for questions as he pivoted and returned to popping nuts into his mouth in his spot under the tent.

Adam smeared his foot in the sand-like dirt as he awkwardly waited for the most beautiful woman he had ever seen to speak to him. She seemed underwhelmed by his presence and her task to show him around and strutted back across the sparring grounds. Adam and Zev followed.

"This is Storm," she said nonchalantly, gesturing to the salamander snoozing on her as she walked. "These are the sparring grounds. Like my father said, we are warriors. Though we attend day school and learn a little bit of everything as children, we are also trained in combat from the time we are small. Our ancestors were at one point too weak to protect themselves, and we paid too high a cost, ending up in exile. We vowed to ensure it would never happen again." As they walked, she pointed out different types of combat on display and the use of various weapons—spears, knives, swords.

It was all entirely unfamiliar to Adam, and his mouth ran dry as he continued to duck and bob out of the way of the fighters. Serafine was completely unaffected, floating through as naturally as a spring flows from its mountain source. She was suddenly barreled into by a woman who was barely more than the height of a child and was howling with laughter. Though he had known her for about five minutes, Adam didn't think Serafine was the type of person to find being nearly knocked over funny. Serafine quickly grabbed the woman's head to put her in a headlock, which was blocked. The women grappled with each other like little boys, aside from the fact that they seemed highly skilled and fairly well matched. Serafine pinned the short woman, who was brawnier, but Serafine's lean muscle won.

"Say it!" Serafine called out, letting out a surprising giggle. "You can't get out of this one, and you know it."

"Ugh, fine, I give. But I'll get you next time, you witch," the smaller woman returned, jabbing Serafine in the ribs harder than looked comfortable, but Serafine just brushed it off. Adam found himself thoroughly dismayed.

"Oh, yeah, this is Adam, and that's Zev. They're visiting. Something about bringing the Jesimi people together and fighting against Xhartana." Serafine shrugged. Adam shot a feeble smile in their direction, the fact that he was totally and completely out of his depth fully sinking in.

The woman stepped forward and grasped both of Adam's hands warmly, then squeezed them too tightly. "I'm Kezia, daughter of Zahava, her best friend," she said, jutting her thumb at Serafine. "Has she been kind to you? She can be a bit icy." Kezia snickered as she delivered the insult with love.

She had the same bronzed skin as Serafine, but her hair was a bright cinnamon red, and it was cut short at her chin. It suited her almond-shaped, amber eyes and plump, flushed cheeks. She wore a fitted, sleeveless white top and tight black pants. Adam wondered what materials they used to make clothes here, as he had never seen garments like these before. She had a carved, dark-wood bow slung across her shoulder, and on the opposite shoulder, she carried a leather quiver full of arrows. An enormous black-and-white bird with the wildest beak circled the air above them, its wingspan likely larger than Kezia's height, then gracefully landed on her arm just as she extended it. The bird faced her; it had beady red eyes and a long, prehistoric beak with a large bump at the top. It was actually quite striking, if not terrifying. Its face was lined with royal blue, black, and white, and its beak started at a deep tangerine, fading into a warm saffron at the tip. The bird leaned into Kezia, nuzzling the crook of her neck lovingly.

Adam figured she must be very strong to be able to remain standing while holding the weight of a bird that size.

"This is King," she said proudly, running the back of her hand across his head. "So, the real question is, can you fight?" Kezia looked Adam up and down with a sly grin.

"Things are pretty different where I'm from; we aren't really the physical types. Well, most of us on the Isle. Of course, there are some guardians, and they train, but we really focus on strength of the mind," Adam said honestly, fiddling with his keys. Both women stared back at him with raised eyebrows.

"You mean to tell me that your tall butt is crossing this whole continent, facing who knows what, and you don't know how to fight?" Kezia asked, truly taken aback by his words. A thickness grew in the air between them as the very evident differences between the Jesimi people settled there.

"I am amazed by this place and what you are capable of. It's just so very different. I have this dagger my uncle gave me before I left," Adam responded, patting the dagger strapped to him and trying to reconcile what he had always known, or what he thought he had known, about his people. About safety, about violence.

"Do you know how to use it?" Serafine asked, placing her hands on her round hips.

"Erm, well, I guess not. I figured it would be self-explanatory if the need arose, and I'm hoping it doesn't." Adam blushed at his own naivete.

Kezia and Serafine stopped to look at each other, then burst out laughing, as if he had said the funniest thing in the world. Once they had caught their breath, they looked back at Adam.

"One should not bear a weapon they are not prepared to use properly; you are far more likely to injure yourself than protect yourself," Serafine instructed. "It's ridiculous to think you won't face danger on your journey. The realms may be amazing, but danger lurks around every corner. Not to mention, those numbskull Xhartanian soldiers show up from time to time, demanding everything from money to food stores, and if we don't deliver, we pay the price in blood."

"Well, it's a bit too late now, seeing as how I'm already well on my way. I have Zev here, and he's pretty ferocious," Adam assured them, though he was really attempting to assure himself.

"He is huge, and looks pretty fierce, but he was subdued pretty quickly the second you stepped through the gates. Yeah, I heard; nothing stays quiet around these parts," Kezia said with a smirk. "You should both be trained." As the words left her mouth, Serafine's head whipped toward her with the speed of a tornado.

"Surely you don't mean *we* should train him here. Our training rituals and methods are sacred; you know that." Serafine brusquely bumped her shoulder.

"Well, how else is he going to learn? We can't let them go on the rest of the journey like this. He is Jesimi, after all; we are all one under El. You know that as well as I do," Kezia replied. Adam watched their exchange, trying to look just a little broader than he was and trying extra hard not to fidget too much.

"We'll have to discuss this with Father. He wanted me to show them the village and then bring them back for a feast in their honor," Serafine acquiesced with a vague expression.

"Welp, I'll see you later then, training buddy," Kezia joked, reaching out to punch Adam's arm.

He had to resist the urge to grab the spot where she hit him, as it hurt way more than she probably intended. *What an odd way to show affection,* he thought. She split off toward the archery range, and Serafine glided through the village, pointing out different places with an air of boredom—their gardens; their corral full of chickens, goats, lambs, cows, and even a few horses; the water well. Kezia's cottage, and then her cottage in a prominent position in the very center. Adam found it surprising that it didn't appear to be much different from the others, very unassuming from the outside. Behind it, just inside the fence surrounding the village, she led them to a tiny abode with a rounded roof, unlike the grass thatching covering the rest. She whisked the door open, and for a tiny place, it was rather elegantly appointed. There was an intricately carved, dark-wooden dresser near the entryway of the circular room, with a golden bowl full of gleaming fruit atop it. There was a chunky, dark-wooden chair with thick white cushions opposite it. The majority of the room was taken up by a large wooden bed with a tall frame attached, billowing translucent-white fabric hanging from the frame on all sides. The bed was made up with white silky bedding edged in gold embroidery and piled with far too many pillows. Behind the bed, hidden from plain view and a step down from the rest of the solid floor, was a small washing area, complete with all the necessities. A far cry from home, it seemed to be fit for a king. Zev circled on the cool tiled floor and sprawled out languidly.

"My father has offered you the use of our guest cottage. I'll wait out here for you while you clean up," Serafine said politely, but without warmth.

"Thank you very much. This is so nice," Adam replied, trying to keep his cool, or whatever cool he had left.

She flipped her hair behind her back as she turned and left the cottage quickly, as if she couldn't have gotten out of there fast enough. Adam was honestly too enamored with her to care; he loved a strong woman. Zev wore an expression that looked dangerously close to a smirk as he watched Adam's reaction.

Adam quickly stripped off his messy clothes and stepped into the washing area to scrub the dirt off, finding it had made its way into every single crevice of his body. He made use of the luxurious, earthy-scented soaps and shaving products, then dried off with the plush white towels, the softest he had ever felt. Finally clean, he strode over to the foot of the bed, dragged his rucksack up onto it, and dumped out its contents, then became aware of the dirt he'd smeared across the bed and tried to wipe it off.

He looked over his clothing options, wanting to make a good impression. He certainly hadn't packed for a party. The closest thing he could find was a pair of black trousers and a black collared cotton shirt that fastened up the front with neat brass snaps, the one the maker had designed for him. He threw it all on, tucking in the shirt, which felt a little foolish and very out of character but appropriate for the occasion. He laced up his boots and finger-brushed his still-dripping hair into place, swooping it across his forehead. Zev nodded his approval as he too exited the washing area, having cleaned the filth from his paws.

They didn't have a moment to think before going to the gathering being held in their honor. Serafine had been impatiently waiting, back and one foot up against the mud siding of the house, and led Adam and Zev back through the sparring grounds, Adam once again dodging a wayward spear that sailed across the path directly over his head, nearly close enough to slice a bit of hair off. Serafine covered her mouth, trying to suppress a giggle. She brought him back before Arnon as people swarmed the tent, draping it with rich ruby and gold fabrics.

"What did you think of our home, son?" Arnon asked, clapping Adam on the arm in the same place that Kezia had just punched him, causing him to wince.

"It's incredible what you've built here. Thank you for the tour and for allowing me to stay in your beautiful home."

Zev let out a low growl as Spike lumbered closer; he was still very much on edge in this new place. Adam found they both missed the comfort of the rainforest and its inhabitants but reminded himself that growth didn't come from staying comfortable. He had a mission, and he intended to follow through.

"Come, join us, our guest of honor" Arnon gestured dramatically.

Adam sat in the intricately carved, light-wooden chair he was led to, and all around him, he watched the space transform. Long tables with many chairs flanking the sides appeared, carried by well-muscled men and women. Children scurried around them, laying fine linens also of ruby and gold. It was quite the ordeal, and Adam was touched by their effort.

His stomach grumbled with hunger; he had not eaten since gnawing at the chocolate from Lian. Though they hadn't stayed anywhere long, those that they had encountered thus far had etched themselves into his heart, and he thought they might stay there for a long time.

The seats at the tables began to fill in, the villagers all turning to look at Adam and Zev curiously. When the seats were nearly full, the most delectable feast was delivered to each table in turn: endless platters of fruits, roasted vegetables, meats, and glamorous-looking combinations of foods that were unfamiliar to Adam. The scents filled his nostrils, and he couldn't wait to dig in.

Serafine wore a long-sleeved, full-length periwinkle dress with eye-catching gold stitching all over the bodice, tiny jewels hidden among the embroidery. He looked around, and most of the women wore a similar dress in various colors. The men did not appear to be as dressed up, wearing simple but nice shirts and trousers. Many of them had the head covering that spiritual Jesimi men often wore.

Serafine and Arnon stood from the seats to his side and raised their golden chalices of wine. They murmured a prayer in the ancient Jesimi tongue in unison.

"Next year reunited in Avaria!" Arnon shouted across the many tables, and everyone returned, "Next year reunited in Avaria!" They all clinked each other's glasses and drank deeply.

Adam did not usually like wine all that much because it was so sweet, but this wine was rich and full, even a little bitter, and he found himself quite fond of it. After a quick prayer over the bread, Arnon filled his golden plate high, and everyone followed suit. Adam attempted to snag a little of everything: mouthwatering mutton that had been roasted over the fire for hours, spicy couscous, chickpea soup, juicy green grapes, figs, and ten varieties of olives. As he ate, his taste buds danced with the novel spices that embellished the food and took him on an adventure all their own.

The Kiritum warriors seemed to be more spiritual than Adam was, as he noted the spread followed the rules laid out in the Great

Scroll: Meat was present; therefore, dairy was absent. Once the platters had emptied, which not so long ago hadn't seemed possible, they were replaced with trays of sweet treats—rich, jam-filled pastries and candied dates and figs. The group seemed to collectively shift back in their chairs, stuffed full, glad for the chance to celebrate.

Arnon called for the tables to be taken away, and they disappeared as quickly as they had come. An enormous fire was built, and an entire band of musicians assembled out of nowhere to play an alluring tune. The crowd gathered around the fire, chatting with each other excitedly.

"How about something a little more upbeat, boys?" Arnon rumbled, and the musicians quickly responded, looking at each other and knowing which song they would play next.

The tune was certainly fast and dulcet, and many of the villagers began to gather and perform some kind of rhythmic dance. They moved together to the beat as they swayed and kicked, shimmying their shoulders and hips, laughing and circling around the fire. Their soul-sealed animals wove underfoot as if trying to participate and avoided being stepped on.

The beat of the drums was beguiling, and Adam was beaming as he looked on, the similarities between the different groups of Jesimi people becoming much clearer again. He wondered how many groups of Jesimi were gathered, in spite of Xhartana banning it, dancing, singing, loving each other, and most of all, just living.

Kezia just about pulled his arm out of its socket as she dragged him into the circle to dance, laughing as he stumbled time and time again, trying to kick at the right times. He laughed too, and Zev's shoulders shook as he looked on. Adam wished he could share this moment with his mother, and when he looked up and saw the brilliant stars smeared across the sky, he was sure she was there.

He finally got away from Kezia and snuck back to his seat. As the dance subsided, Arnon moved beside Adam.

"I would like to hear more about your great journey now," he said, not really asking, but telling.

"Xhartana attacked my village again not long ago. They burned homes to the ground, including mine, and murdered about twenty of our people, my mother included." Adam hung his head, and Arnon, though oversized and daunting, gently placed a hand over Adam's. "She left me a letter informing me that I had a gift, a gift that would bring the Jesimi people together again to rise up and fight for the freedom of our home. She said that I was fated to journey across the continent, using my gift to gather the twelve enchanted keys and prepare for the battle that is now imminent. My gift allows me to see the collective past of a people, to better understand who they truly are and speak directly to their soul from mine. I also must warn you that my uncle and I overheard despicable Xhartanian guards discussing their plans to take their reign even further, controlling the remainder of the continent, destroying all Jesimi at last. They found platinum, so the ones whose powers aren't completely gone can use it to make themselves stronger." Adam felt like he was improving a little each time he gave this speech.

Arnon listened intently, and for a warrior, he seemed truly kind. "We would love to behold your gift, but how do you manage to wield it without garnering the attention of certain mass-murdering empires?"

"My uncle is . . . unique, and he accidentally created a substance that coats one's magical signature, keeping it from being discoverable," Adam said. He jogged over to where he'd stashed his rucksack, rummaged around for the jar, and brought it over to show him. "I simply smear it over my hand, and then I am able to safely access the amount of magic I need."

"That is an incredible invention. I wonder if you might be willing to share the formula with us; we would greatly benefit from being able to safely wield our gifts," Arnon said, with a twinkle in his brown eyes.

"Uh, sure, I don't see why not. I don't have much left, but my uncle has asked me to find a rare magical herb when I am in the Forest of Rian. I will pluck as much as I am able and figure out how to have it delivered to you. It requires a couple of other easier-to-obtain items; I'm happy to share the formula," Adam explained.

"What better time to use your gift than now, when everyone is gathered?" Turning to the crowd, Arnon said, "Behold, everyone, Adam has come to us on fate's whim. He has a rare and powerful gift. I have offered for him to observe our story using his gift. Let us watch."

Profoundly uncomfortable with the countless pairs of eyes watching him, Adam began to prepare. He drew the jar of muck from his pocket, smearing it across his left palm. Arnon leaned away from him, turning up his nose at the smell. Adam let out a nervous laugh, shrugging.

He tried to center himself, highly distracted by being the center of attention, especially the center of a certain woman's attention. It took him longer than usual to focus and call his gift. Trying to clear his mind was a lot easier before he was trekking across the continent, facing down evil arachnids, foes that turned out to be friends, and beautiful women.

He peeked an eye open to see everyone leaning toward him, waiting, and Serafine with her arms folded across her chest, in her seemingly constant state of being underwhelmed. He shook it off and refocused, leaning into Zev for help centering. Finally, his gift unlocked itself and sprung free from his chest, looping its way through his body and into the lengths of every limb. He heard gasps, and through his closed eyes, the white glow of his palm shone pink under his eyelids. He let himself bask in the sheer power of it, now that it troubled him less. Then he moved to focus it on the people before him, envisioning their faces, their home, the details he had observed, to home in on them.

As Serafine's face floated through Adam's mind and threatened to distract him, the sepia-filled display that revealed memories unfolded itself like a scroll. He knew right away this first memory took place in ancient Avaria by the wildly different landscape to where he currently sat. He noticed he was getting better at controlling his gift and remaining grounded while wielding it. This must have been before Avaria split off the continent, right before the dark time. He beheld people being viciously attacked and, not having any way to fight back, brutally stamped out of existence. His heart pinched as the memory shifted to people training, learning to fight, similar to what he had observed in this village, but less skilled and with more primitive weapons not dissimilar to those Xhartana used today.

It faded again, recollections coming in quick succession now. He saw the new warriors trying to fight before being forced to flee Avaria to survive, as there were too few of them against the many radical Marre fighters. Then came a steady flow of visions of coming to the southern part of the Zokhara Savanna and building their village, rebuilding their lives. He heard their warrior code recited and their motto repeated over and over: "We don't live to fight; we fight to live." This was in sheer opposition to their shared foes, who lived to destroy the Jesimi. Living out their promise to always be able to fight back, constantly training, but also rejoicing, celebrating life, worshipping El, praying for Elia the Light Bringer to come and end the Xhartanian reign. His body flooded with warmth as he watched naming ceremonies, holidays, the love that flourished within this community. Again, the details were different, but the values of the Jesimi were the same. The images ceased, and Adam found himself a bit woozy, but that was nothing new. He slowly opened his eyes to find everyone gaping at the receding glow of the symbol on his palm.

"I have never seen a gift symbol glow so brightly. You must be very powerful, son," Arnon pronounced in a tone near to deference.

"As I said, I was fated to receive this gift and to take this journey now, at this exact time. I was meant to be here with you. I have witnessed your pain and beheld your joy. I know who you are as a people, because I am one of you. We are all Jesimi, though you are warriors, and we may eat different foods, dance different dances; we may look different, but we treasure life above all just the same. Our shared values transcend our differences. That is the most valuable lesson I have gathered thus far on my great adventure, and I want to impart it to you. Though we have been scattered across the continent, we must join together to take back our homeland, the place you long for from the depths of your souls, like birds freed from a cage finding their flock again. The time is nigh." Adam inhaled as he realized he had been aided in forming the right words by his gift that curled around his heart. He surveyed the crowd and found many eyes damp, including Arnon's, surprisingly.

"That's just beautiful, Adam. You see right into our warrior hearts. Though we wear thick armor, underneath it, we are all one. I feel I can speak for all of us when I say we have been preparing for this moment, for your arrival, long before we knew of your existence. Those who came before us prepared for the day we would rise up as one. We cannot do it alone, but we will join you. You will have our precious key," Arnon said, earning a round of roaring applause from the people. Adam made eye contact with Serafine again, accidentally, and he was glad to see something besides contempt or disinterest in her hazel eyes, even if he wasn't sure what it was. "Let us celebrate our alliance!" Arnon boomed, indicating jovially to the musicians to resume their playing.

The people didn't need encouraging as they drank and danced and embraced. Many of them came to meet Adam and squeezed him tightly. He felt like Kezia might be right: If he was going to hang around this lot, he might need to toughen up. The people surrounding him decimated any preconceived notions he had held regarding the supposed merciless nature of warriors.

They continued to celebrate until the early hours of the morning, when the chill had made its way into the marrow of Adam's bones, as he sat too far from the bonfire. People began to trail off. Adam stumbled from the wine and caught Arnon's elbow, then thanked the towering man profusely.

Adam and Zev meandered back to the guest cottage slowly, taking their time and breathing in the fresh air, relieved that they had further succeeded in their mission. Adam had a strong inkling that his uncle would be very proud if he were here to see this, and Adam kind of wished he was.

After entering the cottage, Adam kicked off his boots and, arms out to the side, let himself fall onto the nicely made bed. It felt a lot like he imagined lying on a cloud would feel like, and he let out a deep sigh. Memories from his gift mingled with his new ones from the day, and the rush he felt from so much excitement was intoxicating. He patted the bed for Zev to jump up; it was maybe the largest bed he had ever been in, and there was room. Zev hopped up and made a few tight circles before settling in with his back flush along Adam's legs. They had slept like this when Adam was younger and they were first soul-sealed, and it calmed them both. They fell fast asleep, on top of the covers and all the pillows, Adam still fully dressed, fingers woven through thick, white fur.

CHAPTER 14

"Come on, up you get! It's getting late!" The shouting echoed through the crack under the door and off the walls. Adam and Zev stirred, not having budged all night, wondering what the racket was. Adam peeled his eyes open slowly and looked out the very small window. The dawn was just straining to break through the darkness—an ungodly time to be awake. Especially true as a steady drone of pain built in his head from imbibing that third chalice of wine not enough hours ago.

"Let's go! You will seriously regret it if you make us late to training," the female voice said in a singsong that was still somehow threatening.

What training? Adam wondered. Surely Kezia's idea that he should train hadn't been taken seriously; he hadn't even agreed. He wouldn't, would he? He knew he had strengths, though they were at times difficult to notice, but he was very clear about his weaknesses. He was no warrior but a gentle giant, as some had called him. He was immediately brought all the way back to the field behind the day school, when his lanky, gawky self had been even more so, taller and less coordinated than his peers. He had certainly not been any good at running or playing ball with the others. Samuel, his childhood bully, had never let him forget.

He shuddered at the memories and whipped back to the present, desperate to figure out what to do. He couldn't hide; these people had taken him in, they were going to help him. He quickly threw on some loose trousers and an ivory short-sleeved shirt, then laced his boots, cursing as he missed a hole, in too much of a hurry to fix it. He splashed some cold water on his face, ran it through his hair, and tossed open the door, pressing a finger to his temple to quiet the pounding blood rushing around up there. Kezia and Serafine stood before him, mirroring each other with their hands on their shapely hips and annoyed expressions.

"Well, are you ready to go yet? Took you long enough," Kezia teased, her cinnamon hair standing on end.

"I didn't know I needed to be ready. It's a bit early for people who like to sleep, you know, at night," Adam retorted sharply. "Where are we supposed to be going?"

"Training, silly. Arnon agreed it was important. I was right, as usual. I am rather brilliant," she said with a hint of a smile, eyes looking up and showing off her long eyelashes. Serafine rolled her eyes, not involving herself in the conversation.

"I didn't agree to training. I told you, I'm not really the physical type," Adam said, self-consciously crossing his arms over his chest.

"Everyone is the physical type if they try. You are tall; we just need to pack some muscle on there. You'll have to eat more. I saw you last night at the feast; you pick at food like a girl." Kezia poked at Adam's upper arm with an air of tough love.

"Ouch!" Adam jested as he grasped his heart and stumbled back dramatically. "I am willing to try, but just be warned, I am the least agile human alive. I am dangerously prone to tripping, sometimes over nothing. So, I imagine asking me to wield weapons might be risky for me and anyone else in the vicinity." His words dripped with self-deprecation, half joking, half serious.

Kezia and Serafine looked at each other and burst out laughing. Adam was getting the idea that was kind of their thing, but he found he didn't much mind.

"You are too much, Beanpole," said Kezia.

"What did you call me?" Adam laughed, finding theirs to be contagious.

"Beanpole. That's your name. Until you look less like one. Let's get a move on, people." Kezia spun around and started toward the sparring grounds. Serafine followed behind her, trailed by Adam and Zev. Kezia caught Adam's eye as he failed to not stare at Serafine's long chestnut hair sweeping across her shoulder blades in earnest. "Don't worry about her, she is a woman of few words. She doesn't really talk to anyone, except me of course. Don't take it personally!" Serafine shot a smirk back at Adam, and he knew he was in for a world of hurt with her.

I don't know how I feel about this. I like the idea of you being physically stronger and safer, but you are a klutz. These people are warriors; they are intense. I couldn't bear you getting hurt, Zev said into Adam's head.

Adam clutched his head, the wine still making it pound. *What a day to start training,* Adam thought.

"I'll be okay. These people won't hurt me; they just want to help. If it doesn't go well, we'll continue along the journey," Adam whispered to Zev.

Dawn had barely broken, and the orange glow gave way to a flood of steel-blue sky, foretelling of a storm to come. Adam stopped just short of where Kezia and Serafine stood at the edge of the massive sparring grounds. Some sort of chalk marked eight different squares on the ground. Within each square, a pair of warriors, men and women alike, charged at each other, battling fiercely. Around the squares stood many of the other villagers, some jumping in place, some delivering series of punches to the air, some running in circles around the entire training grounds. Beyond the eight squares was the shooting range: a long field with another line of chalk and, hundreds of yards away, red, yellow, blue, and white burlap targets. No one was currently using the range, but next to it, an unremitting woman threw axe after axe, striking another set of targets right in the center every time as she moved back and forth.

Adam was equally awed and terrified by their brute strength. He looked on as a pair of teenagers entered the square, likely near the age where they would go on their quest to find a soul-seal. They danced around each other with their fists locked tightly near their chins; one of them lunged for the other with a stiff uppercut to the jaw that Adam was sure would knock him over. The other one brushed it off as if it was nothing and delivered a blow equally as intense. They continued like that until time was called.

"We figured just observing for the first couple hours would be most helpful before we get you started. That is Edria," Kezia said with a tone of respect, pointing at a woman who was both beautiful and severe, currently locked in a sword battle with a man twice her size. "While Arnon generally runs the show around these parts, she leads warrior training. If we were to go to battle, she would lead us. Her name means 'mighty,' and while she has a gift of vast strength, she doesn't need magic to kick some tail."

Edria struck down the man she was sparring with and held her sword to his throat, drawing a drop of blood from his stubbled flesh. He immediately pled, "I give." She turned her back and stalked toward Adam, Kezia, and Serafine.

She had light-brown skin similar to Serafine's and Kezia's, dark-brown hair shorn close to her head, and piercing brown eyes. She was of average height, but lean muscle rippled under the black bra top and tight black pants she wore. As she folded her arms across her chest, looking Adam up and down, a striking impala trotted up next to her, claiming its place. The lithe, taupe antelope seemed to be posing to be admired, with its wide-set spiraled antlers and delicate facial markings.

When Edria finished observing, never breaking from a straight face, she reached out to take Adam's hand, and he hesitantly accepted, shaking it quickly before she pulled back.

"I am Edria; this is Flash. I hear you have no training," she said, getting directly to the point, no words minced.

"That's correct. Never found reason to," Adam responded.

"You were right; he is delusional," Edria said to Kezia. Then to Adam, she said, "Everyone needs training. Xhartana could strike at any time, and they will. You will observe for a short time, and then we will begin with the fundamentals, like I do with the young ones." With that, she strode away just as quickly as she had come.

Adam stood to the side as Kezia and Serafine took to the nearest square, dropping their weapons before entering. As he looked around, he realized some pairs were practicing hand-to-hand combat, while others wielded spears, daggers, swords, or large wooden sticks. That feeling of being so far in over his head that he was drowning was alive and well within him as he did as he was asked and observed. It was hard to focus on anything while Serafine was half dressed in front of him, her skin glistening with sweat as she easily darted out of Kezia's way time and time again. They laughed, even when one of their strikes landed or they were pinning each other to the cold, hard dirt. He had never found watching people beat each other up to be heartwarming before, but there was a first time for everything.

He slunk backward slowly, leaning against the wall behind him and into the shadows, hoping Edria would conveniently forget her plan to teach him the fundamentals. But after some time had passed and the blazing sun had risen higher above them, Edria came back over with a foreboding look on her face.

"First things first. You can't wear that to fight. The shirt, fine, but those baggy pants will catch on everything," Edria said.

"This is all I have. I wasn't planning on training, and I wouldn't have known what I needed even if I had," Adam said, exasperated.

"We'll have to dig something up for you when you begin sparring. For today, just roll them up to your knees so you don't trip over them," she demanded in a tone that had him reaching for his hems rather quickly. He rolled them up as requested, knowing how it probably looked. That was confirmed by Kezia and Serafine looking over at him with hands covering their mouths, pointing.

"All right, give me five laps to warm up," Edria ordered, signaling a circle in the air.

"You mean running?" Adam asked, eyebrows creeping closer to his hairline.

"Of course I mean running," she said, irritated.

"I don't really run unless I'm running from something," he joked.

"Well, I suggest you change that today." She took a step toward him, flexing her muscular frame, and that was enough impetus to at least try.

Feeling rather ridiculous in his boots and rolled-up pants, he jogged to the edge of the sparring squares and began to make his way around the circle. He was already well out of breath halfway through his first lap as Edria shouted after him to run faster. Zev had apparently decided to join him just to make him look bad and lapped him for the second time before Adam had completed his first loop. He was drawing quite a bit of unwanted attention—well, most attention was unwanted on his part. There was one exception, and the only attention she had paid him wasn't all that desirable.

By the time he rounded out his final lap, his feet were nearly dragging, his chest heaving, but he wasn't going to let these people see him fail. As he finished, he was desperate for water, bent over and clinging to his knees while Zev ran around him excitedly.

"Water's over there." Serafine deigned to give him a moment of attention, but it was useful information.

He made his way over to the pump, cupping his hands full of water a few times before he came close to catching his breath. He warily looked back over at his taskmaster, Edria, wondering what torture she had for him next before inching back over to her with his hands folded over his head. His head was pounding far worse than before, and his shins were on fire. Edria still hadn't moved a single muscle in her face other than when she spoke her commands, leaving him curious as to whether she ever did.

What came next made him long for lap running. Edria ran him through a series of basic exercises to test his strength and agility, as she did with young warriors beginning their training to determine their needs and abilities. He did his very best, which was honestly not much. He attempted to hop sideways through a series of ropes tied into patterns just off the ground, tripping and falling on his face more than once. His hands were raw from catching himself in the dirt, and his wrists throbbed. He writhed and fought to lift a large stone above his head, narrowly pulling his toes back before dropping it where they had been a millisecond before. Edria simply shook her head and issued challenge after challenge, leaving Adam shattered and shaking where he stood by the end. He honestly had no idea how he would even make it back to the guest cottage, as putting one foot in front of the other seemed unmanageable.

"You have much to learn, but you didn't give up. You hold the Jesimi spirit within you; we just have to break it free," Edria encouraged, which felt strange after nearly killing him. He was lifted by her words but had a feeling he wouldn't much like the breaking part.

"Hey, Beanpole, you weren't kidding. I think I saw you bite it ten times!" Kezia laughed. It wasn't filled with spite, however; that just seemed to be how these warriors related to each other. They fed off competition.

Adam casually laughed her off, noting to himself to refrain from laughing so his insides wouldn't fall out like it felt they would.

She clapped him on the shoulder. "At least you didn't run away. Not that you could have. You look like you need to be carried back!" She and Serafine, who had joined her, howled with laughter.

"So, you'll be back tomorrow at the break of dawn?" This time, Serafine issued the challenge casually, surveying her nails, not even making eye contact. The more serious counterpart to her best friend's goofiness.

"I suppose I'll be back if I don't drop dead in my sleep," Adam returned with a grimace.

He all but dragged himself back toward the cottage, deeply thankful the ground was flat; pain raged in his legs, which threatened to give right out from under him. He made it to the cottage and grabbed the wooden doorframe to propel himself over the threshold, then hauled himself to the bed and dropped onto it, steeped in the agony of so many muscles he hadn't known existed before today. He clawed his way to a seated position—also torture—and leaned over to loosen the laces of his boots and kick them off. He used his hands to pull his legs up onto the bed and lay there staring at the rounded ceiling of the tiny mud hut, endlessly grateful for the cloud bed, pondering what he had gotten himself into.

A short time later, a soft knock came at the door, and a female voice piped up to let him know she had brought him some food. The only thing that could have gotten him out of that bed was the promise of a full belly, and Zev stood grumbling near the door in agreement. Adam flopped off the bed, limped across the room, and opened the door to a sumptuous silver tray piled high with bread, fruit, nuts, olives, meat, and figs. The delicious scent drew him to bend and pick it up, with a serious groan as his back protested. He brought it in and managed to tug the door shut. He and Zev shared the delicacies, and even though he struggled to bring each bite to his lips, it was worth it. Once again, he fell asleep hard, fully clothed, with the tray of food next to him.

What felt like moments later, though it was a number of hours, he woke to "Beanpole, time to go!" As consciousness took root and the bliss of being asleep faded, the pain seared deeper. Even if he wanted to keep going, he didn't know if he possibly could.

"Come on, then! Second day is always the worst—well, maybe the third day, I dunno—but it'll get better eventually," Kezia called through the thin wooden door. He noticed for the first time that it had a design etched into it: a vivid rendering of a part of the desert that once was in Avaria and now lay on the island of Xhartana. He thought that must be where these warriors had come from before being exiled. How deep their roots ran; how much they missed a place that they had never been but that flowed through their veins as it did Adam's.

He hoisted himself up, gathering the strength from who knew where and wobbling as he stood, trying not to tip over, because he wasn't sure could get back up again if he fell. He dressed as quickly as his throbbing limbs would allow and walked to the door, creaking it open slowly. Kezia stood on the other side, holding something behind her back and giggling.

"Aren't you gonna ask what I brought you?" she blurted out.

"What did you bring me, Kezia?" Adam asked, playing along with only a mild eye roll.

She whipped something out from behind her back and shoved it into Adam's hands with force, causing him to stumble backward. She was like a child who didn't know their own strength as they barreled into you. He looked down and realized it was clothing and odd black shoes, similar to what the other warriors wore when they trained. He supposed anything would be better than the rolled-up pants that flapped in the wind and did, in fact, get caught on everything.

Adam flipped the door closed again in her face and peeled his clothes off slowly, then replaced them with the tighter-fitting sleeve-less shirt and stretchy pants, which stuck to places he didn't really want them to be sticking, both in black. He pulled on the new shoes, which covered his feet up to the ankle bone. He had never felt more uncomfortable mentally in clothing, but they were fairly breathable, and the shoes were much better than wearing leather boots to train in the heat. It might have been late autumn by this time, but there was still an unrelenting, dry heat during the day on the savanna.

He reopened the door to a perturbed Kezia, her arms crossed and her foot tapping, a judgmental scowl on her face. She looked him up and down, seemingly satisfied with the fit.

"Are you ready yet, Your Highness?" She feigned a bow.

"I don't think there is any way I could possibly be ready for the special form of torture your people have decided to inflict on me," Adam poked back at her.

"You big baby. You haven't seen anything yet." She winked and took off at a pace far too quick to be kept up with. But Adam and Zev knew exactly where their fate awaited them and marched off to Adam's doom.

It was just past dawn again, and the villagers were already sparring and training together when he arrived. This early rising thing was almost as tough to swallow as the physical training thing was. He moseyed over to where Serafine, Kezia, and Edria stood together. The way the morning sun bounced off Serafine's sharp cheekbones made her look like a regal statue, and he tried again not to stare. He marveled at how different these women were to the ones he'd grown up with, and even though they were the harbingers of his torment, he found he didn't mind. In a way, he was very inspired by their collective passion for ensuring the safety of their people to the best of their abilities.

"You came back." Edria didn't bother to turn toward him.

"Well, I didn't have anything better to do today," Adam joked as he stretched his arms as far above his head as he could muster.

"It won't get easier for a while. Are you sure you're up to the challenge?" she prodded, the others now looking on with vague interest.

"I committed, at least for some time, until I must continue my journey," Adam vowed, pressing a hand to his chest.

"All right, then, same thing as yesterday. You'll start with laps, and then we will work on getting you agile enough to even consider sparring or wielding a weapon. Let's see what you can do," Edria instructed, eliciting a deep groan from Adam.

Nevertheless, he figured out how to place one foot in front of the other, and he began running, about as fast as a snail, but running nonetheless. Zev joined him for moral support, and maybe a little bit because he found it funny. The rest of the day went about as poorly as it had the day before, but Adam wouldn't quit.

This routine grew painfully familiar over the next number of days. He was rudely awoken from his slumber by a far-too-perky Kezia, who was sometimes joined by Serafine (those times were his favorite, even though he didn't think he was making a great impression on her, warrior that she was). He dressed in the tight but surprisingly comfortable gear, dragged himself to the sparring grounds, ran, nearly died, and did a wild combination of exercises and agility training that Edria guided him through until he was nearly dying again. Then he dragged himself back to the guest house, ate a little, too tired to even talk to Zev, and fell asleep on the cloudlike bed. Rinse and repeat.

Eventually, Edria began to teach him various punching, kicking, and blocking combinations, talking him through the basics and getting him used to the motions. Though Edria's demeanor and expression never seemed to change in the slightest, she wasn't entirely unpleasant. Her imposing impala, Flash, was much the same and stood tall by her side.

Soon, Adam found himself waking naturally just before dawn, and he nearly shocked the life out of Kezia one morning when he swung the door open just before she knocked. He practiced the fight combinations when he was washing, eating, and sometimes just lying in bed, much to Zev's dismay. Sometimes Arnon would pull himself away from utterly annihilating any and all opponents in sword fighting to watch Adam's training for a moment, often providing words of encouragement, which were much appreciated.

Kezia had really grown on Adam, and her constant ribbing, though unfamiliar to him, did seem to make him want to try harder. And Serafine . . . Ugh, Serafine. Even her name was beautiful. He had never felt so drawn to someone, especially someone who barely acknowledged his existence, though he had caught her watching him curiously a time or two. That didn't seem to stop him from daydreaming like a silly teenager about her long, springy curls and her unending hazel eyes.

He thought of his mother often, knowing she would have had a good laugh at this whole situation.

After a few weeks, he felt ever so slightly less winded when he ran, and it was somewhat easier to lift the large stone over his head. These seemed like important life skills, especially if he wanted to do more than simply gather his people and actually fight Xhartana himself. It wasn't something he had ever considered, but watching these brave people, he wanted to. He recalled holding his mother's lifeless body, how helpless he had felt. He didn't want to feel like that again, not ever.

"It's time for your first sparring match," Edria announced one morning, running her hand over Flash's twisted antlers with a tenderness Adam didn't know she possessed. He went wide-eyed, clenching his teeth. Practicing fighting and punching was very different from actually fighting and punching. "Remember what I told you, and listen for me. I'll be beside the square, guiding you the entire time."

He'd come quite a long way in a short time; if he backed down now, he wasn't sure he could face these people, or himself. So, he sucked in a deep breath through his nose and stepped into the chalk square. Zev darted to his side with a stern and protective growl.

"It's okay, Zev. I have to do this," Adam said, hoping his words would also convince himself.

He couldn't help but think of the many people who left these squares bleeding and broken every day without complaint. He knew that they didn't use any healing elixirs, because the pain was apparently part of being a warrior. He shook out his arms and legs as he tried to prepare, and a man who was probably around his same age and the same height entered the square and faced him. The man was carved from steel; he was bare chested, and his skin had a sheen of sweat slicked across it already. His long hair was tied back with maroon fabric, which somehow made him look more intimidating.

"Fight!" Edria called out with no warning, and the well-sculpted man charged Adam.

Adam tried to recall absolutely anything Edria had taught him, but his mind was empty, save for the blinding panic from this man swinging his fists at him. He dodged the first rush, jumping to the side and raising his fists, mostly out of pure instinct to protect his face. He did notice that, blurred out in the background, a crowd had gathered to watch.

His opponent's fist thrust up under Adam's ribcage on his left flank, catching him unprepared. He doubled over and tried to protect himself from the man as he peppered Adam's shielding arms with fierce punches. Adam vaguely heard someone yelling in the background, but the pain shattered him; he was frozen.

"Come on, Adam! Keep your arms tucked to your sides, like we practiced. Protect your weak spots!" Edria screamed to try to get Adam to listen, but the pain and the panic clouded together to fog his vision and his hearing. "Hit back! Come on, left, right, left!" He heard the words as if they were coming from miles away and tried to gather his bearings.

His opponent danced on his feet, back and forth, trying to figure out a way pin Adam and end this, as if toying with his prey. Adam shook his head, and his vision cleared enough to try to attack, letting his left arm loose with a tight fist like he had been shown. He didn't make contact but tried again and hit the man's shoulder. This didn't faze him at all; he leaped forward and gave Adam a swift right hook to the ear, setting it to ringing, and Adam felt a trickle of what he feared was probably blood. He continued to protect his head and his middle, only striking a time or two more before his opponent swiped Adam's feet out from under him and his tall frame thundered to the ground. The man hopped on top of his chest, pinning him to the ground. Adam couldn't see straight enough to bother fighting at this point, wanting it to be over. He didn't hear anything besides high-pitched ringing and focused on the searing pain in his side and his head as he barely made out Kezia and Edria leaning over him.

"It was your first fight. No one does well," Kezia assured Adam as he lay wilting, but he could barely hear her and honestly didn't much care.

"Kezia, you're up next. Serafine, get Adam to the cottage and cleaned up, will you?" Edria ordered. Serafine was finishing a sparring match that she, of course, won, and she strolled over to Adam.

"Come, then, let's get up," she said, with about as much warmth and care as the dirt he lay upon.

She moved to where his head lay and slid her arms under his, easily standing him upright. He was incredibly dizzy and unstable, so she wove her arm under his and behind his back. With her strength, she was able to drag him back to the guest cottage and flop him onto the bed. While Adam felt his eyes glaze over from the pain and the head injury, she went to the washroom, wetting some towels and bringing them over. Serafine pulled his shirt over his head; he was aware enough to be glad she was the one tending to him, though he wished it were under different circumstances. She perched herself beside him on the bed, moving a displeased Storm from his roost at the base of her throat to the top of her shoulder so he didn't fall forward. Remaining aloof, she scrubbed the blood that had escaped from his ear and down his neck and chest. Her gaze lingered for a moment; the extra food and training had already begun to chisel themselves into somewhat defined pectoral muscles.

"We live by a warrior code, you know? We don't ever want to spill blood, but we have to sometimes to make sure we stay safe. We don't live to fight; we fight to live, and we never start a fight, but we always finish it . . ." Serafine trailed off uncertainly, as if she wasn't sure why she was sharing this.

"When I used my gift on your people, I heard those words over and over again. I get it, I do. I just don't seem to be cut out for the warrior life myself," Adam squeezed out between breaths.

Serafine cleaned his arms and face roughly as he tried hard not to wince. Once she was satisfied that all that was left on him were blossoming bruises, she grabbed the bloody towels and strode right out the door, leaving him lying there, broken. Zev whimpered at his side. Adam had thought that the pain from training was pretty bad, but he was pretty sure he had a broken rib, and that pain was only matched by the furious rhythm thrashing in his head. Moving was too painful, and when he heard someone leave food at the door, he couldn't bring himself to get up. That night, he was in and out of consciousness like a fever dream; he couldn't find peace for a moment as he questioned all his life choices up to this point.

As he saw the first whispers of light floating through the window, the wooden door to the cottage was thrust open, slamming against the dresser behind it, and in waltzed Kezia, like any other day, as if nothing had happened. Adam even found forming words too painful and just moaned at her.

"Well, isn't this just pathetic? You get beat up one time, and you can't move," she joked, moving to slug him in the shoulder but thinking better of it as she eyed him. Much of the tan skin covering his arms; one side of his face, ear, and neck; and his whole left side were covered with deep, scarlet bruising. She flinched. "That actually does look nasty. My first fight was even worse. I mean, I got in a bunch of shots too, but I did get pretty destroyed—broke my arm, a couple fingers, but I ended up fine. I learned quickly to not let anyone get in those kinds of jabs." She pointed at his side.

"Are you seriously telling me I need to get back on the horse right now? My ribs are broken, I'm fairly sure. Contrary to what you might believe about my solo adventure, I do not, in fact, have a death wish. I intend to keep all of body parts intact," Adam seethed through his teeth, breathing in spurts and grasping his side.

"Well, you get off easy today. Once a month, one of our best warriors is allowed to wield their gift. For a very short time, of course, without letting off too much power. Arnon feels it's important that they are familiar with using their gifts in combat situations," Kezia explained, twirling her cinnamon hair around her finger as if she wasn't a savage warrior. "It's Serafine's turn today." Her eyes glowed with pride for her friend.

Adam wished he had experienced that type of friendship, but he found people to be generally difficult. More difficult than Zev, at least. This girl was a perfect example; she drove him absolutely crazy, making fun of him and competing in a one-sided competition he wanted no part in, but he was growing fond of her. Like a little sister that he didn't really want.

"What about you? Do you get a turn?" Adam asked.

"I don't have a gift," she said matter-of-factly, shrugging her sculpted bronze shoulders. "My name means 'cinnamon'; it was inspired by my hair. Turns out I'm also pretty spicy, so it worked out." She giggled, dramatically fluffing her short, bright hair. Then she seized her bag off the floor and pulled out what appeared to be some bandages. She yanked Adam to a seated position by his very sore neck, despite his many qualms, and wrapped the gauze cotton material tightly around his injured core, sending lightning bolts of agony through him. Although, once she was finished, it did seem he could breathe a bit easier, at least shallow breaths.

"Thanks for nothing," he muttered under his breath, forcing a half smile.

"What was that, Beanpole? I couldn't hear you," she sang out, cupping her hand behind her ear. "Come on, we gotta go. We gotta get you a shirt. No one wants to see all that." She pretended to shield her eyes and went riffling through the dresser by the door, tossing stuff behind her, until she found a short-sleeved shirt.

"Hey, those are my things. Who's going to clean that mess up?" Adam complained, and she ignored him as she helped him pull the shirt over his head and stick his battered arms through.

He decided to leave the pants on from yesterday; it wasn't worth the hassle to change. She pulled him upright and marched him toward the door. As soon as they walked outside, King descended from the top of the grassy roof of another cottage to roost on Kezia's shoulder. Adam wanted to back away from the gigantic bird, but he needed Kezia's assistance to stay standing. He leaned his head away; birds were scary, especially ones with beaks bigger than his head. Zev glared at King apprehensively, seeming to agree with Adam's assessment.

They meandered up to the sparring grounds, but this time, everyone stood around the edges; no one was engaging in any kind of training. Adam leaned against the fence's tall wooden stakes, desperate for relief but not wanting to be seen as weak by sitting.

Arnon parted the crowd with Serafine at his back. They looked like the very picture of warriors that Adam had spent his life reading about in the scrolls: fearless and vicious opponents no one would want to face. Serafine wore something very similar to when he had first laid eyes on her, maroon leather crisscrossed over her chest, swooping around her neck, tying at its delicate nape. The short pants came up to right below her belly button, displaying the gently carved lines of her stomach that were feminine and alluring and showing off her muscular, long legs. As always, her two spears were fastened to her back. Her father matched her, wearing maroon leather studded with gold around the collar and waistband, and he had a sword sheathed at his hip. There was a strong family resemblance, both equally forbidding. Spike circled Arnon's feet, gnashing his teeth menacingly, while Storm rode on his soul-seal's shoulder, uninterested.

"You all know what today is. We look forward to this day every month when one of our best warriors wields their gift. We don't chance being caught by Xhartana more often than that, but we will ensure we are able to fight to the best of our ability when the time comes." Arnon's thunderous voice reverberated across the crowd. "It is my beloved daughter's turn, and she has selected me to spar with, which was a poor choice, as she well knows."

"You wish, old man. I have been waiting for this moment for a long while. My time has come to take you down," Serafine said with a smirk on her face.

They stood mere inches from each other, not breaking eye contact for a moment, before turning their backs and taking measured paces apart. They finally swung around to face each other. Serafine closed her eyes for a moment, centering herself to access her gift, raising her left palm. A red-orange symbol began to glow brighter and brighter, a circle with a flame in the middle. As Adam looked on, he thought he had never seen her look more beautiful as when her gift enveloped her.

She swiftly used both hands to pull her spears forward across her shoulders. She waved her left palm over the razor-sharp steel point of each spear, setting them alight, grasping the dark-wooden handles set with garnets. She gripped the spears firmly in her hands, and the irises of her eyes matched the blazing fire before her as she stared down her father.

Arnon unsheathed his well-crafted sword. The hilt was gold, of course—that was his kind of thing—the handle inlaid with giant rubies. These people loved their gold and shiny things, but Adam had learned the hard way not to tangle with them.

"Fight!" Edria shouted from the midst of the crowd, and the second the word tumbled from her lips, Serafine released the spears toward her father at a speed that was inhuman.

Apparently, they both were inhuman, because Arnon raised his sword and slashed it through the air, driving the spears onto the dirt beneath his feet and dampening their fire. A smile tugged at the corner of his mouth as his daughter dashed toward him, bellowing some kind of warrior call before she dodged right, then left, picking up her spears and effortlessly whirling around.

What played out between them was nothing less than a ferocious dance, doling out what would have been devastating blows to anyone else time after time. The sound of Arnon's unflinching sword clashing with the heads of Serafine's twin spears, which she managed to keep ablaze, was deafening. They appeared to be evenly matched; every time Arnon plunged his sword toward Serafine with the might of a dragon, she gracefully sidestepped it, striking back with unparalleled precision and speed. Every time Serafine leaped to tower over her much-taller father, driving her flaming spears down on him, he spun out of the way. Adam wasn't certain how long the match had been going, but he had even forgotten temporarily about his debilitating pain—it was so fascinating, beautiful even, in a dark way. Oddest of all, they seemed to be having a great deal of fun.

The ground was suddenly swallowed by stirring shadows, which was odd, considering there hadn't been a cloud in the sky. Macabre squawking echoed from above. Adam looked up, shielding his eyes, and though he couldn't make out what they were due to the glare from the sun, enormous creatures circled above their heads, more and more of them coming seemingly out of nowhere. They began to swoop down as Arnon barked orders and the villagers scattered in different directions. They all remained calm and focused on their tasks, most of them gathering their weapons and preparing for a fight, the way they had been trained to do. Arnon stood at Serafine's side, flanked by Edria, who suddenly had at least eight daggers strapped to her sides and legs—and those were just the ones Adam could see.

Arnon caught a glimpse of Adam out of the corner of his eye and shouted, "Adam! Stay out of the way; keep yourself safe!"

He stood paralyzed with fear, his back pressed tightly against the wooden fence, buried in shadows. Zev had moved in front of him to protect him from whatever these giant birds were. They began to dive down into the village, and Adam gasped aloud as he realized they had descended out of a dark fairy tale. They were griffins, half eagle and half lion. Upon their backs rode Xhartanian soldiers in their signature blood red, heavily clad with primitive weapons. Adam kicked himself for not offering the magical signature–blocking concoction to Serafine, assuming that was why they had been attacked.

He didn't know what to do; there were so many of them, and painful memories of past attacks by Xhartana, his mother's life ending in his arms, swirled in his mind. Even if he wanted to defy Arnon's wishes to stay out of the way, he had been in exactly one fight in his life, and he had been destroyed. He was entirely immobile, his feet cemented to the ground.

As the griffins came in for their landings, spreading their mighty dark-brown and patchy-white eagle wings, soldiers jumped from the height of their ghastly backs, striking mercilessly at the warriors of Kiritum, who stood at the ready. The griffins reared up on their powerful lion back legs and screeched as they attacked in time with the soldiers they seemed to serve. The soldier's weapons looked to be handmade: roughly hewn spears with long wooden handles and sawtooth iron tips tied on haphazardly with twine, shoddily crafted swords, rusted knives.

Savage voices pierced the air, roaring, "Praise the Deity! Praise the Deity!" with sadistic, remorseless expressions.

These soldiers wore different uniforms than the guards Adam had seen before, and he wondered if these attackers were higher up in the ranks. Xhartana was a fully militaristic society of religious extremists, and it was common knowledge that since the dark time, they had been brutal rulers over not just the realms but also over their own people, caring more about the ruin of the Jesimi people than about the success and safety of their own. Three men were in charge of their regime, and the rest fell into a hierarchy of men beneath, only earning their way up through number of kills. He watched as the people that he had been growing to care for fought against the nearly fifty men and the fifty beasts that were just as malicious, aiming for the throats of their foes.

"Sef, Zimra, Nuhro! Use your powers, now! It's time to take out the trash. Jesimi scum!" bellowed a brutish man, disgust rolling off his tongue with the words as he spit into the dirt that was stirred up many feet below his position, saddled atop his griffin a safe distance from the fight.

He was shrouded in different dress from his soldiers; he wore a full-length, blood-red robe piped with intricate silver detailing and a matching blood-red scarf covering his head and neck. He had medium-tan skin, a full beard, and dark features. Adam couldn't tell whether it was a reflection off his clothing or if his hooded eyes were truly deep red around the pupil. The man pursed his lips, as if he were displeased by being called away from something very important to come attack this village.

"Right away, Namtar, sir!" three soldiers responded, bowing their heads in reverence.

The three pushed back those they had been fighting, and other soldiers filled in for them. They stood together and raised their left palms. Adam slumped back deeper into the fence, as if he were melting into it. This had happened far too quickly, and his head spun at the sheer violence he was witnessing.

The soldier on the far left shot a massive wave of water from his palm, pushing it over Kiritum, upending many of the warriors. The Xhartanian soldiers grabbed on to the griffins and stayed upright, giving them the upper hand for a moment. Adam watched as the man tried to continue pushing water out, but the glow of the wave symbol on his hand dulled, flickering until it puttered out completely.

The next soldier, a look of pure malice seeping from him, waved his now-glowing hand to rip the wooden posts of the fence from the ground, the sharpened end hurtling through the air toward the warriors. Adam screamed a warning, hoping it would be enough. It was the least he could do. Zev hadn't budged from his place guarding Adam, though he bucked up and down, desperately wanting to jump into the fight but contracted to protect his soul-seal.

The warriors were mostly were able to dodge the fence posts, with only a few skinned arms and close calls. Adam's eyes desperately darted around, looking for Serafine and Kezia, and he found them fighting back-to-back with unimaginable strength.

The same soldier flicked his wrist again, uprooting another wave of posts and sending them out before the mustard glow of his symbol petered out. While most were able to duck out of the way, one of the wooden stakes plunged into the back of a Kiritum warrior who had just speared a Xhartanian soldier. Adam's heart shredded as he heard the shriek of horror from the person fighting by his side. The woman lay with her legs folded beneath her, eyes wide open. Heat bristled behind Adam's eyes, and he willed tears not to fall, not here, not now. He couldn't just stand here; he had to do something, and he looked around for something to grab that might help. He didn't want to get in the way, though, and his feet remained firmly planted beneath him, his mind and his body at odds.

The third Xhartanian lifted his palm up to the sky, and dark, threatening clouds loomed overhead. Lightning struck just outside the village, and a nauseatingly loud crack of thunder followed. The sky opened and emptied itself across the village. The Kiritum warriors fought with the fierceness of their ancestors, struggling to remain afoot as the dirt turned to thick, slippery mud. Though they numbered far higher and were led valiantly by Arnon and Edria and surrounded by their soul-seals, it was uncertain whether they would prevail.

Next to Edria, Flash charged forward in a repeated attempt to impale the enemy with her antlers. Spike, Arnon's trusty crocodile, snapped his jaws down on someone's legs with the might of El, dragging him to the ground and rolling him around at a dizzying speed before swiftly clamping down on his head.

Adam looked back to the three monsters who had been wielding magic, and their hands remained plain, without a glow. The storm the soldier had created broke apart, and sunlight streamed through once more. The man they had called Namtar screamed in fury—they had failed him. Adam knew that if magic was used for dark purposes, the glow and its magic would begin to fade and eventually disappear forever, but he had never seen it before. There were whispers of them enslaving Jesimi people to work the old platinum mine that sat beneath the surface of what was now Xhartana, constantly searching for platinum, the only substance that could recharge waning powers, but it had never been found since Avaria split off the continent. Or so he had thought, before the conversation he and Ben had overheard. At least they didn't seem to have access to it yet, judging by the display of waning powers today. You could only use platinum to recharge if there was lingering magic; if it was completely gone, there was no remedy. It was more proof the barbarians before him truly were the face of evil, though he didn't need any more than he already had.

A thought occurred to Adam as he remained fixed in his spot, and he shouted, "Arnon, use your gifts! They're already here!"

Arnon didn't seem to hear him from the thick of battle. Out of the corner of his eye, Adam caught a glimpse of fiery cinnamon hair as Kezia fired an onslaught of arrows at the soldiers, King circling the air above her before spiraling downward to dive-bomb them. He threw his fist in the air at his awesome friend and was hit with a wave of nausea and worry—he really cared.

Not a moment later, he saw a soldier sneaking up behind her with a rusty, serrated dagger. Adrenaline struck, and freed from his mental restraints, he tore across the sparring grounds that were now thick with mud and blood, screaming her name in warning, with Zev hot on his heels. Kezia whipped around just in time for the monster to plunge the dagger into her side, ripping it back out with a wicked smile and then licking the blood that trickled from the blade. She grasped her side and flashed Adam a look of bewilderment as blood began to spurt from the deep wound.

Adam caught her and lowered her gently to the ground just before she fell. He quickly surveyed the area, but they were too close to the enemy. He fought through the blinding pain, hoisted her into his arms, and carried her behind the nearest cottage to give them some cover as Zev paced, keeping his eyes on the enemy with a snarl.

King dove from the sky, landing gently next to Kezia's head and letting out a heartrending, nearly human cry for his soul-seal.

Adam ripped off his shirt and packed it tightly into the wound, trying to stop the bleeding. Kezia's usually warm complexion grew pale, and her eyes rolled back in her head as she fought to remain conscious.

"Stay with me, Kezia. Don't you dare think about going anywhere, you hear me? Stay with me. You have to stay awake!" Adam all but shouted at her, blinking away tears. He wished he were a healer more than anything. He didn't know what to do, so he kept trying to stem the flow of blood. She bled through his shirt, so he snatched a few items off a nearby clothesline and used all his might to press them to her wound. Her eyes fluttered; her grit was evident as she held on.

"Oh El, Kezia. What happened?" Serafine cried as she slid through the mud to Adam's side, Storm's beady black eyes popping out of his head as he tried to grip her collarbone.

"I couldn't get to her on time. I tried to warn her. I'm trying to stop the bleeding, but if we don't do something, she will bleed out before too long," Adam told her, trying to remain calm.

Serafine did some kind of special whistle, and mere moments later, Arnon charged around the corner, bloody sword in hand.

"Father, she's bleeding out. What do we do?" Serafine asked, the crushing pain etched into her face and voice.

"Oh, how I wish we had a healer. She needs help, and fast. Pack the wound really well and wrap her waist very tightly. You'll have to get away somehow. Get her to the River of Pyxis; its waters are healing. Take the horses, both of you. It's only a couple hours' ride, and just past the river is a village. My friend Tuvia will welcome you there," Arnon calmly instructed, his brow furrowed and his sword-free hand curled tightly into a fist.

"What about you? What about everyone else?" Serafine asked, her fierce loyalty to her people scored into her very being.

"We are mighty warriors, descended from mighty warriors. We are Jesimi; we always survive," Arnon vowed.

"I was trying to shout to you earlier to use your gifts. What more can they do to you? Fight them off!" Adam implored Arnon.

"Of course! Thank you, dear Adam. Go with El, my loves." He kissed his daughter's and Kezia's foreheads before rushing back into the heart of the battle with a cry that was dredged from the depths of the Jesimi collective soul.

They watched for a moment as Arnon struck down a soldier like a blade of grass before bobbing out of the way and slicing into another. Then he bellowed for the gifted warriors to unleash their powers. A rainbow of dazzling colors burst from the village into the sky above, humming with power, sowing into them seeds of hope.

Serafine easily lifted her best friend into her arms and wove in and out of the shadows, then quickly dipped into her house and came out with a large canteen of water, a shirt she tossed to the half-dressed Adam, and a bundle of bandages to temporarily stop the bleeding. Bandages just like Kezia had brought to Adam that very morning. He couldn't bring himself to acknowledge just how much he needed her to be okay. The guilt for not having done more sunk deeper under his skin, and he followed quietly as they made their way to the stable.

"Can you ride?" Serafine asked.

"I have a couple times. I'm sure I can figure it out," he responded.

"She'll ride with me. Just try to keep up." She gently put Kezia down in the wet hay, tossed aside the bloodied garments, packed the wound full, then wrapped the bandages around Kezia's waist tightly as Adam kept lookout. He then knelt at Kezia's side, brushing her hair out of her face, as Serafine led two great mares their way. She saddled them silently and said, "You're going to have to lift her to me," slipping her foot through the stirrup and hoisting her other leg across the chestnut mare.

Adam bent down, sucking in a breath as he braced for the pain, and lifted Kezia up once more, attempting to bring her high enough for Serafine to grab her. Thankfully, Serafine was strong; she reached down and was able to carefully lift her friend onto the saddle in front of her so she could monitor her bleeding. Serafine gestured to the white mare beside her, and Adam went to imitate her mounting technique. Clumsily, he missed the stirrup and dropped his foot back into the mud, then tried again, and he swore as he used everything he had left to lift himself up into the saddle. Serafine quietly clicked her tongue, gently grabbing the reins and pressing her foot to her mare's side. Adam followed suit, and they were trotting off. King raced overheard, hovering close to Serafine and Kezia.

"We'll have to go really fast now to get away before they notice and catch us. Keep a strong hold of those reins!" Serafine called out, a woman on a mission as she snapped the reins, and they broke into a full-speed gallop. "Kez, you're going to be okay. Just hold on; I've got you."

Adam did as he was asked, leaning forward in the saddle as they flew north across the savanna as fast as the horses would carry them. Zev matched pace with Adam's mare. Adam looked at Serafine, leaving her home under attack to save her best friend, and his hope for humanity began to knit itself back together. He wasn't much of praying man, but he uttered the Jesimi prayer for safety under his breath in the ancient tongue, figuring they seriously needed it.

Serafine, under her warrior façade, cracked like porcelain, all the pieces shattering to the ground, so one could never put them all back together again quite right. She had known loss with her mother and others; she beat its beckoning claws away with her spears and fists every day as she trained. She kept it all buried inside, and the only person allowed to see it all was dying in her arms. If she lost Kez, her other half who made her more palatable, she wouldn't be able to pretend anymore, to pretend she was fine, above emotion. Kezia was the reason people wanted to be around her, because she was part of a package deal with her whip-smart and funny best friend. Serafine was nothing without her. What good was being the fiercest warrior if that was your only merit? She gripped the reins with white knuckles as she looked down; a shell of a girl bobbed up and down in front of her in the saddle. Blood-soaked, but still so beautiful. Serafine silently begged and pleaded with Kezia, with El, anyone who might listen to spare her friend as she choked back sobs. Adam shot her an understanding half smile, and she momentarily allowed herself to be comforted by his presence riding by her side.

CHAPTER 15

The undulating terra-cotta hills blurred together as Serafine and Adam raced across the savanna to save their friend. They kept a brisk pace, knowing that time was running out for Kezia. Adam caught a glimpse of her face, tucked tight in front of Serafine, and all the color and light had drained away, leaving a nearly empty shell. He longed for her to call him Beanpole or make fun of his clothes and was reminded of why he tended to not let people get too close. If they get too close, it hurts too much when you lose them. His mother had always called him out on that, telling him that was no way to live life. She said it was the people around you who made life rich and worth living. He missed her so much it ached, and he knew she'd probably been right, but it had been easier to keep to himself and his scrolls. Until now.

Everything about his reality had changed; he was shaken to his core after having seen Xhartana carry out such a brutal attack in front of his very eyes. He had seen them before as a child but had always been told to hide. This had been different; the throbbing of his soul was deeper as he played the last thirty minutes back in his head. He had just stood there while these good people, his people, were violently attacked for no reason. He had never felt more helpless, more useless. He felt it so keenly, looking in front of him at Serafine's long, dark hair flowing freely in her wake as she charged forward gallantly.

She was everything he wasn't—brave and fearless—and he felt that he could never be worthy of someone like her.

Zev growled lightly at him as he raced alongside Adam's mare, sensing his pity party, and Adam brushed him off. He held the reins tightly with his left hand and his ribs with his right; the pain of riding at this pace was blinding.

"We're almost there. I can feel it in the wind," Serafine called over her shoulder, her husky voice painted with the burden she bore. Adam found himself wishing he could carry some of the burden that was clearly on her shoulders, but he couldn't find the right words, so he kept on in silence.

The wind had grown fiercer, and the air felt thicker. A family of warthogs crossed their path, and they slowed to a canter. Adam directed his mare closer to Serafine's side. The tall grasses that had been shades of brown as they rode past were now flush with color and filled with delicate white blossoms. Adam's white mare let out a whinny as they slowed further. Large, oddly bulbous trees with wispy branches swayed in the wind, lining their path as a wide river came into view. This river was different from the Copper River Adam had struggled to cross in the wood back on the Isle; it was a pure shade of indigo, and it flowed smoothly and calmly as it carved its way across the bleak savanna.

"Whoa!" Serafine guided her chestnut mare, gently threading her hands through her black mane as she came to a stop.

Adam guided his mare beside hers, and when she stopped, he dismounted as quickly as his body would let him before hobbling over to take Kezia from Serafine. She lowered her friend down, and Kezia's head bobbed and then fell limp.

Kezia was covered in blood; she had bled through the bandages. Serafine stuck two fingers onto her neck, listening for a pulse, and told Adam it was there but barely noticeable. Adam bent his knees, hoping to absorb her weight so he wouldn't drop her, and held her tightly to his chest, his stomach churning at how close to the edge she was.

Serafine hopped off her horse, took Kezia from Adam, and rushed to the edge of the water. There was a pool carved into the bank of the river and bathed in lush greenery and swaying cattails. Through the vivid water, Adam could see all the way to the bottom.

Serafine jumped in—clothes, shoes, and all—to kneel on the river rocks and submerge Kezia's body under the water completely, aside from her face. Adam jumped in after them, fully dressed, eager to help, and he reached out to stroke Kezia's colorless face, which contrasted starkly with the bright-indigo water that circled around her. Zev paced the edge of the mystical river, on guard.

"What can I do? How does this work?" Adam said desperately, unfamiliar with the magical healing river.

Serafine was the picture of calm as she held her friend steady beneath the water, though Adam could see the excruciating fear below her practiced expressions. "The more severe the injury, the longer it takes for the River of Pyxis to heal. As long as a person has blood pumping through their veins, the magic should work," she said, faltering only a little.

Considering Kezia was so close to death, he imagined it might take a while. They both metaphorically held their breath, waiting in the surprisingly warm water. He noticed the pool becoming a bit murky around Kezia and assumed it was all the blood seeping out, like spilled ink.

Water started to circle Kezia's body quicker, and it glimmered as watery ribbons of gold formed and wrapped themselves around Kezia's core, as if they were bandaging her. Adam and Serafine locked eyes for a moment, meeting in their desperation and hope, though it looked very different on each of them.

This couldn't possibly be real—sparkly indigo healing river water? Could it? Ivy had been real. Giant, evil griffins were real.

The golden glimmer from the water intensified, and Adam and Serafine both shielded their eyes. There was a sputter followed by a shallow chuckle, and they looked down at Kezia's face. The golden ribbons dissolved in the water, leaving it clear once again, and the warm, rosy color returned to Kezia's cheeks as she peeled her eyes open and chuckled again. Adam lunged for her, helping Serafine pull her up, all three of them grinning from the deepest parts of themselves.

"Something funny, Kez?" Serafine asked her, squeezing her to her chest and trying to brush off King, who was squawking and pecking at them excitedly.

"You two, fully clothed in this river, looking like somebody died," Kezia responded—her attitude seemed to have been returned as well. Adam snorted a laugh, allowing the relief he felt to allay his usual annoyance.

"You almost died!" Serafine shouted at her, still clutching her friend like she was never planning to let go.

"But I didn't; you two saved me," she said, trying to free herself from Serafine.

"How about a thanks, jerk. I didn't know if we would get you here on time," Serafine said, her stone mask starting to slip.

"Thanks, guys," Kezia murmured, punching their arms. Adam preemptively flinched, thinking it would be extremely painful, but it was just the normal level of painful. He poked around his side and his forearms, and the pain had disappeared.

"Hey, my ribs are fixed. My head isn't throbbing anymore!" Adam exclaimed.

"Um, healing river? I just came back from the dead, you know," Kezia said, gesturing to the unnatural water around them and rolling her eyes.

They all burst out laughing and kept laughing longer than usual from a mixture of relief and the fear of what awaited them back in Kiritum.

As they soaked, Serafine lifted her face toward the sun, with her eyes closed, slowly running a finger across the length of the scar that crossed her radiant face. Adam couldn't bring himself to look away, basking in her beauty and strength. Kezia gave him a side-eye as he admired her friend so openly.

Serafine opened her eyes and saw his expression. "I could have had it healed when it happened, but I chose not to. It's a part of me, a part of my story, who I have fought to become."

He simply nodded, fully accepting her as she was, admiring her deeply, not for the scar, but for how she had chosen to keep it. As Serafine really looked at Adam, seeing him clearly for the first time as the man who helped save her best friend, she realized how handsome he actually was. Vastly different to the warriors in Kiritum who had vied for her affections. The way the light struck him, warming his skin, glinting off his nearly black eyes and his thick, jet-black hair. The way he had no idea that he was handsome or what he could be capable of if he tried. The way stubble was pushing through along his suddenly very masculine-looking jaw.

The warm water was so soothing, they were hesitant to get out, but they figured they should get moving and trudged out of the shallow water. Now Adam understood why Arnon had wanted them to go to his friend Tuvia's village just across the river—they were soaked to their cores, and the chill of the late-autumn wind tore through them. As much as Serafine and Kezia wanted to race back home, they needed to dry off and eat first.

Serafine gracefully mounted her mare once again, and Kezia hopped up behind her. Adam found it much easier to move and breathe with mended ribs, and he got on more easily than before. They trotted down the grassy banks of the river, looking for a shallow place to ford it. They found one, and the chestnut mare leaped into the shallow water without so much as a splash. Adam's white horse was not quite as lucky, plunging her hooves into the water and receiving a face full of it in return.

Once across, they began looking for the village Arnon spoke of. They perked up as the wind carried the tantalizing scent of fresh-baked bread under their noses, and they followed it until they found themselves in front of a small village. This one didn't have any kind of barrier like Kiritum; it was tucked under a large hill covered in tall grass. They dismounted and led the horses around the outside of the village, which seemed to be a group of homes constructed of carved wood. As they rounded the corner, a small gathering of people came into view. A short, robust man with rosy skin and a large, white mustache noticed them and waddled their way.

"Hello, children. How might I be of service?" he asked in an accent thick with the ancient Jesimi language as he took in their drenched state. He wore a long black garment that covered him from his neck to his shiny black shoes. An intricately embroidered prayer shawl hung from his neck, and a shiny black hat sat atop his head. Looking around, Adam saw that the other men who had been gathered with him wore similar garments.

"I am the daughter of Arnon. We were attacked by Xhartana. My friend here was grievously wounded, and we had to get her to the River of Pyxis to be healed. Now that she has been healed, he sent us to you," Serafine explained as warmly as she was able to, even cracking a closed-mouth smile that didn't quite reach her eyes.

"Oh, how awful. I am so terribly sorry. I am Tuvia, son of Miriam. Your father and I have known each other for a very long time; he is a good man. You are welcome in Vleskov. We shall get you clothes to wear while we dry yours by the coals. My wife has been preparing a special meal for Nvakh, the Day of Rest. Join us," Tuvia commanded, shooing them forward into the village, with a surprisingly large leopard tortoise lumbering behind him. "We were just finishing up our study of the Great Scroll for the evening; you have perfect timing."

They passed the houses, the spaces between full of children shouting and playing as their exasperated mothers tried to wrangle them inside for the Day of Rest meal that they had spent the entire day preparing.

Tuvia led them to his modest home, where he pressed a kiss to his fingers and touched the mizzur that hung from the doorframe at an angle. He introduced them to his wife and four children, kissing each one on the head. Two of the children were grown up and preparing to marry. His wife was a delicate woman with a fair complexion, light-blue eyes, and graying straw-colored hair that peeked out from beneath a white hair wrap. She wore a high-necked, long-sleeved, floor-length blue dress that matched her eyes and was embellished with tiny white flowers. Tuvia's younger daughters wore different-colored versions of the same, while the sons wore similar black robes, prayer shawls, and hats to their father.

Tuvia took Adam behind a curtain and gave him a robe to wear, and his wife provided the women with dresses that were a bit tight for their curves, but they worked. Tuvia took their wet clothing and footwear over to the hearth, where coals still glowed from the fire that had raged there, and placed them in front of it to dry.

Adam fretted about his lack of piety, of spirituality, but he found he was met only with love and kindness. Tuvia's tortoise hobbled across the floor, as if trying to remain underfoot, as a warthog and a caracal raced around him, and his wife welcomed them to their table, which was now rather full, before rising to answer a knock at the door.

A young man, clad head to toe in black, with tight ringlets tumbling from beneath his top hat, entered nervously, tapping his fingers on his legs. He was introduced as the intended of one of the daughters, and Tuvia's wife shared every detail of their matchmaker story. Serafine and Kezia let out a collective "Aw!" as he made nervous eye contact with his bride-to-be, and her cheeks flushed red. He was seated across the table from the girl, as they could not make any physical contact before they wed; the looks bouncing between them made it clear that wasn't an easy task.

"Hey, it's like you and Tamir," Kezia threw out, looking at Serafine. All eyes landed on Serafine as she began to shift in her chair.

Kezia took the opportunity to explain, "She's betrothed as well. In our village, young warriors compete for their rank as the best of the best. The top-ranked warrior is considered most fit to marry Arnon's daughter, Serafine, because she is the strongest female warrior."

The full little home had fallen silent. This news was a blow to Adam's gut. She was to be married; it sunk in like a bag of rocks. Serafine's discomfort turned to fuming at her friend for bringing it up—her betrothal was clearly a sore spot she hadn't fully reckoned with. Adam had a million questions, but he did not have the right to ask any of them, so he shoved his hands together in his lap, his knuckles turning white, and plastered a fake half smile across his face.

Tuvia's wife said the Jesimi prayer while lighting the candles, covering her eyes. Then she said, "Let us eat!" breaking the painful silence, for which everyone seemed grateful.

Tuvia prayed over the wine and then the bread, breaking the beautifully braided loaves and passing them around before laying down the rest of the food, taking up every inch of the packed table and covering the white linen tablecloth embroidered with tiny blue flowers.

The bounty that lay before them was familiar to Adam, much of it similar to what he had eaten on the Day of Rest at home. Another meat meal, sans dairy: hearty stews full of meat and vegetables, brisket, fluffy potatoes. They all helped themselves, Adam, Serafine, and Kezia thanking their generous hosts endlessly as they were restored by the meal. Delicious apple cake followed, and they all but licked their plates, making sure they didn't miss a morsel.

As they ate, Tuvia and his family regaled them with tales of how they lived their lives in their modest little village on the savanna. Tuvia's wife was trying to convince them to stay for a while so Kezia and Serafine could go with her and the rest of the women and girls to the nearby hot springs while the men gathered to study the Great Scroll. They would have all liked to stay with this lovely family, but the longing to know what had happened in Kiritum after they had left was unyielding.

Before they took their leave, Adam decided to share a bit about his great journey to gather the twelve keys and their people. He also thought it pertinent to warn the kind people about the horrors they might face if Xhartana's new plans took shape.

Tuvia wove a thin black ribbon around his arm and then his head before facing north, toward Avaria, and bowing repeatedly, praying in the ancient Jesimi tongue. Tuvia asked Adam to wield his gift, so he did. Adam went through all the steps to protect his magical signature with the mixture and set his gift free within him, tapping into the community. He was honored with a barrage of visions of these people who so deeply loved El; they believed that Elia the Light Bringer would return from the bottom of their souls, and every action they took as a people was so full of love and intention toward that end. These kind people had been endlessly persecuted, like all other Jesimi, sometimes more for the intensity of their beliefs, and it only strengthened their steadfastness. It was deeply inspiring, and Adam found himself so grateful for this strange gift and wild journey he had been sent on.

"Thank you for allowing me the gift of learning about your people. While your struggles are your own, all Jesimi share the same dream: to be free and safe to be who we are. Your love, piety, and dedication have deeply inspired me," Adam shared as Tuvia looked on, blinking quickly as if holding back tears.

"You are the gift, Adam. El handpicked you to be the one to bring our people together once more and to rise up against those who wish us ill. Although it is our life's goal to follow the Great Scroll as closely as possible, it is written that we must protect our lives above all. We would never leave our village for any other reason or sway away from our prayers and studies, but we must do what we can for our people. We would be proud to give you our key for safekeeping, and when the time comes, you can count on us," Tuvia vowed solemnly.

The weight of his words hung in the air; his willingness to sacrifice a lifestyle that was so precise was deeply meaningful.

"I am honored. Thank you," Adam responded, placing his hand on his heart, touched by the people who didn't know him but were willing to pledge themselves to fight evil by his side. An evil that had tainted their peace for too long.

As they all said their goodbyes and Adam's group thanked their hosts for the hundredth time, Tuvia hurried over to Vleskov's Temple to grab the key. When he returned, he handed Adam an unassuming silver key with a lion soldered into the bow. Adam slid the fifth key onto the twine and embraced the stout man who had slid his way into Adam's heart in a few short hours.

As they left, Adam fell deep into his thoughts; he knew something had to change within him. He could never allow himself to be in the situation he had been in before, frozen in place as he watched his people fight, doing nothing. As they walked back toward their horses, his resolve was strengthened with each step. He would train harder, no matter how much it broke him, until the weakness and guilt he felt washing back and forth inside him with his meal were banished forever. He might not be a warrior like Tamir, but he would learn how to fight. When the time came to face Xhartana as a people, he would lead the charge, front and center. His eyes steeled over as he mounted the white mare, clicking his teeth and pressing his heel to her side gently, and he took off before Serafine and Kezia as they looked on in pleasant surprise. They caught up to him and galloped by his side, laughing as they raced toward Kiritum, blanketed by darkness.

Something changed in you, my friend, Zev said to Adam breathlessly as he bounded at his side.

"Everything changed, Zev," he responded, and pulled the reins tighter.

CHAPTER 16

"Whoa, girl, whoa!" Serafine called out to the chestnut mare as they closed in on Kiritum, just making out the shadows of the village from afar. They hopped off their horses so as not to make much sound when they approached, as they weren't certain it was safe yet.

They rounded what remained of the fence and silently entered the gate at the front, but they heard nothing, saw next to nothing, aside from the glow of a fire toward the back edge of the village. They quickly returned their mares to the stable and ensured the animals had ample food and water in their troughs before tiptoeing through the gloom toward the fire. Adam tripped over his own feet, catching himself on the wall of a mud hut just before falling, and Kezia snorted, quickly covering her face, trying not to laugh. Serafine glared at them as they proceeded.

"Who goes there?" Arnon barked.

"Father? It's just us," Serafine responded, and she flew across the sparring grounds into his arms. Adam surveyed the place, and though the mud had crusted over, traces of blood coated the ground. People and their soul-seals scurried around, trying to clean it up.

"Thank El; I have been so worried! Kez, my dear, you're all right," he sighed, pulling Kezia into his chest next to his daughter. Adam's heart squeezed again; how lucky they were to have each other.

"Jeez, I'm fine. You've been worried? We've been worried! What happened here? We've been dying to know," she said dramatically, withdrawing herself from his embrace, stroking King's wings as he stretched them from the flight he had just taken.

"It wasn't long after you left that we took the upper hand by wielding our magic, thanks to Adam. They didn't have any magic left, and the griffins seemed to grow uninterested in the fight. We were tearing them all asunder one by one before their leader—that coward who didn't even have the guts to face us himself—called them away, roaring a warning to not try anything again or they would hunt every last one of us. We've been dealing with the bodies for hours. We lost one of our own . . ." He trailed off, visibly trying to gather himself. Adam felt strongly that Arnon wasn't an emotional man, so this moment was all the more harrowing as his haunted eyes fixed upon them. "I suppose we have been careless, trying to exercise our gifts under their radar. I would never have endangered our people intentionally. But it was a valiant effort; I am so very proud."

"I will make sure to gather extra magical herbs when I am in the Forest of Rian, enough to send back plenty for you to make your own magical signature protectant," Adam promised, wanting to say so much more, how sorry he was, how much he wished he would have done more. That wouldn't change anything now, though; he had to be braver, and he would give everything he had to try.

"Thank you, dear Adam. I am glad you were able to help our Kezia; you're a good man." Arnon patted him on the back and Adam blushed, feeling undeserving.

All the same, it made him want to be the person Ben thought he could be, the person his mother thought he would be, same with this gentle warrior. So, he committed to becoming that man.

They sat the zayin for the incredible warrior they had lost; they ate, drank, danced, and celebrated life, but most of all, they trained harder. Adam woke up earlier, ran farther and faster, lifted heavier, practiced his fight combinations harder and quicker. He took every word of Edria's advice and put it to use. He fought any opponent, and every time he was knocked down, shattered, he used it forge himself anew. His feet grew quicker; the muscles across his arms and chest rippled under his skin. He remained lean, but his once-spindly legs grew thicker with sinewy muscle. The young women in the village certainly took notice as he began to occasionally win a sparring match, as he began to wield his dagger with finesse. Kezia endlessly teased him about the attention he was receiving, as any good friend would, their bond deepening. She even retired his Beanpole nickname, saying he had outgrown it, literally. Serafine watched with disdain from afar, though Adam couldn't be sure if it was pointed at him or his new following. He certainly didn't mind beautiful warrior women paying him heed, but there was only one woman who had him completely enraptured, and he could never have her.

As time went on and winter fell upon them, it became clear that it was time for Adam to continue his great journey; he still had many a key to collect. It pained him deeply, as he had grown fond of these people, more than fond of others in general. This would forever be the place that molded him from the strongest steel, altering his course for the rest of his life.

When he told Arnon he was leaving, Arnon responded, in true Arnon style, by demanding to throw him a goodbye feast, just as he had been welcomed many weeks before. As much as Adam didn't want to be the center of attention again, he wanted the chance to say goodbye to everyone and properly thank them for what they had meant to him.

This feast was just as extravagant as his welcome, if not more so. An enormous tent was erected near where the fence had been repaired to protect them from the bitter chill that had set in. Though it never snowed on the savanna, it always felt like it was just on the precipice.

Each morning, a blanket of thick frost coated the sandy dirt, melting into droplets as the first of the warriors awakened.

The tent was splashed with ruby and gold, the tables laden with ruby linens and golden plates, chalices, and utensils. Adam wore a highly decorative, ruby-red outfit marked with gold embellishments he had found on his bed earlier that morn. Serafine looked enchanting as she strutted across the tent, wearing a dress spun from the same material as what he wore. Kezia was at her side in a golden dress that clung to her curves.

"So, this is it, huh? You're just going to up and leave us now?" Kezia said, half joking, as she tried to jab him in the arm. He jumped out of the way just in time, though, having learned his lesson many times over.

"I must continue on; I've stayed too long already. I would never change it for anything. My time here has changed my life. *You* have changed my life," he said in return as they all took their seats at the table.

Arnon moved to stand, and everyone, dressed in their finest, fell into silence. "The time has come for our Adam to continue on his great journey and take his leave of us. He came to us pure of heart but altogether too gangly. He leaves as one of us, a Jesimi warrior, whom I will be proud to fight beside when the day comes." The warriors cheered. "We shall miss you, some of us more than others." He raised an eyebrow at Serafine and Kezia. "And now, as promised . . . our most sacred key is yours." Arnon slipped an ornate, gilded box with claw feet in front of Adam. All eyes fell on Adam once again as he sheepishly unfastened the latch and the lid creaked open. The gold box was lined with a luxurious ruby velvet, and in the center was the fanciest key Adam had ever beheld. He squinted as it threatened to blind him with its gleam. He very gently removed the key from its much-too-large box and admired it; it had been cast from the finest gold and adorned with several sparkling rubies. Adam rode the swell of pride that soared through him as he added the sixth key to his makeshift necklace, more certain than ever that the piece of twine was not the appropriate vessel to be holding the treasures of the Jesimi people.

"There are no words to express what this time in your home has meant to me. I may have been pure of heart, but I was weak. I had always thought enemies should be fought with the mind alone. Your trials, and mine, all Jesimi people's, illustrate how wrong I was. You motivated me to become tougher, stronger, more like you, and it's been a gift. Even the moments when Edria was making my life completely miserable." Adam laughed, smiling warmly at the woman he had befriended. He could have sworn the corners of her mouth turned up ever so slightly in return before flashing back to the cold, hard warrior she was. "Thank you, all of you. I look forward to the day we are reunited to take back our homeland. Next year reunited in Avaria!" He lifted his chalice of wine, a couple of drops sloshing over the rim, and everyone echoed him boisterously, clashing their drinks together.

"Wait!" Everyone froze as Kezia shoved back her chair and stood. "What if we go with you?" she asked with a straight face, cocking her head to the side and pulling up the back of Serafine's collar so she stood beside her. Serafine looked at her like she was crazy; everyone looked at her like she was crazy. "Listen, I know he's sort of stronger now, and he can kinda fight, but he's not us. He still has to cross Imiris, where the Marre people of Xhartana are from. If he was fated to take this great journey, he was fated to end up here and meet us. He needs to complete his journey safely and gather the other half of the keys and more Jesimi for the battle. He needs bodyguards, and we love an adventure! The guy did help save me," Kezia said convincingly. The silence hung over their heads as everyone was pondering how to find the right words to respond.

"Yes," Arnon quietly pronounced. "She is right. Xhartana will come again, whether we break their ridiculous laws or not. Our best hope of defeating them for good is Adam. If you want to go with him, I approve of it."

"Um, well. We have so much going on around here; it would be very inconvenient to leave," Serafine stuttered, trying to offer a half-hearted explanation as to her discomfort with the idea.

"Come on, Ser; we need an adventure. Clearly, our people are more than capable of handling themselves. We can train on the way—heck, I'll carry your nifty spears for you. We could see the other realms; we've always dreamt of this," Kezia argued, with stars in her eyes.

"If you are certain you'll be okay here, Father, I suppose we could go," Serafine said, not even half as enthused as her best friend. This had obviously stirred something buried deep within her; Adam could tell by the glint in her eyes that she was keen to figure out what it was. Adam didn't bother to hide his ear-to-ear grin.

"It's settled, then. You'll all six leave for Imiris in the morning. Tonight, we have much reason to celebrate!" Arnon clapped his hands, leaving it at that, and the villagers took that to heart and did what they did best: rose from the ashes of their pain and celebrated life, full of hope.

The next morning, Adam and Zev naturally rose with the break of dawn as it peeked through the tiny window in the mud hut that had become their home. He pulled on some thicker taupe pants that were not as roomy as they once had been and ran his fingers over the muscular slope of his abdomen, still surprised by the changes. He donned a black long-sleeved top and the black knit sweater he had worn to start this whole journey and quickly stuffed what was left out into his rucksack, then pulled the drawstring tight, fastened the flap, and hoisted it onto his back for the first time in a while, noticing how much lighter it felt, though it was fuller than it had been before. He had begun to grow comfortable with the glimmer of pride that was growing within him as he looked around the hut and made to exit. He would really miss that bed.

"Are you ready to go again?" he asked Zev.

More than ready. Zev prowled behind him, and both were more determined than ever.

They made their way to the entrance of the village, where the large majority of Kiritum stood to send them off. Kezia dashed up and shoved into him with glee. She wore tight-fitting black clothing, black boots, and a charcoal cloak and had a rust-colored leather rucksack that dwarfed her short stature on her back. She had her bow slung around her shoulder and her full quiver at the ready.

Serafine flipped her mahogany curls off her shoulders, draping them across the hefty bag that had been specially made to accommodate her spears, of which there were now six. She turned, showing her tight-fitting, midnight-blue clothing and an intricately embroidered pewter cloak.

Arnon strode over to Adam and placed a bundle of thick, soft black material in his hands. It was a cloak to stave off the cold, similar to the women's but without the floral details. Adam stripped off his rucksack, dropping it into the dirt unceremoniously, and flung the cloak around his shoulders, fastened the gold clasp at his neck, and whirled around to show it off.

"Thank you. You have done too much for me; you are too generous," Adam said, humbled once again.

"You deserve it; you are doing so much for us. Don't lose track of how far you've come. You are brilliant *and* strong. I wish you a safe and successful journey until we meet again. Watch out for my girls." Arnon warmly embraced Adam, smacking him on the back before turning to the others.

"My girls. I am so proud of you both. There is no one I would trust more with the future of the Jesimi people. Now, go forth into the realms, but come home safely." Arnon kissed Kezia on the forehead and pulled his daughter close to his chest, resting his chin on her head for a moment and closing his eyes, soaking up the love between them.

Tamir lurked around the edge of the crowd, trying to catch Serafine's attention, his expression showing just how furious he was at the present arrangement. Adam couldn't help but smirk.

The three of them with King, Storm, and Zev in tow started off, shouting goodbyes and waving furiously until Kiritum fell from view. They walked side by side toward the border of the Imiris Tundra, with intensity and purpose driving their every step. Adam felt renewed, strengthened in his resolve to complete this epic journey, even more so now that he wasn't alone.

Kezia beamed from deep within, like a child with a new toy. Serafine's brow was furrowed as complex emotions stirred in her, part of her excited for what lay ahead, the other part confused about the odd man they had decided to cross the realms with. He had more nerve than she had expected; that had been clear since they had returned from the River of Pyxis. He represented the opposite of the life she had expected for herself, and that made her endlessly uncomfortable, but also something else she hadn't yet identified.

They had checked his map of the continent and the enchanted bronze compass. Serafine and Kezia had heard rumblings about some of the dangers that Imiris possessed, so they suggested they skirt across the north side of the realm, then make their way through the Kokhav Valley and into the Forest of Rian. Adam readily agreed, not wanting to face unnecessary dangers. Imiris was the original home of the Marre people, some of whom had become radical and dangerous in their ideology, though many didn't share their tyrannical views. Xhartana maintained an active presence across Imiris more than the other realms because of their connection to that land.

They kept walking. King circled overhead, casting huge shadows in the wake of his immense wingspan. Zev strolled between Kezia and Adam, hoping for snacks from both of them, as he had bonded quite a bit with Kezia. Storm napped on Serafine's collarbone, his body tucked warmly under her shirt, as his shiny black head with red orange spots stuck out. What an odd team they made, Adam thought as he scanned them over, traversing the open plains. But he was relieved to be part of a team made up of more than just him and his wolf. Zev had told him the night before that he wasn't thrilled to be in King's company, as the large bird unnerved him, but it was more than worth it for companionship.

They sheltered for the first night from the beating of a winter rainstorm. Sheets of frigid water drove into them, freezing the hair on their heads, forcing them to erect their tent quickly. Once they had warmed, they laughed and ate the plentiful food that Arnon had sent from the feast the night before. They ate like kings and queens under that soaked tent in the muddy savanna.

It was only a couple days' journey before the temperature dropped significantly; any traces of the tall grasses and living soil of the savanna vanished, replaced by gray, jagged terrain dotted with sharp, volcanic-looking rocks covered in moss. In a similar way to the rainforest, but tens of degrees colder, water clung to the air, fogging their path as they forged ahead. Adam was very glad he'd listened to the women and that they were only crossing the top of this realm; it was eerily foreboding. The fog prevented them from seeing any potential dangers ahead, forcing them to move at a glacial pace. It was also one of the largest realms, spanning nearly the entire southern part of the continent before its rocky landscape plunged into the southern Sea of Tehom.

The days passed quickly, thanks to good company, no matter how deeply the chill nestled in their bones. Kezia and Adam heckled each other constantly as Serafine pretended to disapprove, but she always ended up laughing just as hard. Adam hoped he wasn't imagining that Serafine had started actually looking at him and even speaking to him directly. He constantly had to remind himself she was betrothed, no matter how bewitching her presence was and how much he longed to take her hand as her arms swung back and forth next to his.

One day was particularly cold, and their breath froze in the air as soon as it was expelled. The scenery hadn't changed in the few days since they'd crossed into Imiris, not one bit. They rubbed their hands together for warmth and hoped the next place would be a little warmer.

As they walked along through the murky, frosted air, Adam trying to step carefully to avoid tripping, the ground suddenly gave way beneath them. They screamed as they plummeted about twenty feet before hitting cold, hard earth below. The wind was knocked from their lungs as they landed flat on their backs, the massive fall only broken by their rucksacks. Serafine swore louder than a sailor in a sea storm as she reached for her ankle. She'd twisted it, and it was already beginning to swell. Zev, thankfully, had landed on his feet like a cat.

"What the hell! What is this?" Kezia cried out as she winced, standing and running her hands along the ragged earthen walls that surrounded them before turning to tend to Serafine.

"It must be some kind of trap. Usually, I can see a trap coming, but this one was very clever, plus that damned fog. We could have died, we fell so far." Serafine cursed under her breath as she stripped a bandage from her pack and shirked any attempt to help her bandage her ankle. "It's not broken. I'm fine; leave me be."

Adam groaned as he stood, fairly sure he had bruised his tailbone when he'd landed, and ran his hand across his backside.

"You think we can climb out of here somehow? How are we going to get Ser out?" Adam asked as Kezia tried to dig into the walls of their prison and feel out rocks they could use to climb. She couldn't get more than a few feet off the ground before crashing back down, as the walls were reinforced by rock that had been shaved down to prevent exactly what she was attempting to do.

Not the type to give up, she kept trying as Serafine struggled with her bandage and the more practical Adam sat back down beside Zev, leaning to one side to take the pressure off his tailbone, and waited. The small span of sky above them began to blacken with dusk.

Adam cried out as what appeared to be a single head popped out over the edge, though he could barely make it out from so far down in the dark, damp hole in the earth. Kezia ripped her bow off and strung up an arrow at the same time as Serafine drew two spears from her back.

A female voice echoed off the walls down to them. "What do we have here?"

"Let us out this instant. You could have killed us!" Serafine shouted.

"There is a reason I have this trap set: Most of the people or animals crossing Imiris mean me harm. Why should I release you?" the woman called, her voice brimming with suspicion.

"We are simply trying to cross this hellscape to get to the Forest of Rian. You will let us out now," Serafine demanded, stomping her good foot on the hard-packed ground before collapsing against the wall.

Serafine's words went unanswered for some time as she fumed. Kezia kept searching for a way to gain purchase on the wall.

Unexpectedly, a giant wooden ladder pierced the center of the hole, just missing Adam's feet as he jumped backward, hitting the wall.

"Great, a ladder. And how are we supposed to get Zev out of here?" Adam asked, and Zev let out a little whimper. Zev was very large, even for a wolf, and they all deliberated how to get him up the ladder. Serafine brushed off further attempts to help her, deciding to limp one-footed to the top and check to see if it was safe up there. Once she'd made it, she called down for the rest of them to follow.

Kezia shimmied up the ladder backward, holding on to Zev's front haunches while Adam supported his significant weight from behind. Zev climbed one rung at a time with his paws, his weight balanced by his people. It took quite some time, but they finally popped out of the top of hole just as the sun sank beneath the mossy, gray horizon.

Serafine glowered at the woman who stood casually near the edge. "Are you crazy, digging a hole like that? I wrecked my ankle!"

"Like I said, you were not my target. Imiris is full of dark people and dark creatures. I have to protect my home and my family," the woman explained, lifting both hands up. She was rather tall and had light-brown skin with an olive undertone and a round face scored with dark-brown eyes. She wore a full-length white robe that covered her from her neck to her slipper-clad toes, and her hair was completely covered, wrapped in a white scarf. She bared a narrow smile, as she seemed to be waiting to see what they were going to do. Serafine seemed to warm slightly to the notion of protecting one's family, and her shoulders dropped the slightest bit.

"Since it's dark, is it all right if we make camp here for the night before we get back on our way?" Adam asked.

"Why don't you come stay with my family? I know you can't see it from here, but all of our homes and buildings in Imiris are underground for safety and warmth," she offered kindly.

Serafine's, Kezia's, and Adam's eyes darted back and forth among themselves as they wondered whether to trust the woman who had just trapped them twenty feet underground. The cold won out, and they silently agreed to go with the woman and hope for the best.

"You may call me Dalila," she said, the words floating off her tongue in the most ethereal way.

They followed her a matter of feet before she warned them to watch their step, and Kezia muttered a joke about how that would have been nice before they fell. Dalila pointed out a very narrow staircase carved into earth; each step was an uneven, moss-covered black rock. Serafine kept swearing as she hobbled along. They squeezed after the woman down the tight, nearly vertical entrance, and when they reached the bottom, Kezia forcing Serafine to let her help, their jaws slackened as they beheld the subterranean home that lay behind the round wooden door Dalila held open. They stepped in and looked around in awe as the warmth and coziness enveloped them, drawing them in further.

The home was etched out of the earth itself. Gray and black stone walls with intricate carvings jutted up around them, meeting in a circular shape above their heads, and the space was full of light from a fire roaring in the hearth. A soft blanket of moss graced the floor beneath their feet, and Dalila waved them inward toward a tiny kitchen, where a man and a woman sat on a bench carved from the wall.

"Welcome to our home. This is my husband, Rafi. That is our dear friend, Cora." Both people stood to shake hands. "They fell into our trap accidentally, so I thought we owed them some hospitality. Let's get you some ice for now, and we know a healer nearby. We'll take you in the morning." Her cheeks flooded with rosy red.

"We are always happy to have guests. I am guessing you are Jesimi, by your soul-seals?" Rafi said. Adam, Serafine, and Kezia all looked at each other again, unsure of whether to answer. The Marre people tended to have unfavorable views of the Jesimi, in their experience. They were fairly certain that these people were Marre as well, except for this Cora, maybe. Rafi sensed their hesitation and continued. "All are welcome here; we do not judge people with differing beliefs, unlike those who persecute and abuse you. You are safe here."

"Thank you. Yes, we are Jesimi," Adam responded. I am on a great journey across the continent to use my gift to gather our people, rise up against Xhartana, and reclaim our freedom and our homeland." He sighed with relief, hoping it wasn't a mistake to be so naturally trusting.

"Well, that is a noble undertaking and one we can stand behind. Though we are Marre, we rebuke the actions of those monsters on Xhartana acting in the name of our beliefs. We are horrified by them and their hatred of your people, not to mention their treatment of their very own people. They often manage to patrol these parts, since we are right on the edge of the city. That's one reason for our trap before you can get to the entrance to our home," Rafi explained. He was rather tall and broad, and he had a thick, dark-brown beard and penetrating gray eyes. His head was covered with a white wrap similar to his wife's.

"I'm Cora Rose Yarrow. Are you looking for only Jesimi support or other people who may become your allies as well?" Cora piped in timidly, her voice high-pitched, like a field mouse's.

"Well, we are attempting to visit many Jesimi villages across the realms to gather the twelve enchanted keys, but I have encountered many non-Jesimi people who plan to join us. Xhartana is evil; they may hate us the most, but they oppress all people who don't share their extreme beliefs. We would be proud to have any righteous support," Adam said, Serafine looking at him in a new way that made him shift his stance.

She couldn't help but be impressed by him when he spoke with such passion, such kindness. He was so much gentler than the men she had been raised by and with. She had thought that to be weakness, but maybe she had been wrong; she pursed her lips at the thought.

"I only ask because I am on the run from Pax," Cora whispered, and they all whipped around to look at her in shock. Pax was very mysterious; very few people knew anything about it. Nothing but rumors ever made their way off of the shores positioned between Xhartana and the Isle of Ori, all of which had been Avaria before the dark time. "I was very lucky to escape; as far as I know, no one had ever succeeded before me, and few had ever tried." She shuddered as the words came out.

She was a petite, bony girl with overly large blue eyes that made her appear doll-like, pale-pink skin, and waves of fading lavender hair that tumbled nearly to her waist. She wore a modest white dress that buttoned up to her neck and fell to the floor with a delicate trim. She attempted a feeble smile, but Adam had to wonder what she had been through to need to escape—what she had seen.

"Rafi was trading in Zokhara and saw her wandering aimlessly, and he offered to help her. She wasn't well, so he brought her to me. We've been working to make sure she feels safe again and grounded. No pun intended." She gestured around her.

"They brought me back to life. I'm so lucky Rafi found me. It's been so healing to finally be free. Pax may be very different from Xhartana, but they are equally dangerous; that's probably how they ended up teaming up during the dark time to take over," Cora said, ghosts dancing in her eyes.

"Let's all have something to eat. You've had quite the scare, thanks to me," Dalila said with an apologetic expression, and she waved for them to follow her.

There was another massive, round wooden door at the far end of the living space. She pushed it open, and beyond it were endless rows of greenery in long metal planters or in stone boxes embedded into the sides of the walls. Water flowed through copper tubes above their heads, releasing a steady spray of mist atop the plants, and the air was ripe with fertilizer and damp, thick heat. Who knew an underground greenhouse existed? They were fascinated; even Serafine was temporarily distracted from her bitter anger over her injury.

"This is amazing," Kezia said as she walked through the rows of plants, brushing her fingers across the tops.

"We do all of our farming beneath the earth here, as above ground is too unforgiving; it could never yield crops. We have figured out how to grow our own food, and we are mostly self-sufficient. Like I said, Rafi does travel to trade sometimes to get other goods we need," Dalila explained, casually tending to her plants as she moved through the rows, whispering to them.

At the back end of the greenhouse, in a separate space, a large circular bench was carved from the stone walls, its cracks filled with moss. There was a dark-wooden table that seemed carefully designed to fit it, and Rafi encouraged everyone to sit. They all slid in around the bench, and Dalila disappeared and reappeared with tea and dark bread flecked with seeds and berries. They talked while they snacked and drank their tea before Dalila slid a heaping platter of food in front of them. There was a different kind of round, puffy bread next to skewers of succulent meat and spicy vegetables.

Once they'd had their fill, she brought out a thin pastry filled with soft cheese and soaked in a sweet syrup. Adam had one and licked his fingers, fully delighted with the situation, but Kezia and Serafine skipped the dessert so as not to mix dairy and meat.

They were all struggling to stay awake after dessert. Dalila noticed and giggled, then led them to their sleeping quarters. Kezia and Serafine would share with Cora, and Adam would sleep on a make-shift bed on the mossy floor of the ethereal living space.

Kezia and Serafine followed Cora to her room, which should have felt constricting and cold, as it was clearly carved out of rock, but the intricate carvings of animals, flowers, and people seemed to be almost moving, coming to life. The thick, mossy floor was so soft under their feet. Cora made a huge nest of blankets and pillows on the floor for herself, insisting the girls take her bed, which was also carved from the gray stone, with a mattress of thick, cotton-like material on top of it. It was so comfortable, both of them started to snore a little before long. Cora snickered and blew out the candle illuminating her little den, bursting with hope for the first time in a long time.

Adam bid their hosts good night as he rolled up in his little cocoon, bundled up with Zev, grateful for how warm and comforting this home beneath the earth was. He was getting to the point where he wasn't surprised by much anymore, but it wasn't any less exciting. Though he fell asleep easily, his dreams turned to nightmares, Namtar's punishing eyes circled in blood haunting him from atop his mighty griffin. This same scene disturbed them all but, in equal measure, drove them forward with a shared, fervent purpose.

CHAPTER 17

Adam and Zev woke to an outpouring of giggles that filled the eerie stillness beneath the surface of the realms. They looked up, and Cora, Serafine, and Kezia stood over them, covering their mouths and laughing hysterically, as thick as thieves. Adam realized that in the night, he and Zev had gotten all tangled up in the bedding, and the scene was pretty silly to behold. He chuckled, shoving Zev off of him and pushing his hair back to try to get back any semblance of appearing unflustered. He put his hand back to casually prop himself up, and it slid across the mossy surface, causing him to tumble onto his back. This sent the women over the edge, howling and gasping for air as Adam's cheeks turned scarlet and his lips grew thin.

Dalila and Rafi came into the room to see what the hubbub was about and, much to Adam's dismay, joined in when Kezia was kind enough to retell the story in great detail for them through her tears. As annoyed as Adam was, Cora looked different today, less like glass that was about to shatter into a million pieces. Through his embarrassment, he swelled with pride in his friends for making Cora feel that way.

They all shuffled into the small, plant-saturated stone kitchen and shoved in around the table there for delicious coffee and breakfast. Kezia chattered nonstop, and Serafine rolled her eyes at her so hard and so many times, Adam thought they really might stick, as his mother had warned. Cora watched them with fascination and just a hint of melancholy, as if looking at the life she could have had if she hadn't been born on Pax.

They really couldn't afford to stay, though Adam found it harder and harder to leave each place. They still had to stop at a healer for Serafine's ankle; she couldn't complete the journey like this.

As he started to remind them it was time to go, the lavender-haired wisp of a girl cried out awkwardly, "Wait! I was thinking, well, I was wondering if maybe there was any way it might be possibly possible, I mean, if you would consider, maybe, letting me come with you?"

She'd rushed through the last part, and they had to ask her to repeat it three times before they heard her. They all paused, taking her surprising request in.

"I love it here, I mean, Dalila, Rafi, you gave me life again. I mean, blasting banshees, I was a shell of a girl when you found me. But, but, if I stay, I'm afraid I'll never get the courage to leave. And you three, you three are so brave, and I want to be brave too. I want my people to be free, if there is a chance of that happening. Xhartana has to fall. See, we have the same goal. I mean, I totally understand if you don't want me to come with you; I would totally, completely get that." And with that, Cora started weeping, throwing herself into Dalila's welcoming arms as the woman brushed a hand over Cora's long hair.

Serafine, Kezia, and Adam looked at each other silently, trying to decide what to do. Serafine and Kezia clearly had taken to Cora, but how would she affect their journey? She was another person they would have to protect. Adam was overwhelmed at the thought of being surrounded by so many women, and Cora seemed like a bit of a loose cannon, if he was honest. On the other hand, who was he to turn away an ally? Someone who had suffered at the hands of the oppressive regime of Pax that had worked with Xhartana to take over Avaria during the dark time and was similarly evil.

He had always been surrounded by strong women, and as he looked at each of them—the incredibly fierce Serafine, the funny and loyal Kezia, and this waiflike girl who had been the first to ever escape Pax—he had his answer. The other two had clearly come to the same conclusion, as they nodded to each other and went to hug Cora.

"We are in no position to turn away allies who share our mission to free the Jesimi people—all people, from all kinds of tyranny. We must tell you, this great journey has been fraught with danger, and it is harsh and cold out there. But if you are up for an adventure, you are more than welcome to join us," Adam said, patting Cora on the shoulder awkwardly, sending her into further waves of sobs. He sincerely hoped they wouldn't regret this. "Let's get you packed up, and we'll be on our way, then. Time is running thin, and we still have much to accomplish."

"Come on, girl, we'll help you pack up and get ready. We'll have all kinds of fun. Maybe we can even teach you to fight like we taught Adam, put some meat on those bones," Kezia said as she gripped Cora's thin upper arm. She put her arm around the frail girl, and they wandered toward her quarters, with Serafine shuffling behind. Dalila pushed back tears as she rushed off into the greenhouse to collect some food to send with them.

Rafi shifted in his seat. "She's strong, you know. When I found her, she was so confused. Those tyrants in Pax really did a number on her. She had no education whatsoever; they are only taught the propaganda that they fill their heads with to keep them in line. She may be naive, but she has fire in her. This will be good for her and good for all of you. We will miss her, though; we'll look forward to reuniting when the time comes, and we'll stand by your side in your righteous battle. Dalila holds a special power; she is able to cast an illusion over herself or someone else to make them appear differently. Never know when that might come in handy. The healer we are taking you to is Jesimi; she works from an underground marketplace with all kinds of makers and healers and preservers. She may have an idea where this key you're looking for might be. It's really the only place Jesimi live in Imiris; this far north is a bit safer," Rafi shared openly.

"Thank you, Rafi. You should know as well, I overheard some Xhartanian guards saying they finally found platinum, and they have big plans to exert control over the remainder of the continent, wiping out the Jesimi people. Likely wiping out any non-Xhartanian people."

"There have been rumblings, and I'd wondered. You have good timing. You can do this; make sure they don't succeed," Rafi encouraged.

They firmly shook hands, and Adam wished so very deeply that more people were like Rafi and Dalila. He deeply understood the hatred Xhartana had for the Jesimi people, but it all seemed so unnecessary when they coexisted so peacefully with Marre people like these.

Adam got himself dressed and packed quickly, soaking up the last of the cozy warmth of the home, flinging on his cloak as he and Zev impatiently waited for the women. Eventually they emerged, Serafine and Kezia in their usual travel garb and Cora clad in a thick gray tunic and black trousers. Dalila rushed over to her with charcoal boots and a warm, woolen coat of hers and helped bundle her up. She yanked open Cora's supple russet-leather satchel and stuffed in a bunch of food she had just plucked from the greenhouse. And when Dalila couldn't find anything left to pick at, she smashed Cora to her chest, tears making their break down her face, before leading them all out.

They exited through the large, round wooden door and wound up the incredibly narrow, slick rock staircase. Adam went behind Serafine, not allowing her an out from his assistance as he boosted her up.

They shared a collective shiver as the freezing air settled into their lungs once again. It was midmorning, though the thick, near-constant cloud cover and fog made it almost impossible to tell.

"It's not far, but stick close to us," Dalila informed, her dark features becoming obscured in the weather.

They hadn't been walking across the treacherous landscape for long before Rafi signaled for them to slow, and he dissolved into the belly of the earth. Another staircase. They each followed him down,

Dalila taking up the tail. Adam half expected something similar to Dalila and Rafi's cozy home, but they descended into a bustling marketplace, seemingly in an underground city. Marre people and Jesimi people alike shouted and shoved past, and the low ceiling and dim light made Adam, Serafine, and Kezia hesitant to plunge into the hectic crowd.

Dalila gestured for them to follow Rafi, and they did, bumping up against people who were bartering and haggling for leather goods and handcrafted silk garments. Kezia and Cora were distracted by a jewelry stand before Adam dragged them away. Piles of colorful spices with scents to match adorned endless tables.

Rafi vanished between the booths, and they followed him into a small room that smelled of the loam surrounding them and the bevy of herbs and plants lined up along a wall. Only a few candles lit the place, leaving it spooky and dim, and all of them and their menagerie scarcely fit inside. Along another wall, iron vessels shaped like cauldrons brewed a mix of scintillating and repulsive solutions, and up against the third wall, a rotting wooden desk was a mess of parchment, quills, and ink. A tiny woman, shorter than Kezia, flew through the door into their midst.

"What have we here?" the woman croaked, her spindly, wrinkled fingers pointing to the uninvited guests.

"Arashel, we have come to seek your expertise. Our friend injured her ankle. We know there aren't any better healers with or without a gift than you," Dalila said, clearly stroking the ancient woman's ego.

"You need not flatter me, child. I shall heal any who are able to pay, simple as that." Arashel fixed her beady black eyes on each of them before turning to tend to her brews.

"I can pay," Adam said, unsure whether they should be afraid of this witchy woman. She turned at the words, her thin, timeworn lips turning up at the edges.

"Very well. Be seated, girl, and quickly. I haven't all day." Arashel could barely reach Serafine's shoulders but shoved her into a small wooden chair, then yanked her leg up to remove the bandage and survey the damage of her incredibly swollen ankle.

Arashel swiftly shoved most of the parchment from her desk, slopping her ink over the wood, and grasped what appeared to be some type of recipe. She sped around the wall of herbs and plants, plucking them out and thrusting them over her shoulders with surprising speed and strength for what appeared to be rather advanced age. Each of her pickings somehow landed in the same boiling pot.

Adam, Serafine, and Kezia all looked at each other. Adam wondered if she was some type of witch, but she wasn't using her magic—her palm wasn't glowing.

Arashel leaned over the pot, studying its contents while she stirred and wiping the sweat from her brow. A heady, herbaceous scent overtook the room, clouding the air as if with smoke and perfume. She scooped some of the glittering, goldenrod elixir out of the bubbling vessel and into a vial, then spread it onto the swollen joint. Serafine looked as if she was ready to fight, which wasn't that different from usual. Adam wasn't sure whether to intervene or not but ultimately trusted Rafi and Dalila.

"That shall do the trick. You are quite welcome, girl. Now, for payment, five lyat." Arashel snidely unfurled her hand to Adam. He rummaged around in his rucksack, found the right pouch, and withdrew the copper coins, which he dropped into her hand to avoid contact with the withered healer.

"It's fixed—completely fixed," Serafine said as she scanned her no-longer-swollen ankle, then jumped up and down to be sure. "Thank you."

"Thank you, Arashel," Rafi said. "Now, one other matter. You don't happen to know anything about keys given to twelve Jesimi representatives in Avaria during the dark time, before they went into exile, would you? Adam here is on a great journey to collect them, and we happen to know one is here in Imiris. I figured this would be a likely place, since most Jesimi who live in Imiris are here in the city." Rafi politely inquired, lacing his fingers together.

"Of course I know of it. I know of all. I have no use for the old thing; it's from a time past, a time we all best forget. Follow me," Arashel beckoned, leading them into the damp, earthen hallway and through a series of tunnels behind the marketplace. She stopped suddenly, pressing her brittle fingertips to a chunk of earth that seemed much the same as all the others in the subterranean city. She gave it a push, and they gasped as a hidden door swung through to the other side.

"Secret door, cool," Kezia muttered, and Adam chuckled.

The room was some kind of musty library, but it was Adam's version of heaven, stuffed floor to ceiling with scrolls, mold be damned. With little decorum, which seemed called for in a secret room hiding what was supposed to be a prized key, Arashel's short legs carried her to the far side of the room, where she ripped a few scrolls from their places, rapping her knuckles against the rotting wood. Her knocking released a mechanism, and a tiny door popped out. She yanked the key from its well-hidden spot and tossed it to Adam, and he and Serafine both furiously raced to catch it before it fell. Serafine snatched it just in time and handed the fragile-looking key to Adam gently, staring daggers at the careless old woman. Adam traced the outline of this key; it was unlike any he'd seen to this point. Strange material, eerie, but incredible.

"It's made of caribou antler. They shed them each year. Now, take it and leave me to my business." Arashel left the room and led them back to the hubbub of the thrumming market before disappearing into the crowd.

"Well, that was weird," Kezia commented.

"Thank you!" Adam called after her, stunned by the whole experience. He found it odd that she seemed to care so little for the key; it was so deeply important to the Jesimi, to him, although he still wasn't entirely sure why. He fastened it beside glimmering rubies and emeralds, silver and wood, tucking it carefully beneath his shirt.

Rafi and Dalila led them back to the exit, weaving through the scenes and scents of the crowds to the staircase, which Serafine easily climbed, and they were back on the frozen tundra.

"I can't thank you enough, really," Adam said as he embraced Rafi and Dalila.

"There are other Jesimi and non-Jesimi people here who will want to fight by your side," Rafi told him. "Their freedom is at stake as much as yours is. Leave it to me to gather as many as I can, and when the time comes, we'll be there." The conviction in his eyes confirmed how genuine he was.

"You will always have a home here with us. All of you will always have a safe place with us, should you need it. We will meet again," Dalila managed to say through her steadily increasing stream of tears as she and Cora fell to their knees, holding each other tightly.

"I can't, I can't find the right words. I just, I couldn't have done any of this if it weren't for you. You gave me life again, you know? I am gonna miss you so much," Cora wailed as Dalila helped her stand and unthreaded her hands from her thin lavender hair.

"You can do this, Cora Rose Yarrow. You were made for bigger things than Pax; it's time to find out just what."

Dalila and Rafi waved goodbye and turned to return home.

"Are you ready for an adventure?" Serafine asked Cora mischievously, like Kezia would.

"It's about time I had a new adventure. Let's go!" Cora half yelled, then sheepishly grinned. "I get kind of excited. I had to be quiet and perfectly behaved for so long, Dalila says it's hard for me to read the room."

"It's adorable, *but* there are going to be times where you'll have to be more careful. Don't worry; we'll tell you when," Kezia said, slinging her arm around Cora's shoulder and leading what was becoming quite the procession of people and soul-seals.

The group started forward, using Adam's enchanted compass to ensure the correct course. According to the map, it wouldn't be long before they crossed through the valley and made it to the next realm. Adam couldn't tell if Kezia was still shivering or buzzing with excitement, as if her short stature could barely hold it in.

They watched their footing across the extraterrestrial-looking terrain, and Cora began to open up to them about Pax. They would never have asked her to share such personal and painful memories, but she seemed like it was helpful for her to be open, so they listened raptly to every bit as she confirmed and even exceeded the vile rumors they had heard.

Pax had been plagued by famine once Avaria had split into three off the continent, the once-fertile ground lifeless, blackened. Kezia shared with Cora the tales they had been told: that the lands of Xhartana and Pax were no longer blessed by El and the magical hands of the Jesimi people, and that's why nothing would grow.

Cora told them about what Pax looked like: colorless and flat. The buildings they lived in were hewn from gray stone and filled with gray, uncomfortable furniture, as the premise of the place was sameness—equality, so to speak. While the self-proclaimed sage of Pax trained its people to believe that everyone was equal and accepted, the opposite took root. No one had any individual rights; difference was punished in a rigid and unforgiving manner. Everyone dressed in the same baggy gray tunics and loose pants. Everyone worked a job the sage assigned to them, day in and day out. Everyone attended daily "informational" meetings, where they were fed propaganda. Cora's eyes glazed over a bit as she told them about these meetings, as if the memory of being involved in a cult was carved so deeply into her psyche, she would never fully shake it. There was no joy, no celebration, no learning or growing, simply conforming and fitting in.

Cora shared that from the time she was small, she felt out of place; she questioned things no one else seemed to question. She was brutally punished by her mother and the sage regularly for asking these questions, while her father was too weak to protest. She desperately wanted her parents to be proud of her, so she tried to lose herself in the teachings, but she could never fully let go. It didn't fit; the teachings were morally wrong. So, she meticulously planned for over a year to escape. She managed to get across the Channel of Arcturus, and Rafi eventually found her, broken at the tender age of eighteen.

Adam, Serafine, and Kezia spent the majority of that first day just listening to Cora talk and noticing that as the day went on, the heavy burden she carried seemed the slightest bit lighter.

"Cora, you are so brave. I know you've been through hell, but you escaped. How amazing is that? And you chose to go with us on this crazy escapade," Kezia blurted out after Cora had spilled her heart across the tundra all day. She reached out and grasped Cora's hand, squeezing it and holding on for a few moments.

As the muted light from above the clouds began to dim further, they heard the distant roaring of water. Far ahead, the beginnings of mountains jutted up out of the ground, looking like giants sleeping, curled up on their sides. They gave each other a round of high fives, as the Kokhav Valley lay just ahead.

They walked side by side, King oddly perched on Kezia's cinnamon-colored head, Zev eyeing him warily, until they reached the mouth of the valley. The River of Pyxis had gained a great deal of velocity from where they'd bathed in it on the savanna, and it thundered through the valley floor at the base of the Latros Mountains. The water remained an intense indigo in stark contrast to the taupe and ash colors of the granite mountains that sprawled out before them.

Adam looked at the map. Ben had marked a very small village, a key holder, at this very location. He looked up to scan the area and, on second glance, narrowly made out a grouping of tents that camouflaged seamlessly with the foot of the mountains.

Time was of the essence, so they approached quickly, introducing themselves and Adam's great journey to the first villagers they saw. The villagers were nomads who moved through the area like the night itself, never staying anywhere for too long, unwilling to trust anyone. Their reception of Adam and his friends was no different: They were met with icy indifference. Similar to Arashel, they seemed disconnected from the Jesimi people. They did not want anything to do with Adam or his gift and vehemently denied any interest in a fight they said was not theirs. They readily handed over their key, saying it had only been a burden trying to carry their past with them and they wanted to move forward, alone.

Adam graciously received the key, which was cast of iron ore from the very mountains they neared and had an eye etched into the center of the bow. He and the group respected the villagers' wishes and moved on quickly, leaving with more questions than answers, but they brushed it off and chose to focus on their successes. They had collected the eighth key and had found far more friends than foes along the way.

They set up camp for the night nearby, tucked in between the bank of the river and the edge of the vast mountains. They feasted on the food that Dalila had sent with Cora. It was not lost on Adam that without the kindness of many strangers, this adventure would have been much more challenging on so many levels.

After they ate, Serafine demanded that they train, and neither Adam nor Kezia put up a fight. He had come so far, and the last thing he wanted was to lose progress; he wanted to grow stronger still, and he was fairly sure it was for himself, not just to impress Serafine. Cora cheered them on giddily, promising to consider trying next time.

They made an early night of it, leaving the fire smoldering in the pit they had dug for warmth. It was far too cold for Adam and Zev to sleep away from the women; they needed as much body heat as they could get. They all shoved into one tent, Zev on the far end, then Adam, Serafine and Storm, Kezia, and Cora on the other end. Adam was thrilled with the setup—his first opportunity to be close to Serafine without getting punched, he hoped. He turned to his side for body heat purposes—definitely body heat purposes. Not because her curves fit perfectly within the large shape of him. Not because her springy pile of hair was in his face and smelled like an enchanting combination of morning dew and stargazer lilies.

Serafine was decidedly less thrilled, and she was vocal about it as they all shifted around, trying to warm up and get comfortable. She stewed under the heavy blankets, shoved in between her best friend and this infuriating man like a sardine. It wasn't actually him who was infuriating, more her confusion about odd feelings that percolated within her when he was near. Especially when he was trying to spoon her, she was rabidly torn between sinking into the comfort of his warm, awkward embrace and why in all the realms she had any feelings about him holding her at all. Her drifting thoughts felt traitorous while she was betrothed to another, even if he was a dimwitted wall of muscle. Not just because she fit Adam like a puzzle piece but because the infuriatingly delicious scent of papyrus and freshly chopped wood emanated off of him, making her dizzy.

Kezia giggled at Serafine as she huffed and puffed, rolling over repeatedly like meat on a spit. Kezia was a smart woman; she knew exactly what was going on with lovestruck Adam and her confused best friend, who sort of didn't hate Adam, but also sort of did, and kind of liked him, but didn't really want to. Even if she did want to, she couldn't because of Tamir. Kezia found it all rather amusing; she was just so glad to be observing the situation and to have no stake in it whatsoever.

Eventually, they all slept, though they were rudely awakened more than once to the tune of Zev's snores, and they flopped their arms over to wake him.

The next morning, Serafine thought she awoke just before the rest and was horrified to find Adam's arms wound tightly around her and his leg hitched over her hip. Even worse, her fingers were intertwined with his where his arms came across her chest. She gently tried to pry his arms open and push his leg back so she could sneak out of the tent before, El forbid, anyone else noticed. As she turned to the side, she saw Cora propped up on her elbow, smirking at her. They both ducked out of the tent and went to tend the fire.

"So . . . what's that about?" Cora inquired, wide-eyed and literally bobbing up and down on the rock she sat upon. Serafine looked at her with pursed lips, ignoring the question. "Come on. We were never allowed to date on Pax; we were married off by the sage as adults, if it suited her wicked plan. I've never even kissed a boy." She held her head in her hands, her large blue eyes twinkling with dreams. Serafine pondered how truly childlike she was, not having been allowed to grow up.

"I'm betrothed to another. And there is less than nothing between Adam and I; he could not be any less of what would interest me." Serafine cocked her chin up, asserting herself.

"Floundering fairies! This is quite the love story. Betrothed to another, but the heart, the heart wants what the heart wants," Cora said, one hand across her chest, the other lifted toward the sky as the first peek of dawn crept across it.

"Shhhhh! Who talks like that, honestly? Where do you come up with those sayings?" Serafine pressed a finger to her lips with urgency, speaking in a whisper.

"I've always been like this, a little different. I used to get punished for it, so now, I just let it fly," Cora said, flinging her arms wide. Serafine's icy heart melted a little as she took in this frail girl who had chosen them to help continue to free her from her past.

The others piled out of the tent, Adam grinning from ear to ear, having slept more soundly than he had in months. Serafine rolled her eyes.

They ate some berries, packed up, and started along the wide bank of the river through the Kokhav Valley. The ground under them was a combination of shale, dirt, and fallen rocks from the steep face of the mountain to their left. The river roared too loudly for them to converse, so they walked along, thawing their hands by blowing warm air into them. Zev's thick white coat flowed in the arctic breeze as he ambled along.

The valley swallowed them whole for a time, and they were unable to see beyond its staggering walls and taciturn beauty. Eventually, it spit them out on the other side, marking the beginning of the Forest of Rian. The unforgiving mountains fell away, leaving spongy, green grass sprawling before them. Bare trees speckled their path forward, and as they moved farther in, the bite of the bitter cold began to abate. As it got warmer, the trees bore leaves and fruit; the endless meadows were filled with lilacs, peonies, tulips, and daffodils; and the grass grew thicker, longer, more fragrant. It was impossible not to smile, and Cora even sang a little ditty about a manticore who loved a unicorn, which made them all laugh.

"I'm not surprised by anything anymore since I started this journey. Maybe a unicorn will come strolling by. If they lived anywhere, it would be here." Adam spun around with his hands flailing at his sides.

"Unicorns." Kezia snorted. "Unicorns aren't real." She shoved his arm with her shoulder before descending into fits of laughter with the other girls. Even Zev seemed amused.

"Listen, before I left the Isle, I didn't think anything was real. Then I met a pixie and was attacked by fist-sized, vividly colored arachnids. We were attacked by griffins, and you were healed by a magical river. All bets are off now!" he said in his defense, clenching his fists tightly, which just had them laughing harder. He was not enjoying being ganged up on by three women, instead of just the two—those two had been more than enough.

They went farther into the fantastical forest, and each stripped off a layer as the sun strengthened its grip on the sky, bathing them in warmth. The trees grew thicker and threaded closer together as they reached the edge of another village Ben had marked on Adam's map. Adam wondered when he would run out of awe, but as they stepped through an ancient stone archway covered in lichen, with female figures carved into it like a doorway to the past, he knew it wouldn't be today.

Ahead lay an entire town that had been raised from these incredibly intricate ruins. Long ago, faded gray stone had been wielded to create picturesque buildings and temples, and over what had to have been hundreds of years, life and the forest had grown in around it. Trees had burst from the midst of the stone, casting webs of sprawling roots. Vines and more roots had twined their way through doors and windows and across the walls of what had been. Giant, gnarled trunks had melded with the stone in a way that defied logic. The ruins had been too lovely to be left to rot, so the earth itself had taken hold of them, forging them anew. And now, it seemed, man had returned to reclaim this mysterious place, and life flowed through its veins once more. People inhabited the structures, honoring the meeting of the past and the present.

Intermixed with the tree-swept ruins were small, intricately carved wooden homes. The carving seemed to match the incredibly detailed designs on the stone of old.

A small collection of people caught a glimpse of their visitors, and they strode over to receive them. Three men and three women beelined for them, no clear leader among them. They wore simple, neutral-colored robes, unassuming in nature.

"Welcome to Hilat, young visitors. What brings ye here on such a fine morn?" said the person in the middle, a portly man with round pink cheeks, extending a hand to shake.

"Well, thank you, sir. My name is Adam, son of Rachel, and this is my Zev; that is Serafine, daughter of Rivka, and her Storm; Kezia, daughter of Zahava, and King; and that is Cora Rose Yarrow," Adam introduced, accepting the man's hand, and then launched into his usual speech.

"Well, that is rather a fanciful adventure, I quite admit. Let me introduce me friends: Ezra, son of Eliora, the healer." An older man stepped forward and bowed, holding a carved wooden cane. Between his feet was a large tawny-brown snowshoe hare.

"Malachi, son of Elizabeth, holder of a whisper gift." The man sneered and bowed mockingly. They all took notice that he had no soul-seal, setting the wheels turning in their heads. To fail the quest set for you by your potential soul-seal was incredibly rare.

"Roni, daughter of Malka, can sing an angelic hymn, captivating all who listen." A woman stepped forward, bowing deeply, accompanied by a great white barn owl.

"Aya, daughter of Eliora and sister of Ezra, possesses the gift of flight." Another woman bowed, smiling, as a tiny forest-green hummingbird with a white-tufted chest buzzed around her head.

"Sydelle, daughter of Hannah, gently sends any enemy off to their dreams." The final woman stepped forward, gracefully bowing, a spotted lynx purred at her side.

"Omri, son of Sarai, is my moniker. I make fruitful the harvest with only the flash of me palm." A tiny puff of a vole was cradled safely in his hands.

Adam, Serafine, Kezia, and Cora stood there blinking, waiting to see if he was finished. They had never quite heard anyone speak like this, although it was very Jesimi to be introduced by gifts they couldn't even currently use. Cora had retreated behind Kezia as her burst of confidence dissipated among this new group.

"Ye steadfast voyagers are welcome to stay for a time and rest yer weary bones from a lengthy journey."

"Uh, sure, we would love to stay, if it is not an inconvenience," Adam responded, twiddling his thumbs, wholly uncomfortable with this display.

"I shall hear nothing further of it. Ye shall be our guests. Come, I bid ye follow me."

They did.

The robed townspeople they had met peeled off one at a time, Malachi looking Adam deeply in the eyes before stalking off, leaving him inexplicably unnerved. The only ones left were Omri and Sydelle, guiding them toward the town across the thicket.

"Our town is unlike others. We are one community; we do everything together as a team. We eat most of our meals together, our children are raised together, we farm the land together, and we prosper as one."

Cora shuddered as Sydelle described the town, and Adam wondered if she was thinking of Pax. Kezia reached out and squeezed her hand, reminding her she was not alone anymore, and Cora gave her a timid smile.

Sydelle and Omri showed them the town, bursting with pride at the life they had built since exile. They passed an ornate building that was open to the air, with a colossal tree jutting out of the ceiling, its dark-green leaves casting patchy shade below. The vivid foliage and mild climate took Adam and his friends by surprise, considering it was the dead of winter.

They heard peals of young laughter dancing across the stone courtyard where the children were reared. As they trailed through the ruins that had been reborn and now boomed with life, Cora's shoulders lifted; it was clear that Hilat's idea of living equally and peacefully was wildly different from Pax's.

The women were led to Sydelle's modest oak cabin, while Adam and Zev followed Omri to his home that he had crafted from the ruins themselves, a tree sitting square in the middle of his living space.

After a period of rest that Omri had insisted upon, they were led to a communal dining space for an evening meal. The townspeople were dressed casually, mostly in neutral, earthy colors, some still smudged with dirt from tilling the fields. The meal was as casual as the dress, and Adam, Serafine, Kezia, and Cora followed suit as the people served themselves from platters atop a table lining the half-destroyed, but no less beautiful, ancient stone wall. They went to sit down, and Malachi shoved in at the last moment, clad in black, his olive skin leaning yellow under his cold, brown eyes. He sat next to Adam, flashing him a false smile full of crooked, yellowing teeth surrounded by a thick, dark goatee. Something about him made Adam's skin crawl.

Kezia, Cora, and Serafine seemed oblivious as they ate the hearty food they were provided, grown by the hands of these people. Many others hated the Jesimi, for some reason, but they were hardworking, creative, and deeply resourceful.

After they had eaten, Sydelle introduced the newcomers to the town and shared a bit about Adam's purpose, inviting him to stand and use his gift. He complied, pulling the jar from his pocket and smearing the mixture on his left palm. He called to his gift, untethering it, swathing the room in the brilliant glow.

"Leaping leviathan," Cora muttered under her breath, beholding Adam's power for the first time.

Adam attached to the faces of the people he had met and was plunged into a series of visions of their communal story. Like before, he first saw sepia-tinged scenes of the townspeople's ancestors, desperate for peace as they escaped war-torn Avaria. They ventured far and wide, seeking a place where they could begin anew, with a clear vision for a future where they connected with the land and each other in harmony. Adam watched them take the once-infertile land surrounding these abandoned ruins and pour their souls into it as they worked it day after day until it thrived, and they reaped harvest after bountiful harvest. He saw more recent visions of celebrations—a wedding where a bride and a groom beamed at each other across the room as their chairs were lifted up by their guests, stars in their eyes. He bore witness to their pain, their losses, their attempts to gather enough lyat to pay Xhartana the taxes they demanded, though they did not tend to deal in money in Hilat. He watched them pay the consequences. Like always, he watched them rise again. He watched them dance again. It ended with a flash, and he let the bright-white tentacles of his gift curl back up in his chest, his palm dimming. He blinked away his single tear and allowed his gift to shape his words.

"Thank you for allowing me to behold your story; it is beautiful and uniquely yours. However, the more Jesimi collective truths I have faced, the more convinced I am of a shared Jesimi soul. The way we celebrate may be different, and the way we have suffered may be different, but the threads that flow through them bind us nevertheless. We share the same enemies, and most importantly, we share the same dreams. We are crafted from the well of hope itself. I can see how deeply your values and your way of life run in your veins, and I wonder, would you consider relinquishing your key and standing with us to ensure that the peace you sow can remain intact forever? With Xhartana in power, we will never know true peace. We have recently learned of their plans to use newly discovered platinum and infiltrate the rest of the continent to the farthest reaches, destroying anyone they can't control." Adam imparted the words the townspeople needed to hear as they looked at each other and toward the six people he had met earlier that day, who sat at Adam's table, with varying expressions.

"Ye are wise fer being young folk," Omri said, rubbing his chin between two fingers, deep in thought. He rested a plump arm atop his round belly.

"We shall have to discuss this amongst ourselves," Roni added. "You see, we abhor any type of violence, so although you may well be correct, standing with you in battle flies in the face of our steadfast values. The large majority of us have no fighting skills, and those of us who have gifts are not able to practice wielding them. We have a few weapons for emergencies, which are kept with the community tools just there." She pointed to a large shed just out the window and behind the gathering hall they stood in, her barn owl on her shoulder, hooting loudly. "Stay for a couple of days while we meet, and we will have a decision for you."

"We will stay for a couple more days, but then we really must be on our way. Time is running out," Serafine said, her hazel eyes narrowing.

They visited for a bit longer. Malachi took great interest in the details of Adam's gift and his great journey, which Adam offered hesitantly, as he continued to feel a tug in his gut. Malachi even extended a long, greasy finger with a yellowing nail toward the keys around Adam's neck before Adam quickly blocked him, earning a scowl.

Adam's group went their separate ways for the evening, which also didn't feel right to Adam. For someone who had spent much of his time alone, he was growing rather fond of the ragtag assortment of people and soul-seals he had gathered. He felt protective over them, though he knew Serafine and Kezia could still beat him senseless one-handed, if they wanted to.

The next couple of days, they grew to know the people in this magical little town and witnessed the ins and outs of their unique routine. The people met for hours each day that Adam, Serafine, Kezia, and Cora were there, trying to come to a community decision on whether they would hand over their key and aid in the battle to take back their homeland, banishing malevolent Xhartana forever.

Adam had felt the pressure that had been birthed in him the first time he'd read his mother's letter grow bit by bit as he had gone along, gathering speed and size within him over the length of his journey. It was his fate to do this most important work, and he felt as if an imaginary clock was posted in the air right above his head at all times, ticking, ticking, ticking. It was time to move on, and though the people of Hilat hadn't come to a decision, they agreed to continue to consider it. Adam promised to send word when the time came and hoped that at least some of them would take the chance and come, bringing their key with them. He knew what he asked of his people: to look fear itself in the face, stare it down, and fight back with all that they had. He didn't judge these people for being wary of risking their lives, and it did not quell the hope that he held on to.

The group packed up, having received directions to the Bei Llai Glade deeper within the forest, and they had been forewarned to watch out for the Tigris that guarded it. That was where they could procure more weeping heart, the magical herb they needed to make more protectant.

As they said their goodbyes, Malachi snuck past, like a snake in the grass, with a pack on his back dressed for travel and disappeared to the north. Adam scratched his head, wondering what it was about that man that gave him the creeps.

They left the village and sank farther into the otherworldly Forest of Rian. Adam had fire in his steps as he picked up the pace, easily matched by Kezia and Serafine, and poor Cora had to nearly run on her short, skinny legs to keep up. The leafy, plush trees gathered closer together still, darkening the path forward as they followed Aya's directions to the glade.

CHAPTER 18

The forest buzzed with life. All manner of animals bounded across the springy, dew-swept grass. A dreamy meadow popped up like a bubble between the thick, ropy trunks of the trees; it appeared untouched, with knee-high grasses that bent and blew in the wind. Boundless vivid amethyst irises stood tall against the grass, with streaks of gold through their centers. The meadow was begging to be frolicked in, and Zev was the first to be tempted, tunneling through the tall grass, carving a path through the blooms. The rest followed close behind, running and jumping, forgetting for a time that they were adults on a crucial mission. They laughed and played, lying back in a circle and looking up at the azure sky, trying to figure out what animals the clouds were shaped like. Serafine was the one to break the spell, dragging them out of a beautiful dream and into the glade ahead.

They crossed into the thicket and toward a towering, willow-like tree whose roots sprawled messily, interspersed with weeping heart and a variety of other magical herbs. This tree was unlike any other in all the realms, as its umbrella of wispy branches held unnatural, twinkling cerulean leaves twirling to and fro. It stood in stark contrast to the rich, boundless layers of green, and its beauty drew them in slowly, raptly at attention.

Before they knew it, the frail branches sprang to life, snatching them and propelling them toward its hulking trunk. Kezia was the only one who leaped out of the way, just in time, ripping an arrow from her quiver, placing it in her bow, and sweeping it back to hold the feathers against her mouth in one seamless motion, though it wasn't clear how she would use a bow against a tree.

Adam, Serafine, and Cora screamed as they were held against the tree, but the sound was drowned out by Zev's guttural howls. Serafine violently thrashed against the formidable branches that lashed both her hands and her feet, while Adam froze. Cora rested her head back against the trunk and sobbed. Kezia darted back and forth, trying to get close to her friends as the branches with the lustrous cerulean leaves attempted to ensnare her as well. King swooped in time after time, trying to peck the branches, but they caught hold of his beak and pinned him next to Adam, who began to squirm against the constricting manacles.

As they fought valiantly against this most unlikely foe, a centaur crashed through the trees from the direction they had come, galloping toward them as if off the parchment of a fairy tale. He slowed to a stop in front of them, shaking his long strawberry-blonde locks over his brawny shoulders and giving them a smirk. He looked as if he had been carved from stone, and his golden muscles matched his golden coat. Kezia hopped away from the tree and pointed her arrow directly at the centaur.

"I mean you no harm, humans," he rumbled. "I am Cyrus. I have come to deliver a message from your uncle. I see you have found yourselves in some trouble." Adam stared blankly in shock; he would never get used to these odd, magical occurrences. Somehow his uncle was having a message delivered by a centaur deep in a far-off realm while they were being held against their will by a tree.

"What, no cute centaur catchphrase?" Kezia muttered to Cora. Cora simply let out a little squeak as she shook from her position against the tree.

Cyrus reached out and grasped a single branch, his defined biceps rippling, and whispered something in a foreign tongue. The tree seemed to fall fast asleep, releasing its prisoners. Adam fell like a plank, and Serafine fell directly on top of him. He caught her by her elbows, gently brushing her hair out of her face. For a moment, they stayed like that, everyone else looking on silently, until Serafine sprang up to help Cora to her feet. Kezia checked King for any damage to his delicate wings. Then they all turned their curiosity to Cyrus.

Cyrus reached for his leather satchel and removed a small glass bottle, which he held before them steadily. He uncorked it, and an ashy-gray cloud of smoke came billowing out, forming a thick cloud above them. The outline of Ben's face emerged from within the smoke itself, smiled cautiously, and began to speak as Adam, Serafine, Kezia, and Cora moved closer, listening intently.

"Nephew, you've been gone for awhile. I hope you've been successful and found some happiness to take for yourself along the way. No time for messing around, as it is of the utmost importance that this message reaches you. Listen closely.

"You might remember me telling you about Adala, the young seer I helped to practice her gift before she disappeared into the ether of her mind. She came to me, clear as day, finally understanding the vision she'd had all those years ago. She told me that what she had once seen was a mighty weapon, one that would one day be wielded to turn the tide of the impending battle between good and evil. She was kinda cryptic, but she saw that Xhartana hadn't found the weapon yet, but they know of its legend and have hunted its power to keep their reign of tyranny and destroy all Jesimi once and for all. Her visions didn't show where the weapon has been hidden all these hundreds of years, but she saw what it was. It's a mighty bronze sword said to be imbued with powerful magic gifted from El himself. One strike of its blade, and hundreds of foes will fall. Continue your journey—time is running out—but you've gotta find more information about the sword. It'll be the end of all of us if Xhartana finds it first.

"Oh, by the way, that idiot from Kesil in the south popped by for a little visit. Their village was attacked by Xhartana; their 'mighty' wall fell like it had been made of paper. He realized no one is invincible and they can't fight Xhartana alone, so he's in, and he gave me their key. Cyrus has it. I'll see you soon," Ben said ominously as his likeness vanished in the wisps of smoke that were released to the sky.

Cyrus reached for the bottom of his satchel and withdrew a key fashioned from glossy, tumbled cobalt, which was found in droves beneath the heart of what had been Avaria. He presented it to Adam, who hurriedly added it to his growing collection, the weight of which was growing heavier, physically and mentally.

Kezia broke the lengthy silence. "What in all the realms was that about?"

"I wish I knew more, but this message is all that I have to relay," Cyrus said. "My kind have suffered at the hands of this evil regime, and we will take our place at your side when the time comes to fulfill your righteous quest." He crossed his heart with his hand and bowed his head lightly.

"Thank you, Cyrus, for everything," Adam said, at a loss for any other useful words as his mind spun with the news, and Cyrus galloped off, ducking under the brush.

Taking advantage of the tree still being stunned, each of them shoved as many of the spring-green herbs with heart-shaped, fuchsia blossoms as they were able into the tops of their bags, then hastily began the trek north once again, toward Terebet.

The harrowing weight of his people rested on Adam's shoulders, bogging him down as he walked. The anxiety that had been building in him was quickly growing unmanageable. Not only did they face the wicked Xhartana, but there was also some sword that could determine their fate just lying around somewhere.

The ladies talked about how handsome Cyrus had been, batting their eyelashes over his muscles, making Adam grit his teeth. Then they began rattling off all the places across the continent where they thought a magical sword might be hidden. Adam retreated within himself, as was his habit when he became too overwhelmed to think straight.

Kezia seemed to notice and hung back next to him. "You're not alone in this anymore, you know? There is a reason we're with you. And it's not just because you need bodyguards. You're our friend."

"Friends, huh? Does Serafine know? Not sure she would agree. And Cora would be best friends with a fruit fly," Adam bit back sarcastically.

Kezia snorted a laugh. "Serafine is definitely your friend; she's just a complicated gal. Anyway, quit hiding what you're thinking from us. I know you've been alone a long time, but it doesn't have to be like that anymore."

"Thanks, Kez. I'm just gathering my thoughts; I have no idea what to make of all that. It was already so much, and I don't want to mess it up," Adam said as he wrung his hands together.

"One step at a time, man. You heard your uncle; he just wanted it to be on your radar. We'll ask around when we get to Terebet, but there is nothing you can do until then. Look at all you have done. And you made us like you." She smiled from her eyes, jamming her shoulder into him and knocking him aside lovingly. Adam laughed with her, knocking her back, and they went on like that for a while until he felt his load lessen just a little with this fireball by his side.

The sun dropped beneath the cover of trees, and the light dimmed between the branches. They decided to make camp in a clearing for the eve. There was a slight chill that descended when it grew dark, but they wanted to sleep under the millions of sparkling stars that had come to life, splattered across the sky.

Adam built a blazing fire, and they ate and talked and laughed together before rolling out their blankets close to the waning fire, pointing out constellations to each other until they fell fast asleep. They all slept fitfully as Xhartanians, griffins, centaurs, and magical swords played in their heads on an endless loop.

The pace gradually increased as the pressure of the ticking clock grew. They made good time across the forest and into the realm of Terebet, and they were disheartened to find the temperature dropping and the air thinning as they climbed higher in altitude. Their breath began to catch more often as they wound across and around the hills that rose in front of them until they reached the foot of the Latros Mountains. They had passed through the very southern tip of the mountain range on their way to the Forest of Rian, and now the cold and unforgiving mountains stood between them and the finish line.

Ben had marked a small city tucked among the mountaintops on the map, and they scanned the mountains jutting from the ground above them for any sign of life. Adam and Cora struggled to stay on their feet a bit more than Kezia, Serafine, and Zev as they traversed the narrow, shale-filled pathways up the mountainside.

Suddenly, a small city came into view from above, dwellings shorn from the steel-hued granite of the mountain itself. A generous dusting of snow graced the peaks, blustering in the frigid wind, whipping into the stark blue sky and muting its brilliance. Oxen roved the barren landscape between the peaks, along with the odd goat and chicken, trying not to topple over the steep edges.

"Hollering hydra!" Cora screeched, clamping her hand over her mouth as she beheld the mysterious city tangled in the clouds.

"Couldn't have said it better myself," Kezia responded as they took it in, not entirely sure why people would choose to live up this high. King seemed to agree with her and circled their heads, squawking madly, his vivid royal blue coloring very much out of place in the stark gray landscape. But as he looked around at the panoramic view of the Kokhav Valley and across all of Terebet, Adam understood.

Spurred on by the aching cold, they climbed higher until they reached the beginnings of the city, a life that was etched in stone among the clouds. As they approached, they were intercepted by a tall, thin man with his arm wrapped around a very pregnant woman—his wife, Adam assumed. They both smiled warmly, putting their visitors at ease.

"Why, hello there, brothers and sisters. What brings you all the way up here, to our great city of Lasuron?" The man asked.

Adam gave a version of his well-practiced speech about his gift and their great journey as well as delivered the warning of the developments in Xhartana's destructive plotting. Seeing as Jesimi were nothing if not hospitable and excellent hosts, they were readily embraced.

"I am Aryeh, son of Zia. My name means 'lion'; I hold a gift that feeds me endless courage, and I am able to impart it to others around me. This is my beautiful wife, Estee; she was named because of her natural shine, like a star that fell from the sky and landed in my arms." Aryeh looked at her as if she had done just that.

Estee did shine, her medium-brown skin alight with love for her husband and the growing life she held within her. Her hair was fully covered, wrapped tightly in delicate white cotton, and a fluffy chocolate-brown alpine marmot stretched across her rounded belly. Aryeh towered above her, his rich umber skin the perfect canvas for his curly black hair that poked out from under the white prayer shawl with sky blue stripes that was draped over his head. An enormous white mountain goat emerged from Aryeh's shadow and perched at the very edge of the cliff, setting Zev on edge, as he growled softly. Adam had to say, Zev's attitude toward other soul-seals had definitely improved, though he still tried to bite King's head off every time he landed on Zev's broad back.

Serafine looked back and forth between Aryeh and Estee, realizing that their eyes were almost an exact match—glistening pools of amber—and found herself pondering the concept of soulmates. She pushed the thought away; she knew full well that her betrothed had never looked at her the way Aryeh looked at Estee, or the way Adam looked at her, which she shoved even further down.

Aryeh swept them into the village, cautioning them to watch the edge, which dropped off at a dizzying height. They were introduced to many Jesimi residents, similarly dressed to Aryeh and Estee, with covered heads and varying shades of warm brown skin. They took in the bustling market, full of people selling their wares, and the sounds of rhythmic drumming echoed across the mountaintops.

Adam used his gift, and the people readily accepted his invitation to join in the looming battle and graciously offered their obsidian key with a sculpted flame symbol.

Adam's head spun that it was already the month of Te'umim, signaling the Jesimi celebration of Alaz, the Day of Triumph. The day before, they all fasted with the people of the city, though Kezia grew ill. She was tended to by a healer and was given some healing plants from the mountains, her illness forcing her to break her fast early. However, El looked kindly on his people; El was not a punishing god, and Jesimi who were not well enough to fast for any reason were encouraged not to. Life and health came first. Kezia used it as an opportunity to crack endless jokes about how it was very Jesimi to have an upset stomach.

Adam again quickly felt an affinity for his people, these people. An undeniable connection through their shared heritage, a shared connection to Avaria.

When the fast was broken, the city celebrated their lost queen from thousands of years ago, who had triumphed over an evil ruler. It seemed particularly relevant to celebrate today. Xhartana was certainly not the first foe that had sought to destroy the Jesimi people, and Adam was certain they wouldn't be the last.

The group went door-to-door, helping Aryeh and Estee share gifts with their neighbors and friends. They helped Estee deliver food to their Temple, carved out of the apex of the mountain, to be served to those who were unable to feed their families.

That eve, they donned intricate masks and drank wine and bitter beer. They supped on succulent lamb, chicken stew with eggs and potatoes, vegetables stuffed to the brim, and pastries stuffed with spiced dates.

Kezia entertained the crowd while Cora looked on in adoration and Serafine snuck off on her own. Adam noticed her absence and went to check on her, his cheeks flushed from the wine. He didn't usually let himself have more than one or two cups, but tonight, he had let the alcohol silence that mounting fear within him. He stumbled over a rock as he traced his hand over the granite, wading through the inky shadows to find Serafine.

She stood, bathed in the glow of the moon, tossing pebbles down the mountainside and rubbing her arms. A delicate snow fell, each flake resting on her skin and melting from her warmth. She was swathed in ruby, one of the colors of her people. Her dress hid much of her bronzed skin beneath, but it clung to her every curve, the fabric pooling at her feet. Adam's breath, already thin, disappeared as he allowed himself to truly take in her beauty The glint of the moonlight bounced off her mahogany curls as she whipped around toward him.

"Don't sneak up on me like that!" Serafine spat at Adam, her cheeks a bit rosier than usual from the nip of the frost, and maybe the wine.

"Sorry, you just look so beautiful right now. Well, always, but especially right now," Adam mumbled as he shrugged off the black velvet jacket he had borrowed from Aryeh and swung it over her shoulders. She inhaled, closing her eyes for a moment, apparently consumed by his masculine scent and the delicate caress of the snow upon her face.

He stepped toward her, one foot at a time, emboldened by drink and the feelings she had shaken awake when he'd first laid eyes on her. She said nothing as the gap between them closed, the words stuck on her full lips. Once he stood mere inches from her, she finally really looked at him. The moon made his nearly black eyes glow and highlighted his strong, stubbled jawline; seemingly mindlessly, she ran a finger across it before dropping her hand back to her side. That was all that he needed to thread his hands behind her neck, through her silky, lily-and-dew-scented hair, and tilt her head up to press his lips to hers. He had waited so long for this moment, and he had never had a happier one; their kiss felt like the most natural thing in the realms, like their lips had been forged just for this moment, so they could rendezvous beneath the moonlight on the top of a snowy mountain. He thought he might float away just as she suddenly broke the kiss, shoving him away and ripping off the jacket, which she tossed back to him. She looked at him for a moment and then took off back toward the gathering, leaving him confused and broken in a whole new way.

Serafine rushed back inside and squeezed into the seat beside Kezia, plastering on a fake smile while the whole world churned within her. What in all the realms had just happened? She had been in control of the stirring of feelings she'd felt creeping in around Adam; she knew that the way she saw him, as a fighter, as a man, had shifted. Storm scampered back and forth across her shoulders excitedly, stirred up by the whirling emotions of his soul-seal.

Serafine's knees went a bit weak when Adam wore black; it brought out the darkness of his eyes and accentuated the depth of his soul. Why had she stroked his jaw in that way? Why hadn't she pushed him away when he'd first kissed her? Why had she felt like her heart might burst when he had grabbed her with such vigor and pulled her toward him? She was betrothed; she was going to marry Tamir. It was set. Why did the thought of that make her want to sob uncontrollably? It was mere weeks ago that Adam's lanky self had turned up in their village. Yes, he had learned to fight, but he wasn't a warrior who had been training his whole life, and that was the kind of match her father wanted for her. That was what she wanted, wasn't it?

"Room for two in there?" Kezia said, tapping on Serafine's snow-covered head.

"Adam kissed me," Serafine whispered.

"What?!" Kezia shrieked, and the majority of the room swung their heads around to look before she shooed their attention away.

"I heard that!" Cora sang out. "I knew it; I saw you two all snuggled up that morning."

"Again, what?" Kezia cried, slightly quieter this time. "I'm your best friend, and I'm the last to know everything. I mean, I knew the man had goo-goo eyes for you from day one. I also knew that you had conflicting feelings over the whole thing. I just tried to stay out of it, but it's getting juicy now. Give me the details!"

Cora looked on, resting her chin on her fist.

"I don't know how it happened; I was just out there, thinking about everything. About, you know, what's going to happen next. He strolled out there, all suave all of a sudden, and just walked over to me, grabbed me by the back of my neck, and kissed me. I did push him away . . . eventually. I don't know what I'm thinking. I *am* sure I'm done talking about it. Pass me some more wine, please, not that I need my head to be clouded any more, but I do need to forget." Serafine fanned herself, as she was suddenly a bit warm.

Adam strolled back into the cavernous granite room with his hands folded behind his back and a sheepish look on his face. The second he laid eyes on Kezia and Cora, he knew Serafine had told them, and he was even more appalled. It was bad enough Serafine had pushed him away, but the smirks their friends wore were too much. He swung around and headed to their sleeping quarters, Zev silently judging him. Adam pretended to be asleep when the women arrived later that night, too embarrassed to face them.

The next very awkward morning marked the day they would leave to finish crossing the Latros Mountains and descend into the Ma'adim Desert, which fell away into the Sea of Orion at the final village, marking the end of their journey. Knowing it was so close petrified Adam. He had asked Aryeh to ask around about the sword, but they had only heard whispers of its existence. He was nearing the end of the journey, close to facing a vile enemy but no closer to finding the weapon that could defeat them, and he had kissed Serafine. The most perfect moment of his life, before it was ruined.

They hugged their new friends and bid them goodbye before pressing deeper into the mountains. The air was so thin, they couldn't bring themselves to talk much, simply watching the air freeze as it left their lungs.

They treaded higher and wove through the treacherous mountain pass with Zev in the lead, as he had demanded, ensuring the route was reinforced and safe. Their path was now dusted with a thin coat of snow that swirled around them furiously in the sharp wind. Adam found himself grateful that his uncle had talked him into the leather boots that he had cursed during his time in the muggy rainforest.

They only made camp once at this altitude, sharing a tent and leaving the fire ablaze all night. Although, much to Adam's chagrin, Serafine forced her way into the far opposite side from him this time. They broke camp before dawn; the chill had buried itself so deep within their bones, they couldn't wait to descend on the other side.

The path soon became a very slick, narrow strip of earth. On one side, the granite face protruded far above their heads. On the other side, it fell away, plunging hundreds of feet into an abyss below. They each steadied themselves against the rock face to their right and took their time crossing this precarious spot. Zev, Serafine, Kezia, and Cora had stepped off onto safer ground, and just before Adam followed, the ground beneath them shook violently. Serafine desperately jumped, grabbed his hands, and pulled him to safety, nearly flinging Storm off his perch in the nook of her collarbone, then brushed it off and pretended it hadn't happened.

They tried to keep their balance as the mountains swayed like a ship on the ocean. A gargantuan shadow cast over them as they huddled together and pulled Zev and King close to the mountainside. They looked up to see what could possibly possess a shadow so massive, and what they beheld stunned them all.

CHAPTER 19

One after another, what appeared to be five giants, each the size of ten men, unfurled themselves from the rocks at the base of the mountains they had seamlessly blended into. They stood, dwarfing the mountain under their feet, swallowing the group in darkness and dread in equal measure. Adam's throat bobbed as he worked to swallow, flinching for what might come next. He had intuitively unsheathed his dagger and stood hunched protectively over Cora. Kezia and Serafine were at the ready, bearing their bow and spears. It did not seem that their small weapons would even faze these colossal beings, who appeared to have been hewn from stone, like the city they had just left behind.

The largest of the giants suddenly swung his fist, crushing the earth beside them, turning the granite into dust before their eyes in a dizzying show of power. It let out an inhuman bellow that shook each of them to their very cores.

"Who dares disturb our peace?" another of the otherworldly beings yelled, causing the group to slam their hands over the ears in an attempt to dampen the deafening pitch.

Serafine made to step forward, but Adam narrowly beat her to it, wanting to stand between her and danger, no matter the cost. Palms trickling with sweat, he said, "We come peacefully, to traverse your mountains on our way to complete a great journey across the continent. A righteous quest. We mean you no harm." He allowed his gift to aid him, and it hummed to life within his veins. He wasn't quite sure if it was the power anymore, or if he inherently knew what to say.

The largest giant, a veritable mountain, was clothed around the waist with an enormous swath of russet-colored fabric fastened at one hip. The other four donned similar coverings in shades of brown and green. The largest one leaned closer to Adam, Serafine, Kezia, and Cora, looking each one in the eyes as they all held their breath. He paused for a moment, as if considering their fate.

"We are Nephilim, the fallen ones. We are descended from the meeting between angels and humans. We, the semidivine, guard this mountain and man's most valuable treasure so that no one with ill intent shall pass, or the scourge that is our wrath will befall them." He paused, looking to the ten keys hanging from Adam's neck, leaving just enough time for Adam and his friends to brace themselves for the ground to quake when he resumed speaking. "I can sense that you are pure of heart, humans; your quest is just. You shall pass unharmed. Afore you go, unburden yourselves of your woes before us; the weight of your future hangs heavily around your necks like a noose."

For some reason, this set them each in turn sharing bits and pieces of the lives that had led them here. Adam shared the fruits of his journey, its purpose, perched atop this snowy mountain. What he didn't say was that debilitating fear was nearly consuming him as his great journey came to a close. He had learned to fight, he was stronger, but he had no idea what he had done to deserve the allegiance he had been granted from so many of his people. Familiar self-doubt crept up from its cage that he had kept locked tight for some time, taking hold of him once again. He did not have what it took to organize them and lead them into battle. He could only hope that when the time came, his uncle, his friends, and the experienced warriors would take over. He tried to remind himself of his mother's words, Ben's words, that he could not do it alone, and that it wasn't weakness—it was strength. He would do whatever he could to be worthy of his people's trust, of Serafine's trust, and he gazed at her longingly before quickly pulling away.

"Just as we have a responsibility to safeguard the treasure, so too must we act against evil in the name of our fathers, on behalf of our mothers, who lived among you many a year ago. We pledge ourselves to your noble cause; we will fight fearlessly at your side. With our tremendous abilities to aid you, you shall prevail," one of the Nephilim in the back thundered. He ceremoniously plunged an enormous hand into the ground and, between two stony fingers, unearthed an ancient, rectangular box, gray stone with black veining. The giant smashed the box against the side of the mountain with an immense clatter and a landslide of rocks and pebbles. They all peered over the edge as the Nephilim presented his staggeringly large open palm to them. On it was a simple bronze sword, greenish with patina from age.

They all looked at each other, and Adam said, "This isn't . . . It can't be, can it?" He reached out, tentatively tracing his finger across the unassuming blade, then hoisted its significant weight in front of him.

"I assure you, it very much is. The mighty bronze sword of ancient lore, said to fell hundreds with one strike. I see the keys laced around your neck; you are fated to wield the weapon and save your people. We have been awaiting your arrival. All twelve enchanted keys are required to unlock its true power; for now, it remains but a simple blade, like any other."

Without warning, all five Nephilim suddenly sprouted magnificent white-feathered wings from their backs, displaying an unimaginable wingspan.

"Dazzling dragons," Cora said, wide-eyed, before returning to shuddering against the rock face behind her. Kezia giggled and rubbed her shoulder.

"We would be honored to have you by our side. Thank you." Serafine stood proudly, hands on her shapely hips as usual, seemingly unaffected by the massive creatures that dwarfed her.

"When the time comes, we shall heed your call. You need only listen for the hum of our wings, and we shall stand stalwart on the side of honor to abolish the plague that has caused your people such destruction." With those words echoing off the steel wall of the mountain into the distance, the Nephilim curled back up into the earth. It was as if they had never even been there. They all looked at each other, as if to be certain it wasn't a dream.

"Like I told you, apparently anything can be real here." Adam smirked and continued to brandish the bronze sword, whipping it through the air. "I cannot believe we got it. Ben will be thrilled. We can actually win, be free!"

"Don't forget, we still have to get two more keys. One from the village in the desert, and the other from Hilat, if they decide to come. Otherwise, that's just a sword you don't know how to use well," Serafine told him, as if he didn't think about it every moment of the day.

"I thought we were goners for sure," Kezia announced, lightening the tension, trying to coax Cora out of the trance she seemed to have been lulled into. "You're safe. They're going to help us." King hopped off her shoulder and onto Cora's, nuzzling his long, orange beak in her neck.

"Sorry, I just, it's just that I . . ." Cora trailed off, absent behind her doll-like blue eyes.

"You have nothing to be sorry for; this journey is not for the faint of heart. You're doing great," Kezia responded lovingly, and Serafine patted Cora's arm.

"Let's get going. We have to get farther down the other side of this mountain before nightfall," Adam encouraged, taking up the rear and walking side by side with Zev as he threaded the bronze blade through his rucksack.

I can see the wheels turning in your head. You're still worried you can't do this, even after all you have accomplished, Zev spoke into Adam.

"I just can't help but think I haven't done anything to earn the blind trust that Jesimi in most of the realms are pledging to me. Even non-Jesimi—Ivy, the centaurs, Dalila and Rafi, Cora, the damn giant angels we just met. What if I lead them to their deaths? I am not capable of leading anyone into battle; I can barely disarm Kezia still," Adam whispered in return, quietly enough that only Zev could hear as the group traced the switchbacks down the mountain.

I thought we had gotten past this. I have seen your confidence grow beyond what I could have ever dreamed for you as a boy. You earned their trust by being willing to trek across the realms and risk your life day in and day out to answer fate's call. You are pure of heart, and anyone who meets you can plainly see that. That is why your enemies hate you, hate us, so deeply. They could never invoke the kind of trust and love the Jesimi people share. This is your moment. Look at this family you've built upon the ashes of the one you lost. These people would follow you anywhere. That has always included me. Zev's eyes bore into Adam, his fur particularly striking in this blinding sunlight as it glared off the snow.

"You are the best thing in my life; you know that, right? I would never want you to think that the girls or anyone could ever replace you. Sealed or not, I choose to keep you etched into the depths of my tarnished heart." Adam stopped for a moment to lean down and scratch behind both enormous ears.

I know, Adam. You never have to worry about me. Seeing you become the person I always knew you could be is the greatest gift. Your happiness is all I could ever wish for. Zev sniffed as tiny droplets formed in his melted-caramel eyes.

With no further words left between them, they raced each other to catch up, guffawing heartily. The bold sun slid behind the crest of the mountains, blanketing them rapidly in darkness. They found a suitable spot to camp, shielded from the wind in a small, shallow cave.

They had been training at least twice daily, faster and harder with Serafine in the lead. Cora had even begun some very basic fight techniques, and Adam's heart warmed to see that the harsh lines of her face had begun to fill in with food and time and love.

Tonight, they faced off in hand-to-hand combat around the raging fire they had built in the center of the granite cave. Adam had beaten Kezia, catching her off guard for a moment and slamming her to the ground, victorious at last. The winner was to face Serafine. He looked her up and down, clad in her burgundy fighting leathers, and tried to suppress the overwhelming desire to press his body to hers in the flickering fire light in favor of taking her down.

"Don't go easy on me," Serafine goaded as she began to circle around him like a predator, fists balled tightly at her chest.

"I wouldn't dare," Adam shot back as he casually watched her, a sly smile unfolding.

She darted out with a double right jab, left hook combination, and he rolled just out of her reach. Her own fire flared in her irises as she gathered herself for her next move. Knowing she was lighter and quicker on her feet, he let her come to him, and as she leaped for him again, he hooked onto her upper arm, flinging her around and pulling her arms tight behind her. She thrashed against his grip, but he didn't falter as he held her back flush against him. She looked for a way out, hooking her foot around the back of his knee, making it buckle, loosening his grip. One arm free, she swung her fist into his side, and he let go of her other arm, tucking his arms tight to his sides to protect himself from her onslaught.

"It would help if you would hit me back, you know," she said breathlessly, hammering punches that he blocked with his forearms.

"I can't hit you, okay? I give." Adam winced as he pressed a hand to his tender flank.

"Idiot," Serafine muttered under her breath, sinking to the ground, casually resting on her elbow by the fire.

Kezia and Cora looked at each other, snickering, and joined her. Adam groaned as he folded himself onto the ground carefully.

He thought he might prefer being hit in the face to the ribs; the ribs were always so painful.

"You're getting better still. You never could have held me off like that even a couple weeks ago," Serafine said, surveying her slightly bloody fingernails before gazing over to Adam, who sat shirtless on the other side of the fire. She scanned his lean muscles as they pulsed with the pain she had inflicted, the flames making his deep-tan skin glow. When she met his eyes, she quickly looked away. She had not stopped thinking about their kiss since the moment it happened, much to her alarm, as she had done everything possible to scrub it from her memory. It had taken up residence in her very skin, reminding her of the meeting of their souls that had occurred for a brief moment.

"Because of you—both of you. Edria and Arnon as well. Your training has made me strong. I will stand a chance in battle, and it's because of you," Adam said, without looking up at them.

"You sorta told us about Xhartana attacking your village and your mother, but you've never talked about it again. What could have driven you to leave your home and take on this kind of obligation?" Kezia inquired, shoving her bright-cinnamon hair behind her shoulder and warming her hands over the crackling fire.

"Cora, I suppose you never heard the story either." Adam paused, as opening up like this was not natural for him. "I grew up in a little village on the Isle of Ori. It was just my mother and I, and we were very close. She was an incredible preserver, and I was an apprentice, following in her footsteps. We didn't have much, but we were happy. Xhartana inhabits and controls much of the Isle, so over the years, there were frequent attacks of varying degrees. I was certainly no stranger to their cruelty. Just months ago, some of us had gathered together in secret to celebrate the Day of the Great Scroll, as all worshipping and gathering on the Isle was banned. Someone must have turned us in, because Xhartanian soldiers struck that eve with a fury, the likes of which I had never seen. They burned many homes to the ground and viciously murdered anyone who crossed their path. I was with my mentor, working, when they struck. By the time I got home, it was too late. I found my mother there among the ruins of our little home. She spoke a few final words and sent me to dig up a letter she had left beneath the ashes of our life. Once she took her last breath, I unearthed the letter and learned about how I was fated to gather the twelve keys and bring our people together once again, because only together can we defeat Xhartana and take back our homeland. She told me about my naming ceremony and my gift, which I had known nothing about; I'd assumed I didn't have a gift when it hadn't manifested along with the others when I was younger.

"She sent me to her estranged brother, my uncle, whom I had never met. He took me in and used his gift to help coax mine out and teach me to wield it. He prepared me for my great journey. And you know most of the rest." Adam quickly wiped away the weighted tears that clung to his lower eyelids, despite his desire to barricade them deep within. He licked the salt from his lips and peered up at his friends, who were watching him thoughtfully.

"The Isle is so close to Pax; you can see it when the fog rolls away once in a while," Cora said. "I can't believe that all my life in that suffocating place, you were so close. I am so sorry about your mother; she sounds like she was wonderful." She wiped away a few tears that rolled down her face before they could fall into her web of long faded-lavender hair.

"She really was," Adam responded, feeling the grief threaten to crack him open, as if he was still holding her body as her last breath escaped her lungs.

Kezia scooted around the fire to put her arm around him, and he let her warmth in, her embrace like glue holding him together. He looked at her, the tiny warrior, and the shell of his broken heart swelled for how easily she offered love.

"I would have loved to have had a mother like her. My parents were cold and distant; my mother was . . . punishing." Cora shuddered, as if envisioning a dark memory, her eyes glazed over. Kezia reached out, yanked her to her other side, and gently stroked her hair.

"My mother died too," Serafine said, looking shocked at herself as the words spilled from her lips. "When I was young, she was killed by a Xhartanian soldier while she was on a warrior mission. I can barely remember her anymore, but I know that I miss her. My father misses her terribly."

"I'm sorry. I'm glad you told us," Adam responded, with a heartening smile.

"If we're talking about dead parents, I've got two. Similar story to Serafine's; no need to go into the details. It was a long time ago. I was lucky that my aunt took me in and treated me like one of her own. And, of course, that I got to grow up with my best friend." Kezia looked at Serafine. "What a sorry lot we are. Tonight, we can wallow in our pain. But tomorrow, we live to fight again. We journey on."

Wallow they did; they allowed their fears and their pain to crack through the thinly veiled surface and take shape among the company of friends, and they worked to banish their demons together in this cave on the side of a mountain. They fell asleep in a heap of wayward limbs, leaving the fire roaring to warm them.

The next day, they took Kezia's declaration to heart, and not another word was uttered of their pain. They pushed forward as one, further united and keeping a quick pace as they spiraled down the remainder of the mountain. They surveyed the path below as they grew closer to the bottom, realizing that the River of Pyxis had wound back this way and carved its path up against the base of the mountain range, blocking their way to the mouth of the Ma'adim Desert. They took the last few turns down and stood surveying the vast indigo river. It was far too deep and wide to ford at this point. They were well and truly pinned in. The water was not as still as it had been when they waded in its waters to heal Kezia, but thankfully it wasn't raging, as it had been through the heart of the Kokhav Valley.

"What are we going to do now? We have to get across somehow; I'm not going back up that mountain," Kezia warned through clenched teeth.

"We aren't going backward; we don't have time," Adam said. He studied the map as Serafine paced up and down the narrow bank, trying to come up with a solution.

"You know the answer is staring you in the face, right?" Cora said, stunning them all, and they whipped around to look at her. "We have to swim, silly sirens! It's not moving that fast; we'll be fine."

Kezia chuckled. "The water *is* warm. The current isn't very strong here. I don't know that we have any other choice. It's not like we can build a boat out of rocks, and that's all we have on this side."

"There has to be a more practical solution," Serafine returned warily.

"I think they're right. As much as I wish they weren't." Adam started to check his rucksack, making sure everything was closed and tied on tightly, especially the massive, aged bronze sword. The supposed key to their survival, if only he could get his hands on the last two keys. He removed the ten precious keys from his neck, fastened the twine they hung from carefully to a strap inside the bag, and looped the rucksack's straps more than once around his shoulders to ensure it remained secured to him. The rest followed suit as Serafine grumbled, but she secured Storm inside her rucksack and pressed it to her chest.

"This is going to be so much fun!" Cora shouted as she wrapped her satchel tightly around her shoulder and launched herself in, causing an indigo wave to crash over Adam's head. The rest quickly followed, Kezia first, then Adam and Zev, then Serafine begrudgingly hopping in after them.

The water was as warm as bathwater, banishing the chill that had taken up residence in their limbs since entering Terebet. They floated along, attempting to paddle their way across to the other side. The current was sneakily strong and refused them leverage, keeping them firmly in the river's center. At least it was taking them in the right direction; the air grew balmy to match the temperate waters. Cora and Kezia's laughs resounded across the surface as they floated on their backs, letting themselves be carried away. Adam and Serafine watched in amusement as King attempted to land on Kezia's foot repeatedly, only to be dunked every time her feet were swept under her. Adam swiftly remembered the healing properties of the indigo waters as the bruises inflicted by the object of his desire faded.

They began to pick up speed as the river narrowed and began to twist and turn. They tried harder to earn their release from its grip to no avail, and they were dunked under white-capped rapids. Large boulders began to pop up from the depths of the mighty river, dotting their path with peril.

"Feet first!" Adam screamed, and everyone scrambled around, trying to gain control of their bodies as they tumbled through the coursing water.

The river grew wilder as it carried them violently, and they used their feet to push back from the rocks. Kezia was shouting a string of curses, while Adam and Serafine scanned for any branches hanging over the river, anything they could grab on to. As the landscape melded from mountain to plains, the trees were few and far between. Their hearts shot into their throats as they were plunged over small drop-offs time and time again, fighting to stay afloat. Kezia grabbed Cora, who was not as strong a swimmer as the rest, locking their arms together. Adam thought for a moment, as they dodged yet another giant boulder, that this might actually be fun if their deaths didn't seem quite so imminent.

The mouth of the river grew wider once again, and deeper, and the boulders fell away below. There was a roaring sound in the distance, and the group desperately tried to get their exhausted heads far enough out of the water to see what lay ahead. They made another attempt for the bank, which seemed farther out of reach than ever, as they hurtled toward the unknown, facing their fate together.

Adam began to fill with dread as the wide river ploughed them faster and faster toward the roar that drowned out every thought in their heads. Cora let out a piercing shriek, and if the rest had been capable of making that sound, they would have as well, as just ahead, the water ended. It appeared to drop straight off the face of the realms themselves.

The thunder grew as the water swelled beneath them, forcing them closer to the edge. Kezia held fiercely to Cora, who clung on like a baby to its mother, her eyes shut tightly. Adam flung his arm out in a desperate attempt to latch on to Serafine's leg as she floated just behind him. He grasped her and used all his might to pull her closer, wrapping his fingers around hers as they neared the edge. She didn't fight him. None of them knew how far the drop would be.

Adam kept grabbing for Zev, who paddled the water easily, but couldn't grasp his wet fur. Would it be too far to survive? This couldn't be it, after all they'd faced.

Kezia and Cora spilled over the edge, disappearing in a tangle of limbs and leaving only ear-piercing shrieks in their wake. Serafine and Adam looked at each other, their hands clutched together frantically. The deceivingly soothing water dragged them to the precipice and launched them over a towering waterfall. They tried to scream, but the air was ripped from their lungs as they plunged an unimaginable distance downward, toward a surface they couldn't make out through the thick mist of the roaring falls. They fell through space and time, and Adam's stomach was in his chest. It seemed fairly certain they couldn't survive a fall this far as they were thrust deep into the waiting pool at the bottom.

Serafine puffed her cheeks to hold a bubble of air as she clawed her way to the surface, breathing as much air as she could muster as she tried to gain her bearings once again. She looked around for Adam. Zev popped up, having been pitched over the falls last, and he paddled easily to the shore.

Serafine desperately dove beneath the surface of the water, opening her eyes to search for him, catching a glimpse of his limp body sinking to the bottom. She tore through the water, as if she were a mermaid with a fin, her heart catching as his thick black hair danced through the water atop his expressionless face. She mustered all her strength, grasped him under his arms from behind, and kicked her legs as ferociously as she could, slowly propelling them upward. She breached the surface, dragging his body up, begging him to take in a breath of the air that was now readily available. Kezia and Cora came crashing through the shallow water to meet her, helping her to bring Adam's body onto the pebbled, sandy shore. The murky water churned up in the waterfall lapped at his feet as Serafine grabbed his face in her hands.

"Please, Adam. Your great journey isn't over yet. We need you," Serafine whispered as she leaned in close, her lips almost touching his ear. "I need you," she admitted, and the pang of agony that resounded through her body at the thought of living in a world where he didn't exist threatened to topple her. "You can't die, stupid. We haven't had enough time."

All of the impenetrable walls she had built around herself to prevent allowing someone to get close enough to her that she could feel this devastation turned to dust. Kezia placed her hand on Serafine's shoulder while Cora stroked Adam's hand, both with panic-laden expressions. Zev wound his body against Adam's side, hoping his warmth would reach him, wherever he was, and reminding him he was needed. Storm, who never left the comfort of his soul-seal's skin, hopped onto Adam's chest and rested against its newly broad plane. Serafine closed her eyes and pressed her forehead to his, willing him to find the spark that lived within him, flickering, guiding him and those around him out of the dark. It was that spark that had ignited something deep within her soul and suddenly made everything else seem ordinary.

Adam trembled, his blue lips filling with pink. He began to sputter as indigo water spurted from his lungs, and he continued to choke as he opened his eyes to see his beloved friends, his Zev. The love he saw in their eyes made nearly dying almost worth it. Cora and Kezia threw their arms around his neck, squeezing him and laughing in relief. Serafine snapped out of it, snatched Storm, and moved to stand up and walk away. He grabbed her wrist before she could pull away, looking deeply at her, past the walls she had reconstructed anew in an instant.

"You saved me," Adam uttered, relaxing his firm grip and running his fingers gently along hers. "Thank you."

"I would have done it for anyone," Serafine said, pulling her hand away and shrugging.

"Yes, you would have. But you did it for me," he said, letting her walk away.

He sat up with Kezia's help and gave Zev a squeeze, his nose filled with wet-dog scent as Zev stood and shook himself out. Adam moved to stand; his legs were weak beneath him, but he was buoyed by his win in this bout with fate.

They all looked about, unsure where the river had taken them, and they turned at the same time. They had been delivered to the mouth of the Ma'adim Desert. The vast copper plain loomed ahead, looking as if it might swallow those who enter whole, never to return again.

This was it. The last stop on his great journey, Adam's mind clouded with thoughts, worries, memories, but he cleared all of it, making way for the thing that was most important now: determination. He was going to complete the great journey he had been fated to, for his mother, for his people, for Serafine. He was going to ignore all that might live beyond this singular hope, this singular goal. He drew in a deep breath of the dry air that was now ample, as they had returned to sea level. He had to free his people.

CHAPTER 20

The group quickly filled their water canteens before forging ahead, Adam embracing the tornado of warring emotions within himself about what came next. And what was to come after that.

They had stripped out of their sopping wet clothes in favor of those more suitable for the desert they were entering. Cora donned a pale-blue dress that was fitted on top and fell loosely to her ankles. Kezia and Serafine had taken to wearing fighting leathers underneath layers to keep them warm, but now the tight black leather, in their own individual styles, was all they needed for the endless sand that lay before them. Their signature weapons remained affixed to them, as always; Storm and King took up their usual positions.

Adam wore a fitted white T-shirt that showed off his newly defined musculature, noticeably snagging Serafine's attention, which drifted his way a few times. His lightweight tan trousers that had once been baggy now traced the outline of his thicker core and ropy, vascular thighs. The dagger was sheathed at his side, as his uncle had requested when he had bestowed it upon him what seemed like a lifetime ago. As they neared the end of the journey, they grew increasingly on edge, prepared for anything. Or, at least, they hoped so.

The sand grew thicker, swallowing their feet a little with each step as they pressed into the Ma'adim Desert toward the Sea of Orion.

The last Jesimi village lay there, folded between the dunes at the end of the continent.

"My legs are on fire," Cora complained, wicking away the sweat that had beaded on her forehead with a swipe of her delicate hand.

The sun had risen high, seeming to chase them across the sand, which reflected its thick heat and left them missing the grip of the cold. They rose and fell across the infinite terra-cotta dunes toward their date with destiny. Kezia cracked jokes to try to keep spirits up as their plight grew more fervent, weighing down each painstaking step they took.

They hunkered down and shielded themselves from a massive sandstorm as one, a team working seamlessly together to overcome the onslaught of challenges that continued to come their way. After being mercilessly pelted by walls of sand, they came out mostly unafflicted, aside from sand in their eyes and blisters covering their feet.

As they made their way to the top of a dune, Zev threw himself downhill, sliding on his backside, howling as he flew down the slope. Everyone laughed, and Cora tried to follow suit but discovered quickly that her flowy dress was not conducive to sliding down a sand dune.

They only had to make camp once, as the desert was a fairly thin strip of land that had once connected Avaria to the continent before the dark time. The stars were somehow even more brilliant above the inhospitable desert, and the group danced around the blazing fire that night as if it wasn't all about to end, one way or another. As if the survival of their people wasn't at stake.

The next day brought an intensity, an air of foreboding as they crossed the remainder of the desolate landscape. They closed in on the Sands of Sivan, the great sand dunes that lined the edge of the continent before falling away into the sea that lay just beyond. There were few signs of life, save for some scattered reptiles, the flies buzzing about their heads, and sparse trees with cracked grayish-brown trunks and olive-green foliage that looked less than alive. It was enough to remind them periodically that even in the harshest conditions, life finds a way to grow and thrive.

As Adam's enchanted compass edged them closer to their destination, the dry breeze laced with kernels of sand began to carry the scent of salt. They crested the final dune that stood between them and the final village at the edge of the realm. Kezia looped her arms into Adam's and Serafine's, and Serafine grabbed on to Cora, Zev peeking between them. They steadied themselves as trails of sand toppled down the sides of the dune from the imprints of their feet.

What they beheld, they could have never predicted. A shudder rippled down Adam's spine. Kezia looked as if she was a fragile ceramic, ready to splinter into a million pieces. Serafine's expression went cold; her heart dropped to her stomach, and in its place, the need for revenge that had taken root so many years ago now raged within her. Cora fell to her knees, and a fount of tears escaped her eyes; she made no move to stop it. The brokenness her friends had worked so hard to banish dug its claws into her to stake its claim.

What remained of the little Jesimi village, and any hope of gathering their key, was nothing more than piles of soot and ash that billowed up in thick clouds, carrying on the wind and raining down over their heads. There was no question who had laid waste to this place. Like the trees they had passed along the way, life had existed here, despite the harshness of the conditions; an entire world had blossomed from grains of sand, out of the ingenuity of the Jesimi. And now it had been stamped out of existence, torched to the ground.

They stood at the crest of the hill, ash accumulating in their hair. They grasped on to each other, desperate to anchor themselves, else the despair might carry them away forever. They mused about the people they should be meeting, the stories they might have shared. Adam may not have known these people yet, but it was as if a part of his own soul was being shredded into fine ribbons; they had been his people.

Before they'd even had a chance to collect themselves from the horrors they were seeing, the cloud of smoke lifted, revealing what lay beyond the smoldering remnants of the village built upon the crux of the Sands of Sivan.

The reapers of destruction themselves, the very depiction of all that was evil, spread behind it, as far as the eye could behold. They had wreaked their chaos and violence, and now they stood across the valley between the dunes, scattered about in small groupings, wielding a variety of primitive weapons and facing down Adam, Serafine, Kezia, and Cora—just the four of them and their soul-seals. The soldiers covered the valley floor between the dunes and across the very top of the sands that stood between the group and the inky Sea of Orion, which sprawled out beyond until it kissed the sky. Adam felt his heart stop beating as he took in the vast, bloodthirsty army that had assembled before them.

"Did they know that we were coming somehow? How is this possible?" Serafine whispered, trying not to move her lips, as if the soldiers could read them from afar.

"There is no way they could have found out; we've been so careful," Adam replied in hushed tones, debilitating fear coursing through his veins.

It was too soon. They needed time to prepare for the battle; they needed their people. He had known it was imminent, but it wasn't supposed to come so soon. They had *just* been given the mighty bronze sword that had the power to change the tide of the battle, but he only had ten keys around his neck, rendering it nearly useless. He sighed deeply, eliciting a love slug on the shoulder from Kezia. The realization that he had failed sent him reeling so far, he thought he might never make his way back.

Adam squinted across the valley to try to make out the faces of their enemies. There had to be hundreds of them, all of whom had been infused with extremist religious beliefs and military training from the time they were very young. Many of the men appeared to be no older than teenagers, rearing for another fight even after stealing the lives of so many and standing upon their ruin. The destruction of the Jesimi people was their lifeblood, their purpose, and it looked like Adam wasn't going to be the one to put a stop to it.

The vicious crowd slashed their weapons menacingly. The men in the front sat atop griffins, as they had when they'd attacked Kiritum. One of them Adam recognized as Namtar, one of their leaders, the man with dark eyes ringed in blood red. He and two others rode the largest griffins and were draped in gilded red cloaks. The rest of the soldiers were in varying states of dress in bold red and black. It was hard to tell what state of dress they had been in before bathing themselves in the blood of the villagers whose lives they had just taken, wearing it like a sick badge of depravity. Just as Adam went to tear his gaze away and try to figure out how he might save his friends, his eyes landed on a familiar yellow-olive face, trimmed with a dark goatee. The man stared at him with a twisted smile from afar and Adam's gut wrenched. He grabbed Serafine's wrist and pointed.

"It's Malachi, from Hilat," Adam said, his voice dripping with disgust. "He must have told Xhartana everything about me, us, this journey. He must have looked at my map somehow. It's all my fault. The village and everyone in it were destroyed because of me." He collapsed onto his knees, the dizzying realization setting in.

"Despicable traitor," Serafine spit, her hands forming into iron fists as if they were desperate to spill his blood.

"How is this your fault?" Kezia asked. "You said something wasn't right about him; you had the right gut instinct. He is the treasonous bastard, not you. He betrayed his own people, and for what? Power? Does he think they won't kill him too? He is still Jesimi, whether he stands with us or against us. They will hate him for his blood either way." Her words came out in a gust of fury, matching her best friend's.

"You cannot blame yourself," Cora murmured, unable to form further words from her place slumped in the sand, tears still streaming down her flushed cheeks.

"Well, what are we going to do now?" Serafine pressed Adam. "They're just toying with us, watching us like this. There are hundreds of them and a few of us. I don't even know if we could flee back across the desert fast enough, not with their griffins." She gripped his forearm so tightly, it began to turn white.

"I am no leader. I wasn't prepared for this. This wasn't how it was supposed to go," Adam said. Zev nuzzled his hip, taking a momentary break from his predatory stance toward the enemy. "What the hell are they even doing over there? Why aren't they coming for us?"

"Whoa, you kiss your mother with that mouth?" Kezia joked, trying to dispel the tension.

"You are a leader; you've proven that. You have to act like it now. Get it together; figure something out!" Serafine cried with desperation.

As the words exited her lips, they noticed a figure racing across the sand toward them from the way they had come. Too numb to react, they simply awaited the arrival of whatever was coming, weapons at the ready.

A striking ocelot came into view and bounded across the last dune before sliding into place in front of them. Adam had seen this animal before, recalling its unique black facial markings and green eyes that should have been feline and cold but instead were full of warmth and knowing. This was Phineas's soul-seal, from the Mesios Rainforest. He didn't know what this could possibly mean, but the ocelot turned sideways, showing a large pouch that had been fastened across its spine. Adam removed it and pulled out a scroll, and the group carefully read each word together.

Adam,

I have seen what has now come to pass. A vicious enemy has betrayed your righteous quest, and you now face the vast army of Xhartana alone, at the edge of the world, where the Sands of Sivan slip into the darkest sea. As I have foreseen this outcome,

I procured this magical object that you will use to call forth your own army of Jesimi and non-Jesimi alike. One long, resounding blast should do it. Those who have pledged to fight at your sides will come to your aid. Xhartana shall strike at any moment; the time is nigh!

Yours, Phineas

Adam staggered back a couple steps and had to catch himself before he tumbled down the backside of the copper-colored dune. He looked at his friends, a mixture of fear, pain, loss, courage, and the last grain of hope swirling between them, and reached into the pouch, retrieving a large ram's horn with gold filigree.

"This will call our people forth? Am I supposed to blow into it or something?" Adam asked as they passed it around and back to him, leaving him unanswered.

He felt a hum of power flowing from the twisted horn that sat heavy in his hands, and he lifted its gilded edge to his lips. He drew in a deep breath, trying not to choke on the ash that still lingered, and blew out with all his might for as long as he was able. The depth of the sound resounded within him and echoed across the endless sands. The Xhartanian army looked on, as the blow had sounded like a call to battle. And it was; they just didn't know how. The ocelot rested in the warm sand beside Adam and his friends, satisfied at having completed his assignment.

They waited, Adam battling within himself to let hope rise to the top, as it always had, even in unimaginable circumstances such as these. He reread Phineas's letter over and over again in case there was something left to glean from it.

A loud crack sounded, and a familiar group of large, leather-clad warriors dropped out of thin air, deposited into the sand beneath them. Kezia let out a squeal of excitement as she realized it was Arnon, Edria, Spike, and Flash, surrounded by every last warrior from Kiritum. Serafine hurtled down the side of the dune, throwing herself into her father's arms, nearly knocking him over despite his enormous stature. Storm unrolled his tongue and licked Arnon's cheek, which he quickly wiped off. Kezia shoved her way into the hug from behind them, laughing maniacally.

"I see you've kept up with your training," Arnon boomed, surveying Adam's muscular frame at the top of the dune.

"That's all you have to say?" Serafine thrust out the words. "We find ourselves facing battle far sooner than we had imagined, and that's what you have to say? We've been betrayed. A Jesimi man we met in the Forest of Rian stabbed us in the back and told Xhartana of our plans."

"You're not alone; we're here now. We felt your call resounding in our souls," Edria said. She sent sentries in all different directions to keep watch of the Xhartanian army, should they advance.

They all climbed the dune to where Adam and Cora stood. Adam greeted everyone quickly and Cora was introduced, shaking. Adam scanned their surroundings as another crack brought a much larger cohort of people, dropping them into a pocket of desert ahead. Lian shrieked as she made eye contact with Adam, rushing forward to meet him, her golden hair flying behind her as Lily the giant otter bounded playfully through the sand. They embraced, and Raviv followed behind her, his red howler monkey jumping and howling his excitement.

Phineas emerged from their midst, rejoining his ocelot and whispering to him affectionately before turning to Adam. "I see you received my letter and heeded my advice." He placed a large hand on Adam's shoulder.

"I can't even imagine what would have happened if . . ." Adam trailed off, his mind wandering to the dark places that lived in its nooks and crannies. "Thank you; thank you." Phineas simply nodded his head and retreated; the mysterious man had given them a chance.

A couple more brassy cracks sounded, depositing more people into the sand. They stood and spat out mouthfuls, brushing themselves off. Dalila and Rafi set their sights on Cora, who sat with her feet buried in the sand, and darted toward her. They collected her in their arms, all of them sobbing at their ill-timed reunion.

Trailing behind them were tens of people from Imiris, wearing thick, fur-lined clothing that they began to strip off as the desert heat descended upon them. They were accompanied by a menagerie of soul-seals—reindeer, ptarmigan, an enormous caribou. All of these animals looked wildly out of place in this setting, but the soul-seal bond would ensure their safety in climates they were not built for.

"Told you they would come through," Rafi said, clapping Adam on the back. "Many of the exiled people in the Imiris Jesimi community have joined us. Some of them are Marre and, much like us, have no stomach for the hateful direction Xhartana's leaders took our beliefs."

Adam and Serafine explained to the newcomers what had happened with Malachi and that Xhartana had leveled the village before they'd arrived. Arnon and Edria began to organize the people into ranks based on weaponry, magical gifts, and fighting abilities, consulting with Adam regularly.

The cracking sound was earsplitting at this point, but each time it sounded, it meant they had a better chance of success. This crack dropped Uncle Ben and George right before Adam. Adam hopped back in surprise before dropping down to his knees to embrace him, and Ben squeezed him tightly. Ben felt Adam melt into him and could only imagine the weight he was carrying from his great journey, especially considering it hadn't ended the way they had planned. But life never went that way, and they could roll with the punches as well as anyone. They had missed each other dearly, and though the words were left unspoken, the love clung to the dry air between them. Ben cracked a joke about how Adam left a boy and was now a brawny man with all his facial scruff. Zev bounded up to George, rolling his giant tongue across the water monitor's entire head in excitement. George seemed to roll his beady eyes but nuzzled Zev's giant paws as Ben and Adam looked on warmly.

Lemuel, David, Sela, Samuel, and a handful of others from Zera came next, soul-seals in tow. The next wave from the Isle included Gideon, his mighty ibex, and his warrior friends from the city on the Isle, surrounded by other brawny builders Gideon worked with. Next, Irena and much of Mezarim came forward to greet Adam and Ben. Adam couldn't believe how far he had come since the first time he'd used his gift on a group of his people, Irena's people. That idyllic little village at the edge of the sea. Her sand cat scampered around at her feet, chasing a mongoose that had come out of the midst of the newly forming crowd. Ethan, the arrogant man who hadn't let them through the gate in Kesil, appeared with a large guard of burly men and women.

Observing Adam, Ben asked, "You received my message from Cyrus? And the key from Kesil?" Intensity laced his gruff demeanor.

"We did. It wasn't supposed to happen like this." Adam creased his forehead and pushed a lock of hair out of his face. "We also found this. The Nephilim guarded it in the Latros Mountains; they said we were worthy." He removed the bronze sword from his still-wet rucksack and showed it to his uncle. "A lot of good it does us, since Hilat didn't give us their key, and the village here was demolished. Their key will likely never surface."

"You found it," Ben muttered as he studied every inch of the plain blade in awe. "You did good, kid. I'll always bet on you, magical sword or not."

The next crack brought a mighty herd of centaurs atop a nearby dune, led by Cyrus, the sun glinting off his golden skin. He waved hello to Adam and the women, who remained together as they watched their righteous army accumulate.

Tuvia and the Vleskov faction arrived, dressed head to toe in black and uncomfortably handling farming tools as weapons. Serafine looked at Adam, her expression for once giving way to her feelings and showing her approval at what he had built here, in this stark desert, where they would face off against fear itself. He looked back into her hazel eyes, and the world fell away for a moment; all he could see was her. He knew she cared for him; she had tried to hide it, to pretend otherwise, but there was no hiding it now. This moment was raw, real, terrifying, and they might lose each other forever, but it was enough, just knowing that she was proud of the man he had become. The moment ended as they tore their gazes away to greet the newest group, the villagers from Lasuron in Terebet.

As Adam's glance moved to Kezia, he realized his life had not been complete until she was flying through it, filling the dark and broken parts of him with color. Cora stood now; she had stopped shaking, and he couldn't help but be impressed by her resilience. He had brought these people together. He closed his eyes and connected to the memory of his mother that flowed within him, alive, and he knew with certainty that she was proud too. He had done what he'd set out to do, regardless of the outcome.

Omri, Sydelle, Aya, Ezra, Roni, and a couple of the others from Hilat in the Forest of Rian arrived next, rushing to Adam, Serafine, Kezia, and Cora.

"Oh, woe are we, my young friends. Had we known there was a double-crosser, a rapscallion among us, we would have banished him many a moon afore! Alas, his end is nigh; he will meet it by my very hand," Omri pronounced, grabbing Adam's hands and falling at his feet, his vole tucked in the back of his oatmeal-colored tunic.

"We are so terribly sorry; we had no idea he was capable of this level of evil." Sydelle shook her head. "We couldn't convince much of the town to battle, but we will stand by your side and wield our gifts with such power, Malachi will rue the day he turned his back on his own people." Her lynx batted her paws at Aya's humming-bird soul-seal. "We've brought you something we hope will begin to make amends." Sydelle reached into her floral-patterned cotton bag and removed an ethereal-looking circular container fashioned from branches and vines, true to Rian. Tiny purple blossoms burst from the gaps. She gently handed it to Adam, and he pried the bramble of branches and vines open, careful not to crush the blooms. On a bed of white petals lay the eleventh key, minted out of gleaming brass, with a flame symbol hammered into the bow.

"Thank you, really," Adam said, struggling to find enough breath to speak as he added the key to the collection. So close yet so far away to unlocking the answer to their prayers, it was impossible not to feel like he came up short.

A significant drone hummed in the air; Adam looked around, wondering who was left. Seemingly plucked out of the azure sky, a cloud of brightly colored pixies slowly descended from above them. A tiny pixie with red hair and jade wings landed on Zev's snout. He thrashed back and forth a few times before she spoke.

"Adam, Zev, my dears. I've missed you," Ivy said with the signature lilt to her voice. "We felt your call on the winds, and we thought we might be of aid."

"We missed you too, Ivy," Adam said fondly, deeply meaning it. Ivy had signaled the beginning of his understanding that anything was possible. He gave her a bright, genuine smile and brushed a finger gently across her wings. "I'm glad you came. Thank you."

He looked across the valley at the Xhartanian army, who appeared to be thoroughly confused and violently angry as they began to assemble more closely. A few of the griffin riders flew across the sand dune toward an approaching ship, which sidled up to the massive dune that fell away to the sea and flopped a plank from the deck onto the sand. Dozens of people clad in loose-fitting lifeless-gray uniforms crossed the precarious plank onto the sand, one by one. They climbed the dune single file and filled in the space in front of Xhartana. In contrast to the heathens behind them, they formed perfect ranks, walking at the same pace. Adam felt a shiver brush a finger across the back of his neck. As the last of at least a hundred people crested the dune to fall into formation, they stood silently, waiting for direction. Adam and Serafine cast a glance at each other as they squinted to see what this meant, who these people were, barricading the monsters behind them, shielding them. They were altogether void of any human expression, almost faceless as they stood at attention, hands folded just so behind their backs, blankly staring forward. They all blended into one.

Cora yelped, and Adam, Serafine, and Kezia flew to her side, holding her up as she nearly buckled again.

"It's, it's my . . . my parents." She shuddered as the words left her lips, the old familiar ghosts floating in the irises of her childlike eyes.

"Those people are from Pax?" Kezia asked.

"Yes," Cora breathed, withdrawing into herself, face-to-face with the people she had worked so hard to escape. Adam clearly understood why, looking at the husks of people who stood before them. Suddenly, a tall blond man broke from their ranks and tore away from the army toward them.

Cora shrieked again. "That's my father. What is he doing, why is he running this way? They'll kill him!"

The man raced through the sand, tripping and picking himself back up again. His once-stone face had now been cracked open and oozed with desperation. He had gotten too far ahead for the Xhartanians on foot to catch him, but a sharp-toothed griffin took flight after him.

"No!" Cora yelped.

Aya lifted her left palm, and it was enveloped in a glowing coral symbol of a bird in a circle. "Not much point in hiding our gifts anymore; they'll kill us either way." She pushed off from the sand and took flight, barreling through the air to reach the man before the griffin could unleash its nasty talons on him. She swooped him up under his thin arms, flew him back, and deposited him before Cora, whose lavender hair was now stringy and wet from her tears. Adam, Kezia, Zev, and Serafine formed a circle around her, and King flew scarily close to the man's head in warning.

"Cora, my Cora. Is that you?" The man wept, lowering his head into his hands. He had the same large, piercing blue eyes as his daughter, though from what Cora had told her friends about him, he wasn't much of a father. Cora simply whimpered in Kezia's arms. "I never thought I would see you again. When I did, it was like something broke inside of me. I've been lost for so long. Seeing you like this, so strong . . . I wanted to be strong for you."

Cora gestured for her friends to move aside, and the man stepped closer. "I know you could never forgive me; I've been so cold and distant. I allowed your mother to be cruel to you. I believed every lie they ever told, and you paid the price. At least let me stand by your side now. On the side of good, for the first time in my life," he begged. Cora closed the gap between them and pulled her father in for a hug, and he held her like she was the most precious treasure in all the realms. And to him, she was.

Cora looked over his shoulder at the woman he had been standing next to before he ran—her mother. She remained a statue.

"She's lost, Cora. But I'm not anymore, and I will never leave you until the very moment you ask me to. I haven't really ever used my gift—you know anything that sets us apart from one another is banned—but I suspect it's fairly strong. I can move things by just thinking about it. Maybe it can help," he offered as Cora clung to him. It was evident that a place deep within her was sewing itself back up that very moment.

Cora introduced her father, Ellis Yarrow—by full name, of course—to everyone, and they all tried to be gracious. Serafine looked upon the pair and was so blown away by Cora's ability to forgive, by her kindness. It wasn't something that came naturally to Serafine, and she respected it deeply. She surveyed the rather large army they had amassed and allowed the seed of hope that Adam had planted and relentlessly watered to bloom within her. She looked across the valley, trying to ascertain what the first strike might be, and she noticed Malachi holding his left palm up, its glow an almost completely faded shade of rust. His other hand circled his revolting mouth as he whispered over the people of Pax, standing as human shields before the Xhartanians.

"Look, see what he's doing?" Serafine smacked Adam's shoulder to get his attention, pointing at Malachi.

Adam remembered that Omri had introduced him as having some kind of whisper power. The gray people weren't budging; they weren't even blinking. As the rust glow petered out, Malachi quickly tried to hide his obvious frustration and grinned maliciously, standing between Namtar and the other two leaders of Xhartana. Namtar slid his sword from its sheath and swiftly drew the blade clean across Malachi's throat. Blood bubbled from it as he dropped to his knees and then slumped dead in the sand, blood pooling beneath his limp body. Namtar looked at Adam with a sneer and began ferociously calling out orders.

"The traitors always think they're different than us, more special if they betray us. But they always end up paying for it one way or another. We stand together, we fight together, we may die together, but we will never turn our backs on each other!" Adam cried out to resounding whoops and cheers from across the oddest collection of people, magical creatures, and soul-seals he had ever laid eyes on.

They stood steadfast in this harrowing desert at the edge of the dark sea, poised to battle those who sought to destroy them. Tears swam in Adam's eyes as thoughts of grief and failure were replaced with pride for these people putting their lives on the line. They had formed into some semblance of ranks organized by Arnon, Edria, Ben, and Gideon and now stood arm in arm, and they smiled at Adam, the man who had stood before them and bared his soul, pairing his with theirs as he collected their secrets and empowered them to face their tormentors. He turned to face his destiny.

As soon as Malachi had fallen, the shackles of the spell he had woven over his unwitting victims from Pax was dispelled, leaving hollow shells who, in an attempt to believe in everything, stood for nothing.

The gray people of Pax began to take in their surroundings, realizing they were the first line of defense in a war they wanted no part in. Forgetting the treaty their ancestors had signed after the dark time over a hundred years ago, agreeing to come to Xhartana's aid should they go to war again in return for living on Pax undisturbed, a frenzy began. The Pax soldiers ran in every direction, attempting to escape their fate, drenched in cowardice. Adam and Kezia chuckled a little; they looked like chickens that had escaped their coop, aiming not to get caught and butchered, and Adam supposed that Namtar should have waited a little longer to take out Malachi, because Xhartana had lost their initial defense.

Some of them took off toward the ship, attempting to fling themselves off the dune onto it. Some fled into the desert. Most were mercilessly disposed of by Xhartanian soldiers, who easily caught them.

Namtar looked over, with the first traces of unease on his face, but his forces still far outnumbered the clan that Adam had built. Namtar called his army to order, as much order as they ever had. Adam, Serafine, Ben, and Arnon did the same. Adam thought this would be a great time for Elia the Light Bringer to make his appearance.

Aryeh used his gift to imbue the Jesimi people and their righteous allies with ample courage. It coursed through their veins—no going back now. Whatever happened was meant to happen, Adam thought, feeding off Aryeh's imparted courage. He would fight valiantly beside the people who had forged him from the ashes. He whispered a prayer to El, but he was ready to make a deal with a Mazzik, if that's what it took to keep his people safe.

CHAPTER 21

"Charge! Praise the Deity!" Namtar roared, thrusting a jewel-crusted sword in the air, its grandeur a stark contrast to the weapons his army carried.

"For Avaria! Charge!" Arnon bellowed in response, his words echoing across the dunes.

The army that stood behind him cried, "Next year in Avaria!" in unison, filling them all with passion and purpose that drove their footsteps through the viscous sand toward their shared destiny. They had survived together, and now they might die together, as one.

Serafine held a spear ablaze in her hand, and with the other, she slid her fingers through Adam's, and he squeezed her hand tightly as they sprinted toward the battle, leading their people from a place of life, of love, and of hope for a better future. The living embodiment of the Kiritum warriors' code—they don't live to fight; they fight to live.

The soul-seals raced furiously at the sides of their people as if they were rushing for their place on Noah's ark. Adam's people cried out from the depths of their souls their dreams for peace, giving voice to the collective pain that drove them to these lengths to protect themselves, to break their chains for good.

The three Xhartanian leaders had peeled off to the sides like the cowards they were, the malevolence that defined them clinging to them as if it was the air they breathed. Adam looked to Arnon, Edria, and Ben at his side for guidance, for leadership, as they crossed the gap between them and their mortal enemies.

"Lead, Adam. It's your purpose." Ben nudged his arm as they continued to propel themselves forward through the sand.

Adam flashed to holding his mother in the ashes as she took her last breath, helpless to stop it. To Kezia, bleeding, helpless again. He had promised himself he would never feel helpless again, and he transcended past revenge; he would fight for the future his mother had dreamed of. These people had all come here to fight at his behest, and he had to stand strong beside them now. The woman at his side believed in him—all of his people did.

Adam called to the line of archers, which included Kezia and the centaurs, that had formed to one side atop the dune: "Archers, release!"

They released their arrows, which sailed over the heads of their people and met their target, taking down a number of Xhartanian soldiers as they scrambled to get their makeshift shields up. The archers seamlessly notched more arrows and freed them with such precise aim, not a single one missed.

On the opposite side of the dune from the archers stood a group of people with unique gifts. Phineas stood apart from the rest, his hands pressed to his temples in an attempt to foresee anything that might be helpful during the battle. Raviv held out his palm as it glowed a vibrant sky blue with a single rain drop, forming an eternal storm cloud over the enemy that blasted them with sheets of perpetual rain. Irena sat barefoot in the sand, casting a sense of harmony and unity over their people, building upon the togetherness that is inherent to the Jesimi people. A luminous, multihued dome covered them and radiated out toward their targets; it was oddly beautiful.

Adam charged along with the front line, made up of himself and Zev, Ben and George, Serafine with Storm strapped under her fighting leathers, and those with strength-based powers, including Arnon and Spike, Edria and Flash, Gideon and his giant Ibex and friends,

Ethan with his strength power, and Sela, her menacing black viper draped around her shoulders. Adam held the dagger Ben had given him tightly in one hand and another Arnon had forged for him in the other, determined to never let his fear stand in his way again. The simple bronze sword was fastened to his back; he had not trained with it enough for battle, and without the twelfth key, it was just a sword. He focused on breathing and putting one foot in front of the other as he raced toward an army that was twice the size of his and had been training since they were children.

Just as they were about to clash with the enemy, Omri beamed a golden-yellow flower symbol from his palm and blossomed a wall of towering sunflowers from the depths of the sand between the sides— a final obstacle. Adam and Serafine looked at each other, laughing, and watched the strange, jovial man who wielded his magic in this beautiful way.

Xhartanian soldiers used their rusty, primitive weapons to slash their way through the giant stalks of sunflowers, and Adam's army was finally face-to-face with their hated foes. Adam slashed down the soldier in front of him; the skills he had learned in Kiritum from his friends had become second nature. He hesitated as he watched the soldier crumple into a pile before him, then pushed forward to close in on the next one.

The Xhartanian soldiers slid back and forth, trying to maintain their footing under the pummeling rain Raviv was sending their way, as they let out a flurry of "praise the Deity" battle cries. Adam attempted to observe the battle at large while facing off against Xhartanian soldiers out for his blood. A number of Xhartanians wielded gifts: super strength, speed, shield, water blasting, fire. Adam supposed they *had* struck platinum in their mine, allowing many to recharge their misused powers. He wiped his hands on his worn pants to regrip his daggers as they continued to slick with sweat.

Serafine flicked her flaming spears at the oncoming soldiers with a ferocity that clearly ran in her blood. Spike swung his enormous jaw down on a soldier that Arnon had run through, splattering blood across the sand. Arnon quickly swept the blood from his face, wiping his ruby-studded blade across his burgundy fighting leathers, and struck again with a resounding clang. Flash impaled a man who went wide-eyed, dropping his rusty sickle into the sand before following it. Edria made combat look like a dance as she twirled her daggers, slashing through her enemies like butter.

An electric shiver struck Adam as he watched the Xhartanians delight in bloody combat; they smiled as blood spurted from their victims, Adam's people. Adam's army fought back fiercely, but how could they realistically compete with an army of this size and this level of evil? The odds were stacked against them, even as the archers, the gift wielders, and the front-line warriors battled fervently for their lives. It didn't look good; Adam wasn't naive enough to think otherwise, and a shared look with Serafine said she knew it as well.

The red-orange glow of Serafine's left palm shone brightly as she shot a line of fire at the next set of attackers. They leaped backward, and Adam caught a glimpse of something blinding and silver over to the far side of the sandy battlefield. The flames allowed him to take a second look and realize that Namtar and his tyrannical co-leaders were beside a large, gleaming heap of raw platinum. A line of soldiers stood waiting to recharge their powers and return to battle—a revolving door Adam's forces couldn't beat. If they couldn't find a way to get rid of the platinum, they would lose. Xhartana's numbers, the griffins spiraling out of the sky to strike, plus their magic were too much for Adam's ragtag army, and it was showing in blood.

"Ser, Sela, with me! The rest of you, fall in line, push forward!" Adam shouted. Serafine and Sela pulled back to tail him, making their way toward Namtar. The rest clashed violently against Xhartanians, who were now hopping over Serafine's flames as they grew lower, licking the copper sand.

Adam's pulse thrashed in his neck as he dipped into a part of him that seemed so natural, as if it had always been there. He was Jesimi.

He would lead his people to freedom, to peace. His palms slickened under his blades as he heard Namtar speak to the other two dastardly leaders, in their gilded blood-red robes, too weak to fight their own battles. Adam briefly recalled being frozen against that fence in Kiritum, watching these brutes attack his people and doing nothing. Zev let out a fierce growl in warning of the hell Adam was about to unleash. He would make them pay, for his mother, for his people and their suffering.

Adam's hair whipped around with a violent wind, and five mountainous shadows were cast over both armies as the Nephilim appeared above. The giants tucked their mighty wings behind their towering, sculpted frames and faced Xhartana with the fury of El himself as they descended into the heat of the messy battle. The flock of steel-eyed griffins that had been decimating everything in their path took flight in a feeble attempt to face the giants before them. The Nephilim plucked them out of the air with their stony hands and slammed them and their riders deep into the sand, sending out tremors that set everyone unsteady.

The clash continued at an earth-shattering volume, the Nephilim uttering roars so deep that the sand shifted under everyone's feet as Adam and his people worked to regain their composure. A smile turned up the corners of Adam's mouth; their giant friends had kept their vow.

"Balian, Vardas, quickly, we must keep recharging their powers, before they lose them completely. They are stronger than we suspected, and we must crush the Jesimi pigs and their friends beneath our feet. As we always do, praise the Deity," Namtar seethed, dripping with malice, his eyes darting around with trepidation at the entrance of the Nephilim.

Adam didn't need to direct Serafine or Sela, as the harmony that lived between them had them moving as one behind enemy lines, buoyed by Irena's gift, which hung like a glittery veil above them. They looked at each other knowingly, and Adam and Serafine simultaneously struck a fighter holding a large fragment of platinum, currently recharging. Serafine plunged a gold, flaming spear into his heart, dropping him to his knees and sending the platinum flying through the air. It was a race toward fate as Sela and Balian atop his griffin soared toward it and each other. Sela stuck out her glowing palm with the strength of the army she had become part of, smashing it into Balian and snatching the platinum out of the air before he could grab it. She crushed it into dust in her fist as if it were glass. Balian flew off his griffin, clutching his chest from Sela's powerful blow. Namtar swung over on his griffin and grabbed him before he could hit the dune.

Meanwhile, Serafine had snuck behind the mountain of platinum and was setting it alight, piece by piece, her eyes glowing a red-orange like her palm. The platinum turned the shade of a fiery sunset but didn't disintegrate the way Sela's had. Sela wove in and out of the Xhartanians to attempt to smash the rest, but it was too hot and burned her hand. Serafine, Sela, and Adam looked at each other desperately, surrounded by the enemy.

At that very moment, the wind picked up again, and the leader of the Nephilim flapped his massive white angel wings to get to them in a single bound. His monstrous frame had Namtar and the others cowering as he smashed his stone fist into the smoldering platinum, rendering it useless dust. Apparently immune to burns, he simply brushed the ashy substance off his hand and returned to his place in battle. Namtar shrieked in fury, and Adam and Serafine braced for a counterattack, having destroyed Xhartana's chance to recharge the powers they had abused.

"Fall back! Let the rest dispose of these worthless rats," Vardas commanded in a grating voice that clawed under the skin of all those who heard it. Self-preservation was clearly his highest priority.

Vardas, Namtar, and Balian—back on his griffin, grasping his side, blood spouting from his nose—flew to safety behind the masses of Xhartanians, who were haphazardly attacking Adam's army.

"That was incredible, Sela," Serafine said, offering a rare compliment to her quick thinking and vast strength.

"Well, thanks. Um, you too." Sela winked, quickly re-braiding her sticky, blood-coated hair. "Let's get back to it. We have a battle to win, for Avaria." Her viper, black as night, loosened its coil around her neck, ready to aid her in her next move.

They stood back for a moment, surveying the battle. The Nephilim had destroyed most of the griffin riders, smashing them into the ether; their bodies lay mangled and mostly buried in the sand. Kezia and the centaurs bellowed back and forth to each other with each wave of arrows they released. Adam caught a glimpse of Lian's golden hair darting through the Xhartanian ranks, always just narrowly out of the beasts' reach, somehow managing to disarm them of their weapons, leaving them vulnerable. Adam caught Samuel's eye. The arbiter of so much pain in his youth, now fighting bravely for justice. They smiled at each other, putting aside their past and making way for a future that was intertwined; they were Jesimi.

A massive black rhino ran two men through at once as they looked on, the gore dripping from the skewered bodies on his horn. Serafine grasped Adam's arm as they began to notice those who had fallen among their ranks, many vitally injured, immobile, strewn across the sand. Much to their surprise, a familiar lavender-haired wisp of a girl wove her way in and out of the brutality with a bravery they hadn't known existed. Her father followed, using his gift to protect her, moving his palm over fallen shields and weapons and sending them reeling toward those who meant harm. Cora was searching for the wounded and dragging them over to the side of the dune, where Ezra floated his glowing-red hand over them in a race against time to heal them. After attempting this on an older man she had brought over, Ezra closed his eyes and shook his head at her, and she burst into tears. The weight of that loss, of any loss, weighed heavily on Adam's shoulders as he fought through the throngs of foes engaged in combat to return to the center once more, flanked by his longtime friend and the woman whom he now couldn't live without.

Even with the Nephilim taking out the griffins, he wasn't sure it would be enough; there were just so many of them. He wished for a moment that blood did not have to be spilled to succeed, but he quickly remembered that freedom isn't free. There is a price, and he would gladly take payment in the form of their enemy's blood in place of their own.

He set his sights on a weasel of a man, spattered with blood, who used a slingshot to fire rocks and pellets at Adam's people. He called on his training as he slashed at the hand holding the primitive weapon, causing him to drop it to the sand. Adam slammed his boot down on it, crushing the carved wood, before returning to the gaze of the man. Only, he wasn't a man; he couldn't have been more than sixteen, and terror seeped out from deep within his cold brown eyes as he stood there. Adam hesitated; this was a teenager.

Before he knew it, the boy had lashed his leg out, trying to hook it behind Adam's to drop him. Adam had seen this move in his training and easily hopped out of the way. The glimpse of terror he had seen in the boy's eyes had transformed into hatred. The boy wanted to kill him at any cost; that was all he had ever known. It wasn't fair to any of the Xhartanian kids.

The boy pulled a rusty knife from his pocket, and reality flashed before Adam: The boy would kill him and then others. As the boy darted forward, slashing at his stomach, Adam grabbed his shoulder and redirected him. The boy bucked within his grasp, swiping again before Adam plunged a dagger cleanly into his heart, hoping he would meet a swift and painless end. The boy dropped to the ground, and Adam saw the life leave the limp body at his feet, blood spilling over his black-leather boots. Tears formed behind his eyes, burgeoning to be released at the cruelty of this world. His heart sank deep into the cavity of his chest, regret and sadness flowing from within, and anger at the Xhartanian people for abusing their children this way, turning them into weapons. He vowed to be part of a new age, filled with peace and kindness. But first, he had to finish this, or the Jesimi people and innocent Marre people would never be free. His eyes narrowed.

Serafine looked over at him as she lit spear after spear on fire and skillfully tossed them into the chests of oncoming enemies. Her heart cracked open as she watched Adam realize what she had always known: Most Jesimi people would never choose battle. But if they did nothing and chose not to fight back against the tyranny imposed upon them, then eventually, they would all be stamped out, relegated to a distant memory of a people. Though she was born a warrior, she took no pleasure in spilling blood; she simply refused the alternative, which was the spilled blood of her family, of the people who stood beside her.

Though the battle between the two sides produced a deafening roar—weapons clanging, battle cries, shrieks announcing the fallen—Adam only heard a dull buzz. His other senses were as sharp as a dagger, but sound fell away as he pushed forward in pursuit of freedom. He bumped into Rafi, who stood proudly among a line of Imiris warriors commanding lethal atlatls—spear-throwers constructed from reindeer antlers in Imiris—to propel spear after spear at an incredibly high velocity, plummeting into the hearts of their enemies, ending them before they even knew what hit them.

"Adam, be careful! Dalila is using her illusion to breach Xhartana's ranks, taking on the appearance of one of their soldiers so she can catch them off guard and finish them," Rafi shouted, wearing the love he held for his wife across his face.

Adam shot him a shaky smile and moved over a couple of paces, where he was reunited with his uncle, who looked at the crimson stains of blood smudged all over Adam with an expression of pride tinged with sadness. Ben tore through enemies with the speed and tenacity of a warrior, viciously slashing his blade across their throats and into their guts as he wheeled around, facing multiple opponents at a time with agility and grace. Fighting next to him was Gideon, who needed no weapons aside from the steel-enforced gloves that covered his ebony knuckles. He drove them up into the chins of those who approached, sending them flying, with the strength of his gift flowing through his veins.

Adam realized that arrows had stopped sailing over their heads, and he looked back at the archers. They must have been out of arrows, as Kezia and the centaurs had galloped into the heart of the fray.

Dusk made itself known—the color of the blood that had been shed on the sand was now painted across the sky, a harsh crimson reminder of those who had fallen. Adam glanced around fleetingly while Serafine watched his back. They looked at each other grimly. Though the gifts of Xhartana had faded with the destruction of the platinum, and they had sustained major casualties, their numbers still held strong. Bodies littered the valley of sand the Xhartanians fought in. Their supposed brothers-in-arms must not have meant much to them, as they were stomping on their dead to get to their next victims.

Adam's side had suffered significant loss as well, but there were still many functioning gifts and warriors on their side; they couldn't give up, no matter how bleak it looked, standing on the blood of their people. The bronze sword felt as if it were melting a hole in Adam's back, and he desperately wished they had been able to save this last village and obtain the final key. He hoped that his people's deep belief in each other and desperation to be free and safe in their homeland would be enough at this point.

The darkness in the sky met the darkness of the sea just beyond the battle that waged into the eve against the copper Sands of Sivan. Kezia crashed into Serafine as they were reunited, and King dive-bombed those who attacked them, slamming his knobbed hornbill into each target with precision. Sydelle from Hilat unfurled her glowing left palm beside them and blew across it, sending mauve wisps dancing toward a throng of Xhartanians who were clawing their way forward. The wisps infiltrated their heads through every open orifice, dropping them like flies as they fell fast asleep, surely dreaming of blood and glory they would never know.

Tamir emerged from the masses, merging his way closer to his betrothed, which she didn't acknowledge. Tamir's eyes darted between her and Adam, who seamlessly fought by each other's sides in a way he could only have dreamed of. She had been promised to him, but she had never really been his. Adam did not indulge Tamir in the nonexistent battle for Serafine's attention that he was seeking. Serafine shot her flaming spears out of her hand, fast as lightning, ignoring Tamir completely and winking at Adam, filling him with an aching hunger to win, for her.

Kezia twirled her sword around a few times before following King and clashing it against an opponent. They went back and forth, a look of contempt on the soldier's face as he was matched move for move by the tiny ball of energy. She had quickly realized that this was the bastard who had attempted to gut her in Kiritum, and she delighted in the opportunity to return the favor. He had no idea who she was or what she was about to do to him. Women were nothing in Xhartana, simply suited for tucking away in a kitchen and breeding. That wasn't Kezia, and if her friends knew anything about her, she was about to teach him a lesson about underestimating her.

Adam lunged to help her, remembering the man's sneer as he had licked his blade dripping with her blood. Serafine moved to stop him, and he nodded in understanding; he had to let Kezia fight her own battle.

Kezia grazed the soldier's arm with her short silver sword and, taunting him, pretended to lick the blade as he had. He roared in fury, lumbering at her, but she was far too quick, easily sidestepping the attempt. She bounced back and forth, somehow remaining light on her feet in the sand, and feigned a strike up and to the left before quickly slashing her blade downward and thrusting it deep into his chest. She held on to the handle as he fell, then pressed her foot to his chest to free her blade.

Cora brushed her long fingers across each of their arms lovingly as they fought with every shred of vigor they could muster, though they were nearly depleted. Ellis hung on to his daughter's every step, giving her friends a small smile. She grabbed Omri, who had fallen, and dragged him through the maze of fighting to Ezra. Omri had been attempting to use his harvest magic to block their foes while simultaneously wielding a scythe. He had been struck down from behind and lay bleeding from his rotund middle. Aya had seen him fall and called Cora over.

Adam was certain his arms were going to fall off as he slammed his blade toward his opponent time and time again, getting a bit slower each time. The monster in front of him dragged his caveman-like stone spear across Adam's chest, and he cried out as it pierced his skin. He went to lash back, but Zev coasted through the air and leapt onto the soldier's chest, brutally ripping out his throat with a guttural snarl—his soul-seal had been marked.

They heard a loud buzzing overhead and looked upward. Just as darkness encroached on the battle, a swarm of pixies bloomed in the sky above, fronted by a tempestuous Ivy, and dropped down over a scattered Xhartana. They beat their wings furiously and flew into the soldiers' faces, glowing at full blast to blind them.

"Yes, Ivy!" Adam hollered over to her as she attempted to blind and maim a nearby solider clad in blood-red rags.

Ben swooped in and thrashed a man who had attacked Adam, allowing him cover to call out orders to the slapdash ranks of his people's army. It was hard to see now, the stakes growing ever higher as the darkness loomed. Adam squinted to catch a glimpse of Namtar, Vardas, and Balian in the back, the only Xhartanians still sitting aboard griffins, as the Nephilim had decimated the ranks of the rest. The rest of the Xhartanians seemed less threatening, running rampant without real guidance. But they still held the upper hand in numbers, and it would be stupid to count them out. Adam knew destroying Namtar, Vardas, and Balian would end this battle and fulfill his duty to his people. He also hoped it might lead to a new future for the kids of Xhartana, without hatred and violence.

"One last push, my fellow righteous friends! We are hanging over the precipice of victory; it is nearly ours! Onward!" Adam shouted over the strangest mishmash of people and soul-seals and magical creatures that had likely ever assembled in one place, warming his weary, blood-tinged soul. The message was passed along, and they all pressed forward with renewed spirits toward victory. They would prevail.

"We must take the leaders out," Adam said in the direction of Ben, Arnon, Edria, Kezia, and Serafine.

"We'll follow you anywhere," Serafine said stoically beside him, looking at him as if he were hers.

He could argue, but he knew that wouldn't be a successful venture, so he looped around the outside of the remaining skirmishes toward the cowards in the back, trailed by his family. His loving, strong, ferocious family. Dusk provided some cover as they skirted around the battle silently and surrounded the three fiends who had wreaked so much pain and destruction on all of them and their land for over a century.

Adam gave the signal, and the six of them struck in one blinding attack. Arnon and Ben slashed their swords at the hind legs of the griffins, causing them to drop their passengers many feet to the ground. Adam, Zev, Serafine, Kezia, and Edria descended upon their reviled adversaries the second they tumbled to the ground. Namtar, Balian, and Vardas appeared temporarily shocked as they scrambled to fight back, truly cornered. Their cloaks were torn to shreds in a moment by blades, revealing molded brown armor that covered their medium-tan, yellow-tinged skin, which matched their rotted teeth. They clearly hadn't expected to have to fight themselves, and Adam and his family quickly gained the upper hand as they fought with the will of El.

"Bahir, Aelius, Magen, Diya! Come, quickly!" Balian squealed, in an incredibly high pitch, toward the fighting Xhartanians.

A dozen bulky soldiers retreated from the fight and rapidly surrounded them, fighting their way between Adam, Edria, Serafine, and Kezia and their leaders while Arnon, Spike, Ben, and George still worked to take down the three formidable griffins. George snapped his jaw closed over the throat of one that Ben held close, his bite bursting with powerful venom, ending the beast's life.

Adam clenched his jaw as he gripped his daggers more firmly, fighting through the pain to end this. They grappled with the guards with all their might as Namtar, Vardas, and Balian once again stood back with their arms crossed, as if they were bored by this whole spectacle. Adam and his friends were outmatched here in number, and Adam started to grow increasingly afraid that they might not be able to take the leaders and escape with their lives. His movements and jabs remained steadfast as he allowed the fear to turn to fuel within him. With one quick move, the tall, menacing guard he had been facing kicked his legs out from under him, and a second guard dropped down over him in an attempt to slam his knife into Adam's chest. Another guard had managed to trap Zev, who was thrashing against him furiously. It was over now. Adam wouldn't be able to protect his people. He had failed.

Serafine tore across the space between them, wild-eyed, desperate to intervene. Her father tossed her a sword, and she slashed it across the throat of the tall guard who had Adam pinned to the ground, then lunged for the man who held Zev, freeing him in one swing. Zev turned around, took a chunk of the man's side, and dropped it into the sand before turning away. He tried to push through the guards once more to get to their rotten leaders, but to no avail.

Adam squeezed Serafine's hand to thank her and shouted, "Arnon, now is the time! We have to do something!"

Arnon nodded, quickly shoving everyone behind him so anyone in his path was the enemy. He narrowed his eyes and lifted his left hand, and a brilliant sapphire glow lit the dimming valley between the dunes. An oceanic tidal wave formed out of thin air, and with a shove of his hands, it surged forward through the desert valley before them. A torrential valley, truly living up to the meaning of his name. Balian, Namtar, and Vardas swiftly took flight on the two remaining griffins before the wave could carry them away, and they hovered above, watching as the screams and cries of their soldiers gave way to bobbing beneath the bubbles as they were swept across the sandy valley. Some Xhartanians scampered up the dunes on both sides, narrowly avoiding the wall of water, while others attempted to outrun its fury.

"Welp, I think it's safe to say the tides have turned." Kezia chuckled.

"You didn't." Serafine shook her head at her best friend's joke.

It was difficult to tell how many soldiers had survived, as many had been swept out of sight, but Adam wasn't putting his guard down yet and called to his people to do the same. This wasn't over. The water left thick, clumpy sand in its wake as they watched the Xhartanians in the distance attempt to gather again, their cowardly leaders circling above them.

"What's that?" Ben asked as he kicked at the wet sand before them.

Adam looked down, and at his feet, something was stuck in the sand, flapping unnaturally. It stood more on end the closer Adam got to it. He reached down and realized it had a sheer glow. He freed it from the muck, and it shot to his neck, to the other eleven keys, like a magnet.

"Oh my El," Ben gasped, staggering back.

Adam looked down, and all the keys were glowing a vivid white, like the symbol on his palm when he used his gift. The twelfth key had wanted Adam to find it. It was the most fascinating yet, and everyone formed a circle around Adam, desperate for a glimpse. He brushed the sand off the key; it was chiseled out of fossil, with a large chunk of topaz embedded in it. Fossils were often found buried beneath Avaria, indicative of the Jesimi people's thousands of years in their homeland. As he held all twelve keys in his hands, watching them shimmer and glow, he held the history of his people, their trust.

Time was running out; the Xhartanians were amassing in the distance, angrier than ever. Adam ceremoniously pulled the bronze sword from the leather straps across his back and held it in both hands. Before he could do anything to try to unlock it, the twine holding the keys around his neck ripped off, and the entire valley filled with a blinding, pulsing white light. Everyone ducked, shielding their eyes. Adam struggling to maintain his grip on the sword as something far beyond his imagining happened: The keys fixed themselves to the blade, six on each side, threading themselves into the metal of the mighty bronze sword. Flashes of ruby, emerald, cobalt, shell, wood—pieces of all the villages and cities, pieces of his people, forged the sword anew. It lifted from his hands, finishing its magical work as it spun above their heads, shooting out beams of light. Spellbound by this miracle, Adam's attention was only momentarily torn away as he caught the back end of Namtar, Balian, and Vardas flying off into the darkness above the sea. His heart dropped, knowing what this meant, but he faced forward, the sword dropping into his calloused, bloody hands, a perfect fit. He brandished it, to the cheers of his people. Only a shadow of a glow remained, but it thrummed with power Adam had only heard of in the scrolls.

He saw bands of Xhartanians, bloody and waterlogged, creeping back toward them, looking to finish this, and he stepped forward, planning to do just that. Kezia on one side, Serafine on the other, flanked by Ben, Arnon, Edria, Gideon, and the rest of their war-torn people left standing.

Adam leaped forward, slicing the mighty bronze blade across the highest-ranking Xhartanian. As the sword met its target, an immeasurable explosion of white, shimmering magic crashed across the ranks of the Xhartanians behind him. The blast was so intense, it sent Adam's front line flying into the wet sand. It was as vast as Arnon's wave, and each soldier, one by one, crumpled to the sand under the power of the blade. It was just as Ben's former student Adala had foreseen: A single strike of the blade felled hundreds of Xhartanian soldiers—in fact, every last one. Edria and a few others moved forward at Adam's behest to ensure they were no longer a threat. The relief Adam felt took the form of slumping over in the sand, staring at the mighty sword that had saved them. Kezia fell into bouts of laughter; her relief showed more awkwardly than most.

"Adam, quick!" Arnon cried, hunched over a figure sprawled out in the sand.

Adam threaded the mighty bronze sword through the straps on his back once again and turned, dropping to his knees. "Uncle! How did this happen? I didn't think anyone else got close enough!" He leaned over his uncle, who was steadily bleeding from his chest and leg. "Ben, come on. Not after mother. We won; we did it. I need you." Serafine and Kezia dove to his side.

"Ezra, Cora! We need a healer, fast . . . please. He's losing too much blood!" Adam let the tears that had been brimming go free. The thought of losing the first man who had felt like a father to him was unimaginable. The anguish pierced his already-shredded heart, and Serafine held his hand tightly, as if she knew there were no words. Adam and Arnon held scraps of cloth to Ben's wounds to allay the bleeding as Ezra hurried over; Cora and Ellis were tending to others who were wounded up on the dune.

"I'll be honest, Adam. He has lost a lot of blood, very quickly. I will do my best, but I'm not certain it will be enough," Ezra said seriously as he started to work on Ben.

Ezra skimmed his hands cautiously over Ben's wounds, summoning all his focus as the crowd remained silent. Adam silently begged El—begged anyone listening—to let his uncle live. His uncle deserved a second chance, to not be alone anymore. Adam needed him.

Ben's wounds continued weeping as Ezra squeezed his eyes tighter, a single tear falling from the corner of his eye and landing on Ben's cheek just as it began to fill with pink again. Adam leaned forward in awe as Ben's wounds began to visibly knit together, not altogether different from what had happened to Kezia in the River of Pyxis. Ben pried his eyes open and looked up at the many faces watching him. Adam hoped that he realized just how many people cared whether he lived or died and that it changed him, for good. Just like his nephew had. Adam flopped over on his uncle's chest, crying from relief and overwhelm.

"Ooh, ouch, still hurts, kid," Ben croaked, but he chuckled at Adam's zealousness.

"Sorry. I'm just so glad you're okay. We weren't sure for a minute there . . ." Adam trailed off, gazing into the distance.

"I'm not going anywhere; you're stuck with me for good. Now, can I get outta this wet sand? We gotta celebrate." Ben reached for Adam's hand, and Arnon used his vast size to push Ben up and help support him.

"You still need to rest, or that will rip open again. Come over to where I have the others healing up," Ezra suggested, and Ben nodded. Arnon helped him limp over to the painfully crowded part of the dune, where Ezra was tending to the wounded and the dead.

Adam looked down at his blood-caked boots, standing on blood-soaked sand in the pitch black of night. The stars, one at a time, made their entrances, emblazoned there by El himself to light the way of his people and their allies on this most painful of nights. That was the thing about the Jesimi people: There had always been those who sought to destroy them, and they never knew peace for long. Throughout history, they had joined together to vehemently fight those trying to bring them down, as they had this very day.

Adam reached deep within, grabbing hold of his gift, and spoke. "Words would never be sufficient to thank you for what you have given to your people, what you have each sacrificed to stand with us today. We have prevailed in this battle, but I fear a war looms on the horizon. The Xhartanian leaders escaped when the twelve keys unlocked the magic within the sword; they may have more platinum. We must stand steadfast together. I was fated to take a great journey to gather our people together because alone, separate, we stand no chance. Together, we are unstoppable, an immovable force.

We will take back our homeland; we are one giant step closer. Next year reunited in Avaria!" His words echoed across the valley, pinging straight from his soul to theirs. Zev brushed up against his leg, his great white snout covered in blood.

Adam, Ben, Serafine, and Kezia checked on Cora, who was aiding Ezra courageously as they tended to the many wounded and doting specifically on Uncle Ben. They watched as the timid girl they had known for such a short time had burrowed her way deep into their hearts. She worked side by side with her father, the first step toward healing their painfully broken relationship.

The four of them milled about, bone tired but lifted by their victory, checking in with all of their friends and their people, comforting them and thanking them. The Nephilim had long returned to their eternal mountain pass, and Ivy and the pixies had headed home, closely followed by the centaurs. The humans who were uninjured began to make plans for transporting the dead home, to bury them as quickly as they possibly could. Kezia rushed around, helping them all as much as she could, managing a significant amount of her humor despite what they had been through, as was the Jesimi way.

Serafine and Adam climbed, side by side, up the last sand dune under the sliver of a silver moon, cresting the top, their steps casting copper sand into the sea. The water was peaceful, as if the beginnings of war hadn't been waged against its very shores. The sea was one with the night, only given away by its gentle lapping against the dunes. The battle ended the way it had begun as Adam ran his fingers down Serafine's slender arm, then laced his bruised and calloused fingers through hers, sticky with blood. Anchoring each other to a new day. Still fraught with apparitions from their pasts, but grateful to be alive to see what tomorrow might bring. Both equally, for the first time, hoping they would see it together.

Adam brushed his fingers across Serafine's full cheek, sliding them into her mahogany curls. He wiped away some of the blood that tainted the scar beside her eye.

She traced her finger across the outline of his muscular arm. As much as she admired the way he looked, that wasn't what drew her to him. She gazed at the man who stood before her, and she wanted him because he firmly believed in himself the way she had known he could. She snaked her other arm around his waist and tugged him down toward her, their lips meeting gently at first, tasting of salty sweat mixed with the metallic edge of blood. The kiss grew deeper and more desperate, Serafine's fingers threading through Adam's hair as he gripped her hips firmly, pulling her closer. An unspoken promise ignited between them. Atop that dune at the edge of the world, after a brutal battle filled with loss, they clung to each other as it all fell away for a finite moment.

Kezia's laugh rang out, and Adam pulled back, holding tight to Serafine's hand. Kezia, Cora, and Zev moved to join them, looking like mischievous kids as they caught the private moment between their friends.

"Tamir is going to love this," Kezia joked, lightening the mood that toed the line between passion and panic.

"Meddling mermaids, Kez, they will figure out for themselves that they are destined to be together and to guide the Jesimi people and the rest of us to peace. I knew it the moment we met," Cora said with a breathy tone as she pressed her hands together under her chin, swelling with her usual hopefulness and dreams. They were all glad to see that her spirit remained intact after the horrors of the day.

"Yea, quit it!" Serafine lashed out, smacking Kezia's hand. Storm flew off her neck, and Kezia caught him just before he fell to the sand, stroking his orange-speckled black skin.

"Your father will understand," Kezia said, more seriously this time, placing a hand each on Adam's and Serafine's shoulders.

Serafine brushed her off. "I'll tell him soon. But we have more important things to worry about."

And they did. They stood side by side, leaning on each other, a family, an unshakeable team looking out over the blackness of the sea.

They were better together. Adam realized he hadn't remained alone by preference all those years; he had been protecting himself, thereby preventing this kind of goodness, camaraderie. He had a sneaking suspicion that even with his mother gone, he would never be alone again.

Out of the depths, the moon cast a light over the endless water, and they caught a glimpse of a spine lined with monstrous, golden scales gliding through the gentle waves before plunging below, creating a whirlpool in its wake. The ground quaked beneath their feet. They reached out for each other and hopped over to the other side of the dune before the ground steadied, then raced back to join their people in the valley. They had won the battle, but Adam couldn't shake the sinking feeling that the war still brewed before them. From the Leviathan to the earth itself, they could face anything, just like this. Avaria would be theirs again; they would be reunited on holy ground. From the heart of the battered and bloodied ranks, their people stood and solemnly, but proudly, joined hands, swaying back and forth, singing the old song of Avaria. Together.

The End

ACKNOWLEDGMENTS

Special thanks to Rachel A. Hellman who generously contributed her artistic talents to the book. She turned a very rough sketch into a beautifully drawn map to guide readers through the realms of Avaria.

Appreciation to Andy Symonds, Lauren Green, Kayleigh Rucinski, and the rest of the talented team at Ballast Books. Their support, insight and guidance made publishing this book possible.

ABOUT THE AUTHOR

Jennifer Paller Girard wrote *Next Year in Avaria* in a twenty-day period during the last months of her life while fighting the symptoms of several debilitating diseases. Her inspiration for writing the book was the October 7 Hamas attack on Israel. Her hope was that the story would lift the spirits of the affected families and those who support Israel.

Jennifer was born in Vail, Colorado, and lived in Eagle, Colorado, most of her life. After receiving a doctorate in behavioral health from Arizona State University, she embarked on a career of helping people, including orphans in Vietnam, the homeless in Denver, cystic fibrosis patients in Children's Hospital Colorado, and many clients in her private counseling business.

One of her favorite passions was travel. She visited forty-seven countries on six continents.

This was her final message in her own words:

"I may be thirty-eight, but I lived the life of someone twice my age. I wouldn't change it for anything. I mean, except the becoming incurably, chronically ill.

Thank you to everyone who touched my life in some way or taught me some kind of lesson. Live big, and don't waste a moment—I didn't. Bring our hostages home. Keep fighting for the Jewish people. You are loved." —Jenn